Son of the religious philosopher Henry James, Sr., and brother of the psychologist and philosopher William, Henry James was born in New York City, April 15, 1843. His early life was spent in America; on and off he was taken to Europe, especially during the impressionable years from twelve to seventeen. After that he lived in Newport, went briefly to Harvard, and, in 1864, began to contribute both criticism and tales to the magazines. In 1869, and then in 1872–74, he paid visits to Europe and began *Roderick Hudson*. Late in 1875 he settled in Paris, where he met Turgenev, Flaubert, and Zola, and wrote *The American*. In December 1876 he moved to London, where two years later he achieved international fame with *Daisy Miller*. Other famous works include *Washington Square* (1880), *The Portrait of a Lady* (1881), *The Princess Casamassima* (1886), *The Aspern Papers* (1888), *The Turn of the Screw* (1898), and the three large novels of the new century, *The Wings of the Dove* (1902), *The Ambassadors* (1903), and *The Golden Bowl* (1904). In 1905 he revisited the United States and wrote *The American Scene* (1907). He also wrote many works of criticism and travel. Although old and ailing, he threw himself into war work in 1914; and in 1915, a few months before his death, he became a British subject. In January 1916 King George V conferred the Order of Merit on him. He died in London in February 1916, and his ashes were buried in the James family plot in Cambridge, Massachusetts.

HENRY JAMES

What Maisie Knew
and
The Spoils of Poynton

A MERIDIAN CLASSIC
NEW AMERICAN LIBRARY

NEW YORK AND SCARBOROUGH, ONTARIO

Introduction copyright © 1984 by New American Library

MERIDIAN TRADEMARK REG. U.S. PAT. OFF. AND FOREIGN COUNTRIES
REGISTERED TRADEMARK—MARCA REGISTRADA
HECHO EN WINNIPEG, CANADA

SIGNET, SIGNET CLASSIC, MENTOR, PLUME, MERIDIAN
and NAL BOOKS are published *in the United States* by
New American Library, 1633 Broadway, New York, New York 10019,
in Canada by The New American Library of Canada Limited,
81 Mack Avenue, Scarborough, Ontario M1L 1M8

First Meridian Classic Printing, January, 1985

1 2 3 4 5 6 7 8 9

PRINTED IN CANADA

INTRODUCTION

In the first volume of his autobiography, Henry James recounts one of the turning points in his young life. When he was twelve, his father went to the home of a New York aunt in an attempt to comfort another aunt who was staying with her in a time of crisis, and the young boy accompanied him. The visiting aunt's husband was dying of a contagious disease in Albany and, against her wishes, she had been ordered by her doctors to forsake her husband in his final days. Against this separation from her spouse on his deathbed the Albany aunt protested passionately, and it was to convince her not to sacrifice her own life by running back to her husband's bedside that James' father had been called in by the family. In his account of the visit, James gives full measure to his grieving aunt's state of hysteria and desolation, and to his own sense of his anomalous position as a young boy in the house:

> I recover but my sense, on our arrival, of being for the first time in the presence of tragedy, which the shining scene, roundabout, made more sinister—sharpened even to the point of my feeling abashed and irrelevant, wondering why I had come. . . . Vivid to me still, as floating across the verandahs into the hot afternoon stillness, is the wail of [my aunt's] protest and her grief; I remember being scared and hushed by it and stealing away beyond its reach. I remember not less what resources of high control the whole case imputed, for my imagination, to my father; and how creeping off to the edge of the eminence above the Hudson, I somehow felt the great bright harmonies of air and space becoming one with my rather proud assurance and confidence, that of my own connection, for life, for interest, with such sources of light.

But the sheer realities of death and his aunt's mourning are too distant and emotionally intangible to make the ultimate impression on a twelve-year-old boy. As James confesses with a certain degree of chagrin, the most momentous passage of his young life came not as a result of his aunt's state of despair or his uncle's subsequent death, however, but in an entirely different context, involving himself and the New York aunt's young daughter one evening around bedtime:

The great impression, however, the one that has brought me so far, was another matter: only that of the close, lamp-tempered, outer evening aforesaid, with my parent again, somewhere deep within, yet not too far to make us hold our breath for it, tenderly opposing his sister's purpose of flight, and the presence at my side of my young cousin Marie, youngest daughter of the house, exactly of my own age, and named in honor of her having been born in Paris, to the influence of which fact her shining black eyes, her small quickness and brownness, marking sharply her difference from her sisters, so oddly, so extravagantly testified. It had come home to me by some voice of the air that she was "spoiled," and it made her in the highest degree interesting; we ourselves had been so associated, at home, without being in the least spoiled (I think we even rather missed it:) so that I knew about these subjects of invidious reflection only by literature—mainly, no doubt, that of the nursery—in which they formed, quite by themselves, a romantic class; and, the fond fancy always predominant, I prized even while a little dreading the chance to see the condition at work. This chance was given me, it was clear—though I risk in my record of it a final anticlimax—by a remark from my uncle Augustus to his daughter: seated duskily in our group, which included two or three dim dependent forms, he expressed the strong opinion that Marie should go to bed. . . . It had been remarked but in the air, I feel sure, that Marie should seek her couch—a truth by the dark wing of which I ruefully felt myself brushed; and words seemed therefore to fall with a certain ironic weight. What I have retained of their effect, at any rate, is the vague fact of some objection raised by my cousin and some sharper point to his sentence supplied by her father; promptly merged in a visible commotion, a flutter of my young companion across the gallery as for refuge in the maternal arms, a protest and an appeal in short which drew from my aunt the simple phrase that was from that moment so preposterously to "count" for me. "Come now, my dear; don't make a scene—I insist on your not making a scene!" That was all the witchcraft the occasion used, but the note was none the less epoch-making. The expression, so vivid, so portentous, was one I had never heard—it had never been addressed to us at home; and who should say now what a world one mightn't read into it? It seemed freighted to sail so far; it told me so much about life. Life at these intensities clearly became "scenes"; but the great thing, the immense illumination, was that we could make them or not as we chose. It was a long time of course before I began to distinguish between those within our compass more particularly as spoiled and those producible on a different basis and which should involve detachment, involve presence of mind; just the qualities in which Marie's possible output was apparently deficient. It didn't in the least matter accordingly whether or not a scene *was* then proceeded to—and I have lost all count of what immediately happened. The mark had been made for me and the door flung open; the passage, gathering up *all* the elements of the troubled time, had been itself quite a scene, quite enough of one, and I had become aware with it of a rich accession of possibilities.

It is important to an appreciation of this passage to realize that this is, in the context in which James locates it, a moment trivial in the extreme, a "scene" apparently all the more trivial in comparison with the "scene" of his aunt's despair that has been narrated immediately preceding it, the echo of whose wail from the house's inner chambers resonates throughout it. And yet it is to this second sort of scene-making, and not the first, that James is directing our attention. Both his wailing aunt and his whining cousin "make scenes," but they do it in something close to the vulgar sense of the phrase, not at all with the "detachment" and "presence of mind" that James is invoking here.

What is it to make a scene in this other sense? What is it to make a scene on a different basis from the scenes which the grief-stricken aunt was making with his father in an inner room, or to produce one with "the qualities in which Marie's possible output was apparently deficient"? One answer is that it is to be able to do exactly what this passage itself does: to be able to sort, arrange, and shape experience into the form of a brilliantly creative, interesting, and personal expression. The scene is not something being described by this passage, it is the passage itself. "It didn't in the least matter accordingly whether or not a scene *was* then proceeded to" precisely because the "passage" (in a pun on the word that James implicitly sanctions in the final lines of the paragraph) is "itself quite a scene, quite enough of one." The playful periphrases, the syntactic elaborations and qualifications, the wittily nuanced and half-facetious observations, the extravagantly launched metaphoric flights are evidence, in short, of James' triumphant capacity to "make a scene" of even such outwardly unpromising material. But it is a "passage" in the other sense of the word as well, and James the seventy-year-old autobiographer is only repeating, in his own way, the scene-making performed by the twelve-year old boy. The boy is a scene-maker in his own right, in his ability to turn what would otherwise be merely a childish squabble about going to bed into a momentous psychological and moral "passage" in his life, a passage "freighted to sail so far" with its rich and strange cargo of impressions.

The similarities between the wondering little boy in this passage and the central character of *What Maisie Knew* are unmistakable. *What Maisie Knew* is, in a strikingly similar way, a study of the possibilities of redeeming even the least promising material through scenic arrangements of it. Maisie (and her author) are given as their *donnée* the coarsest material possible to work with, the stupidest puppets of parents and their friends (I take for granted that it is impossible to judge Beale and Ida Farange, Mr. Perriam, the Captain, and Mrs. Cuddon in any more generous terms), and yet it is the achievement of the novel that she (and he) manage to make something perpetually interesting and at times almost delightful of them. In his preface to the volume of the New York edition in which *What Maisie Knew* appears, James observes as much, explicitly commenting on Maisie's talent for making a scene (which, needless to say, is his own talent for making a scene):

I lose myself, truly, in appreciation of my theme on noting what [Maisie] does by her "freshness" for appearances in themselves vulgar and empty enough. They become, as she deals with them, the stuff of poetry and tragedy and art; she has simply to wonder, as I say, about them, and they begin to have meanings, aspects, solidities, connections—connections with the "universal!'"—that they could scarce have hoped for. [A thing] has but to become a part of the child's bewilderment for [the] small sterilities to drop from it and for the *scene* to emerge and prevail—vivid, special, wrought hard, to the hardness of the unforgettable; the scene that is exactly what Beale and Ida and Mrs. Cuddon, and even Sir Claude and Mrs. Beale would have never for a moment succeeded in making their scant unredeemed importances—namely *appreciable*.

Just as in the passage from his autobiography, it is the difference between two kinds of scene-making—the vulgar and the artistic, the mindless and the mindful, the spoiled and the mature—that James calls our attention to in *What Maisie Knew*. The petty, vain, selfish, imbecilic characters circling around Maisie make plenty of tawdry, squalid "scenes" with her and each other throughout the novel, just as James' young cousin and his bereaved and hysterical aunt made their scenes at home, but Maisie's and her author's scene-making capacities are of another sort entirely. Chapter Eighteen, describing the accidental meeting between Mrs. Beale and her husband out with another woman at the Earl's Court Exhibition and its aftermath in which Maisie is spirited off to Mrs. Cuddon's boudoir by Beale Farange, pointedly presents both kinds of "scenes" in the closest proximity, back to back. First there is the spitting and hissing match between Beale and his wife, with their banal attempts at insulting each other, in all its pettiness and venom. And then there is the scene Maisie creates all for herself, the Arabian Nights vision of exoticism and splendor that James gloriously works up for her and a reader to revel in:

The child had been in thousands of stories—all of Mrs. Wix's and her own, to say nothing of the richest romances of French Elise—but she had never been in such a story as this. By the time [her father] had helped her out of the cab, which drove away, and she heard in the door of the house the prompt little click of his key, the Arabian Nights had quite closed around her.

From this minute the pitch of the wondrous was in everything, particularly in such an instant "Open Sesame" and in the departure of the cab, a rattling void filled with relinquished step-parents; it was, with the vividness, the almost blinding whiteness of the light that sprang responsive to papa's quick touch of a little brass knob on the wall, in a place that, at the top of a short soft staircase, struck her as the most beautiful she had ever seen in her life. . . . In the middle of the small bright room and the presence of more curtains and cushions, more pictures and mirrors, more palm-trees drooping over brocaded and gilded nooks, more little silver boxes scattered over little crooked tables and little oval miniatures hooked upon velvet screens that Mrs. Beale and her ladyship together could, in an unnatural alliance, have dreamed of mustering, the child became aware, with a sharp foretaste of compassion, of something that was strangely like the relegation to obscurity of each of those women of taste. It was a stranger operation still that her father should on the spot be presented to her as quite advantageously and even grandly at home in the dazzling scene and himself by so much the more separated from scenes inferior to it.

The facts upon which this scene is based are as sordid as can be imagined. Mrs. Cuddon (if that is even her real name) "keeps" Beale as her lover, and he has had the incredible bad taste and effrontery to wisk Maisie off to her sitting room to meet her in the middle of the night. He is using Maisie in the basest, most craven way, simply to save his own face, and "score points" against his wife. But as the writing in this passage makes clear, in a sense, none of this matters. It is Maisie's scene-making capacity that carries the day. Her scenic powers are sufficient to transform even the most tawdry material into something rich and strange and wonderful. She (in collaboration with her author) can make something out of this mess, something delightful, mysterious, and valuable.

It is in this respect that the character of Maisie foreshadows James' most inspiringly imaginative voyager, Lambert Strether of *The Ambassadors*, written five years later. It seems entirely appropriate that only a few paragraphs following the episode quoted above James' narration momentarily shifts into the rhetorical mode of that later novel, in which retrospective appreciation enriches and changes present experience. If we disregard the gender of the observer, we might almost imagine ourselves sitting in Gloriani's garden or standing in front of the *Cheval Blanc* with Strether, when we read:

The whole hour was to remain with her, for days and weeks, ineffaceably illumined and confirmed; by the end of which she was able to read into it a hundred things that had been at the moment mere miraculous pleasantness.

Maisie, like Strether, exists to be able to do this to life—and to allow Henry James to do this—to convert it into something of imaginative value through an act of consciousness. And the miracle of the golden alchemical transformation he and Maisie work in the course of the novel is that it is performed on such truly leaden figures. It consummately succeeds in working its magic on such thoroughly prosaic material.

Or to put it in a slightly different way, Maisie's accomplishment is that she succeeds in making free, creative, and imaginative "scenes" out of such boring and cartoon-like characters. She makes her scenes despite all of the corruptions and debasing influences around her. Mrs. Wix might seem to be an exception to this group, and many a reader driven almost to desperation to seize the moral high ground in a novel of such rampant immorality has been betrayed into sympathizing with her and seeing her as an elevating influence in Maisie's life. But it is vital to recognize that Mrs. Wix is only playing a deeper game than the rest of the characters, a moral shell-game in which Maisie is the pea, and "morality" is used to hold an individual hostage to her schemes and to blackmail anyone who won't play according to her rules. Like many another moral opportunist in American society before and since, her lectures, sermons, and harangues represent only a subtler form of manipulation, coercion, and regimentation, not an alternative to such things or an escape from them.

With her "straighteners" (both optical and behavioral), her school-marmish tones, and her iterative tics and habits of expression, she is a character out of a Dickens novel, but it is a measure of James' enormous difference from Dickens that precisely insofar as she is imaginable in such Dickensian externalities and fixities of social behavior and expression, she is fundamentally uninteresting to James. It would be just possible for her to be a respectable, positively valued character in a Dickens novel, morally high-minded as she is, since Dickens values such publically enactable and dependable social and moral stances. But James, as much as Melville, Thoreau, or Whitman, is indifferent to the social consistency and coherency of a character, and in fact usually positively antipathetic to it. One always knows what Mrs. Wix's moral or social position will be on any subject (just as one usually knows what that of one of Dickens' characters will be); but that is just the fundamental problem with her in the Jamesian universe. While Maisie opens up unpredictable, unprogrammatic possibilities of appreciation, action, and wonderment, Mrs. Wix closes them down. While James is devoted to freeing imagination and desire from encumbering end-points and destinations, she is busily inscribing a road map for development. While James is interested in finding ways of moving beyond the narrow definitions and limiting categories of social life, she is formulating rules and codes of conduct. As one of those who limit the free movements of imagination, and "straighten out" messy exuberances of scenic appreciation, substituting in their stead morality play rigidities of meaning, she takes her place in a long line of oppressive moralists in James' fiction, extending from Mr. Wentworth in *The Europeans* to Strether's friend Waymarsh in *The Ambassadors*.

No writer had a greater distrust of prefabricated schemes of relationship and understanding, and Mrs. Wix's moral system is as much a narrowing of the imaginative possibilities of life and human relationship as Beale's and Ida's plots against one another. For Maisie to be able to improvise a free imaginative performance in a scene of her own making, it is necessary for her to free herself as much from the coercions of Mrs. Wix's morality as from the manipulations of the Faranges' immorality. The one system is as stifling and oppressive as the other, in James' view. If there are any lingering doubts about how he and Maisie both feel about Wixian morality, Chapter 26 makes the case with a delicacy and tact with which the self-righteous governess would be incapable. Halfway through one of her annoying inquiries into Maisie's "moral sense" and what she "knows," James inserts a lovely and suggestive passage that reminds a reader of all that Mrs. Wix's moral sense leaves out of life. It is a passage that joyously, reverently celebrates Maisie's power to escape from Mrs. Wix's moral pedantry momentarily, and to move, beautifully and deftly, into a world with the mysteriousness, sensuousness, and openness to interpretation of a painting by John Singer Sargent. Almost in mid-question Maisie escapes from Wix's catechism, and a world of imaginative possibilities opens up beyond anything the dowdy governess would be capable of understanding:

> Mrs. Wix's comments had the effect of causing Maisie to heave a vague sigh of oppression and then after an instant and as if under cover of this ambiguity pass out again upon the balcony. She hung again over the rail; she felt the summer night; she dropped down into the manners of France. There was a cafe below the hotel, before which, with little chairs

and tables, people sat on a space enclosed by plants in tubs; and the impression was enriched by the flash of the white aprons of waiters and the music of a man and a woman who, from beyond the precinct, sent up the strum of a guitar and the drawl of a song about "amour." Maisie knew what "amour" meant too, and wondered if Mrs. Wix did: Mrs. Wix remained within, as still as a mouse, and perhaps not reached by the performance.

The relative positions of the two characters are blatantly symbolic, as is Maisie's leaning outward over a balcony metaphorically indicative of her general openness and receptivity to experience. But one can't avoid commenting on a passage like this sheerly as a piece of evocative writing. James' style of writing opens up possibilities of scenic appreciation and imaginative evocation in this passage that are as obviously enticing and interesting for him as a writer, as the experience depicted is meant to be for Maisie as an observer. James' writing at such a moment, that is to say, is accomplishing for him the same thing Maisie's hanging over the balcony does for her. It is a way of escaping from the logic-chopping of dialogue, the intricacies of plot development, and the complex choreography of the entrances and exits of the characters in the novel, and simply hovering, hanging, wondering, or speculating for a few moments of freedom from such narrative burdens. Just as Maisie disencumbers herself from Mrs. Wix's social and moral schemes briefly, James, in effect, disencumbers himself and his writing momentarily from the social and moral presentation and analysis of action and dialogue. He stills his novel and allows his plot to dangle briefly in such a lovely passage, just as Maisie stills herself and allows herself to dangle over the railing in silence. His momentary visionary freedom as an author is as satisfying to him as her brief visionary freedom as a character is to her.

To say the obvious, Henry James (and not Maisie Farange) is the real scene-maker and scene-appreciator in *What Maisie Knew*. But moments of meditative stillness are not the only, or even the principal, self-pleasuring acts in the novel. James seems to get even more delight in, and to be attracted more repeatedly to, scenes of nearly frantic activity and zany agitation. *What Maisie Knew* is the wildest, most kinetic, and high-spirited of James' fictional creations (with a high-spiritedness that at moments borders on becoming indistinguishable from a kind of craziness, hysteria, or mania). It is a novel of dazzling, and seemingly endless, metaphoric transformations, of preposterous coincidences and farfetched narrative parallels, and of a succession of delightful, involved permutations and variations on a few basic themes and events in chapter after chapter. James obviously revels in working out the intricate, baroque choreography of the intertwined entrances, exits, and movements of the small number of characters jockeying for position around Maisie and for power over her. All of these aspects of his novel testify to his powers of making something imaginatively interesting, and at times quite breathtaking, of the most paltry and diminished things. James delightedly trumpets his own ability to move freely and creatively in a world of confining moral, social, and psychological boundaries, sides, and categories with his outrageous imaginative swerves and endless substitutions of one thing or character for another within the text. Not only is he able to make a zany, wonderful, or thrilling "scene" out of anything it seems, but his parody shows that he is able to prevent himself from being trapped by any of the social structures and forms that tyrannize over his characters. His exuberant comedy shows how undaunted he is by these fierce manipulators and their brutalizing social forms. *What Maisie Knew* is a passionate demonstration of both its author's and its central character's ability to stay free and on the move imaginatively in a world in which wonder is always in danger of being reduced to knowledge and vision is threatened with being congealed into a selfrighteous moral stance.

But having said all that, and compared Maisie with Lambert Strether, one of the greatest creations in all of literature, one must finally confess to having fundamental reservations about the novel, precisely because of the exuberance, promiscuity, and glibness of the imaginative activity in the book. *What Maisie Knew* is the most brilliant and sustained *jeu d'esprit* in all of James' work, but its problem is that it seems to be little more than a *jeu d'esprit*. The material Maisie and her author work in seems finally too thin, and James seems, frankly, too easily satisfied with quite superficial imaginative flourishes and thrillingly surprising imaginative movements. Maisie doesn't sufficiently feel the resistance of the objects of her imaginative transformations, and in the cartoon characters around her James has chosen too easy targets for his manipulations. It is all too much a childish, delightful, yet frivolous, game. Maisie (or James?) doesn't suffer or pay for these acts of imaginative conversion in a mature, adult way. (One has only to compare the cost to Strether of his imagination to immediately see the difference.) Maisie's imaginative activity becomes, rather, a way to avoid adult problems and complications. It provides her with a means of escape from the situations around her, not with a mode of finer, more sophisticated engagement with them.

Of course, the reply to all of this is that Maisie is not an adult but a child. But that is only another way to name the fundamental limitation of *What Maisie Knew*. Maisie's consciousness is too sheltered and separated from the adult realities around her to engage our deepest interest. Her imaginative "scenes" are too childish, too superficial, trivial, and disengaged from those realities to count for very much. And that James should, apparently, not have felt this limitation in his novel as a potential shortcoming is revealing and significant. Maisie, and the novel in which she is featured, defines a recurring danger in James' work, albeit it one at times invisible to James. *What Maisie Knew* is, at certain moments, perilously close to disengaging itself from an interest in anything but its own self-delighting artistic arrangements. It comes surprisingly close at times to resembling a document like Walter Pater's *A Child In the House*. There are echoes of the Aesthetic Movement of the 1890s in many of James' writings, and his work repeatedly courts a kind of Pateresque aesthetic connoisseurship—a disengagment from moral and ethical concerns for the sake of living the autonomous life of art, an attempt to free the imagination from the encumberments and limitations of social categories and roles. But at his best, James—unlike Tennyson, Wilde, Pater, or Woolf, slightly later—resisted this tendency in his work, and that is why it is appropriate that *What Maisie Knew* does not stand alone in this volume.

The Spoils of Poynton was written within a year of *What Maisie Knew* and in fact slightly antedates the other novel, so there is no question of artistic "development" between them (if such a concept ever explains anything), but it unmistakeably shows James to be wrestling with the problem I described in the other book. *The Spoils of Poynton* deliberately attempts to make the imagination count in society, and to explore its capacities of social expression in practical human relations, as *What Maisie Knew* didn't. In many respects Fleda Vetch is a character extremely similar to Maisie Farange. Not only is she the absolute center of consciousness in her novel, more interesting by far than any of the characters arrayed around her, but she is, like Maisie, defined as being explicitly a wonderer, a stimulatingly imaginative appreciator, and an enobling spiritual redeemer of the tawdry and sordid aspects of experience. Fleda, however, is much more interesting than Maisie to the degree that James won't let her simply retreat into a world of fantasy and Arabian Nights entertainments. Her enrichments of life are expressed to and enacted upon the characters around her. If Maisie resembles Lambert Strether in that her imaginative scenes are expressed principally in plays of consciousness, Fleda resembles another late James heroine, Maggie Verver of *The Golden Bowl*, in that she is forced to enact her scenes in public social forms with other adults. While most of Maisie's "scene-making" was merely private and visionary, Fleda must express her freedom and independence in the time-bound, realistic, public forms of dialogue and personal interaction with other characters. Fleda is a would-be "free spirit" (as James' preface to the New York edition describes her), but her freedom must be asserted and maintained not as an escape from the social and personal pressures around her, but within the forms and structures of them.

Furthermore, as a mature adult, and moreover someone who falls in love with another character in the course of the novel, Fleda is emotionally involved in scenes and events from which Maisie was able to remain childishly detached. Fleda pays the full emotional cost of her imaginative investments in others, while Maisie had the luxury of treating almost everything as a story-book tale, a game, or a fantasy. Social life is imagined to be almost inevitably coercive and manipulative, and intimate human relations, especially those of love, are almost always potentially predatory for James. That is as true in *What Maisie Knew* as in *The Spoils of Poynton*, but Fleda feels and suffers from the pressures around her as Maisie never does.

Fleda, like Maggie Verver, is forced to become a more interesting actress, improvisor, and scene-maker precisely to the extent that her performances are imperiled by the resistance of, and the counter-plots and counter-performances of others attempting to stage their own alternative scenes. Her scenes are continually threatened with being edited, abridged, re-directed, or re-interpreted by other characters to serve their own ends. Her most important dramatic adversary, however, is neither the willful Mona Brigstock nor her mother, but her closest friend in the novel, Mrs. Gareth. Mrs. Gareth's scenes, both those she stages with the art objects she owns at Poynton, and those she stages with the people around her, more often than not treating them as if they were no more than art objects themselves, are expressions of sheer force, desire, and self-serving possessiveness.

The harrowing conclusion of Chapter Three shows Mrs. Gareth taking a scene out of Fleda's hands entirely. The imaginatively imperious older woman scripts, blocks, and mounts a scene "starring" Fleda (that Fleda doesn't want to be the star of it doesn't make any difference to her of course) to serve her own tyrannical purpose of marrying the younger woman off to her son, and that in itself principally only to protect her "old things." Just as Mrs. Gareth treats the works of art at Poynton as if they were pieces of portable property that could be packed up, picked up, carted about, and plunked down at will, she treats Fleda as if she were only another "find." She is the crowning piece in the Poynton collection, but only a piece nonetheless. In the theater of cruelty that Mrs. Gareth stages at the end of that chapter, Fleda is reduced to being a piece of scenery with which to stage her scene. She is a stage property to be "knocked into position" to support her performance and carry the day dramatically. (Mrs. Wix, Ida, and Beale Farange tugged and pulled on Maisie in this way too, as if she were a disputed piece of inherited furniture, but the difference was that Maisie was too innocent to perceive the dehumanizing horror of her predicament or to suffer the emotional anguish of it. Fleda has no such saving ignorance or naivete.)

Fleda, for her part, is a scene-maker who contrasts in every way with Mrs. Gareth. While the older woman narrows scenes down to a dramatic point that will serve her own selfish purposes, typecasts actors in stereotypical roles, and forces her own interpretations on everyone around her, Fleda attempts to stage free, imaginative, and uncoercive scenes in which others can participate freely. She represents the possibility of a sympathetic imagination of, and a boundless tolerance for the freedom and independence of the actors around her. Her scenes are as altruistic, generous in the liberties of response and interpretation they allow the participants, and imaginatively respectful of the feelings of the other characters, as Mrs. Gareth's are cynical, manipulative, and forced. Fleda's treatment of Owen—allowing him his own freedom of decision, trusting him to plan and execute his own course of action—is meant to make the maximum contract with Mrs. Gareth's treatment of Fleda. Fleda's imagination and her capacities of appreciation, like Henry James', free people and objects to their own independent existences, grant them a saving margin of freedom from too close scrutiny and all psychological, social, and moral predetermination of their behavior.

Completed immediately following James' debacle in the London theater, it is impossible not to read *The Spoils of Poynton*, and indeed much of the late work, including *The Golden Bowl* most notably, as a parable about strategies of acting and directing, and as a series of meditations on what makes for good and bad drama. But perhaps more to the point and even more generally, these late works constitute an extended meditation on novelistic creation itself. Fleda, like almost all of James' most important characters in the late works, is endowed with an imagination that is indistinguishable at many points from that of her creator. She has an appreciation of possibilities of experience and of meanings of other character's actions as rich and fertile as that of James himself, or that of an ideal reader of her book. Almost all of the principal characters in the late novels function as mininovelists in their own right, or as talented readers of their own and each other's stories. They represent alternative fictional strategies for the understanding of experience. They become connoisseurs of possibilities and speculators on possible courses of action for themselves and others. They ideally are able to make surmises about the meanings of events and the motives of other characters as sensitively as a good reader or a good novelist does, and when necessary they are able to revise their surmises and flexibly re-interpret what they have already interpreted. At their best they read symbols and significances in their own lives with the same alertness and subtlety that an ideal reader does, or that a novelist has in using them, and are imaginative appreciators whose capacities of meditation and appreciation are, like Fleda's, as large and noble as those of their creator. At their worst, they are novelists and readers of their own lives as petty, tendentious, self-serving, or dead to certain forms of experience as the worst novelists who write or the worst readers who read.

While Mrs. Gareth, in effect, reduces the works of art at Poynton to the status of melodramatic stage properties, objects to be dramatically grasped at and held on to at all cost, Fleda is capable of imaginatively "possessing" even what she has been physically and tangibly dispossessed of. To "lose" the spoils of Poynton in the worldly sense (Mrs. Gareth's only sense of gain or loss) may actually be the only way to truly "gain" them imaginatively, James suggests: to gain them for appreciation, for wonder, for memory and art. That is why, in two of the most beautiful and revealing passages in the novel, Fleda (and James) can actually succeed in suggesting that not only is worldly loss convertible into imaginative gain, but that the gain in some wonderful and mysterious sense depends upon the loss in the other sense. In the first passage (from Chapter Twenty), Fleda has just learned of Mrs. Gareth's shipment of the works of art back to Poynton for their final rest. In some corner of her being Fleda senses that she will never go to Poynton again, never see a single one of them again. It is an enormous, almost devastating worldly loss; but it is also an almost infinite gain for imagination:

> The loss was a gain to memory and love; it was to her too, at last, that, in condonation of her treachery, the old things had crept back. She greeted them with open arms; she thought of them hour after hour. . . . She too, she felt was of the religion, and like any other of the passionately pious she could worship now even in the desert. Yes, it was all for her; far round as she had gone she had been strong enough: her love had gathered in the spoils. She wanted indeed no catalogue to count them over; the array of them, miles away, was complete; each piece, in its turn, was perfect to her; she could have drawn up a catalogue from memory. Thus again she lived with them, and she thought of them without a question of any personal right. That they might have been, that they might still be hers, that they were perhaps already another's, were ideas that had too little to say to her. They were nobody's at all—too proud, unlike base animals and humans, to be reducible to anything so narrow. It was Poynton that was theirs; they had simply recovered their own. The joy of that for them was the source of the strange peace in which the girl found herself floating.

In the second passage, even more sublime, from the following chapter, Fleda speaks to Mrs. Gareth about the maiden aunt who lived at Ricks before her, and about what her things tell her. She hears a "voice" to which Mrs. Gareth is deaf. Her ability to hear it at all is an indication of all of the ways she differs from Mrs. Gareth. (And note how, in a passage which tests a reader's ability to "hear" voices, James contrasts the voice tones of the two speakers. Mrs. Gareth's smart, chatty responses to Fleda's meditative explorations show that she is as tone deaf to the sort of voice Fleda offers her as she is to the voice the aunt offers.) Fleda begins:

"Ah, the little melancholy, tender, tell-tale things: how can they *not* speak to you and find a way to your heart? It's not the great chorus of Poynton; but you're not, I'm sure, either so proud or so broken as to be reached by nothing but that. This is a voice so gentle, so human, so feminine—a faint, far-away voice with the little quaver of a heart-break. You've listened to it unawares: for the arrangement and effect of everything . . . . you made things 'compose' in spite of yourself. You've only to be a day or two in a place with four sticks for something to come of it!"

"Then if anything has come of it here, it has come precisely of just four. That's literally, by the inventory, all there are!" said Mrs. Gareth.

"If there were any more there would be too many to convey the impression in which half the beauty resides— the impression, somehow, of something dreamed and missed, something reduced, relinquished, resigned: the poetry as it were, of something sensibly *gone*." Fleda ingeniously and triumphantly worked it out. "Ah, there's something here that will never be in the inventory!"

"Does it happen to be in your power to give it a name?". . . .

"I can give it a dozen. It's a kind of fourth dimension. It's a presence, a perfume, a touch. It's a soul, a story, a life. There's ever so much more here than you and I. We're in fact just three!"

"Oh, if you count the ghosts!"

"Of course I count the ghosts. It seems to me ghosts count double—for what they were and for what they are. Somehow there were no ghosts at Poynton," Fleda went on. "That was the only fault."

But James is under no illusions about how much "ghosts" count for in the everyday world, about the difference between imaginative "possession" as Fleda defines it, and physical "possession" as Mrs. Gareth and the Brigstocks understand it. As much of the preface in the volume of the New York edition devoted to *The Spoils of Poynton* argues, life invariably fails to live up to our appreciations of it. To be a character endowed with the imagination of a novelist, or to be a novelist imagining such a character is to be doomed to be repeatedly disappointed by "clumsy Life again at her stupid work." The world won't and can't live up to Fleda's or James' imagination of it. Owen won't live up to her loving appreciation of him, any more than Mrs. Gareth will live up to Fleda's splendid initial conception of her. That is the source of the comedy bordering on tragedy that colors most of Fleda's encounters with both of these others. The conclusion of the novel rubs a reader's nose in the fact—or literally throws soot in Fleda's eyes to emphasize—that in Fleda's life, unlike the lives of characters in novels she has read, she is denied even the final small luxury of possessing either a tangible object or a symbolic token to carry away into the sunset. If there is any final, enduring "possession" for her to console herself with and to summarize all that she has felt and experienced, it can only be imaginative. If there is to be any gain or "richness" for her, it can only be in her consciousness.

The ends of each of James' great, late novels, of which *The Spoils of Poynton* is the first, bring a reader and the principal characters to the same tragic recognition that is forced on Fleda in this final scene: a recognition of the fundamental untranslateability of our imaginations and desires into the languages of social expression and worldly experience. It is a recognition that the only ultimately free act left to us can be one of sacrifice, denial, renunciation, and relinquishment of every form of possession except that of the imagination. There seems to have been a time in James' early work, around the period of *The Europeans*, *An International Episode*, and *The Portrait of a Lady*, when, notwithstanding the specific failures these works document, he felt it might just be possible to live the life of the imagination in the actual forms and structures of social life. The heroines of those three works launch out on extraordinarily daring explorations of the possibility of actually, in the real world of brilliant, glamorous, social intercourse, being able to "make scenes" answerable to their most exalted and passionate dreams of freedom and free self-expression. Neither Eugenia Munster, Bessie Alden, nor Isabel Archer succeed in expressing their extravagant visions of themselves and their ideals of free movement within the particular forms of dialogue, action, and social interchange, but to the very ends of their novels one feels that James, like his heroines themselves, astonishingly hasn't abandoned all hope of it being possible really to succeed, in some way, at some time.

That outrageous American aspiration, that hope, that faith, is what has faded by the time of *What Maisie Knew* and *The Spoils of Poynton*. The earlier work dreamed that the most exalted, liberating, creative "scenes" could be "made" and "appreciated" in real life, but the recognition of the later work, and of these two novels in particular, is that such "scenes" can be "made" and "appreciated" only in our own charged consciousnesses, and that somehow must suffice. The expressive gap that is, apparently almost accidentally, built into *What Maisie Knew* (the difference between what Maisie feels and knows and what she is capable of expressing in any social or linguistic form) becomes the fundamental fact with which all of James' subsequent work begins. It is the basic condition of human existence. There is no way for Maisie to turn her Sargent-like "vision" on the balcony— her appreciation of "amour," her luscious apprehension of the sights and sounds of a French cafe at night, with the sparkling white starched aprons of the waiters and the sounds of a song being sung—into meaningful words or interactions with Mrs. Wix or any other character, any more than James can represent such a moment in terms of the social dialogue and eventfulness of the traditional British novel. He must stop the plot, silence the dialogue, and momentarily arrest the movements of his characters in order to make such a "scene" of scenic insight even momentarily expressible. Such a moment exists as a scene at all only in the scenic consciousness of a character. Similarly there is no way for Fleda to count, inventory, or possess the objects at Poynton except as "ghosts," spiritual realities that can be named or owned in no more tangible or physical way. But that is no reason for James and his heroines to abandon the dream of "scene-making" only an argument that the imagination must be satisfied with its own acts of visionary appropriation and possession.

Nothing is a more graphic illustration of the change I am describing in James' work than his switch, at this point in his career, from central characters who are almost without exception figures in high society to lower- and middle-class protagonists (like Fleda Vetch), and children (like Maisie), who represent a subclass of their own. Upper-class characters like Baroness Munster, Bessie Alden, and Isabel Archer move in worlds in which the stylized, sophisticated, social expression of one's free movements of imagination is at least theoretically possible. Elaborate verbal and social expressions of oneself and possibilities of complex public performance are available to such characters that are denied to the later ones: children, tutors, and governesses (in *What Maisie Knew*, *The Turn of the Screw*, and "The Pupil") and impoverished, disenfranchised, middle-class girls (in *The Spoils of Poynton* and "In the Cage").

For whatever complex personal reasons, and surely James' disastrous attempts to write for the London stage between 1890 and 1895, and the almost unanimous critical and popular failure of his fictional works that led up to it shaped the attitudes of his subsequent work, by the time he sat down to write *What Maisie Knew* and *The Spoils of Poynton* in 1896 and 1897 a youthful dream had died in James. He had abandoned his dream of the free expression of the self in the forms of society. The result, especially manifesting itself in *The Spoils of Poynton*, is the beginning of what has come to be called the late style, but what that means is that from this point on in James' work, authorial style (as distinguishable from social styles of expression and behavior by characters in the novels) is called on to express intensities of desire and richnesses of consciousness that have become novelistically unspeakable in the forms of dialogue, plot, and social interaction.

At the ends of their novels Fleda and Maisie are left with only their freighted consciousness to show for all they have felt and experienced. There are no words either can speak, and no one who would understand to speak them to, to express their consciousnesses in the world. James' prose style has to fill that fundamental expressive gap in order that anything can be expressed in the novel at all. The result is the whole paraphernalia of the late manner—the melodramatic heightenings, the adjectival and adverbial insistencies, and the elaborated cadences of the late work. The passage with which I began—the small "scene" involving the twelve-year-old boy and his cousin Marie—might be read as a veiled parable of this whole process of development in James' work. Marie, like one of the glamorous, gorgeous heroines of the early work, embodies the exhilarating, daring attempt to "make scenes" to express herself in the real world of space, time, actions, events, and dialogue. But the passage itself in which Marie's attempt is recorded—it is a *locus classicus* of James' latest style, written in 1913—communicates the extent to which the real "scene" only exists in the heightened, incommunicable consciousness of the silent, still, passive little boy observing it all (he might be Maisie's twin brother), and in the consciousnesses of the author "making the scene" narratively and of the reader appreciating it. The late style expresses a kind of "scene" that can't be "made" in Marie's sense at all, or that is only misunderstood when it is made (as both Maisie and Fleda are misunderstood by everyone around them). It can be made only as an act of consciousness involving "detachment" and "presence of mind; just the qualities in which Marie's output was apparently deficient."

That, I think, is a way to understand the extraordinary "scene" with which *The Spoils of Poynton* ends. One can feel James applying enormous stylistic pressure to almost every detail and phrase within it. It is a scene that would be easy to object to on account of its melodramatic heightenings, its gothicism, and the purpleness of some of its prose. Everything is made symbolic or significant. Everything is "made" to "speak" to Fleda and a reader. The December dawn, the wild wind, the fierce impending storm, the cataclysmic conflagration engulfing Poynton, the extremity of Fleda's state of feeling, the melodramatic intensifications of the writing (though chastened by the bizarre, comic dialogue of the station master) are right out of a trashy gothic novel (or a Harlequin romance in our day). One could criticize such excessiveness, such a derangement of the style of the novel (how far we have traveled from the style of the first chapters), such gothicism if it were not for the fact that the entire novel has been devoted to getting Fleda and a reader to a point where we can appreciate this expressive predicament. There is no other form of expression available for Fleda's over-charged consciousness than in such an ending. Everything must "speak" for and to Fleda in this way, and to a reader, because all of the other forms of speech have been left behind in the course of the novel. Only in such stylistic intensifications, in such violences of event (and compare the concluding murder of the child in the novel written the year before this one, *The Other House*), in such details of the landscape and the weather can James' "scene," and Fleda's consciousness be expressed. *What Maisie Knew* and *The Spoils of Poynton*, like the later novels *The Ambassadors* and *The Golden Bowl*, in the course of their narratives, deconstruct the novel of manners, the novel of social interchange and the play of dialogue between characters, and in its place, by their ends, offer a new novel, a novel of consciousness alienated and alone, estranged from society and shrouded in silence and the stillness of scenic vision.

Maisie and Fleda must learn to live with this state of affairs. It is on this basis that they in turn anticipate Lambert Strether and Maggie Verver, and that *What Maisie Knew* and *The Spoils of Poynton* respectively anticipate the even more complex tragic achievements of *The Ambassadors* and *The Golden Bowl*. *The Spoils of Poynton* announces in miniature the great resounding theme of all of the late novels. In those works James has awoken with a start from the idealistic dream of his earlier works. but it is possible to argue that the late works, beginning with *The Spoils of Poynton*, offer something richer and more complex than the earlier dream. They represent a profound meditation (to quote part of the preceding statement by Fleda again) on "something dreamed and missed, something reduced, relinquished, resigned." They express "the poetry, as it were, of something sensibly *gone*." They "count the ghosts" that have always haunted the American imagination.

—Raymond Carney
Middlebury College

PREFACE

I RECOGNIZE again, for the first of these three Tales,* another instance of the growth of the 'great oak' from the little acorn; since *What Maisie Knew* is at least a tree that spreads beyond any provision its small germ might on a first handling have appeared likely to make for it. The accidental mention had been made to me of the manner in which the situation of some luckless child of a divorced couple was affected, under my informant's eyes, by the remarriage of one of its parents – I forget which; so that, thanks to the limited desire for its company expressed by the step-parent, the law of its little life, its being entertained in rotation by its father and its mother, wouldn't easily prevail. Whereas each of these persons had at first vindictively desired to keep it from the other, so at present the remarried relative sought now rather to be rid of it – that is to leave it as much as possible, and beyond the appointed times and seasons, on the hands of the adversary; which malpractice, resented by the latter as bad faith, would of course be repaid and avenged by an equal treachery. The wretched infant was thus to find itself practically disowned, rebounding from racquet to racquet like a tennis ball or a shuttlecock. This figure could but touch the fancy to the quick and strike one as the beginning of a story – a story commanding a great choice of developments. I recollect, however, promptly thinking that for a proper symmetry the second parent should marry too – which in the case named to me indeed would probably soon occur, and was in any case what the ideal of the situation required. The second step-parent would have but to be correspondingly incommoded by obligations to the offspring of a hated predecessor for the misfortune of the little victim to become altogether exemplary. The business would accordingly be sad enough, yet I am not sure its possibility of interest would so much have appealed to me had I not soon felt that the ugly facts, so stated or conceived, by no means constituted the whole appeal.

* This Preface forms the major part of the Preface to Volume XI of the New York edition (1909), which also includes *The Pupil* and *In the Cage*.

The light of an imagination touched by them couldn't help therefore projecting a further ray, thanks to which it became rather quaintly clear that, not less than the chance of misery and of a degraded state, the chance of happiness and of an improved state might be here involved for the child, round about whom the complexity of life would thus turn to fineness, to richness – and indeed would have but so to turn for the small creature to be steeped in security and ease. Sketchily clustered even, these elements gave out that vague pictorial glow which forms the first appeal of a living 'subject' to the painter's consciousness; but the glimmer became intense as I proceeded to a further analysis. The further analysis is for that matter almost always the torch of rapture and victory, as the artist's firm hand grasps and plays it – I mean, naturally, of the smothered rapture and the obscure victory, enjoyed and celebrated not in the street but before some innermost shrine; the odds being a hundred to one, in almost any connexion, that it doesn't arrive by any easy first process at the *best* residuum of truth. That was the charm, sensibly, of the picture thus at first confusedly showing; the elements so couldn't but flush, to their very surface, with some deeper depth of irony than the mere obvious. It lurked in the crude postulate like a buried scent; the more the attention hovered the more aware it became of the fragrance. To which I may add that the more I scratched the surface and penetrated, the more potent, to the intellectual nostril, became this virtue. At last, accordingly, the residuum, as I have called it, reached, I was in presence of the red dramatic spark that glowed at the core of my vision and that, as I gently blew upon it, burned higher and clearer. This precious particle was the *full* ironic truth – the most interesting item to be read into the child's situation. For satisfaction of the mind, in other words, the small expanding consciousness would have to be saved, have to become presentable as a register of impressions; and saved by the experience of certain advantages, by some enjoyed profit and some achieved confidence, rather than coarsened, blurred, sterilized, by ignorance and pain. This better state, in the young life, would reside in the exercise of a function other than that of disconcerting the selfishness of its parents – which was all that had on the face of the matter seemed reserved to it in the way of criticism applied to their rupture. The early relation would be

6

exchanged for a later; instead of simply submitting to the inherited tie and the imposed complication, of suffering from them, our little wonder-working agent would create, without design, quite fresh elements of this order – contribute, that is, to the formation of a fresh tie, from which it would then (and for all the world as if through a small demonic foresight) proceed to derive great profit.

This is but to say that the light in which the vision so readily grew to a wholeness was that of a second marriage on both sides; the father having, in the freedom of divorce, but to take another wife, as well as the mother, under a like licence, another husband, for the case to begin, at least, to stand beautifully on its feet. There would be thus a perfect logic for what might come – come even with the mere attribution of a certain sensibility (if but a mere relative fineness) to either of the new parties. Say the prime cause making for the ultimate attempt to shirk on one side or the other, and better still if on both, a due share of the decreed burden should have been, after all, in each progenitor, a constitutional inaptitude for *any* burden, and a base intolerance of it: we should thus get a motive not requiring, but happily dispensing with, too particular a perversity in the step-parents. The child seen as creating by the fact of its forlornness a relation between its step-parents, the more intimate the better, dramatically speaking; the child, by the mere appeal of neglectedness and the mere consciousness of relief, weaving about, with the best faith in the world, the close web of sophistication; the child becoming a centre and pretext for a fresh system of misbehaviour, a system moreover of a nature to spread and ramify: *there* would be the 'full' irony, there the promising theme into which the hint I had originally picked up would logically flower. No themes are so human as those that reflect for us, out of the confusion of life, the close connexion of bliss and bale, of the things that help with the things that hurt, so dangling before us for ever that bright hard medal, of so strange an alloy, one face of which is somebody's right and ease and the other somebody's pain and wrong. To live with all intensity and perplexity and felicity in its terribly mixed little world would thus be the part of my interesting small mortal; bringing people together who would be at least more correctly separate; keeping people separate who would be at least more correctly together; flourishing, to a degree, at the cost of many

7

conventions and proprieties, even decencies, really keeping the torch of virtue alive in an air tending infinitely to smother it; really in short making confusion worse confounded by drawing some stray fragrance of an ideal across the scent of selfishness, by sowing on barren strands, through the mere fact of presence, the seed of the moral life.

All this would be to say, I at once recognized, that my light vessel of consciousness, swaying in such a draught, couldn't be with verisimilitude a rude little boy; since, beyond the fact that little boys are never so 'present', the sensibility of the female young is indubitably, for early youth, the greater, and my plan would call, on the part of my protagonist, for 'no end' of sensibility. I might impute that amount of it without extravagance to a slip of a girl whose faculties should have been well shaken up; but I should have so to depend on its action to keep my story clear that I must be able to show it in all assurance as naturally intense. To this end I should have of course to suppose for my heroine dispositions originally promising, but above all I should have to invest her with perceptions easily and almost infinitely quickened. So handsomely fitted out, yet not in a manner too grossly to affront probability, she might well see me through the whole course of my design; which design, more and more attractive as I turned it over, and dignified by the most delightful difficulty, would be to make and to keep her so limited consciousness the very field of my picture while at the same time guarding with care the integrity of the objects presented. With the charm of this possibility, therefore, the project for 'Maisie' rounded itself and loomed large – any subject looming large, for that matter, I am bound to add, from the moment one is ridden by the law of entire expression. I have already elsewhere noted, I think, that the memory of my own work preserves for me no theme that, at some moment or other of its development, and always only waiting for the right connexion or chance, hasn't signally refused to remain humble, even (or perhaps all the more resentfully) when fondly selected for its conscious and hopeless humility. Once 'out', like a housedog of a temper above confinement, it defies the mere whistle, it roams, it hunts, it seeks out and 'sees' life; it can be brought back but by hand and then only to take its futile thrashing. It wasn't at any rate for an idea seen in the light I here glance

8

at not to have due warrant of its value – how could the value of a scheme so finely workable *not* be great. The one presented register of the whole complexity would be the play of the child's confused and obscure notation of it, and yet the whole, as I say, should be unmistakably, should be honourably there, seen through the faint intelligence, or at the least attested by the imponderable presence, and still advertising its sense.

I recall that my first view of this neat possibility was as the attaching problem of the picture restricted (while yet achieving, as I say, completeness and coherency) to what the child might be conceived to have *understood* – to have been able to interpret and appreciate. Further reflexion and experiment showed me my subject strangled in that extreme of rigour. The infant mind would at the best leave great gaps and voids; so that with a systematic surface possibly beyond reproach we should nevertheless fail of clearness of sense. I should have to stretch the matter to what my wondering witness materially and inevitably *saw*; a great deal of which quantity she either wouldn't understand at all or would quite misunderstand – and on those lines, only on those, my task would be prettily cut out. To that then I settled – to the question of giving it *all*, the whole situation surrounding her, but of giving it only through the occasions and connexions of her proximity and her attention; only as it might pass before her and appeal to her, as it might touch her and affect her, for better or worse, for perceptive gain or perceptive loss: so that we fellow witnesses, we not more invited but only more expert critics, should feel in strong possession of it. This would be, to begin with, a plan of absolutely definite and measurable application – that in itself always a mark of beauty; and I have been interested to find on re-perusal of the work that some such controlling grace successfully rules it. Nothing could be more 'done', I think, in the light of its happiest intention; and this in spite of an appearance that at moments obscures my consistency. Small children have many more perceptions than they have terms to translate them; their vision is at any moment much richer, their apprehension even constantly stronger, than their prompt, their at all producible, vocabulary. Amusing therefore as it might at the first blush have seemed to restrict myself in this case to the terms as well as to the experience, it became at once plain that such an attempt would fail. Maisie's terms accordingly play their part – since her simpler conclusions quite depend on them; but our own commentary constantly attends and amplifies. This it is that on occasion, doubtless, seems to represent us as going so 'behind' the facts of her spectacle as to exaggerate the activity of her relation to them. The difference here is but of a shade: it is her relation, her activity of spirit, that determines all our own concern – we simply take advantage of these things better than she herself. Only, even though it is her interest that mainly makes matters interesting for us, we inevitably note this in figures that are not yet at her command and that are nevertheless required whenever those aspects about her and those parts of her experience that she understands darken off into others that she rather tormentedly misses. All of which gave me a high firm logic to observe; supplied the force for which the straightener of almost any tangle is grateful while he labours, the sense of pulling at threads intrinsically worth it – strong enough and fine enough and entire enough.

Of course, beyond this, was another and well-nigh equal charm – equal in spite of its being almost independent of the acute constructional, the endless expressional question. This was the quite different question of the particular kind of truth of resistance I might be able to impute to my central figure – *some* intensity, some continuity of resistance being naturally of the essence of the subject. Successfully to resist (to resist, that is, the strain of observation and the assault of experience) what would that be, on the part of so young a person, but to remain fresh, and still fresh, and to have even a freshness to communicate? – the case being with Maisie to the end that she treats her friends to the rich little spectacle of objects embalmed in her wonder. She wonders, in other words, to the end, to the death – the death of her childhood, properly speaking; after which (with the inevitable shift, sooner or later, of her point of view) her situation will change and become another affair, subject to other measurements and with a new centre altogether. The particular reaction that will have led her to that point, and that it has been of an exquisite interest to study in her, will have spent itself; there will be another scale, another perspective, another horizon. Our business meanwhile therefore is to extract from her current reaction whatever it may be worth; and for that matter we recognize in it the highest exhibitional virtue. Truly, I reflect, if the theme had had no other beauty it would still have had this rare and distinguished one of its so expressing the variety of the child's values. She is not only the extraordinary 'ironic centre' I have already noted; she has the wonderful importance of shedding a light far beyond any reach of her comprehension; of lending to poorer persons and things, by the mere fact of their being involved with her and by the special scale she creates for them, a precious element of dignity. I lose myself, truly, in appreciation of my theme on noting what she does by her 'freshness' for appearances in themselves vulgar and empty enough. They become, as she deals with them, the stuff of poetry and tragedy and art; she has simply to wonder, as I say, about them, and they begin to have meanings, aspects, solidities, connexions – connexions with the 'universal!' – that they could scarce have hoped for. Ida Farange alone, so to speak, or Beale alone, that is either of them otherwise connected – what intensity, what 'objectivity' (the most developed degree of *being* anyhow thinkable for them) would they have? How would they repay at all the favour of our attention?

Maisie makes them portentous all by the play of her good faith, makes her mother above all, to my vision – unless I have wholly failed to render it – concrete, immense and awful; so that we get, for our profit, and get by an economy of process interesting in itself, the thoroughly pictured creature, the striking figured symbol. At two points in particular, I seem to recognize, we enjoy at its maximum this effect of associational magic. The passage in which her father's terms of intercourse with the insinuating but so strange and unattractive lady whom he has had the detestable levity to whisk her off to see late at night, is a signal example of the all but incalculable way in which interest may be constituted. The facts involved are that Beale Farange is ignoble, that the friend to whom he introduces his daughter is deplorable, and that from the commerce of the two, *as* the two merely, we would fain avert our heads. Yet the thing has but to become a part of the child's bewilderment for these small sterilities to drop from it and for the *scene* to emerge and prevail – vivid, special, wrought hard, to the hardness of the unforgettable; the scene that is exactly what Beale and Ida and Mrs Cuddon, and even Sir Claude and Mrs Beale, would never for a moment have succeeded in making

11

their scant unredeemed importances – namely *appreciable*. I find another instance in the episode of Maisie's unprepared encounter, while walking in the Park with Sir Claude, of her mother and that beguiled attendant of her mother, the encouraging, the appealing 'Captain', to whom this lady contrives to commit her for twenty minutes while she herself deals with the second husband. The human substance here would have seemed in advance well-nigh too poor for conversion, the three 'mature' figures of too short a radiation, too stupid (*so* stupid it was for Sir Claude to have married Ida!), too vain, too thin, for any clear application; but promptly, immediately, the child's own importance, spreading and contagiously acting, has determined the *total* value otherwise. Nothing of course, meanwhile, is an older story to the observer of manners and the painter of life than the grotesque finality with which such terms as 'painful', 'unpleasant', and 'disgusting' are often applied to his results; to that degree, in truth, that the free use of them as weightily conclusive again and again re-enforces his estimate of the critical sense of circles in which they artlessly flourish. Of course under that superstition I was punctually to have had read to me the lesson that the 'mixing-up' of a child with anything unpleasant confessed itself an aggravation of the unpleasantness, and that nothing could well be more disgusting than to attribute to Maisie so intimate an 'acquaintance' with the gross immoralities surrounding her.

The only thing to say of such lucidities is that, however one may have 'discounted' in advance, and as once for all, their general radiance, one is disappointed if the hour for them, in the particular connexion, doesn't strike – they so keep before us elements with which even the most sedate philosopher must always reckon. The painter of life has indeed work cut out for him when a considerable part of life offers itself in the guise of that sapience. The effort really to see and really to represent is no idle business in face of the *constant* force that makes for muddlement. The great thing is indeed that the muddled state too is one of the very sharpest of the realities, that it also has colour and form and character, has often in fact a broad and rich comicality, many of the signs and values of the appreciable. Thus it was to be, for example, I might gather, that the very principle of Maisie's appeal, her undestroyed freshness, in other words that vivacity of intelligence by which she

12

indeed does vibrate in the infected air, indeed does flourish in her immoral world, may pass for a barren and senseless thing, or at best a negligible one. For nobody to whom life at large is *easily* interesting do the finer, the shyer, the more anxious small vibrations, fine and shy and anxious with the passion that precedes knowledge, succeed in being negligible: which is doubtless one of many reasons why the passage between the child and the kindly, friendly, ugly gentleman who, seated with her in Kensington Gardens under a spreading tree, positively answers to her for her mother as no one has ever answered, and so stirs her, filially and morally, as she has never been stirred, throws into highest relief, to my sense at least, the side on which the subject is strong, and becomes the type-passage – other advantages certainly aiding, as I may say – for the expression of its beauty. The active, contributive close-circling wonder, as I have called it, in which the child's identity is guarded and preserved, and which makes her case remarkable exactly by the weight of the tax on it, provides distinction for her, provides vitality and variety, through the operation of the tax – which would have done comparatively little for us hadn't it been monstrous. A pity for us surely to have been deprived of this just reflexion. 'Maisie' is of 1907.

What Maisie Knew

THE litigation had seemed interminable and had in fact been complicated; but by the decision on the appeal the judgement of the divorce-court was confirmed as to the assignment of the child. The father, who, though bespattered from head to foot, had made good his case, was, in pursuance of this triumph, appointed to keep her: it was not so much that the mother's character had been more absolutely damaged as that the brilliancy of a lady's complexion (and this lady's, in court, was immensely remarked) might be more regarded as showing the spots. Attached, however, to the second pronouncement was a condition that detracted, for Beale Farange, from its sweetness – an order that he should refund to his late wife the twenty-six hundred pounds put down by her, as it was called, some three years before, in the interest of the child's maintenance and precisely on a proved understanding that he would take no proceedings: a sum of which he had had the administration and of which he could render not the least account. The obligation thus attributed to her adversary was no small balm to Ida's resentment; it drew a part of the sting from her defeat and compelled Mr Farange perceptibly to lower his crest. He was unable to produce the money or to raise it in any way; so that after a squabble scarcely less public and scarcely more decent than the original shock of battle his only issue from his predicament was a compromise proposed by his legal advisers and finally accepted by hers.

His debt was by this arrangement remitted to him and the little girl disposed of in a manner worthy of the judgement-seat of Solomon. She was divided in two and the portions tossed impartially to the disputants. They would take her, in rotation, for six months at a time; she would spend half the year with each. This was odd justice in the eyes of those who still blinked in the fierce light projected from the tribunal – a light in which neither parent figured in the least as a happy example to youth and innocence. What was to have been expected on the evidence was the

17

nomination, *in loco parentis*, of some proper third person, some respectable or at least some presentable friend. Apparently, however, the circle of the Faranges had been scanned in vain for any such ornament; so that the only solution finally meeting all the difficulties was, save that of sending Maisie to a Home, the partition of the tutelary office in the manner I have mentioned. There were more reasons for her parents to agree to it than there had ever been for them to agree to anything; and they now prepared with her help to enjoy the distinction that waits upon vulgarity sufficiently attested. Their rupture had resounded, and after being perfectly insignificant together they would be decidedly striking apart. Had they not produced an impression that warranted people in looking for appeals in the newspapers for the rescue of the little one – reverberation, amid a vociferous public, of the idea that some movement should be started or some benevolent person should come forward? A good lady came indeed a step or two: she was distantly related to Mrs Farange, to whom she proposed that, having children and nurseries wound up and going, she should be allowed to take home the bone of contention and, by working it into her system, relieve at least one of the parents. This would make every time, for Maisie, after her inevitable six months with Beale, much more of a change.

'More of a change?' Ida cried. 'Won't it be enough of a change for her to come from that low brute to the person in the world who detests him most?'

'No, because you detest him so much that you'll always talk to her about him. You'll keep him before her by perpetually abusing him.'

Mrs Farange stared. 'Pray, then, am I to do nothing to counteract his villainous abuse of *me*?'

The good lady, for a moment, made no reply: her silence was a grim judgement of the whole point of view. 'Poor little monkey!' she at last exclaimed; and the words were an epitaph for the tomb of Maisie's childhood. She was abandoned to her fate. What was clear to any spectator was that the only link binding her to either parent was this lamentable fact of her being a ready vessel for bitterness, a deep little porcelain cup in which biting acids could be mixed. They had wanted her not for any good they could do her, but for the harm they could, with her unconscious aid, do each other. She should serve their anger and seal their revenge,

18

for husband and wife had been alike crippled by the heavy hand of justice, which in the last resort met on neither side their indignant claim to get, as they called it, everything. If each was only to get half this seemed to concede that neither was so base as the other pretended, or, to put it differently, offered them both as bad indeed, since they were only as good as each other. The mother had wished to prevent the father from, as she said, 'so much as looking' at the child; the father's plea was that the mother's lightest touch was 'simply contamination'. These were the opposed principles in which Maisie was to be educated – she was to fit them together as she might. Nothing could have been more touching at first than her failure to suspect the ordeal that awaited her little unspotted soul. There were persons horrified to think what those in charge of it would combine to try to make of it: no one could conceive in advance that they would be able to make nothing ill.

This was a society in which for the most part people were occupied only with chatter, but the disunited couple had at last grounds for expecting a time of high activity. They girded their loins, they felt as if the quarrel had only begun. They felt indeed more married than ever, inasmuch as what marriage had mainly suggested to them was the unbroken opportunity to quarrel. There had been 'sides' before, and there were sides as much as ever; for the sider too the prospect opened out, taking the pleasant form of a superabundance of matter for desultory conversation. The many friends of the Faranges drew together to differ about them; contradiction grew young again over teacups and cigars. Everybody was always assuring everybody of something very shocking, and nobody would have been jolly if nobody had been outrageous. The pair appeared to have a social attraction which failed merely as regards each other: it was indeed a great deal to be able to say for Ida that no one but Beale desired her blood, and for Beale that if he should ever have his eyes scratched out it would be only by his wife. It was generally felt, to begin with, that they were awfully good-looking – they had really not been analysed to a deeper residuum. They made up together, for instance, some twelve feet three of stature, and nothing was more discussed than the apportionment of this quantity. The sole flaw in Ida's beauty was a length and reach of arm conducive perhaps to her having so often beaten her ex-husband at billiards, a game in which she showed a superiority largely accountable, as she maintained, for the resentment finding expression in his physical violence. Billiards was her great accomplishment and the distinction her name always first produced the mention of. Notwithstanding some very long lines everything about her that might have been large and that in many women profited by the licence was, with a single exception, admired and cited for its smallness. The exception was her eyes, which might have been of mere regulation size, but which overstepped the modesty of nature; her mouth, on the other hand, was barely perceptible, and odds were freely taken as to the measurement of her waist. She was a person who, when she was out – and she was always out – produced everywhere a sense of having been seen often, the sense indeed of a kind of abuse of visibility, so that it would have been, in the usual places, rather vulgar to wonder at her. Strangers only did that; but they, to the amusement of the familiar, did it very much: it was an inevitable way of betraying an alien habit. Like her husband she carried clothes, carried them as a train carries passengers: people had been known to compare their taste and dispute about the accommodation they gave these articles, though inclining on the whole to the commendation of Ida as less overcrowded, especially with jewellery and flowers. Beale Farange had natural decorations, a kind of costume in his vast fair beard, burnished like a gold breastplate, and in the eternal glitter of the teeth that his long moustache had been trained not to hide and that gave him, in every possible situation, the look of the joy of life. He had been destined in his youth for diplomacy and momentarily attached, without a salary, to a legation which enabled him often to say, 'In *my* time in the East': but contemporary history had somehow had no use for him, had hurried past him and left him in perpetual Piccadilly. Every one knew what he had – only twenty-five hundred. Poor Ida, who had run through everything, had now nothing but her carriage and her paralysed uncle. This old brute, as he was called, was supposed to have a lot put away. The child was provided for, thanks to a crafty godmother, a defunct aunt of Beale's, who had left her something in such a manner that the parents could appropriate only the income.

20

1

THE child was provided for, but the new arrangement was inevitably confounding to a young intelligence intensely aware that something had happened which must matter a good deal and looking anxiously out for the effects of so great a cause. It was to be the fate of this patient little girl to see much more than she at first understood, but also even at first to understand much more than any little girl, however patient, had perhaps ever understood before. Only a drummer-boy in a ballad or a story could have been so in the thick of the fight. She was taken into the confidence of passions on which she fixed just the stare she might have had for images bounding across the wall in the slide of a magic lantern. Her little world was phantasmagoric – strange shadows dancing on a sheet. It was as if the whole performance had been given for her – a mite of a half-scared infant in a great dim theatre. She was in short introduced to life with a liberality in which the selfishness of others found its account, and there was nothing to avert the sacrifice but the modesty of her youth.

Her first term was with her father, who spared her only in not letting her have the wild letters addressed to her by her mother: he confined himself to holding them up at her and shaking them, while he showed his teeth, and then amusing her by the way he chucked them, across the room, bang into the fire. Even at that moment, however, she had a scared anticipation of fatigue, a guilty sense of not rising to the occasion, feeling the charm of the violence with which the stiff unopened envelopes, whose big monograms – Ida bristled with monograms – she would have liked to see, were made to whizz, like dangerous missiles, through the air. The greatest effect of the great cause was her own greater importance, chiefly revealed to her in the larger freedom with which she was handled, pulled hither and thither and kissed, and the proportionately greater niceness she was obliged to show. Her features had somehow become prominent; they were so perpetually nipped by the gentlemen who came to see her father and

21

the smoke of whose cigarettes went into her face. Some of these gentlemen made her strike matches and light their cigarettes; others, holding her on knees violently jolted, pinched the calves of her legs till she shrieked – her shriek was much admired – and reproached them with being toothpicks. The word stuck in her mind and contributed to her feeling from this time that she was deficient in something that would meet the general desire. She found out what it was; it was a congenital tendency to the production of a substance to which Moddle, her nurse, gave a short ugly name, a name painfully associated at dinner with the part of the joint that she didn't like. She had left behind her the time when she had no desires to meet, none at least save Moddle's, who, in Kensington Gardens, was always on the bench when she came back to see if she had been playing too far. Moddle's desire was merely that she shouldn't do that, and she met it so easily that the only spots in that long brightness were the moments of her wondering what would become of her if, on her rushing back, there should be no Moddle on the bench. They still went to the Gardens, but there was a difference even there; she was impelled perpetually to look at the legs of other children and ask her nurse if *they* were toothpicks. Moddle was terribly truthful; she always said: 'Oh my dear, you'll not find such another pair as your own.' It seemed to have to do with something else that Moddle often said: 'You feel the strain – that's where it is; and you'll feel it still worse, you know.'

Thus from the first Maisie not only felt it, but knew she felt it. A part of it was the consequence of her father's telling her he felt it too, and telling Moddle, in her presence, that she must make a point of driving that home. She was familiar, at the age of six, with the fact that everything had been changed on her account, everything ordered to enable him to give himself up to her. She was to remember always the words in which Moddle impressed upon her that he did so give himself: 'Your papa wishes you never to forget, you know, that he has been dreadfully put about.' If the skin on Moddle's face had to Maisie the air of being unduly, almost painfully, stretched, it never presented that appearance so much as when she uttered, as she often had occasion to utter, such words. The child wondered if they didn't make it hurt more than usual; but it was only after some time that she was able to attach

22

to the picture of her father's sufferings, and more particularly to her nurse's manner about them, the meaning for which these things had waited. By the time she had grown sharper, as the gentlemen who had criticized her calves used to say, she found in her mind a collection of images and echoes to which meanings were attachable – images and echoes kept for her in the childish dusk, the dim closet, the high drawers, like games she wasn't yet big enough to play. The great strain meanwhile was that of carrying by the right end the things her father said about her mother – things mostly indeed that Moddle, on a glimpse of them, as if they had been complicated toys or difficult books, took out of her hands and put away in the closet. A wonderful assortment of objects of this kind she was to discover there later, all tumbled up too with the things, shuffled into the same receptacle, that her mother had said about her father.

She had the knowledge that on a certain occasion which every day brought nearer her mother would be at the door to take her away, and this would have darkened all the days if the ingenious Moddle hadn't written on a paper in very big easy words ever so many pleasures that she would enjoy at the other house. These promises ranged from 'a mother's fond love' to 'a nice poached egg for your tea', and took by the way the prospect of sitting up ever so late to see the lady in question dressed, in silks and velvets and diamonds and pearls, to go out: so that it was a real support to Maisie, at the supreme hour, to feel how, by Moddle's direction, the paper was thrust away in her pocket and there clenched in her fist. The supreme hour was to furnish her with a vivid reminiscence, that of a strange outbreak in the drawing-room on the part of Moddle, who, in reply to something her father had just said, cried aloud: 'You ought to be perfectly ashamed of yourself – you ought to blush, sir, for the way you go on!' The carriage, with her mother in it, was at the door; a gentleman who was there, who was always there, laughed out very loud; her father, who had her in his arms, said to Moddle: 'My dear woman, I'll settle *you* presently!' – after which he repeated, showing his teeth more than ever at Maisie while he hugged her, the words for which her nurse had taken him up. Maisie was not at the moment so fully conscious of them as of the wonder of Moddle's sudden disrespect and crimson face; but she was able

23

to produce them in the course of five minutes when, in the carriage, her mother, all kisses, ribbons, eyes, arms, strange sounds and sweet smells, said to her: 'And did your beastly papa, my precious angel, send any message to your own loving mamma?' Then it was that she found the words spoken by her beastly papa to be, after all, in her little bewildered ears, from which, at her mother's appeal, they passed, in her clear shrill voice, straight to her little innocent lips. 'He said I was to tell you, from him,' she faithfully reported, 'that you're a nasty horrid pig!'

2

IN that lively sense of the immediate which is the very air of a child's mind the past, on each occasion, became for her as indistinct as the future: she surrendered herself to the actual with a good faith that might have been touching to either parent. Crudely as they had calculated they were at first justified by the event: she was the little feathered shuttlecock they could fiercely keep flying between them. The evil they had the gift of thinking or pretending to think of each other they poured into her little gravely-gazing soul as into a boundless receptacle, and each of them had doubtless the best conscience in the world as to the duty of teaching her the stern truth that should be her safeguard against the other. She was at the age for which all stories are true and all conceptions are stories. The actual was the absolute, the present alone was vivid. The objurgation, for instance, launched in the carriage by her mother after she had at her father's bidding punctually performed was a missive that dropped into her memory with the dry rattle of a letter falling into a pillar-box. Like the letter it was, as part of the contents of a well-stuffed post-bag, delivered in due course at the right address. In the presence of these overflowings, after they had continued for a couple of years, the associates of either party sometimes felt that something should be done for what they called 'the real good, don't you know?' of the child. The only thing done, however, in general, took place when it was sighingly remarked that she fortunately wasn't all the year round where she happened to be at the awkward moment, and that, furthermore, either from extreme cunning or from extreme stupidity, she appeared not to take things in.

The theory of her stupidity, eventually embraced by her parents, corresponded with a great date in her small still life: the complete vision, private but final, of the strange office she filled. It was literally a moral revolution and accomplished in the depths of her nature. The stiff dolls on the dusky shelves began to move their arms and legs; old forms and phases began to have a sense that frightened her. She had a new feeling, the feeling of danger; on which a new remedy rose to meet it, the idea of an inner self or, in other words, of concealment. She puzzled out with imperfect signs, but with a prodigious spirit, that she had been a centre of hatred and a messenger of insult, and that everything was bad because she had been employed to make it so. Her parted lips locked themselves with the determination to be employed no longer. She would forget everything, she would repeat nothing, and when, as a tribute to the successful application of her system, she began to be called a little idiot, she tasted a pleasure new and keen. When therefore, as she grew older, her parents in turn announced before her that she had grown shockingly dull, it was not from any real contraction of her little stream of life. She spoiled their fun, but she practically added to her own. She saw more and more; she saw too much. It was Miss Overmore, her first governess, who on a momentous occasion had sown the seeds of secrecy; sown them not by anything she said, but by a mere roll of those fine eyes which Maisie already admired. Moddle had become at this time, after alternations of residence of which the child had no clear record, an image faintly embalmed in the remembrance of hungry disappearances from the nursery and distressful lapses in the alphabet, sad embarrassments, in particular, when invited to recognize something her nurse described as 'the important letter haitch'. Miss Overmore, however hungry, never disappeared: this marked her somehow as of higher rank, and the character was confirmed by a prettiness that Maisie supposed to be extraordinary. Mrs Farange had described her as almost too pretty, and someone had asked what that mattered so long as Beale wasn't there. 'Beale or no Beale,' Maisie had heard her mother reply, 'I take her because she's a lady and yet awfully

25

poor. Rather nice people, but there are seven sisters at home. What do people mean?'

Maisie didn't know what people meant, but she knew very soon all the names of all the sisters; she could say them off better than she could say the multiplication table. She privately wondered, moreover, though she never asked, about the awful poverty, of which her companion also never spoke. Food at any rate came up by mysterious laws; Miss Overmore never, like Moddle, had on an apron, and when she ate she held her fork with her little finger curled out. The child who watched her at many moments, watched her particularly at that one. 'I think you're lovely,' she often said to her; even mamma, who was lovely too, had not such a pretty way with the fork. Maisie associated this showier presence with her now being 'big', knowing of course that nursery-governesses were only for little girls who were not, as she said, 'really' little. She vaguely knew, further, somehow, that the future was still bigger than she, and that a part of what made it so was the number of governesses lurking in it and ready to dart out. Everything that had happened when she was really little was dormant, everything but the positive certitude, bequeathed from afar by Moddle, that the natural way for a child to have her parents was separate and successive, like her mutton and her pudding or her bath and her nap.

'*Does* he know he lies?' – that was what she had vivaciously asked Miss Overmore on the occasion which was so suddenly to lead to a change in her life.

'Does he know – ?' Miss Overmore stared; she had a stocking pulled over her hand and was pricking at it with a needle which she poised in the act. Her task was homely, but her movement, like all her movements, graceful.

'Why papa.'

'That he "lies"?'

'That's what mamma says I'm to tell him – "that he lies and he knows he lies".' Miss Overmore turned very red, though she laughed out till her head fell back; then she pricked again at her muffled hand so hard that Maisie wondered how she could bear it. '*Am* I to tell him?' the child went on. It was then that her companion addressed her in the unmistakable language of a pair of eyes of deep dark grey. 'I can't say No,' they replied as distinctly as possible; 'I can't say No, because I'm afraid of your mamma, don't you see? Yet how can I say Yes after your papa has been so kind to me, talking to me so long the other day, smiling and flashing his beautiful teeth at me the time we met him in the Park, the time when, rejoicing at the sight of us, he left the gentlemen he was with and turned and walked with us, stayed with us for half an hour?' Somehow in the light of Miss Overmore's lovely eyes that incident came back to Maisie with a charm it hadn't had at the time, and this in spite of the fact that after it was over her governess had never but once alluded to it. On their way home, when papa had quitted them, she had expressed the hope that the child wouldn't mention it to mamma. Maisie liked her so, and had so the charmed sense of being liked by her, that she accepted this remark as settling the matter and wonderingly conformed to it. The wonder now lived again, lived in the recollection of what papa had said to Miss Overmore: 'I've only to look at you to see you're a person I can appeal to for help to save my daughter.' Maisie's ignorance of what she was to be saved from didn't diminish the pleasure of the thought that Miss Overmore was saving her. It seemed to make them cling together as in some wild game of 'going round'.

3

SHE was therefore all the more startled when her mother said to her in connexion with something to be done before her next migration: 'You understand of course that she's not going with you.'

Maisie turned quite faint. 'Oh I thought she was.'

'It doesn't in the least matter, you know, what you think,' Mrs Farange loudly replied; 'and you had better indeed for the future, miss, learn to keep your thoughts to yourself.' This was exactly what Maisie had already learned, and the accomplishment was just the source of her mother's irritation. It was of a horrid little critical system, a tendency, in her silence, to judge her elders, that this lady suspected her, liking as she did, for her own part, a child to be simple and confiding. She liked also to hear the report of the whacks she administered to Mr Farange's character, to his pretensions to peace of mind: the satisfaction of dealing them diminished when nothing came back. The day was at hand, and she saw it, when she should feel more delight in hurling Maisie at him than in snatching her away; so much so that her conscience winced under the acuteness of a candid friend who had remarked that the real end of all their tugging would be that each parent would try to make the little girl a burden to the other – a sort of game in which a fond mother clearly wouldn't show to advantage. The prospect of not showing to advantage, a distinction in which she held she had never failed, begot in Ida Farange an ill humour of which several persons felt the effect. She determined that Beale at any rate should feel it; she reflected afresh that in the study of how to be odious to him she must never give way. Nothing could incommode him more than not to get the good, for the child, of a nice female appendage who had clearly taken a fancy to her. One of the things Ida said to the appendage was that Beale's was a house in which no decent woman could consent to be seen. It was Miss Overmore herself who explained to Maisie that she had had a hope of being allowed to accompany her to her father's, and that this hope had been dashed by the way her mother took it. 'She says that if I ever do such a thing as enter his service I must never expect to show my face in this house again. So I've promised not to attempt to go with you. If I wait patiently till you come back here we shall certainly be together once more.'

Waiting patiently, and above all waiting till she should come back there, seemed to Maisie a long way round – it reminded her of all the things she had been told, first and last, that she should have if she'd be good and that in spite of her goodness she had never had at all. 'Then who'll take care of me at papa's?'

'Heaven only knows, my own precious!' Miss Overmore replied, tenderly embracing her. There was indeed no doubt that she was dear to this beautiful friend. What could have proved it better than the fact that before a week was out, in spite of their distressing separation and her mother's prohibition and Miss Overmore's scruples and Miss Overmore's promise, the beautiful friend had turned up at her father's? The little lady already engaged there to come by the hour, a fat dark little lady with a foreign name and dirty fingers, who wore, throughout, a bonnet that had at first given her a deceptive air, too soon dispelled, of not staying long, besides asking her pupil questions that had nothing to do with lessons, questions that Beale Farange himself, when two or three were repeated to him, admitted to be awfully low – this strange apparition faded before the bright creature who had braved everything for Maisie's sake. The bright creature told her little charge frankly what had happened – that she had really been unable to hold out. She had broken her vow to Mrs Farange; she had struggled for three days and then had come straight to Maisie's papa and told him the simple truth. She adored his daughter; she couldn't give her up; she'd make for her any sacrifice. On this basis it had been arranged that she should stay; her courage had been rewarded; she left Maisie in no doubt as to the amount of courage she had required. Some of the things she said made a particular impression on the child – her declaration, for instance, that when her pupil should get older she'd understand better just how 'dreadfully bold' a young lady, to do exactly what she had done, had to be.

'Fortunately your papa appreciates it; he appreciates it *immensely*' – that was one of the things Miss Overmore also said, with a striking insistence on the adverb. Maisie herself was no less impressed with what this martyr had gone through, especially after hearing of the terrible letter that had come from Mrs Farange. Mamma had been so angry that, in Miss Overmore's own words, she had loaded her with insult – proof enough indeed that they must never look forward to being together again under mamma's roof. Mamma's roof, however, had its turn, this time, for the child, of appearing but remotely contingent, so that, to reassure her, there was scarce a need of her companion's secret, solemnly confided – the probability there would be no going back to mamma at all. It was Miss Overmore's private conviction, and a part of the same communication, that if Mr Farange's daughter would only show a really marked preference she would be backed up by 'public opinion' in holding on to him. Poor Maisie could scarcely grasp that incentive, but she could surrender herself to the day. She had conceived her first passion, and the object of it was her governess. It hadn't been put to her, and she couldn't, or at any rate she didn't, put it to herself, that she liked Miss

Overmore better than she liked papa; but it would have sustained her under such an imputation to feel herself able to reply that papa too liked Miss Overmore exactly as much. He had particularly told her so. Besides she could easily see it.

4

ALL this led her on, but it brought on her fate as well, the day when her mother would be at the door in the carriage in which Maisie now rode on no occasions but these. There was no question at present of Miss Overmore's going back with her: it was universally recognized that her quarrel with Mrs Farange was much too acute. The child felt it from the first; there was no hugging nor exclaiming as that lady drove her away – there was only a frightening silence, unenlivened even by the invidious inquiries of former years, which culminated, according to its stern nature, in a still more frightening old woman, a figure awaiting her on the very doorstep. 'You're to be under this lady's care,' said her mother. 'Take her, Mrs Wix,' she added, addressing the figure impatiently and giving the child a push from which Maisie gathered that she wished to set Mrs Wix an example of energy. Mrs Wix took her and, Maisie felt the next day, would never let her go. She had struck her at first, just after Miss Overmore, as terrible; but something in her voice at the end of an hour touched the little girl in a spot that had never even yet been reached. Maisie knew later what it was, though doubtless she couldn't have made a statement of it: these were things that a few days' talk with Mrs Wix quite lighted up. The principal one was a matter Mrs Wix herself always immediately mentioned: she had had a little girl quite of her own, and the little girl had been killed on the spot. She had had absolutely nothing else in all the world, and her affliction had broken her heart. It was comfortably established between them that Mrs Wix's heart was broken. What Maisie felt was that she had been, with passion and anguish, a mother, and that this was something Miss Overmore was not, something (strangely, confusingly) that mamma was even less.

So it was that in the course of an extraordinarily short time she

30

found herself as deeply absorbed in the image of the little dead Clara Matilda, who, on a crossing in the Harrow Road, had been knocked down and crushed by the cruellest of hansoms, as she had ever found herself in the family group made vivid by one of seven. 'She's your little dead sister,' Mrs Wix ended by saying, and Maisie, all in a tremor of curiosity and compassion, addressed from that moment a particular piety to the small accepted acquisition. Somehow she wasn't a real sister, but that only made her the more romantic. It contributed to this view of her that she was never to be spoken of in that character to anyone else – least of all to Mrs Farange, who wouldn't care for her nor recognize the relationship; it was to be just an unutterable and inexhaustible little secret with Mrs Wix. Maisie knew everything about her that could be known, everything she had said or done in her little mutilated life, exactly how lovely she was, exactly how her hair was curled and her frocks were trimmed. Her hair came down far below her waist – it was of the most wonderful golden brightness, just as Mrs Wix's own had been a long time before. Mrs Wix's own was indeed very remarkable still, and Maisie had felt at first that she should never get on with it. It played a large part in the sad and strange appearance, the appearance as of a kind of greasy greyness, which Mrs Wix had presented on the child's arrival. It had originally been yellow, but time had turned that elegance to ashes, to a turbid sallow unvenerable white. Still excessively abundant, it was dressed in a manner of which the poor lady appeared not yet to have recognized the supersession, with a glossy braid, like a large diadem, on the top of the head, and behind, at the nape of the neck, a dingy rosette like a large button. She wore glasses which, in humble reference to a divergent obliquity of vision, she called her straighteners, and a little ugly snuff-coloured dress trimmed with satin bands in the form of scallops and glazed with antiquity. The straighteners, she explained to Maisie, were put on for the sake of others, whom, as she believed, they helped to recognize the bearing, otherwise doubtful, of her regard; the rest of the melancholy garb could only have been put on for herself. With the added suggestion of her goggles it reminded her pupil of the polished shell or corslet of a horrid beetle. At first she had looked cross and almost cruel; but this impression passed away with the child's increased

31

perception of her being in the eyes of the world a figure mainly to laugh at. She was as droll as a charade or an animal towards the end of the 'natural history' – a person whom people, to make talk lively, described to each other and imitated. Everyone knew the straighteners; everyone knew the diadem and the button, the scallops and satin bands; everyone, though Maisie had never betrayed her, knew even Clara Matilda.

It was on account of these things that mamma got her for such low pay, really for nothing: so much, one day when Mrs Wix had accompanied her into the drawing-room and left her, the child heard one of the ladies she found there – a lady with eyebrows arched like skipping-ropes and thick black stitching, like ruled lines for musical notes, on beautiful white gloves – announce to another. She knew governesses were poor; Miss Overmore was unmentionably and Mrs Wix ever so publicly so. Neither this, however, nor the old brown frock nor the diadem nor the button, made a difference for Maisie in the charm put forth through everything, the charm of Mrs Wix's conveying that somehow, in her ugliness and her poverty, she was peculiarly and soothingly safe; safer than anyone in the world, than papa, than mamma, than the lady with the arched eyebrows; safer even, though so much less beautiful, than Miss Overmore, on whose loveliness, as she supposed it, the little girl was faintly conscious that one couldn't rest with quite the same tucked-in and kissed-for-good-night feeling. Mrs Wix was as safe as Clara Matilda, who was in heaven and yet, embarrassingly, also in Kensal Green, where they had been together to see her little huddled grave. It was from something in Mrs Wix's tone, which in spite of caricature remained indescribable and inimitable, that Maisie, before her term with her mother was over, drew this sense of a support, like a breast-high banister in a place of 'drops', that would never give way. If she knew her instructress was poor and queer she also knew she was not nearly so 'qualified' as Miss Overmore, who could say lots of dates straight off (letting you hold the book yourself), state the position of Malabar, play six pieces without notes and, in a sketch, put in beautifully the trees and houses and difficult parts. Maisie herself could play more pieces than Mrs Wix, who was moreover visibly ashamed of her houses and trees and could only, with the help of a smutty forefinger, of doubtful legitimacy in the field of art, do the smoke coming out of the chimneys.

They dealt, the governess and her pupil, in 'subjects', but there were many the governess put off from week to week and that they never got to at all: she only used to say, 'We'll take that in its proper order.' Her order was a circle as vast as the untravelled globe. She had not the spirit of adventure – the child could perfectly see how many subjects she was afraid of. She took refuge on the firm ground of fiction, through which indeed there curled the blue river of truth. She knew swarms of stories, mostly those of the novels she had read; relating them with a memory that never faltered and a wealth of detail that was Maisie's delight. They were all about love and beauty and countesses and wickedness. Her conversation was practically an endless narrative, a great garden of romance, with sudden vistas into her own life and gushing fountains of homeliness. These were the parts where they most lingered; she made the child take with her again every step of her long lame course and think it beyond magic or monsters. Her pupil acquired a vivid vision of everyone who had ever, in her phrase, knocked against her – some of them oh so hard! – every one literally but Mr Wix, her husband, as to whom nothing was mentioned save that he had been dead for ages. He had been rather remarkably absent from his wife's career, and Maisie was never taken to see his grave.

5

THE second parting from Miss Overmore had been bad enough, but this first parting from Mrs Wix was much worse. The child had lately been to the dentist's and had a term of comparison for the screwed-up intensity of the scene. It was dreadfully silent, as it had been when her tooth was taken out; Mrs Wix had on that occasion grabbed her hand and they had clung to each other with the frenzy of their determination not to scream. Maisie, at the dentist's, had been heroically still, but just when she felt most anguish had become aware of an audible shriek on the part of her companion, a spasm of stifled sympathy. This was reproduced by

33

the only sound that broke their supreme embrace when, a month later, the 'arrangement', as her periodical uprootings were called, played the part of the horrible forceps. Embedded in Mrs Wix's nature as her tooth had been socketed in her gum, the operation of extracting her would really have been a case for chloroform. It was a hug that fortunately left nothing to say, for the poor woman's want of words at such an hour seemed to fall in with her want of everything. Maisie's alternate parent, in the outermost vestibule – he liked the impertinence of crossing as much as that of his late wife's threshold – stood over them with his open watch and his still more open grin, while from the only corner of an eye on which something of Mrs Wix's didn't impinge the child saw at the door a brougham in which Miss Overmore also waited. She remembered the difference when, six months before, she had been torn from the breast of that more spirited protectress. Miss Over-more, then also in the vestibule, but of course in the other one, had been thoroughly audible and voluble; her protest had rung out bravely and she had declared that something – her pupil didn't know exactly what – was a regular wicked shame. That had at the time dimly recalled to Maisie the far-away moment of Moddle's great outbreak: there seemed almost to be 'shames' connected in one way or another with her migrations. At present, while Mrs Wix's arms tightened and the smell of her hair was strong, she further remembered how, in pacifying Miss Overmore, papa had made use of the words 'you dear old duck!' – an ex-pression which, by its oddity, had stuck fast in her young mind, having, moreover, a place well prepared for it there by what she knew of the governess whom she now always mentally character-ized as the pretty one. She wondered whether this affection would be as great as before: that would at all events be the case with the prettiness Maisie could see in the face which showed brightly at the window of the brougham.

The brougham was a token of harmony, of the fine conditions papa would this time offer: he had usually come for her in a hansom, with a four-wheeler behind for the boxes. The four-wheeler with the boxes on it was actually there, but mamma was the only lady with whom she had even been in a conveyance of the kind always of old spoken of by Moddle as a private carriage. Papa's carriage was, now that he had one, still more private, somehow, than mamma's; and when at last she found herself quite on top, as she felt, of its inmates and gloriously rolling away, she put to Miss Overmore, after another immense and talkative squeeze, a question of which the motive was a desire for information as to the continuity of a certain sentiment. 'Did papa like you just the same while I was gone?' she inquired – full of the sense of how markedly his favour had been established in her presence. She had bethought herself that this favour might, like her presence and as if depending on it, be only intermittent and for the season. Papa, on whose knee she sat, burst into one of those loud laughs of his that, however prepared she was, seemed always, like some trick in a frightening game, to leap forth and make her jump. Before Miss Overmore could speak he replied: 'Why, you little donkey, when you're away what have I left to do but just to love her?' Miss Overmore hereupon immediately took her from him, and they had a merry little scrimmage over her of which Maisie caught the surprised perception in the white stare of an old lady who passed in a victoria. Then her beautiful friend remarked to her very gravely: 'I shall make him understand that if he ever again says anything as horrid as that to you I shall carry you straight off and we'll go and live somewhere together and be good quiet little girls.' The child couldn't quite make out why her father's speech had been horrid, since it only expressed that appreciation which their companion herself had of old described as 'immense'. To enter more into the truth of the matter she appealed to him again directly, asked if in all those months Miss Overmore hadn't been with him just as she had been before and just as she would be now. 'Of course she has, old girl – where else could the poor dear be?' cried Beale Farange, to the still greater scandal of their companion, who protested that unless he straightway 'took back' his nasty wicked fib it would be, this time, not only him she would leave, but his child too and his house and his tiresome troubles – all the impossible things he had succeeded in putting on her. Beale, under this frolic menace, took nothing back at all; he was indeed apparently on the point of repeating his extravagance, but Miss Overmore instructed her little charge that she was not to listen to his bad jokes: she was to understand that a lady couldn't stay with a gentleman that way without some awfully proper reason.

35

Maisie looked from one of her companions to the other; this was the freshest, gayest start she had yet enjoyed, but she had a shy fear of not exactly believing them. 'Well, what reason *is* proper?' she thoughtfully demanded.

'Oh a long-legged stick of a tomboy: there's none so good as that.' Her father enjoyed both her drollery and his own and tried again to get possession of her – an effort deprecated by their comrade and leading again to something of a public scuffle. Miss Overmore declared to the child that she had been all the while with good friends; on which Beale Farange went on: 'She means good friends of mine, you know – tremendous friends of mine. There has been no end of *them* about – that I *will* say for her!' Maisie felt bewildered and was afterwards for some time conscious of a vagueness, just slightly embarrassing, as to the subject of so much amusement and as to where her governess had really been. She didn't feel at all as if she had been seriously told, and no such feeling was supplied by anything that occurred later. Her embarrassment, of a precocious instinctive order, attached itself to the idea that this was another of the matters it was not for her, as her mother used to say, to go into. Therefore, under her father's roof during the time that followed, she made no attempt to clear up her ambiguity by an ingratiating way with housemaids; and it was an odd truth that the ambiguity itself took nothing from the fresh pleasure promised her by renewed contact with Miss Overmore. The confidence looked for by that young lady was of the fine sort that explanation can't improve, and she herself at any rate was a person superior to any confusion. For Maisie, moreover, concealment had never necessarily seemed deception; she had grown up among things as to which her foremost knowledge was that she was never to ask about them. It was far from new to her that the questions of the small are the peculiar diversion of the great: except the affairs of her doll Lisette there had scarcely ever been anything at her mother's that was explicable with a grave face. Nothing was so easy to her as to send the ladies who gathered there off into shrieks, and she might have practised upon them largely if she had been of a more calculating turn. Everything had something behind it: life was like a long, long corridor with rows of closed doors. She had learned that at these doors it was wise not to knock – this seemed to produce from within such sounds of derision. Little by little, however, she understood more, for it befell that she was enlightened by Lisette's questions, which reproduced the effect of her own upon those for whom she sat in the very darkness of Lisette. Was she not herself convulsed by such innocence? In the presence of it she often imitated the shrieking ladies. There were at any rate things she really couldn't tell even a French doll. She could only pass on her lessons and study to produce on Lisette the impression of having mysteries in her life, wondering the while whether she succeeded in the air of shading off, like her mother, into the unknowable. When the reign of Miss Overmore followed that of Mrs Wix she took a fresh cue, emulating her governess and bridging over the interval with the simple expectation of trust. Yes, there were matters one couldn't 'go into' with a pupil. There were, for instance, days when, after prolonged absence, Lisette, watching her take off her things, tried hard to discover where she had been. Well, she discovered a little, but never discovered all. There was an occasion when, on her being particularly indiscreet, Maisie replied to her – and precisely about the motive of a disappearance – as she, Maisie, had once been replied to by Mrs Farange: 'Find out for yourself!' She mimicked her mother's sharpness, but she was rather ashamed afterwards, though as to whether of the sharpness or of the mimicry was not quite clear.

6

SHE became aware in time that this phase wouldn't have shone by lessons, the care of her education being now only one of the many duties devolving on Miss Overmore; a devolution as to which she was present at various passages between that lady and her father – passages significant, on either side, of dissent and even of displeasure. It was gathered by the child on these occasions that there was something in the situation for which her mother might 'come down' on them all, though indeed the remark, always dropped by her father, was greeted on his companion's part with direct contradiction. Such scenes were usually brought to a climax by Miss Overmore's demanding, with more asperity than she applied to any other subject, in what position under the sun such a person as Mrs Farange would find herself for coming down. As the months went on the little girl's interpretations thickened, and the more effectually that this stretch was the longest she had known without a break. She got used to the idea that her mother, for some reason, was in no hurry to reinstate her: that idea was forcibly expressed by her father whenever Miss Overmore, differing and decided, took him up on the question, which he was always putting forward, of the urgency of sending her to school. For a governess Miss Overmore differed surprisingly; far more, for instance, than would have entered into the bowed head of Mrs Wix. She observed to Maisie many times that she was quite conscious of not doing her justice, and that Mr Farange equally measured and equally lamented this deficiency. The reason of it was that she had mysterious responsibilities that interfered – responsibilities, Miss Overmore intimated, to Mr Farange himself and to the friendly noisy little house and those who came there. Mr Farange's remedy for every inconvenience was that the child should be put at school – there were such lots of splendid schools, as everybody knew, at Brighton and all over the place. That, however, Maisie learned, was just what would bring her mother down: from the moment he should delegate to others the housing of his little charge he hadn't a leg to stand on before the law. Didn't he keep her away from her mother precisely because Mrs Farange was one of these others?

There was also the solution of a second governess, a young person to come in by the day and really do the work; but to this Miss Overmore wouldn't for a moment listen, arguing against it with great public relish and wanting to know from all comers – she put it even to Maisie herself – if they didn't see how frightfully it would give her away. 'What am I supposed to be at all, don't you see, if I'm not here to look after her?' She was in a false position and so freely and loudly called attention to it that it seemed to become almost a source of glory. The way out of it of course was just to do her plain duty; but that was unfortunately what, with his excessive, his exorbitant demands on her, which every one indeed appeared quite to understand, he practically, he selfishly prevented. Beale Farange, for Miss Overmore, was now ~ver anything but 'he', and the house was as full as ever of lively

38

gentlemen with whom, under that designation, she chaffingly talked about him. Maisie meanwhile, as a subject of familiar gossip on what was to be done with her, was left so much to herself that she had hours of wistful thought of the large loose discipline of Mrs Wix; yet she none the less held it under her father's roof a point of superiority that none of his visitors were ladies. It added to this odd security that she had once heard a gentleman say to him as if it were a great joke and in obvious reference to Miss Overmore: 'Hanged if she'll let another woman come near you – hanged if she ever will. She'd let fly a stick at her as they do at a strange cat!' Maisie greatly preferred gentlemen as inmates in spite of their also having their way – louder but sooner over – of laughing out at her. They pulled and pinched, they teased and tickled her; some of them even, as they termed it, shied things at her, and all of them thought it funny to call her by names having no resemblance to her own. The ladies, on the other hand, addressed her as 'You poor pet' and scarcely touched her even to kiss her. But it was of the ladies she was most afraid.

She was now old enough to understand how disproportionate a stay she had already made with her father; and also old enough to enter a little into the ambiguity attending this excess, which oppressed her particularly whenever the question had been touched upon in talk with her governess. 'Oh you needn't worry: she doesn't care!' Miss Overmore had often said to her in reference to any fear that her mother might resent her prolonged detention. 'She has other people than poor little *you* to think about, and has gone abroad with them; so you needn't be in the least afraid she'll stickle this time for her rights.' Maisie knew Mrs Farange had gone abroad, for she had had weeks and weeks before a letter from her beginning 'My precious pet' and taking leave of her for an indeterminate time; but she had not seen in it a renunciation of hatred or of the writer's policy of asserting herself, for the sharpest of all her impressions had been that there was nothing her mother would ever care so much about as to torment Mr Farange. What at last, however, was in this connexion bewildering and a little frightening was the dawn of a suspicion that a better way had been found to torment Mr Farange than to deprive him of his periodical burden. This was the question that worried our young lady and that Miss Overmore's confidences and the frequent observations of her employer only rendered more mystifying. It was a contradiction that if Ida had now a fancy for waiving the rights she had originally been so hot about her late husband shouldn't jump at the monopoly for which he had also in the first instance so fiercely fought; but when Maisie, with a subtlety beyond her years, sounded this new ground her main success was in hearing her mother more freshly abused. Miss Overmore had up to now rarely deviated from a decent reserve, but the day came when she expressed herself with a vividness not inferior to Beale's own on the subject of the lady who had fled to the Continent to wriggle out of her job. It would serve this lady right, Maisie gathered, if that contract, in the shape of an overgrown and underdressed daughter, should be shipped straight out to her and landed at her feet in the midst of scandalous excesses.

The picture of these pursuits was what Miss Overmore took refuge in when the child tried timidly to ascertain if her father were disposed to feel he had too much of her. She evaded the point and only kicked up all round it the dust of Ida's heartlessness and folly, of which the supreme proof, it appeared, was the fact that she was accompanied on her journey by a gentleman whom, to be painfully plain on it, she had – well, 'picked up'. The only terms on which, unless they were married, ladies and gentlemen might, as Miss Overmore expressed it, knock about together, were the terms on which she and Mr Farange had exposed themselves to possible misconception. She had indeed, as has been noted, often explained this before, often said to Maisie: 'I don't know what in the world, darling, your father and I should do without you, for you just make the difference, as I've told you, of keeping us perfectly proper.' The child took in the office it was so endearingly presented to her that she performed a comfort that helped her to a sense of security even in the event of her mother's giving her up. Familiar as she had grown with the fact of the great alternative to the proper, she felt in her governess and her father a strong reason for not emulating that detachment. At the same time she had heard somehow of little girls – of exalted rank, it was true – whose education was carried on by instructors of the other sex, and she knew that if she were at school at Brighton it would be thought an advantage to her to be more or less in the hands of masters. She turned these things over and remarked to

40

Miss Overmore that if she should go to her mother perhaps the gentleman might become her tutor.

'The gentleman?' The proposition was complicated enough to make Miss Overmore stare.

'The one who's with mamma. Mightn't that make it right – as right as your being my governess makes it for you to be with papa?'

Miss Overmore considered; she coloured a little; then she embraced her ingenious friend. 'You're too sweet! I'm a *real* governess.'

'And couldn't he be a real tutor?'

'Of course not. He's ignorant and bad.'

'Bad – ?' Maisie echoed with wonder.

Her companion gave a queer little laugh at her tone. 'He's ever so much younger – ' But that was all.

'Younger than you?'

Miss Overmore laughed again; it was the first time Maisie had seen her approach so nearly to a giggle. 'Younger than – no matter whom. I don't know anything about him and don't want to,' she rather inconsequently added. 'He's not my sort, and I'm sure, my own darling, he's not yours.' And she repeated the free caress into which her colloquies with Maisie almost always broke and which made the child feel that *her* affection at least was a gage of safety. Parents had come to seem vague, but governesses were evidently to be trusted. Maisie's faith in Mrs Wix, for instance, had suffered no lapse from the fact that all communication with her had temporarily dropped. During the first weeks of their separation Clara Matilda's mamma had repeatedly and dolefully written to her, and Maisie had answered with an enthusiasm controlled only by orthographical doubts; but the correspondence had been duly submitted to Miss Overmore, with the final effect of its not suiting her. It was this lady's view that Mr Farange wouldn't care for it at all, and she ended by confessing – since her pupil pushed her – that she didn't care for it herself. She was furiously jealous, she said; and that weakness was but a new proof of her disinterested affection. She pronounced Mrs Wix's effusions, moreover, illiterate and unprofitable; she made no scruple of declaring it monstrous that a woman in her senses should have placed the formation of her daughter's mind in such ridiculous hands. Maisie was well aware that the proprietress of the old brown dress and the old odd headgear was lower in the scale of 'form' than Miss Overmore; but it was now brought home to her with pain that she was educationally quite out of the question. She was buried for the time beneath a conclusive remark of her critics: 'She's really beyond a joke!' This remark was made as that charming woman held in her hand the last letter that Maisie was to receive from Mrs Wix; it was fortified by a decree proscribing the preposterous tie. 'Must I, then, write and tell her?' the child bewilderedly asked: she grew pale at the dreadful things it appeared involved for her to say. 'Don't dream of it, my dear – I'll write: you may trust me!' cried Miss Overmore; who indeed wrote to such purpose that a hush in which you could have heard a pin drop descended upon poor Mrs Wix. She gave for weeks and weeks no sign whatever of life; it was as if she had been as effectually disposed of by Miss Overmore's communication as her little girl, in the Harrow Road, had been disposed of by the terrible hansom. Her very silence became after this one of the largest elements of Maisie's consciousness; it proved a warm and habitable air, into which the child penetrated farther than she dared ever to mention to her companions. Somewhere in the depths of it the dim straighteners were fixed upon her; somewhere out of the troubled little current Mrs Wix intensely waited.

7

I T quite fell in with this intensity that one day, on returning from a walk with the housemaid, Maisie should have found her in the hall, seated on the stool usually occupied by the telegraph-boys who haunted Beale Farange's door and kicked their heels while, in his room, answers to their missives took form with the aid of smoke-puffs and growls. It had seemed to her on their parting that Mrs Wix had reached the last limits of the squeeze, but she now felt those limits to be transcended and that the duration of her visitor's hug was a direct reply to Miss Overmore's veto. She understood in a flash how the visit had come to be possible – that Mrs Wix, watching her chance, must have slipped in under protection of the fact that papa, always tormented in spite of arguments with the idea of a school, had, for a three days' excursion to Brighton, absolutely insisted on the attendance of her adversary. It was true that when Maisie explained their absence and their important motive Mrs Wix wore an expression so peculiar that it would only have had its origin in surprise. This contradiction indeed peeped out only to vanish, for at the very moment that, in the spirit of it, she threw herself afresh upon her young friend a hansom crested with neat luggage rattled up to the door and Miss Overmore bounded out. The shock of her encounter with Mrs Wix was less violent than Maisie had feared on seeing her and didn't at all interfere with the sociable tone in which, under her rival's eyes, she explained to her little charge that she had returned, for a particular reason, a day sooner than she first intended. She had left papa – in such nice lodgings – at Brighton; but he would come back to his dear little home on the morrow. As for Mrs Wix, papa's companion supplied Maisie in later converse with the right word for the attitude of this personage: Mrs Wix 'stood up' to her in a manner that the child herself felt at the time to be astonishing. This occurred indeed after Miss Overmore had so far raised her interdict as to make a move to the dining-room, where, in the absence of any suggestion of sitting down, it was scarcely more than natural that even poor Mrs Wix should stand up. Maisie at once inquired if at Brighton, this time, anything had come of the possibility of a school; to which, much to her surprise, Miss Overmore, who had always grandly repudiated it, replied after an instant, but quite as if Mrs Wix were not there:

'It may be, darling, that something *will* come. The objection, I must tell you, has been quite removed.'

At this it was still more startling to hear Mrs Wix speak out with great firmness. 'I don't think, if you'll allow me to say so, that there's any arrangement by which the objection *can* be "removed". What has brought me here today is that I've a message for Maisie from dear Mrs Farange.'

The child's heart gave a great thump. 'Oh mamma's come back?'

'Not yet, sweet love, but she's coming,' said Mrs Wix, 'and she has – most thoughtfully, you know – sent me on to prepare you.'

'To prepare her for what, pray?' asked Miss Overmore, whose first smoothness began, with this news, to be ruffled.

Mrs Wix quietly applied her straighteners to Miss Overmore's flushed beauty. 'Well, miss, for a very important communication.'

'Can't dear Mrs Farange, as you so oddly call her, make her communications directly? Can't she take the trouble to write to her only daughter?' the younger lady demanded. 'Maisie herself will tell you that it's months and months since she has had so much as a word from her.'

'Oh but I've written to mamma!' cried the child as if this would do quite as well.

'That makes her treatment of you all the greater scandal,' the governess in possession promptly declared.

'Mrs Farange is too well aware,' said Mrs Wix with sustained spirit, 'of what becomes of her letters in this house.'

Maisie's sense of fairness hereupon interposed for her visitor. 'You know, Miss Overmore, that papa doesn't like everything of mamma's.'

'No one likes, my dear, to be made the subject of such language as your mother's letters contain. They were not fit for the innocent child to see,' Miss Overmore observed to Mrs Wix.

'Then I don't know what you complain of, and she's better without them. It serves every purpose that I'm in Mrs Farange's confidence.'

Miss Overmore gave a scornful laugh. 'Then you must be mixed up with some extraordinary proceedings!'

'None so extraordinary,' cried Mrs Wix, turning very pale, 'as to say horrible things about the mother to the face of the helpless daughter!'

'Things not a bit more horrible, I think,' Miss Overmore returned, 'than those you, madam, appear to have come here to say about the father!'

Mrs Wix looked for a moment hard at Maisie, and then, turning again to this witness, spoke with a trembling voice. 'I came to say nothing about him, and you must excuse Mrs Farange and me if we're not so above all reproach as the companion of his travels.'

The young woman thus described stared at the apparent breadth of the description – she needed a moment to take it in. Maisie, however, gazing solemnly from one of the disputants to the other, noted that her answer, when it came, perched upon smiling lips. 'It will do quite as well, no doubt, if you come up to the requirements of the companion of Mrs Farange's!'

Mrs Wix broke into a queer laugh; it sounded to Maisie an unsuccessful imitation of a neigh. 'That's just what I'm here to make known – how perfectly the poor lady comes up to them herself.' She held up her head at the child. 'You must take your mamma's message, Maisie, and you must feel that her wishing me to come to you with it this way is a great proof of interest and affection. She sends you her particular love and announces to you that she's engaged to be married to Sir Claude.'

'Sir Claude?' Maisie wonderingly echoed. But while Mrs Wix explained that this gentleman was a dear friend of Mrs Farange's, who had been of great assistance to her in getting to Florence and in making herself comfortable there for the winter, she was not too violently shaken to perceive her old friend's enjoyment of the effect of this news on Miss Overmore. That young lady opened her eyes very wide; she immediately remarked that Mrs Farange's marriage would of course put an end to any further pretension to take her daughter back. Mrs Wix inquired with astonishment why it should do anything of the sort, and Miss Overmore gave as an instant reason that it was clearly but another dodge in a system of dodges. She wanted to get out of the bargain: why else had she now left Maisie on her father's hand weeks and weeks beyond the time about which she had originally made such a fuss? It was vain for Mrs Wix to represent – as she speciously proceeded to do – that all this time would be made up as soon as Mrs Farange returned: she, Miss Overmore, knew nothing, thank heaven, about her confederate, but was very sure any person capable of forming that sort of relation with the lady in Florence would easily agree to object to the presence in his house of the fruit of a union that his dignity must ignore. It was a game like another, and Mrs Wix's visit was clearly the first move in it. Maisie found in this exchange of asperities a fresh incitement to the unformulated fatalism in which her sense of her own career had long since taken refuge; and it was the beginning for her of a deeper prevision that, in spite of Miss Overmore's brilliancy and Mrs Wix's passion, she should live to see a change in the nature of the struggle she appeared to have come into the world to produce. It would still be essentially a struggle but its object would now be *not* to receive her.

Mrs Wix, after Miss Overmore's last demonstration, addressed herself wholly to the little girl, and, drawing from the pocket of her dingy old pelisse a small flat parcel, removed its envelope and wished to know if *that* looked like a gentleman who wouldn't be nice to everybody – let alone to a person he would be so sure to find so nice. Mrs Farange, in the candour of new-found happiness, had enclosed a 'cabinet' photograph of Sir Claude, and Maisie lost herself in admiration of the fair smooth face, the regular features, the kind eyes, the amiable air, the general glossiness and smartness of her prospective stepfather – only vaguely puzzled to suppose herself now with two fathers at once. Her researches had hitherto indicated that to incur a second parent of the same sex you had usually to lose the first. '*Isn*'*t* he sympathetic?' asked Mrs Wix, who had clearly, on the strength of his charming portrait, made up her mind that Sir Claude promised her a future. 'You can see, I hope,' she added with much expression, 'that *he's* a perfect gentleman!' Maisie had never before heard the word 'sympathetic' applied to anybody's face; she heard it with pleasure and from that moment it agreeably remained with her. She testified, moreover, to the force of her own perception in a small soft sigh of response to the pleasant eyes that seemed to seek her acquaintance, to speak to her directly. 'He's quite lovely!' she declared to Mrs Wix. Then eagerly, irrepressibly, as she still held the photograph and Sir Claude continued to fraternise, 'Oh, can't I keep it?' she broke out. No sooner had she done so than she looked up from it at Miss Overmore: this was with the sudden instinct of appealing to the authority that had long ago impressed on her that she mustn't ask for things. Miss Overmore, to her surprise, looked distant and rather odd, hesitating and giving her time to turn again to Mrs Wix. Then Maisie saw that lady's long face lengthen; it was stricken and almost scared, as if her young friend really expected more of her than she had to give. The photograph was a possession that, direly denuded, she clung to, and there was a momentary struggle between her fond clutch of it and her capability of every sacrifice for her precarious pupil. With the acuteness of her years, however, Maisie saw that her own avidity would triumph,

46

and she held out the picture to Miss Overmore as if she were quite proud of her mother. 'Isn't he just lovely?' she demanded while poor Mrs Wix hungrily wavered, her straighteners largely covering it and her pelisse gathered about her with an intensity that strained its ancient seams.

'It was to *me*, darling,' the visitor said, 'that your mamma so generously sent it; but of course if it would give you particular pleasure – ' she faltered, only gasping her surrender.

Miss Overmore continued extremely remote. 'If the photograph's your property, my dear, I shall be happy to oblige you by looking at it on some future occasion. But you must excuse me if I decline to touch an object belonging to Mrs Wix.'

That lady had by this time grown very red. 'You might as well see him this way, miss,' she retorted, 'as you certainly never will, I believe, in any other! Keep the pretty picture, by all means, my precious,' she went on: 'Sir Claude will be happy himself, I daresay, to give me one with a kind inscription.' The pathetic quaver of this brave boast was not lost on Maisie, who threw herself so gratefully on the speaker's neck that, when they had concluded their embrace, the public tenderness of which, she felt, made up for the sacrifice she imposed, their companion had had time to lay a quick hand on Sir Claude and, with a glance at him or not, whisk him effectually out of sight. Released from the child's arms Mrs Wix looked about for the picture; then she fixed Miss Overmore with a hard dumb stare; and finally, with her eyes on the little girl again, achieved the grimmest of smiles. 'Well, nothing matters, Maisie, because there's another thing your mamma wrote about. She has made sure of me.' Even after her loyal hug Maisie felt a bit of a sneak as she glanced at Miss Overmore for permission to understand this. But Mrs Wix left her in no doubt of what it meant. 'She has definitely engaged me – for her return and for yours. Then you'll see for yourself.' Maisie, on the spot, quite believed she should; but the prospect was suddenly thrown into confusion by an extraordinary demonstration from Miss Overmore.

'Mrs Wix,' said that young lady, 'has some undiscoverable reason for regarding your mother's hold on you as strengthened by the fact that she's about to marry. I wonder, then – on that system – what our visitor will say to your father's.'

47

Miss Overmore's words were directed to her pupil, but her face, lighted with an irony that made it prettier even than ever before, was presented to the dingy figure that had stiffened itself for departure. The child's discipline had been bewildering – it had ranged freely between the prescription that she was to answer when spoken to and the experience of lively penalties on obeying that prescription. This time, nevertheless, she felt emboldened for risks; above all as something portentous seemed to have leaped into her sense of the relations of things. She looked at Miss Overmore much as she had a way of looking at persons who treated her to 'grown up' jokes. 'Do you mean papa's hold on me – do you mean *he's* about to marry?'

'Papa's not about to marry – papa *is* married, my dear. Papa was married the day before yesterday at Brighton.' Miss Overmore glittered more gaily; meanwhile it came over Maisie, and quite dazzlingly, that her 'smart' governess was a bride. 'He's my husband, if you please, and I'm his little wife. So *now* we'll see who's your little mother!' She caught her pupil to her bosom in a manner that was not to be outdone by the emissary of her predecessor, and a few moments later, when things had lurched back into their places, that poor lady, quite defeated of the last word, had soundlessly taken flight.

8

AFTER Mrs Wix's retreat Miss Overmore appeared to recognize that she was not exactly in a position to denounce Ida Farange's second union; but she drew from a table-drawer the photograph of Sir Claude and, standing there before Maisie, studied it at some length.

'Isn't he beautiful?' the child ingenuously asked.

Her companion hesitated. 'No – he's horrid,' she, to Maisie's surprise, sharply returned. But she debated another minute, after which she handed back the picture. It appeared to Maisie herself to exhibit a fresh attraction, and she was troubled, having never before had occasion to differ from her lovely friend. So she only could ask what, such being the case, she should do with it: should she put it quite away – where it wouldn't be there to offend? On this Miss Overmore again cast about; after which she said unexpectedly: 'Put it on the schoolroom mantelpiece.'

Maisie felt a fear. 'Won't papa dislike to see it there?'

'Very much indeed; but that won't matter *now*.' Miss Overmore spoke with peculiar significance and to her pupil's mystification.

'On account of the marriage?' Maisie risked.

Miss Overmore laughed, and Maisie could see that in spite of the irritation produced by Mrs Wix, she was in high spirits. 'Which marriage do you mean?'

With the question put to her it suddenly struck the child she didn't know, so that she felt she looked foolish. So she took refuge in saying: 'Shall *you* be different – ?' This was a full implication that the bride of Sir Claude would be.

'As your father's wedded wife? Utterly!' Miss Overmore replied. And the difference began of course in her being addressed, even by Maisie, from that day and by her particular request, as Mrs Beale. It was there indeed principally that it ended, for except that the child could reflect that she should presently have four parents in all, and also that at the end of three months the staircase, for a little girl hanging over banisters, sent up the deepening rustle of more elaborate advances, everything made the same impression as before. Mrs Beale had very pretty frocks, but Miss Overmore's had been quite as good, and if papa was much fonder of his second wife than he had been of his first, Maisie had foreseen that fondness, had followed its development almost as closely as the person more directly involved. There was little indeed in the commerce of her companions that her precocious experience couldn't explain, for if they struck her as after all rather deficient in that air of the honeymoon of which she had so often heard – in much detail, for instance, from Mrs Wix – it was natural to judge the circumstances in the light of papa's proved disposition to contest the empire of the matrimonial tie. His honeymoon, when he came back from Brighton – not on the morrow of Mrs Wix's visit, and not, oddly, till several days later – his honeymoon was perhaps perceptibly tinged with the dawn of a later stage of wedlock. There were things dislike of which, as the child knew it, wouldn't matter to Mrs Beale now, and their number increased so

49

that such a trifle as his hostility to the photograph of Sir Claude quite dropped out of view. This pleasing object found a conspicuous place in the schoolroom, which in truth Mr Farange seldom entered and in which silent admiration formed, during the time I speak of, almost the sole scholastic exercise of Mrs Beale's pupil.

Maisie was not long in seeing just what her stepmother had meant by the difference she should show in her new character. If she was her father's wife she was not her own governess, and if her presence had had formerly to be made regular by the theory of a humble function she was now on a footing that dispensed with all theories and was inconsistent with all servitude. That was what she had meant by the drop of the objection to a school; her small companion was no longer required at home as – it was Mrs Beale's own amusing word – a little duenna. The argument against a successor to Miss Overmore remained: it was composed frankly of the fact, of which Mrs Beale granted the full absurdity, that she was too awfully fond of her stepdaughter to bring herself to see her in vulgar and mercenary hands. The note of this particular danger emboldened Maisie to put in a word for Mrs Wix, the modest measure of whose avidity she had taken from the first; but Mrs Beale disposed afresh and effectually of a candidate who would be sure to act in some horrible and insidious way for Ida's interest and who, moreover, was personally loathsome and as ignorant as a fish. She made also no more of a secret of the awkward fact that a good school would be hideously expensive, and of the further circumstance, which seemed to put an end to everything, that when it came to the point papa, in spite of his previous clamour, was really most nasty about paying. 'Would you believe,' Mrs Beale confidentially asked of her little charge, 'that he says I'm a worse expense than ever, and that a daughter and a wife together are really more than he can afford?' It was thus that the splendid school at Brighton lost itself in the haze of larger questions, though the fear that it would provoke Ida to leap into the breach subsided with her prolonged, her quite shameless non-appearance. Her daughter and her successor were therefore left to gaze in united but helpless blankness at all Maisie was not learning.

This quantity was so great as to fill the child's days with a sense of intermission to which even French Lisette gave no accent – with finished games and unanswered questions and dreaded tests; with the habit, above all, in her watch for a change, of hanging over banisters when the door-bell sounded. This was the great refuge of her impatience, but what she heard at such times was a clatter of gaiety downstairs the impression of which, from her earliest childhood, had built up in her the belief that the grown-up time was the time of real amusement and above all of real intimacy. Even Lisette, even Mrs Wix had never, she felt, in spite of hugs and tears, been so intimate with her as so many persons at present were with Mrs Beale and as so many others of old had been with Mrs Farange. The note of hilarity brought people together still more than the note of melancholy, which was the one exclusively sounded, for instance, by poor Mrs Wix. Maisie in these days preferred none the less that domestic revels should be wafted to her from a distance: she felt sadly unsupported for facing the inquisition of the drawing-room. That was a reason the more for making the most of Susan Ash, who in her quality of under-housemaid, moved at a very different level and who, none the less, was much depended upon out of doors. She was a guide to peregrinations that had little in common with those intensely definite airings that had left with the child a vivid memory of the regulated mind of Moddle. There had been under Moddle's system no dawdles at shop-windows and no nudges, in Oxford Street, of 'I *say*, look at '*er*!' There had been an inexorable treatment of crossings and a serene exemption from the fear that – especially at corners, of which she was yet weakly fond – haunted the housemaid, the fear of being, as she ominously said, 'spoken to.' The dangers of the town equally with its diversions added to Maisie's sense of being untutored and unclaimed.

The situation, however, had taken a twist when, on another of her returns, at Susan's side, extremely tired, from the pursuit of exercise qualified by much hovering, she encountered another emotion. She on this occasion learnt at the door that her instant attendance was requested in the drawing-room. Crossing the threshold in a cloud of shame, she discerned through the blur Mrs Beale seated there with a gentleman who immediately drew the pain from her predicament by rising before her as the original of the photograph of Sir Claude. She felt the moment she looked

51

at him that he was by far the most shining presence that had ever made her gape, and her pleasure in seeing him, in knowing that he took hold of her and kissed her, as quickly throbbed into a strange shy pride in him, a perception of his making up for her fallen state, for Susan's public nudges, which quite bruised her, and for all the lessons that, in the dead schoolroom, where at times she was almost afraid to stay alone, she was bored with not having. It was as if he had told her on the spot that he belonged to her, so that she could already show him off and see the effect he produced. No, nothing else that was most beautiful ever belonging to her could kindle that particular joy – not Mrs Beale at that very moment, not papa when he was gay, nor mamma when she was dressed, nor Lisette when she was new. The joy almost overflowed in tears when he laid his hand on her and drew her to him, telling her, with a smile of which the promise was as bright as that of a Christmas-tree, that he knew her ever so well by her mother, but had come to see her now so that he might know her for himself. She could see that his view of this kind of knowledge was to make her come away with him, and, further, that it was just what he was there for and had already been some time: arranging it with Mrs Beale and getting on with that lady in a manner evidently not at all affected by her having on the arrival of his portrait thought of him so ill. They had grown almost intimate – or had the air of it – over their discussion; and it was still further conveyed to Maisie that Mrs Beale had made no secret, and would make yet less of one, of all that it cost to let her go. 'You seem so tremendously eager,' she said to the child, 'that I hope you're at least clear about Sir Claude's relation to you. It doesn't appear to occur to him to give you the necessary reassurance.'

Maisie, a trifle mystified, turned quickly to her new friend. 'Why it's of course that you're *married* to her, isn't it?'

Her anxious emphasis started them off, as she had learned to call it; this was the echo she infallibly and now quite resignedly produced; moreover, Sir Claude's laughter was an indistinguishable part of the sweetness of his being there. 'We've been married, my dear child, three months, and my interest in you is a consequence, don't you know? of my great affection for your mother. In coming here it's of course for your mother I'm acting.'

52

'Oh I know,' Maisie said with all the candour of her competence. 'She can't come herself – except just to the door.' Then as she thought afresh: 'Can't she come even to the door now?'

'There you are!' Mrs Beale exclaimed to Sir Claude. She spoke as if his dilemma were ludicrous.

His kind face, in a hesitation, seemed to recognize it; but he answered the child with a frank smile. 'No – not very well.'

'Because she has married you?'

He promptly accepted this reason. 'Well, that has a good deal to do with it.'

He was so delightful to talk to that Maisie pursued the subject. 'But papa – *he* has married Miss Overmore.'

'Ah, you'll see that he won't come for you at your mother's,' that lady interposed.

'Yes, but that won't be for a long time,' Maisie hastened to respond.

'We won't talk about it now – you've months and months to put in first.' And Sir Claude drew her closer.

'Oh, that's what makes it so hard to give her up!' Mrs Beale made this point with her arms out to her stepdaughter. Maisie, quitting Sir Claude, went over to them and, clasped in a still tenderer embrace, felt entrancingly the extension of the field of happiness. '*I'll* come for you,' said her stepmother, 'if Sir Claude keeps you too long: we must make him quite understand that! Don't talk to me about her ladyship!' she went on to their visitor so familiarly that it was almost as if they must have met before. 'I know her ladyship as if I had made her. They're a pretty pair of parents!' cried Mrs Beale.

Maisie had so often heard them called so that the remark diverted her but an instant from the agreeable wonder of this grand new form of allusion to her mother; and that, in its turn, presently left her free to catch at the pleasant possibility, in connexion with herself, of a relation much happier as between Mrs Beale and Sir Claude than as between mamma and papa. Still, the next thing that happened was that her interest in such a relation brought to her lips a fresh question. 'Have you seen papa?' she asked of Sir Claude.

It was the signal for their going off again, as her small stoicism

53

had perfectly taken for granted that it would be. All that Mrs Beale had nevertheless to add was the vague apparent sarcasm: 'Oh papa!'

'I'm assured he's not at home,' Sir Claude replied to the child; 'but if he had been I should have hoped for the pleasure of seeing him.'

'Won't he mind your coming?' Maisie asked as with need of the knowledge.

'Oh you bad little girl!' Mrs Beale humorously protested.

The child could see that at this Sir Claude, though still moved to mirth, coloured a little; but he spoke to her very kindly. 'That's just what I came to see, you know – whether your father *would* mind. But Mrs Beale appears strongly of the opinion that he won't.'

This lady promptly justified that view to her stepdaughter. 'It will be very interesting, my dear, you know, to find out what it is today that your father does mind. I'm sure *I* don't know' – and she seemed to repeat, though with perceptible resignation, her plaint of a moment before. 'Your father, darling, is a very odd person indeed.' She turned with this, smiling, to Sir Claude. 'But perhaps it's hardly civil for me to say that of his not objecting to have *you* in the house. If you knew some of the people he does have!'

Maisie knew them all, and none indeed were to be compared to Sir Claude. He laughed back at Mrs Beale; he looked at such moments quite as Mrs Wix, in the long stories she told her pupil, always described the lovers of her distressed beauties – 'the perfect gentleman and strikingly handsome.' He got up, to the child's regret, as if he were going. 'Oh, I daresay we should be all right!'

Mrs Beale once more gathered in her little charge, holding her close and looking thoughtfully over her head at their visitor. 'It's so charming – for a man of your type – to have wanted her so much!'

'What do you know about my type?' Sir Claude laughed. 'Whatever it may be I daresay it deceives you. The truth about me is simply that I'm the most unappreciated of – what do you call the fellows? – "family-men." Yes, I'm a family-man; upon my honour I am!'

54

'Then why on earth,' cried Mrs Beale, 'didn't you marry a family-woman?'

Sir Claude looked at her hard. '*You* know who one marries, I think. Besides, there *are* no family-women – hanged if there are! None of them want any children – hanged if they do!'

His account of the matter was most interesting, and Maisie, as if it were of bad omen for her, stared at the picture in some dismay. At the same time she felt, through encircling arms, her protectress hesitate. 'You do come out with things! But you mean her ladyship doesn't want any – really?'

'Won't hear of them – simply. But she can't help the one she *has* got.' And with this Sir Claude's eyes rested on the little girl in a way that seemed to her to mask her mother's attitude with the consciousness of his own. 'She must make the best of her, don't you see? If only for the look of the thing, don't you know? One wants one's wife to take the proper line about her child.'

'Oh I know what one wants!' Mrs Beale cried with a competence that evidently impressed her interlocutor.

'Well, if you keep *him* up – and I daresay you've had worry enough – why shouldn't I keep Ida? What's sauce for the goose is sauce for the gander – or the other way round, don't you know? I mean to see the thing through.'

Mrs Beale, for a minute, still with her eyes on him as he leaned upon the chimney-piece, appeared to turn this over. 'You're just a wonder of kindness – that's what you are!' she said at last. 'A lady's expected to have natural feelings. But *your* horrible sex – ! Isn't it a horrible sex, little love?' she demanded with her cheek upon her stepdaughter's.

'Oh I like gentlemen best,' Maisie lucidly replied.

The words were taken up merrily. 'That's a good one for *you*!' Sir Claude exclaimed to Mrs Beale.

'No,' said that lady: 'I've only to remember the women she sees at her mother's.'

'Ah they're very nice now,' Sir Claude returned.

'What do you call "nice"?'

'Well, they're all right.'

'That doesn't answer me,' said Mrs Beale, 'but I daresay you do take care of them. That makes you more of an angel to want this job too.' And she playfully whacked her smaller companion.

'I'm not an angel – I'm an old grandmother,' Sir Claude declared. 'I like babies – I always did. If we go to smash I shall look for a place as responsible nurse.'

Maisie, in her charmed mood, drank in an imputation on her years which at another moment might have been bitter; but the charm was sensibly interrupted by Mrs Beale's screwing her round and gazing fondly into her eyes, 'You're willing to leave me, you wretch?'

The little girl deliberated; even this consecrated tie had become as a cord she must suddenly snap. But she snapped it very gently. 'Isn't it my turn for mamma?'

'You're a horrible little hypocrite! The less, I think, now said about "turns" the better,' Mrs Beale made answer. '*I* know whose turn it is. You've not such a passion for your mother!'

'I say, I say: *do* look out!' Sir Claude quite amiably protested.

'There's nothing she hasn't heard. But it doesn't matter – it hasn't spoiled her. If you knew what it costs me to part with you!' she pursued to Maisie.

Sir Claude watched her as she charmingly clung to the child. 'I'm so glad you really care for her. That's so much to the good.'

Mrs Beale slowly got up, still with her hands on Maisie, but emitting a soft exhalation. 'Well, if you're glad, that may help us; for I assure you that I shall never give up any rights in her that I may consider I've acquired by my own sacrifices. I shall hold very fast to my interest in her. What seems to have happened is that she has brought you and me together.'

'She has brought you and me together,' said Sir Claude.

His cheerful echo prolonged the happy truth, and Maisie broke out almost with enthusiasm: 'I've brought you and her together!'

Her companions of course laughed anew and Mrs Beale gave her an affectionate shake. 'You little monster – take care what you do! But that's what she does do,' she continued to Sir Claude. 'She did it to me and Beale.'

'Well, then,' he said to Maisie, 'you must try the trick at *our* place.' He held out his hand to her again. 'Will you come now?'

'Now – just as I am?' She turned with an immense appeal to her stepmother, taking a leap over the mountain of 'mending', the abyss of packing that had loomed and yawned before her. 'Oh *may* I?'

Mrs Beale addressed her assent to Sir Claude. 'As well so as any other way. I'll send on her things tomorrow.' Then she gave a tug to the child's coat, glancing at her up and down with some ruefulness. 'She's not turned out as I should like – her mother will pull her to pieces. But what's one to do – with nothing to do it on? And she's better than when she came – you can tell her mother that. I'm sorry to have to say it to you – but the poor child was a sight.'

'Oh, I'll turn her out myself!' the visitor cordially said.

'I shall like to see how!' – Mrs Beale appeared much amused. 'You must bring her to show me – we can manage that. Good-bye, little fright!' And her last word to Sir Claude was that she would keep him up to the mark.

9

THE idea of what she was to make up and the prodigious total it came to were kept well before Maisie at her mother's. These things were the constant occupation of Mrs Wix, who arrived there by the back stairs, but in tears of joy, the day after her own arrival. The process of making up, as to which the good lady had an immense deal to say, took, through its successive phases, so long that it heralded a term at least equal to the child's last stretch with her father. This, however, was a fuller and richer time: it bounded along to the tune of Mrs Wix's constant insistence on the energy they must both put forth. There was a fine intensity in the way the child agreed with her that under Mrs Beale and Susan Ash she had learned nothing whatever; the wildness of the rescued cast-away was one of the forces that would henceforth make for a career of conquest. The year, therefore, rounded itself as a re-ceptacle of retarded knowledge – a cup brimming over with the sense that now at least she was learning. Mrs Wix fed this sense from the stores of her conversation and with the immense bustle of her reminder that they must cull the fleeting hour. They were surrounded with subjects they must take at a rush and perpetually getting into the attitude of triumphant attack. They had certainly no idle hours, and the child went to bed each night as tired as from a long day's play. This had begun from the moment of their reunion, begun with all Mrs Wix had to tell her young friend of the reasons for her ladyship's extraordinary behaviour at the very first.

It took the form of her ladyship's refusal for three days to see her little girl – three days during which Sir Claude made hasty merry dashes into the schoolroom to smooth down the odd situation, to say, 'She'll come round, you know; I assure you she'll come round,' and a little even to compensate for the indignity he had caused her to suffer. There had never in the child's life been, in all ways, such a delightful amount of reparation. It came out by his sociable admission that her ladyship had not known of his visit to her late husband's house and of his having made that person's daughter a pretext for striking up an acquaintance with the dreadful creature installed there. Heaven knew she wanted her child back and had made every plan of her own for removing her; what she couldn't for the present at least forgive any one concerned was such an officious underhand way of bringing about the transfer. Maisie carried more of the weight of this resentment than even Mrs Wix's confidential ingenuity could lighten for her, especially as Sir Claude himself was not at all ingenious, though indeed on the other hand he was not at all crushed. He was amused and intermittent and at moments most startling; he impressed on his young companion, with a frankness that agitated her much more than he seemed to guess, that he depended on her not letting her mother, when she should see her, get anything out of her about anything Mrs Beale might have said to him. He came in and out; he professed, in joke, to take tremendous precautions; he showed a positive disposition to romp. He chaffed Mrs Wix till she was purple with the pleasure of it, and reminded Maisie of the reticence he expected of her till she set her teeth like an Indian captive. Her lessons these first days and indeed for long after seemed to be all about Sir Claude, and yet she never really mentioned to Mrs Wix that she was prepared, under his inspiring injunction, to be vainly tortured. This lady, however, had formulated the position of things with an acuteness that showed how little she needed to be coached. Her explanation of everything that seemed not quite pleasant – and if her own footing was perilous it met that danger as well – was that her ladyship was passionately in love. Maisie accepted this hint with infinite awe and pressed upon it much when she was at last summoned into the presence of her mother.

There she encountered matters amid which it seemed really to help to give her a clue – an almost terrifying strangeness, full, none the less, after a little, of reverberations of Ida's old fierce and demonstrative recoveries of possession. They had been some time in the house together, and this demonstration came late. Pre-occupied, however, as Maisie was with the idea of the sentiment Sir Claude had inspired, and familiar, in addition, by Mrs Wix's anecdotes, with the ravages that in general such a sentiment could produce, she was able to make allowances for her ladyship's re-markable appearance, her violent splendour, the wonderful colour of her lips and even the hard stare, the stare of some gor-geous idol described in a story-book, that had come into her eyes in consequence of a curious thickening of their already rich circumference. Her professions and explanations were mixed with eager challenges and sudden drops, in the midst of which Maisie recognized as a memory of other years the rattle of her trinkets and the scratch of her endearments, the odour of her clothes and the jumps of her conversation. She had all her old clever way – Mrs Wix said it was 'aristocratic' – of changing the subject as she might have slammed the door in your face. The principal thing that was different was the tint of her golden hair, which had changed to a coppery red and, with the head it profusely covered, struck the child as now lifted still further aloft. This picturesque parent showed literally a grander stature and a nobler presence, things which, with some others that might have been bewildering, were handsomely accounted for by the romantic state of her affections. It was her affections, Maisie could easily see, that led Ida to break out into questions as to what had passed at the other house between that horrible woman and Sir Claude; but it was also just here that the little girl was able to recall the effect with which in earlier days she had practised the pacific art of stupidity. This art again came to her aid: her mother, in getting rid of her after an interview in which she had achieved a hollowness beyond her years, allowed her fully to understand she had not grown a bit more amusing.

She could bear that; she could bear anything that helped her to feel she had done something for Sir Claude. If she hadn't told Mrs Wix how Mrs Beale seemed to like him, she certainly couldn't tell her ladyship. In the way the past revived for her there was a queer confusion. It was because mamma hated papa that she used to want to know bad things of him; but if at present she wanted to know the same of Sir Claude, it was from the opposite motive. She was awestruck at the manner in which a lady might be affected through the passion mentioned by Mrs Wix; she held her breath with the sense of picking her steps among the tremendous things of life. What she did, however, now, after the interview with her mother, impart to Mrs Wix was that, in spite of her having had her 'good' effect, as she called it – the effect she studied, the effect of harmless vacancy – her ladyship's last words had been that her ladyship's duty by her would be thoroughly done. Over this announcement governess and pupil looked at each other in silent profundity; but as the weeks went by it had no consequences that interfered gravely with the breezy gallop of making up. Her ladyship's duty took at times the form of not seeing her child for days together, and Maisie led her life in great prosperity between Mrs Wix and kind Sir Claude. Mrs Wix had a new dress and, as she was the first to proclaim, a better position; so it all struck Maisie as a crowded brilliant life, with, for the time, Mrs Beale and Susan Ash simply 'left out' like children not invited to a Christmas party. Mrs Wix had a secret terror which, like most of her secret feelings, she discussed with her little companion, in great solemnity, by the hour: the possibility of her ladyship's coming down on them, in her sudden high-bred way, with a school. But she had also a balm to this fear in a conviction of the strength of Sir Claude's grasp of the situation. He was too pleased – didn't he constantly say as much? – with the good impression made, in a wide circle, by Ida's sacrifices; and he came into the schoolroom repeatedly to let them know how beautifully he felt everything had gone off and everything would go on.

He disappeared at times for days, when his patient friends understood that her ladyship would naturally absorb him; but he always came back with the drollest stories of where he had been, a wonderful picture of society, and even with petty presents that showed how in absence he thought of his home. Besides giving Mrs Wix by his conversation a sense that they almost themselves 'went out', he gave her a five-pound note and the history of France and an umbrella with a malachite knob, and to Maisie both chocolate-creams and story-books, besides a lovely great-coat (which he took her out all alone to buy) and ever so many games in boxes, with printed directions, and a bright red frame for the protection of his famous photograph. The games were, as he said, to while away the evening hour; and the evening hour indeed often passed in futile attempts on Mrs Wix's part to master what 'it said' on the papers. When he asked the pair how they liked the games they always replied, 'Oh immensely!' but they had earnest discussions as to whether they hadn't better appeal to him frankly for aid to understand them. This was a course their delicacy shrank from; they couldn't have told exactly why, but it was a part of their tenderness for him not to let him think they had trouble. What dazzled most was his kindness to Mrs Wix, not only the five-pound note and the 'not forgetting' her, but the perfect consideration, as she called it with an air to which her sounding of the words gave the only grandeur Maisie was to have seen her wear save on a certain occasion hereafter to be described, an occasion when the poor lady was grander than all of them put together. He shook hands with her, he recognized her, as she said, and above all, more than once, he took her, with his stepdaughter, to the pantomime and, in the crowd, coming out, publicly gave her his arm. When he met them in sunny Piccadilly he made merry and turned and walked with them, heroically suppressing his consciousness of the stamp of his company, a heroism that – needless for Mrs Wix to sound *those* words – her ladyship, though a blood relation, was little enough the woman to be capable of. Even to the hard heart of childhood there was something tragic in such elation at such humanities: it brought home to Maisie the way her humble companion had sidled and ducked through life. But it settled the question of the degree to which Sir Claude was a gentleman: he was more of one than anybody else in the world – 'I don't care,' Mrs Wix repeatedly remarked, 'whom you may meet in grand society, nor even to whom you may be contracted in marriage.' There were questions that Maisie never asked; so her governess was spared the embarrassment of telling her if he were more of a gentleman than papa. This was not, moreover, from the want of opportunity, for

61

there were no moments between them at which the topic could be irrelevant, no subject they were going into, not even the principal dates or the auxiliary verbs, in which it was farther off than the turn of the page. The answer on the winter nights to the puzzle of cards and counters and little bewildering pamphlets was just to draw up to the fire and talk about him; and if the truth must be told this edifying interchange constituted for the time the little girl's chief education.

It must also be admitted that he took them far, farther perhaps than was always warranted by the old-fashioned conscience, the dingy decencies, of Maisie's simple instructress. There were hours when Mrs Wix sighingly testified to the scruples she surmounted, seemed to ask what other line one *could* take with a young person whose experience had been, as it were, so peculiar. 'It isn't as if you didn't already know everything, is it, love?' and 'I can't make you any worse than you *are*, can I, darling?' – these were the terms in which the good lady justified to herself and her pupil her pleasant conversational ease. What the pupil already knew was indeed rather taken for granted than expressed, but it performed the useful function of transcending all textbooks and supplanting all studies. If the child couldn't be worse it was a comfort even to herself that she was bad – a comfort offering a broad firm support to the fundamental fact of the present crisis: the fact that mamma was fearfully jealous. This was another side of the circumstance of mamma's passion, and the deep couple in the schoolroom were not long in working round to it. It brought them face to face with the idea of the inconvenience suffered by any lady who marries a gentleman producing on other ladies the charming effect of Sir Claude. That such ladies wouldn't be able to help falling in love with him was a reflexion naturally irritating to his wife. One day when some accident, some crash of a banged door or some scurry of a scared maid, had rendered this truth particularly vivid, Maisie, receptive and profound, suddenly said to her companion: 'And you, my dear, are you in love with him too?'

Even her profundity had left a margin for a laugh; so she was a trifle startled by the solemn promptitude with which Mrs Wix plumped out: 'Over head and ears. I've *never*, since you ask me, been so far gone.'

This boldness had none the less no effect of deterrence for her when, a few days later – it was because several had elapsed without a visit from Sir Claude – her governess turned the tables. 'May I ask you, miss, if *you* are?' Mrs Wix brought it out, she could see, with hesitation, but clearly intending a joke. 'Why, *rather*!' the child made answer, as if in surprise at not having long ago seemed sufficiently to commit herself; on which her friend gave a sigh of apparent satisfaction. It might in fact have expressed positive relief. Everything was as it should be.

Yet it was not with them, they were very sure, that her ladyship was furious, nor because she had forbidden it that there befell at last a period – six months brought it round – when for days together he scarcely came near them. He was 'off', and Ida was 'off', and they were sometimes off together and sometimes apart; there were seasons when the simple students had the house to themselves, when the very servants seemed to be 'off' and dinner became a reckless forage in pantries and sideboards. Mrs Wix reminded her disciple on such occasions – hungry moments often, when all the support of the reminder was required – that the 'real life' of their companions, the brilliant society in which it was inevitable they should move and the complicated pleasures in which it was almost presumptuous of the mind to follow them, must offer features literally not to be imagined without being seen. At one of these times Maisie found her opening it out that, though the difficulties were many, it was Mrs Beale who had now become the chief. Then somehow it was brought fully to the child's knowledge that her stepmother had been making attempts to see her, that her mother had deeply resented it, that her stepfather had backed her stepmother up, that the latter had pretended to be acting as the representative of her father, and that her mother took the whole thing, in plain terms, very hard. The situation was, as Mrs Wix declared, an extraordinary muddle to be sure. Her account of it brought back to Maisie the happy vision of the way Sir Claude and Mrs Beale had made acquaintance – an incident to which, with her stepfather, though she had had little to say about it to Mrs Wix, she had during the first weeks of her stay at her mother's found more than one opportunity to revert. As to what had taken place the day Sir Claude came for her, she had been vaguely grateful to Mrs Wix for not attempting, as her mother had attempted, to put her through. That was what Sir Claude had called the process when he warned her of it, and again afterwards when he told her she was an awfully good 'chap' for having foiled it. Then it was that, well aware Mrs Beale hadn't in the least really given her up, she had asked him if he remained in communication with her and if for the time everything must really be held to be at an end between her stepmother and herself. This conversation had occurred in consequence of his one day popping into the schoolroom and finding Maisie alone.

10

HE was smoking a cigarette and he stood before the fire and looked at the meagre appointments of the room in a way that made her rather ashamed of them. Then before (on the subject of Mrs Beale) he let her 'draw' him – that was another of his words; it was astonishing how many she gathered in – he remarked that really mamma kept them rather low on the question of decorations. Mrs Wix had put up a Japanese fan and two rather grim texts; she had wished they were gayer, but they were all she happened to have. Without Sir Claude's photograph, however, the place would have been, as he said, as dull as a cold dinner. He had said as well that there were all sorts of things they ought to have; yet governess and pupil, it had to be admitted, were still divided between discussing the places where any sort of thing would look best if any sort of thing should ever come and acknowledging that mutability in the child's career which was naturally unfavourable to accumulation. She stayed long enough only to miss things, not half long enough to deserve them. The way Sir Claude looked about the schoolroom had made her feel with humility as if it were not very different from the shabby attic in which she had visited Susan Ash. Then he had said in abrupt reference to Mrs Beale: 'Do you think she really cares for you?'

'Oh awfully!' Maisie had replied.

'But, I mean, does she love you for yourself, as they call it, don't you know? Is she as fond of you, now, as Mrs Wix?'

The child turned it over. 'Oh I'm not every bit Mrs Beale has!'

Sir Claude seemed much amused at this. 'No; you're not every bit she has!'

He laughed for some moments, but that was an old story to Maisie, who was not too much disconcerted to go on: 'But she'll never give me up.'

'Well, I won't either, old boy: so that's not so wonderful, and she's not the only one. But if she's so fond of you, why doesn't she write to you?'

'Oh on account of mamma.' This was rudimentary, and she was almost surprised at the simplicity of Sir Claude's question.

'I see – that's quite right,' he answered. 'She might get at you – there are all sorts of ways. But of course there's Mrs Wix.'

'There's Mrs Wix,' Maisie lucidly concurred. 'Mrs Wix can't abide her.'

Sir Claude seemed interested. 'Oh she can't abide her? Then what does she say about her?'

'Nothing at all – because she knows I shouldn't like it. Isn't it sweet of her?' the child asked.

'Certainly; rather nice. Mrs Beale wouldn't hold her tongue for any such thing as that, would she?'

Maisie remembered how little she had done so; but she desired to protect Mrs Beale too. The only protection she could think of, however, was the plea: 'Oh at papa's, you know, they don't mind!'

At this Sir Claude only smiled. 'No, I daresay not. But here we mind, don't we? – we take care what we say. I don't suppose it's a matter on which I ought to prejudice you,' he went on; 'but I think we must on the whole be rather nicer here than at your father's. However, I don't press that; for it's the sort of question on which it's awfully awkward for you to speak. Don't worry, at any rate: I assure you I'll back you up.' Then after a moment and while he smoked he reverted to Mrs Beale and the child's first inquiry. 'I'm afraid we can't do much for her just now. I haven't seen her since that day – upon my word I haven't seen her.' The next instant, with a laugh the least bit foolish, the young man slightly coloured; he must have felt this profession of innocence to be excessive as addressed to Maisie. It was inevitable to say to her, however, that of course her mother loathed the lady of the

65

other house. He couldn't go there again with his wife's consent, and he wasn't the man – he begged her to believe, falling once more, in spite of himself, into the scruple of showing the child he didn't trip – to go there without it. He was liable in talking with her to take the tone of her being also a man of the world. He had gone to Mrs Beale's to fetch away Maisie, but that was altogether different. Now that she was in her mother's house, what pretext had he to give her mother for paying calls on her father's wife? And of course Mrs Beale couldn't come to Ida's – Ida would tear her limb from limb. Maisie, with this talk of pretexts, remembered how much Mrs Beale had made of her being a good one, and how, for such a function, it was her fate to be either much depended on or much missed. Sir Claude, moreover, recognized on this occasion that perhaps things would take a turn later on; and he wound up by saying: 'I'm sure she does sincerely care for you – how can she possibly help it? She's very young and very pretty and very clever: I think she's charming. But we must walk very straight. If you'll help me, you know, I'll help *you*,' he concluded in the pleasant fraternizing, equalizing, not a bit patronizing way which made the child ready to go through anything for him and the beauty of which, as she dimly felt, was that it was so much less a deceitful descent to her years than a real indifference to them.

It gave her moments of secret rapture – moments of believing she might help him indeed. The only mystification in this was the imposing time of life that her elders spoke of as youth. For Sir Claude then Mrs Beale was 'young', just as for Mrs Wix Sir Claude was: that was one of the merits for which Mrs Wix most commended him. What therefore was Maisie herself, and, in another relation to the matter, what therefore was mamma? It took her some time to puzzle out with the aid of an experiment or two that it wouldn't do to talk about mamma's youth. She even went so far one day, in the presence of that lady's thick colour and marked lines, as to wonder if it would occur to any one but herself to do so. Yet if she wasn't young then she was old and this threw an odd light on her having a husband of a different generation. Mr Farange was still older – that Maisie perfectly knew; and it brought her in due course to the perception of how much more, since Mrs Beale was younger than Sir Claude, papa must be older than Mrs Beale. Such discoveries were disconcerting and even a trifle confounding: these persons, it appeared, were not of the age they ought to be. This was somehow particularly the case with mamma, and the fact made her reflect with some relief on her not having gone with Mrs Wix into the question of Sir Claude's attachment to his wife. She was conscious that in confining their attention to the state of her ladyship's own affections they had been controlled – Mrs Wix perhaps in especial – by delicacy and even by embarrassment. The end of her colloquy with her stepfather in the schoolroom was her saying: 'Then if we're not to see Mrs Beale at all it isn't what she seemed to think when you came for me.'

He looked rather blank. 'What did she seem to think?'

'Why that I've brought you together.'

'She thought that?' Sir Claude asked.

Maisie was surprised at his already forgetting it. 'Just as I brought papa and her. Don't you remember she said so?'

It came back to Sir Claude in a peal of laughter. 'Oh yes – she said so!'

'And *you* said so,' Maisie lucidly pursued.

He recovered, with increasing mirth, the whole occasion. 'And *you* said so!' he retorted as if they were playing a game.

'Then were we all mistaken?'

He considered a little. 'No, on the whole not. I daresay it's just what you *have* done. We *are* together – it's really most odd. She's thinking of us – of you and me – though we don't meet. And I've no doubt you'll find it will be all right when you go back to her.'

'Am I going back to her?' Maisie brought out with a little gasp which was like a sudden clutch of the happy present.

It appeared to make Sir Claude grave a moment; it might have made him feel the weight of the pledge his action had given. 'Oh some day, I suppose! We've plenty of time.'

'I've such a tremendous lot to make up,' Maisie said with a sense of great boldness.

'Certainly, and you must make up every hour of it. Oh I'll *see* that you do!'

This was encouraging and to show cheerfully that she was reassured, she replied: 'That's what Mrs Wix sees too.'

'Oh yes,' said Sir Claude; 'Mrs Wix and I are shoulder to shoulder.'

Maisie took in a little this strong image; after which she exclaimed: 'Then I've done it also to you and her – I've brought *you* together!'

'Blest if you haven't!' Sir Claude laughed. 'And more, upon my word, than any of the lot. Oh you've done for *us*! Now if you could – as I suggested, you know, that day – only manage me and your mother!'

The child wondered. 'Bring you and *her* together?'

'You see we're not together – not a bit. But I oughtn't to tell you such things; all the more that you won't really do it – not you. No, old chap,' the young man continued; 'there you'll break down. But it won't matter – we'll rub along. The great thing is that you and I are all right.'

'*We're* all right!' Maisie echoed devoutly. But the next moment, in the light of what he had just said, she asked: 'How shall I ever leave you?' It was as if she must somehow take care of him.

His smile did justice to her anxiety. 'Oh well, you needn't! It won't come to that.'

'Do you mean that when I do go you'll go with me?'

Sir Claude cast about. 'Not exactly "with" you perhaps; but I shall never be far off.'

'But how do you know where mamma may take you?'

He laughed again. 'I don't, I confess!' Then he had an idea, though something too jocose. 'That will be for you to see – that she shan't take me too far.'

'How can I help it?' Maisie inquired in surprise. 'Mamma doesn't care for me,' she said very simply. 'Not really.' Child as she was, her little long history was in the words; and it was as impossible to contradict her as if she had been venerable.

Sir Claude's silence was an admission of this, and still more the tone in which he presently replied: 'That won't prevent her from – some time or other – leaving me with you.'

'Then we'll live together?' she eagerly demanded.

'I'm afraid,' said Sir Claude, smiling, 'that that will be Mrs Beale's real chance.'

Her eagerness just slightly dropped at this; she remembered Mrs Wix's pronouncement that it was all an extraordinary muddle. 'To take me again? Well, can't you come to see me there?'

'Oh I daresay!'

Though there were parts of childhood Maisie had lost she had all childhood's preference for the particular promise. 'Then you *will* come – you'll come often, won't you?' she insisted; while at the moment she spoke the door opened for the return of Mrs Wix. Sir Claude hereupon, instead of replying, gave her a look which left her silent and embarrassed.

When he again found privacy convenient, however – which happened to be long in coming – he took up their conversation very much where it had dropped. 'You see, my dear, if I shall be able to go to you at your father's it yet isn't all the same thing for Mrs Beale to come to you here.' Maisie gave a thoughtful assent to this proposition, though conscious she could scarcely herself say just where the difference would lie. She felt how much her stepfather saved her, as he said with his habitual amusement, the trouble of that. 'I shall probably be able to go to Mrs Beale's without your mother's knowing it.'

Maisie stared with a certain thrill at the dramatic element in this. 'And she couldn't come here without mamma's – ?' She was unable to articulate the word for what mamma would do.

'My dear child, Mrs Wix would tell of it.'

'But I thought,' Maisie objected, 'that Mrs Wix and you –'

'Are such brothers-in-arms?' – Sir Claude caught her up. 'Oh yes, about everything but Mrs Beale. And if you should suggest,' he went on, 'that we might somehow or other hide her peeping in from Mrs Wix –'

'Oh I don't suggest *that*!' Maisie in turn cut him short.

Sir Claude looked as if he could indeed quite see why. 'No; it would really be impossible.' There came to her from this glance at what they might hide the first small glimpse of something in him that she wouldn't have expected. There had been times when she had had to make the best of the impression that she was her-self deceitful; yet she had never concealed anything bigger than a thought. Of course she now concealed this thought of how strange it would be to see *him* hide; and while she was so actively engaged he continued: 'Besides, you know, I'm not afraid of your father.'

'And you are of my mother?'

'Rather, old man!' Sir Claude returned.

IT must not be supposed that her ladyship's intermissions were not qualified by demonstrations of another order – triumphal entries and breathless pauses during which she seemed to take of everything in the room, from the state of the ceiling to that of her daughter's boot-toes, a survey that was rich in intentions. Sometimes she sat down and sometimes she surged about, but her attitude wore equally in either case the grand air of the practical. She found so much to deplore that she left a great deal to expect, and bristled so with calculation that she seemed to scatter remedies and pledges. Her visits were as good as an outfit; her manner, as Mrs Wix once said, as good as a pair of curtains but she was a person addicted to extremes – sometimes barely speaking to her child and sometimes pressing this tender shoot to a bosom cut, as Mrs Wix had also observed, remarkably low. She was always in a fearful hurry, and the lower the bosom was cut the more it was to be gathered she was wanted elsewhere. She usually broke in alone, but sometimes Sir Claude was with her, and during all the earlier period there was nothing on which these appearances had had so delightful a bearing as on the way her ladyship was, as Mrs Wix expressed it, under the spell. 'But *isn't* she under it!' Maisie used in thoughtful but familiar reference to exclaim after Sir Claude had swept mamma away in peals of natural laughter. Not even in the old days of the convulsed ladies had she heard mamma laugh so freely as in these moments of conjugal surrender, to the gaiety of which even a little girl could see she had at last a right – a little girl whose thoughtfulness was now all happy selfish meditation on good omens and future fun.

Unaccompanied, in subsequent hours, and with an effect of changing to meet a change, Ida took a tone superficially disconcerting and abrupt – the tone of having, at an immense cost, made over everything to Sir Claude and wishing others to know that if everything wasn't right it was because Sir Claude was so dreadfully vague. 'He has made from the first such a row about you,' she said on one occasion to Maisie, 'that I've told him to do for you himself and try how he likes it – see? I've washed my hands of you; I've made you over to him, and if you're discontented it's on him, please, you'll come down. So don't haul poor *me* up – I assure you I've worries enough.' One of these, visibly, was that the spell rejoiced in by the schoolroom fire was already in danger of breaking; another was that she was finally forced to make no secret of her husband's unfitness for real responsibilities. The day came indeed when her breathless auditors learnt from her in bewilderment that what ailed him was that he was, alas, simply not serious. Maisie wept on Mrs Wix's bosom after hearing that Sir Claude was a butterfly; considering, moreover, that her governess but half-patched it up in coming out at various moments the next few days with the opinion that it was proper to his 'station' to be careless and free. That had been proper to everyone's station that she had yet encountered save poor Mrs Wix's own, and the particular merit of Sir Claude had seemed precisely that he was different from everyone. She talked with him, however, as time went on, very freely about her mother; being with him, in this relation, wholly without the fear that had kept her silent before her father – the fear of bearing tales and making bad things worse. He appeared to accept the idea that he had taken her over and made her, as he said, his particular lark; he quite agreed also that he was an awful fraud and an idle beast and a sorry dunce. And he never said a word to her against her mother – he only remained dumb and discouraged in the face of her ladyship's own overtopping earnestness. There were occasions when he even spoke as if he had wrenched his little charge from the arms of a parent who had fought for her tooth and nail.

This was the very moral of a scene that flashed into vividness one day when the four happened to meet without company in the drawing-room and Maisie found herself clutched to her mother's breast and passionately sobbed and shrieked over, made the subject of a demonstration evidently sequent to some sharp passage just enacted. The connexion required that while she almost cradled the child in her arms Ida should speak of her as hideously, as fatally estranged, and should rail at Sir Claude as the cruel author of the outrage. 'He has taken you *from* me,' she cried; 'he has set you *against* me, and you've been won away and your horrid little mind has been poisoned! You've gone over to

71

him, you've given yourself up to side against me and hate me. You never open your mouth to me – you know you don't; and you chatter to him like a dozen magpies. Don't lie about it – I hear you all over the place. You hang about him in a way that's barely decent – he can do what he likes with you. Well then, let him, to his heart's content: he has been in such a hurry to take you that we'll see if it suits him to keep you. I'm very good to break my heart about it when you've no more feeling for me than a clammy little fish!' She suddenly thrust the child away and, as a disgusted admission of failure, sent her flying across the room into the arms of Mrs Wix, whom at this moment and even in the whirl of her transit Maisie saw, very red, exchange a quick queer look with Sir Claude.

The impression of the look remained with her, confronting her with such a critical little view of her mother's explosion that she felt the less ashamed of herself for incurring the reproach with which she had been cast off. Her father had once called her a heartless little beast, and now, though decidedly scared, she was as stiff and cold as if the description had been just. She was not even frightened enough to cry, which would have been a tribute to her mother's wrongs: she was only, more than anything else, curious about the opinion mutely expressed by their companions. Taking the earliest opportunity to question Mrs Wix on this subject she elicited the remarkable reply: 'Well, my dear, it's her ladyship's game, and we must just hold on like grim death.' Maisie could interpret at her leisure these ominous words. Her reflexions indeed at this moment thickened apace, and one of them made her sure that her governess had conversations, private, earnest and not infrequent, with her denounced stepfather. She perceived in the light of a second episode that something beyond her knowledge had taken place in the house. The things beyond her knowledge – numerous enough in truth – had not hitherto, she believed, been the things that had been nearest to her: she had even had in the past a small smug conviction that in the domestic labyrinth she always kept the clue. This time too, however, she at last found out – with the discreet aid, it had to be confessed, of Mrs Wix. Sir Claude's own assistance was abruptly taken from her, for his comment on her ladyship's game was to start on the spot, quite alone, for Paris, evidently because he wished to show

72

a spirit when accused of bad behaviour. He might be fond of his
stepdaughter, Maisie felt, without wishing her to be after all
thrust on him in such a way; his absence therefore, it was clear,
was a protest against the thrusting. It was while this absence
lasted that our young lady finally discovered what had happened
in the house to be that her mother was no longer in love.

The limit of a passion for Sir Claude had certainly been
reached, she judged, some time before the day on which her ladyship burst suddenly into the schoolroom to introduce Mr
Perriam, who, as she announced from the doorway to Maisie,
wouldn't believe his ears that one had a great hoyden of a
daughter. Mr Perriam was short and massive – Mrs Wix remarked afterwards that he was 'too fat for the pace'; and it
would have been difficult to say of him whether his head were
more bald or his black moustache more bushy. He seemed also
to have moustaches over his eyes, which, however, by no means
prevented these polished little globes from rolling round the room
as if they had been billiard-balls impelled by Ida's celebrated
stroke. Mr Perriam wore on the hand that pulled his moustache
a diamond of dazzling lustre, in consequence of which and of his
general weight and mystery our young lady observed on his
departure that if he had only had a turban he would have been
quite her idea of a heathen Turk.

'He's quite my idea,' Mrs Wix replied, 'of a heathen Jew.'

'Well, I mean,' said Maisie, 'of a person who comes from the
East.'

'That's where he *must* come from,' her governess opined – 'he
comes from the City.' In a moment she added as if she knew all
about him, 'He's one of those people who have lately broken out.
He'll be immensely rich.'

'On the death of his papa?' the child interestedly inquired.

'Dear no – nothing hereditary. I mean he has made a mass of
money.'

'How much, do you think?' Maisie demanded.

Mrs Wix reflected and sketched it. 'Oh many millions.'

'A hundred?'

Mrs Wix was not sure of the number, but there were enough of
them to have seemed to warm up for the time the penury of the
schoolroom – to linger there as an afterglow of the hot heavy

light Mr Perriam sensibly shed. This was also, no doubt, on his part, an effect of that enjoyment of life with which, among her elders, Maisie had been in contact from her earliest years – the sign of happy maturity, the old familiar note of overflowing cheer. 'How d'ye do, ma'am? How d'ye do, little miss?' – he laughed and nodded at the gaping figures. 'She has brought me up for a peep – it's true I wouldn't take you on trust. She's always talking about you, but she'd never produce you; so today I challenged her on the spot. Well, you ain't a myth, my dear – I back down on that,' the visitor went on to Maisie; 'nor you either, miss, though you might be, to be sure!'

'I bored him with you, darling – I bore every one,' Ida said, 'and to prove that you *are* a sweet thing, as well as a fearfully old one, I told him he could judge for himself. So now he sees that you're a dreadful bouncing business and that your poor old Mummy's at least sixty!' – and her ladyship smiled at Mr Perriam with the charm that her daughter had heard imputed to her at papa's by the merry gentlemen who had so often wished to get from him what they called a 'rise'. Her manner at that instant gave the child a glimpse more vivid than any yet enjoyed of the attraction that papa, in remarkable language, always denied she could put forth.

Mr Perriam, however, clearly recognized it in the humour with which he met her. 'I never said you ain't wonderful – did I ever say it, hey?' and he appealed with pleasant confidence to the testimony of the schoolroom, about which itself also he evidently felt something might be expected of him. 'So this is their little place, hey? Charming, charming, charming!' he repeated as he vaguely looked round. The interrupted students clung together as if they had been personally exposed; but Ida relieved their embarrassment by a hunch of her high shoulders. This time the smile she addressed to Mr Perriam had a beauty of sudden sadness. 'What on earth is a poor woman to do?'

The visitor's grimace grew more marked as he continued to look, and the conscious little schoolroom felt still more like a cage at a menagerie. 'Charming, charming, charming!' Mr Perriam insisted; but the parenthesis closed with a prompt click. 'There you are!' said her ladyship. 'Bye-bye!' she sharply added. The next minute they were on the stairs, and Mrs Wix and her companion, at the open door and looking mutely at each other, were reached by the sound of the large social current that carried them back to their life.

It was singular perhaps after this that Maisie never put a question about Mr Perriam, and it was still more singular that by the end of a week she knew all she didn't ask. What she most particularly knew – and the information came to her, unsought, straight from Mrs Wix – was that Sir Claude wouldn't at all care for the visits of a millionaire who was in and out of the upper rooms. How little he would care was proved by the fact that under the sense of them Mrs Wix's discretion broke down altogether; she was capable of a transfer of allegiance, capable, at the altar of propriety, of a desperate sacrifice of her ladyship. As against Mrs Beale, she more than once intimated, she had been willing to do the best for her, but as against Sir Claude she could do nothing for her at all. It was extraordinary the number of things that, still without a question, Maisie knew by the time her stepfather came back from Paris – came bringing her a splendid apparatus for painting in water-colours and bringing Mrs Wix, by a lapse of memory that would have been droll if it had not been a trifle disconcerting, a second and even a more elegant umbrella. He had forgotten all about the first, with which, buried in as many wrappers as a mummy of the Pharaohs, she wouldn't for the world have done anything so profane as use it. Maisie knew above all that though she was now, by what she called an informal understanding, on Sir Claude's 'side', she had yet not uttered a word to him about Mr Perriam. That gentleman became, therefore, a kind of flourishing public secret, out of the depths of which governess and pupil looked at each other portentously from the time their friend was restored to them. He was restored in great abundance, and it was marked that, though he appeared to have felt the need to take a stand against the risk of being too roughly saddled with the offspring of others, he at this period exposed himself more than ever before to the presumption of having created expectations.

If it had become now, for that matter, a question of sides, there was at least a certain amount of evidence as to where they all were. Maisie of course, in such a delicate position, was on nobody's; but Sir Claude had all the air of being on hers. If, therefore,

Mrs Wix was on Sir Claude's, her ladyship on Mr Perriam's and Mr Perriam presumably on her ladyship's, this left only Mrs Beale and Mr Farange to account for. Mrs Beale clearly was, like Sir Claude, on Maisie's, and papa, it was to be supposed, on Mrs Beale's. Here indeed was a slight ambiguity, as papa's being on Mrs Beale's didn't somehow seem to place him quite on his daughter's. It sounded, as this young lady thought it over, very much like puss-in-the-corner, and she could only wonder if the distribution of parties would lead to a rushing to and fro and a changing of places. She was in the presence, she felt, of restless change: wasn't it restless enough that her mother and her step-father should already be on different sides? That was the great thing that had domestically happened. Mrs Wix, besides, had turned another face: she had never been exactly gay, but her gravity was now an attitude as public as a posted placard. She seemed to sit in her new dress and brood over her lost delicacy, which had become almost as doleful a memory as that of poor Clara Matilda. 'It *is* hard for *him*,' she often said to her companion; and it was surprising how competent on this point Maisie was conscious of being to agree with her. Hard as it was, however, Sir Claude had never shown to greater advantage than in the gallant generous sociable way he carried it off: a way that drew from Mrs Wix a hundred expressions of relief at his not having suffered it to embitter him. It threw him more and more at last into the schoolroom, where he had plainly begun to recognize that if he was to have the credit of perverting the innocent child he might also at least have the amusement. He never came into the place without telling its occupants that they were the nicest people in the house – a remark which always led them to say to each other 'Mr Perriam!' as loud as ever compressed lips and enlarged eyes could make them articulate. He caused Maisie to remember what he had said to Mrs Beale about his having the nature of a good nurse, and, rather more than she intended before Mrs Wix, to bring the whole thing out by once remarking to him that none of her good nurses had smoked quite so much in the nursery. This had no more effect than it was meant to on his cigarettes: he was always smoking, but always declaring that it was death to him not to lead a domestic life.

He led one after all in the schoolroom, and there were hours of late evening, when she had gone to bed, that Maisie knew he sat there talking with Mrs Wix of how to meet his difficulties. His consideration for this unfortunate woman even in the midst of them continued to show him as the perfect gentleman and lifted the subject of his courtesy into an upper air of beatitude in which her very pride had the hush of anxiety. 'He leans on me – he leans on me!' she only announced from time to time; and she was more surprised than amused when, later on, she accidentally found she had given her pupil the impression of a support literally supplied by her person. This glimpse of a misconception led her to be explicit – to put before the child, with an air of mourning indeed for such a stoop to the common, that what they talked about in the small hours, as they said, was the question of his taking right hold of life. The life she wanted him to take right hold of was the public: 'she' being, I hasten to add, in this connexion, not the mistress of his fate, but only Mrs Wix herself. She had phrases about him that were full of easy understanding, yet full of morality. 'He's a wonderful nature, but he can't live like the lilies. He's all right, you know, but he must have a high interest.' She had more than once remarked that his affairs were sadly involved, but that they must get him – Maisie and she together apparently – into Parliament. The child took it from her with a flutter of importance that Parliament was his natural sphere, and she was the less prepared to recognize a hindrance as she had never heard of any affairs whatever that were not involved. She had in the old days once been told by Mrs Beale that her very own were, and with the refreshment of knowing that she *had* affairs the information hadn't in the least overwhelmed her. It was true and perhaps a little alarming that she had never heard of any such matters since then. Full of charm at any rate was the prospect of some day getting Sir Claude in; especially after Mrs Wix, as the fruit of more midnight colloquies, once went so far as to observe that she really believed it was all that was wanted to save him. This critic, with these words, struck her disciple as cropping up, after the manner of mamma when mamma talked, quite in a new place. The child stared as at the jump of a kangaroo.

'Save him from what?'

Mrs Wix debated, then covered a still greater distance. 'Why just from awful misery.'

SHE had not at the moment explained her ominous speech, but the light of remarkable events soon enabled her companion to read it. It may indeed be said that these days brought on a high quickening of Maisie's direct perceptions, of her sense of freedom to make out things for herself. This was helped by an emotion intrinsically far from sweet – the increase of the alarm that had most haunted her meditations. She had no need to be told, as on the morrow of the revelation of Sir Claude's danger she was told by Mrs Wix, that her mother wanted more and more to know why the devil her father didn't send for her: she had too long expected mamma's curiosity on this point to express itself sharply. Maisie could meet such pressure so far as meeting it was to be in a position to reply, in words directly inspired, that papa would be hanged before he'd again be saddled with her. She therefore recognized the hour that in troubled glimpses she had long foreseen, the hour when – the phrase for it came back to her from Mrs Beale – with two fathers, two mothers and two homes, six protections in all, she shouldn't know 'wherever' to go. Such apprehension as she felt on this score was not diminished by the fact that Mrs Wix herself was suddenly white with terror: a circumstance leading Maisie to the further knowledge that this lady was still more scared on her own behalf than on that of her pupil. A governess who had only one frock was not likely to have either two fathers or two mothers: accordingly if even with these resources Maisie was to be in the streets, where in the name of all that was dreadful was poor Mrs Wix to be? She had had, it appeared, a tremendous brush with Ida, which had begun and ended with the request that she would be pleased on the spot to 'bundle'. It had come suddenly but completely, this signal of which she had gone in fear. The companions confessed to each other the dread each had hidden the worst of, but Mrs Wix was better off than Maisie in having a plan of defence. She declined indeed to communicate it till it was quite mature; but meanwhile, she hastened to declare, her feet were firm in the schoolroom. They could only be loosened by force: she would 'leave' for the police perhaps, but she wouldn't leave for mere outrage. That would be to play her ladyship's game, and it would take another turn of the screw to make her desert her darling. Her ladyship had come down with extraordinary violence: it had been one of many symptoms of a situation strained – 'between them all,' as Mrs Wix said, 'but especially between the two' – to the point of God only knew what.

Her description of the crisis made the child balance. 'Between which two? – papa and mamma?'

'Dear no. I mean between your mother and *him*.'

Maisie, in this, recognized an opportunity to be really deep. ' "Him"? – Mr Perriam?'

She fairly brought a blush to the scared face. 'Well, my dear, I must say what you *don't* know ain't worth mentioning. That it won't go on for ever with Mr Perriam – since I *must* meet you – who can suppose? But I meant dear Sir Claude.'

Maisie stood corrected rather than abashed. 'I see. But it's about Mr Perriam he's angry?'

Mrs Wix waited. 'He says he's not.'

'Not angry? He has told you so?'

Mrs Wix looked at her hard. 'Not about *him*.'

'Then about someone else?'

Mrs Wix looked at her harder. 'About someone else.'

'Lord Eric?' the child promptly brought forth.

At this, of a sudden, her governess was more agitated. 'Oh why, little unfortunate, should we discuss their dreadful names?' – and she threw herself for the millionth time on Maisie's neck. It took her pupil but a moment to feel that she quivered with insecurity, and, the contact of her terror aiding, the pair in another instant were sobbing in each other's arms. Then it was that, completely relaxed, demoralized as she had never been, Mrs Wix suffered her wound to bleed and her resentment to gush. Her great bitterness was that Ida had called her false, denounced her hypocrisy and duplicity, reviled her spying and tattling, her lying and grovelling to Sir Claude. 'Me, *me*,' the poor woman wailed, 'who've seen what I've seen and gone through everything only to cover her up and ease her off and smooth her down? If I've been an 'ipocrite it's the other way round: I've pretended, to him and to her, to myself and to you and to everyone, *not* to see! It serves me right to

79

have held my tongue before such horrors!' What horrors they were her companion forbore too closely to inquire, showing even signs not a few of an ability to take them for granted. That put the couple more than ever, in this troubled sea, in the same boat, so that with the consciousness of ideas on the part of her fellow-mariner Maisie could sit close and wait. Sir Claude on the morrow came in to tea, and then the ideas were produced. It was extraordinary how the child's presence drew out their full strength. The principal one was startling, but Maisie appreciated the courage with which her governess handled it. It simply consisted of the proposal that whenever and wherever they should seek refuge Sir Claude should consent to share their asylum. On his protesting with all the warmth in nature against this note of secession she asked what else in the world was left to them if her ladyship should stop supplies.

'Supplies be hanged, my dear woman!' said their delightful friend. 'Leave supplies to me – I'll take care of supplies.'

Mrs Wix rose to it. 'Well, it's exactly because I knew you'd be so glad to do so that I put the question before you. There's a way to look after us better than any other. The way's just to come along with us.'

It hung before Maisie, Mrs Wix's way, like a glittering picture, and she clasped her hands in ecstasy. 'Come along, come along, come along!'

Sir Claude looked from his stepdaughter back to her governess. 'Do you mean leave this house and take up my abode with you?'

'It will be the right thing – if you feel as you've told me you feel.' Mrs Wix, sustained and uplifted, was now as clear as a bell.

Sir Claude had the air of trying to recall what he had told her; then the light broke that was always breaking to make his face more pleasant. 'It's your happy thought that I shall take a house for you?'

'For the wretched homeless child. Any roof – over *our* heads – will do for us; but of course for you it will have to be something really nice.'

Sir Claude's eyes reverted to Maisie, rather hard, as she thought; and there was a shade in his very smile that seemed to show her – though she also felt it didn't show Mrs Wix – that the accommodation prescribed must loom to him pretty large. The next moment, however, he laughed gaily enough. 'My dear lady, you exaggerate tremendously *my* poor little needs.' Mrs Wix had once mentioned to her young friend that when Sir Claude called her his dear lady he could do anything with her; and Maisie felt a certain anxiety to see what he would do now. Well, he only addressed her a remark of which the child herself was aware of feeling the force. 'Your plan appeals to me immensely; but of course – don't you see? – I shall have to consider the position I put myself in by leaving my wife.'

'You'll also have to remember,' Mrs Wix replied, 'that if you don't look out your wife won't give you time to consider. Her ladyship will leave *you*.'

'Ah my good friend, I do look out!' the young man returned while Maisie helped herself afresh to bread and butter. 'Of course if that happens I shall have somehow to turn round; but I hope with all my heart it won't. I beg your pardon,' he continued to his stepdaughter, 'for appearing to discuss that sort of possibility under your sharp little nose. But the fact is I *forget* half the time that Ida's your sainted mother.'

'So do I!' said Maisie, her mouth full of bread and butter and to put him the more in the right.

Her protectress, at this, was upon her again. 'The little desolate precious pet!' For the rest of the conversation she was enclosed in Mrs Wix's arms, and as they sat there interlocked Sir Claude, before them with his teacup, looked down at them in deepening thought. Shrink together as they might they couldn't help, Maisie felt, being a very large lumpish image of what Mrs Wix required of his slim fineness. She knew, moreover, that this lady didn't make it better by adding in a moment: 'Of course *we* shouldn't dream of a whole house. Any sort of little lodging, however humble, would be only too blest.'

'But it would have to be something that would hold us all,' said Sir Claude.

'Oh yes,' Mrs Wix concurred: 'the whole point's our being together. While you're waiting, before you act, for her ladyship to take some step, our position here will come to an impossible pass. You don't know what I went through with her for you yesterday – and for our poor darling; but it's not a thing I can promise you often to face again. She cast me out in horrible language – she has instructed the servants not to wait on me.'

'Oh the poor servants are all right!' Sir Claude eagerly cried.

'They're certainly better than their mistress. It's too dreadful that I should sit here and say of your wife, Sir Claude, and of Maisie's own mother, that she's lower than a domestic; but my being betrayed into such remarks is just a reason the more for our getting away. I shall stay till I'm taken by the shoulders, but that may happen any day. What also may perfectly happen, you must permit me to repeat, is that she'll go off to get rid of us.'

'Oh if she'll only do that!' Sir Claude laughed. 'That would be the very making of us!'

'Don't say it – don't say it!' Mrs Wix pleaded. 'Don't speak of anything so fatal. You know what I mean. We must all cling to the right. You mustn't be bad.'

Sir Claude set down his teacup; he had become more grave and he pensively wiped his moustache. 'Won't all the world say I'm awful if I leave the house before – before she has bolted? They'll say it was my doing so that made her bolt.'

Maisie could grasp the force of this reasoning, but it offered no check to Mrs Wix. 'Why need you mind that – if you've done it for so high a motive? Think of the beauty of it,' the good lady pressed.

'Of bolting with *you*?' Sir Claude ejaculated.

She faintly smiled – she even faintly coloured. 'So far from doing you harm it will do you the highest good. Sir Claude, if you'll listen to me, it will save you.'

'Save me from what?'

Maisie, at this question, waited with renewed suspense for an answer that would bring the thing to some finer point than their companion had brought it to before. But there was on the contrary only more mystification in Mrs Wix's reply. 'Ah from you know what!'

'Do you mean from some other woman!'

'Yes – from a real bad one.'

Sir Claude at least, the child could see, was not mystified; so little indeed that a smile of intelligence broke afresh in his eyes. He turned them in vague discomfort to Maisie, and then something in the way she met them caused him to chuck her playfully under the chin. It was not till after this that he good-naturedly met Mrs Wix. 'You think me much worse than I am.'

'If that were true,' she returned, 'I wouldn't appeal to you. I do, Sir Claude, in the name of all that's good in you – and oh so earnestly! We can help each other. What you'll do for our young friend here I needn't say. That isn't even what I want to speak of now. What I want to speak of is what you'll *get* – don't you see? – from such an opportunity to take hold. Take hold of *us* – take hold of *her*. Make her your duty – make her your life: she'll repay you a thousand-fold!'

It was to Mrs Wix, during this appeal, that Maisie's contemplation transferred itself: partly because, though her heart was in her throat for trepidation, her delicacy deterred her from appearing herself to press the question; partly from the coercion of seeing Mrs Wix come out as Mrs Wix had never come before – not even on the day of her call at Mrs Beale's with the news of mamma's marriage. On that day Mrs Beale had surpassed her in dignity, but nobody could have surpassed her now. There was in fact at this moment a fascination for her pupil in the hint she seemed to give that she had still more of that surprise behind. So the sharpened sense of spectatorship was the child's main support, the long habit, from the first, of seeing herself in discussion and finding in the fury of it – she had had a glimpse of the game of football – a sort of compensation for the doom of a peculiar passivity. It gave her often an odd air of being present at her history in as separate a manner as if she could only get at experience by flattening her nose against a pane of glass. Such she felt to be the application of her nose while she waited for the effect of Mrs Wix's eloquence. Sir Claude, however, didn't keep her long in a position so ungraceful: he sat down and opened his arms to her as he had done the day he came for her at her father's, and while he held her there, looking at her kindly, but as if their companion had brought the blood a good deal to his face, he said:

'Dear Mrs Wix is magnificent, but she's rather too grand about it. I mean the situation isn't after all quite so desperate or quite so simple. But I give you my word before her, and I give it to her before you, that I'll never, never forsake you. Do you hear that, old fellow, and do you take it in? I'll stick to you through everything.'

Maisie did take it in – took it with a long tremor of all her little being; and then as, to emphasize it, he drew her closer she buried her head on his shoulder and cried without sound and without pain. While she was so engaged she became aware that his own breast was agitated, and gathered from it with rapture that his tears were as silently flowing. Presently she heard a loud sob from Mrs Wix – Mrs Wix was the only one who made a noise.

She was to have made, for some time, none other but this, though within a few days, in conversation with her pupil, she described her intercourse with Ida as little better than the state of being battered. There was as yet nevertheless no attempt to eject her by force, and she recognized that Sir Claude, taking such a stand as never before, had intervened with passion and with success. As Maisie remembered – and remembered wholly without disdain – that he had told her he was afraid of her ladyship, the little girl took this act of resolution as a proof of what, in the spirit of the engagement sealed by all their tears, he was really prepared to do. Mrs Wix spoke to her of the pecuniary sacrifice by which she herself purchased the scant security she enjoyed and which, if it was a defence against the hand of violence, yet left her exposed to incredible rudeness. Didn't her ladyship find every hour of the day some artful means to humiliate and trample upon her? There was a quarter's salary owing her – a great name, even Maisie could suspect, for a small matter; she should never see it as long as she lived, but keeping quiet about it put her ladyship, thank heaven, a little in one's power. Now that he was doing so much else she could never have the grossness to apply for it to Sir Claude. He had sent home for schoolroom consumption a huge frosted cake, a wonderful delectable mountain with geological strata of jam, which might, with economy, see them through many days of their siege; but it was none the less known to Mrs Wix that his affairs were more and more involved, and her fellow-partaker looked back tenderly, in the light of these involutions, at the expression of face with which he had greeted the proposal that he should set up another establishment. Maisie felt that if their maintenance should hang by a thread they must still demean themselves with the highest delicacy. What he was doing was simply acting without delay, so far as his embarrassments permitted, on the inspiration of his elder friend. There was at this

84

season a wonderful month of May – as soft as a drop of the wind in a gale that had kept one awake – when he took out his stepdaughter with a fresh alacrity and they rambled the great town in search, as Mrs Wix called it, of combined amusement and instruction.

They rode on the top of buses; they visited outlying parks; they went to cricket matches where Maisie fell asleep; they tried a hundred places for the best one to have tea. This was his direct way of rising to Mrs Wix's grand lesson – of making his little accepted charge his duty and his life. They dropped, under incontrollable impulses, into shops that they agreed were too big, to look at things that they agreed were too small, and it was during these hours that Mrs Wix, alone at home, but a subject of regretful reference as they pulled off their gloves for refreshment, subsequently described herself as least sheltered from the blows her ladyship had achieved such ingenuity in dealing. She again and again repeated that she wouldn't so much have minded having her 'attainments' held up to scorn and her knowledge of every subject denied, hadn't she been branded as 'low' in character and tone. There was by this time no pretence on the part of anyone of denying it to be fortunate that her ladyship habitually left London every Saturday and was more and more disposed to a return late in the week. It was almost equally public that she regarded as a preposterous 'pose', and indeed as a direct insult to herself, her husband's attitude of staying behind to look after a child for whom the most elaborate provision had been made. If there was a type Ida despised, Sir Claude communicated to Maisie, it was the man who pottered about town of a Sunday; and he also mentioned how often she had declared to him that if he had a grain of spirit he would be ashamed to accept a menial position about Mr Farange's daughter. It was her ladyship's contention that he was in craven fear of his predecessor – otherwise he would recognize it as an obligation of plain decency to protect his wife against the outrage of that person's barefaced attempt to swindle her. The swindle was that Mr Farange put upon her the whole intolerable burden; 'and even when I pay for you myself,' Sir Claude averred to his young friend, 'she accuses me the more of truckling and grovelling.' It was Mrs Wix's conviction, they both knew, arrived at on independent grounds, that Ida's weekly excursions were feelers for a more considerable absence. If she came back later each week the week would be sure to arrive when she wouldn't come back at all. This appearance had of course much to do with Mrs Wix's actual valour. Could they but hold out long enough the snug little home with Sir Claude would find itself informally established.

13

THIS might, moreover, have been taken to be the sense of a remark made by her stepfather as – one rainy day when the streets were all splash and two umbrellas unsociable and the wanderers had sought shelter in the National Gallery – Maisie sat beside him staring rather sightlessly at a roomful of pictures which he had mystified her much by speaking of with a bored sigh as a 'silly superstition'. They represented, with patches of gold and cataracts of purple, with stiff saints and angular angels, with ugly Madonnas and uglier babies, strange prayers and prostrations; so that she at first took his words for a protest against devotional idolatry – all the more that he had of late often come with her and with Mrs Wix to morning church, a place of worship of Mrs Wix's own choosing, where there was nothing of that sort; no haloes on heads, but only, during long sermons, beguiling backs of bonnets, and where, as her governess always afterwards observed, he gave the most earnest attention. It presently appeared, however, that his reference was merely to the affectation of admiring such ridiculous works – an admonition that she received from him as submissively as she received everything. What turn it gave to their talk needn't here be recorded: the transition to the colourless schoolroom and lonely Mrs Wix was doubtless an effect of relaxed interest in what was before them. Maisie expressed in her own way the truth that she never went home nowadays without expecting to find the temple of her studies empty and the poor priestess cast out. This conveyed a full appreciation of her peril, and it was in rejoinder that Sir Claude uttered, acknowledging the source of that peril, the reassurance at which I have glanced. 'Don't be afraid, my dear: I've squared her.' It required indeed a supplement when he saw that it left the child momentarily blank. 'I mean that your mother lets me do what I want so long as I let her do what *she* wants.'

'So you *are* doing what you want?' Maisie asked.

'Rather, Miss Farange!'

Miss Farange turned it over. 'And she's doing the same?'

'Up to the hilt!'

Again she considered. 'Then, please, what may it be?'

'I wouldn't tell you for the whole world.'

She gazed at a gaunt Madonna; after which she broke into a slow smile. 'Well, I don't care, so long as you let her.'

'Oh you monster!' – and Sir Claude's gay vehemence brought him to his feet.

Another day, in another place – a place in Baker Street where at a hungry hour she had sat down with him to tea and buns – he brought out a question disconnected from previous talk. 'I say, you know, what do you suppose your father *would* do?'

Maisie hadn't long to cast about or to question his pleasant eyes. 'If you were really to go with us? He'd make a great complaint.'

He seemed amused at the term she employed. 'Oh I shouldn't mind a "complaint"!'

'He'd talk to everyone about it,' said Maisie.

'Well, I shouldn't mind that either.'

'Of course not,' the child hastened to respond. 'You've told me you're not afraid of him.'

'The question is are you?' said Sir Claude.

Maisie candidly considered; then she spoke resolutely. 'No, not of papa.'

'But of somebody else?'

'Certainly, of lots of people.'

'Of your mother first and foremost of course.'

'Dear, yes; more of mamma than of – than of – '

'Than of what?' Sir Claude asked as she hesitated for a comparison.

She thought over all objects of dread. 'Than of a wild elephant!' she at last declared. 'And you are too,' she reminded him as he laughed.

'Oh yes, I am too.'

Again she meditated. 'Why, then, did you marry her?'

'Just because I *was* afraid.'

'Even when she loved you?'

'That made her the more alarming.'

For Maisie herself, though her companion seemed to find it droll, this opened up depths of gravity. 'More alarming than she is now?'

'Well, in a different way. Fear, unfortunately, is a very big thing, and there's a great variety of kinds.'

She took this in with complete intelligence. 'Then I think I've got them all.'

'You?' her friend cried. 'Nonsense! You're thoroughly "game".'

'I'm awfully afraid of Mrs Beale,' Maisie objected.

He raised his smooth brows. 'That charming woman?'

'Well,' she answered, 'you can't understand it because you're not in the same state.'

She had been going on with a luminous 'But' when, across the table, he laid his hand on her arm. 'I *can* understand it,' he confessed. 'I *am* in the same state.'

'Oh but she likes you so!' Maisie promptly pleaded.

Sir Claude literally coloured. 'That has something to do with it.'

Maisie wondered again. 'Being liked with being afraid?'

'Yes, when it amounts to adoration.'

'Then why aren't you afraid of *me*?'

'Because with you it amounts to that!' He had kept his hand on her arm. 'Well, what prevents it is simply that you're the gentlest spirit on earth. Besides – ' he pursued; but he came to a pause.

'Besides – ?'

'I *should* be in fear if you were older – there! See – you already make me talk nonsense,' the young man added. 'The question's about your father. Is he likewise afraid of Mrs Beale?'

'I think not. And yet he loves her,' Maisie mused.

'Oh no – he doesn't; not a bit!' After which, as his companion stared, Sir Claude apparently felt that he must make this oddity fit with her recollections. 'There's nothing of that sort *now*.'

But Maisie only stared the more. 'They've changed?'

'Like your mother and me.'

She wondered how he knew. 'Then you've seen Mrs Beale again?'

He demurred. 'Oh no. She has written to me,' he presently sub-joined. '*She's* not afraid of your father either. No one at all is – really.' Then he went on while Maisie's little mind, with its filial spring too relaxed from of old for a pang at this want of parental majesty, speculated on the vague relation between Mrs Beale's courage and the question, for Mrs Wix and herself, of a neat lodging with their friend. 'She wouldn't care a bit if Mr Farange should make a row.'

'Do you mean about you and me and Mrs Wix? Why should she care? It wouldn't hurt *her*.'

Sir Claude, with his legs out and his hand diving into his trousers-pocket, threw back his head with a laugh just per-ceptibly tempered, as she thought, by a sigh. 'My dear stepchild, you're delightful! Look here, we must pay. You've had five buns?'

'How can you?' Maisie demanded, crimson under the eye of the young woman who had stepped to their board. 'I've had three.'

Shortly after this Mrs Wix looked so ill that it was to be feared her ladyship had treated her to some unexampled passage. Maisie asked if anything worse than usual had occurred; whereupon the poor woman brought out with infinite gloom: 'He has been seeing Mrs Beale.'

'Sir Claude?' The child remembered what he had said. 'Oh no – not *seeing* her!'

'I beg your pardon. I absolutely know it.' Mrs Wix was as positive as she was dismal.

Maisie nevertheless ventured to challenge her. 'And how, please, do you know it?'

She faltered a moment. 'From herself. I've been to see her.' Then on Maisie's visible surprise: 'I went yesterday while you were out with him. He has seen her repeatedly.'

It was not wholly clear to Maisie why Mrs Wix should be pros-trate at this discovery; but her general consciousness of the way things could be both perpetrated and resented always eased off for her the strain of the particular mystery. 'There may be some mistake. He says he hasn't.'

Mrs Wix turned paler, as if this were a still deeper ground for alarm. 'He says so? – he denies that he has seen her?'

'He told me so three days ago. Perhaps she's mistaken,' Maisie suggested.

'Do you mean perhaps she lies? She lies whenever it suits her, I'm very sure. But I know when people lie – and that's what I've loved in you, that *you* never do. Mrs Beale didn't yesterday at any rate. He *has* seen her.'

Maisie was silent a little. 'He says not,' she then repeated. 'Perhaps – perhaps – ' Once more she paused.

'Do you mean perhaps *he* lies?'

'Gracious goodness, no!' Maisie shouted.

Mrs Wix's bitterness, however, again overflowed. 'He does, he does,' she cried, 'and it's that that's just the worst of it! They'll take you, they'll take you, and what in the world will then become of me?' She threw herself afresh upon her pupil and wept over her with the inevitable effect of causing the child's own tears to flow. But Maisie couldn't have told you if she had been crying at the image of their separation or at that of Sir Claude's untruth. As regards this deviation it was agreed between them that they were not in a position to bring it home to him. Mrs Wix was in dread of doing anything to make him, as she said, 'worse'; and Maisie was sufficiently initiated to be able to reflect that in speaking to her as he had done he had only wished to be tender of Mrs Beale. It fell in with all her inclinations to think of him as tender, and she forbore to let him know that the two ladies had, as *she* would never do, betrayed him.

She had not long to keep her secret, for the next day, when she went out with him, he suddenly said in reference to some errand he had first proposed: 'No, we won't do that – we'll do something else.' On this, a few steps from the door, he stopped a hansom and helped her in; then following her he gave the driver over the top an address that she lost. When he was seated beside her she asked him where they were going; to which he replied, 'My dear child, you'll see.' She saw while she watched and wondered that they took the direction of the Regent's Park; but she didn't know why he should make a mystery of that, and it was not till they passed under a pretty arch and drew up at a white house in a terrace from which the view, she thought, must be lovely that, mystified, she clutched him and broke out: 'I shall see papa?'

He looked down at her with a kind smile. 'No, probably not. I haven't brought you for that.'

'Then whose house is it?'

'It's your father's. They've moved here.'

She looked about: she had known Mr Farange in four or five houses, and there was nothing astonishing in this except that it was the nicest place yet. 'But I shall see Mrs Beale?'

'It's to see her that I brought you.'

She stared, very white, and, with her hand on his arm, though they had stopped, kept him sitting in the cab. 'To leave me, do you mean?'

He could scarce bring it out. 'It's not for me to say if you *can* stay. We must look into it.'

'But if I do I shall see papa?'

'Oh some time or other, no doubt.' Then Sir Claude went on: 'Have you really so very great a dread of that?'

Maisie glanced away over the apron of the cab – gazed a minute at the green expanse of the Regent's Park and, at this moment colouring to the roots of her hair, felt the full hot rush of an emotion more mature than any she had yet known. It consisted of an odd unexpected shame at placing in an inferior light, to so perfect a gentleman and so charming a person as Sir Claude, so very near a relative as Mr Farange. She remembered, however, her friend's telling her that no one was seriously afraid of her father, and she turned round with a small toss of her head. 'Oh I daresay I can manage him!'

Sir Claude smiled, but she noted that the violence with which she had just changed colour had brought into his own face a slight compunctious and embarrassed flush. It was as if he had caught his first glimpse of her sense of responsibility. Neither of them made a movement to get out, and after an instant he said to her: 'Look here, if you say so we won't after all go in.'

'Ah but I want to see Mrs Beale!' the child gently wailed.

'But what if she does decide to take you? Then, you know, you'll have to remain.'

Maisie turned it over. 'Straight on – and give you up?'

'Well – I don't quite know about giving me up.'

91

'I mean as I gave up Mrs Beale when I last went to mamma's. I couldn't do without you here for anything like so long a time as that.' It struck her as a hundred years since she had seen Mrs Beale, who was on the other side of the door they were so near and whom she yet had not taken the jump to clasp in her arms.

'Oh I daresay you'll see more of me than you've seen of Mrs Beale. It isn't in *me* to be so beautifully discreet,' Sir Claude said. 'But all the same,' he continued, 'I leave the thing, now that we're here, absolutely *with* you. You must settle it. We'll only go in if you say so. If you don't say so we'll turn right round and drive away.'

'So in that case Mrs Beale won't take me?'

'Well – not by any act of ours.'

'And I shall be able to go on with mamma?' Maisie asked.

'Oh I don't say that!'

She considered. 'But I thought you said you had squared her?'

Sir Claude poked his stick at the splashboard of the cab. 'Not, my dear child, to the point she now requires.'

'Then if she turns me out and I don't come here – ?'

Sir Claude promptly took her up. 'What do I offer you, you naturally inquire? My poor chick, that's just what I ask myself. I don't see it, I confess, quite as straight as Mrs Wix.'

His companion gazed a moment at what Mrs Wix saw. 'You mean *we* can't make a little family?'

'It's very base of me, no doubt, but I can't wholly chuck your mother.'

Maisie, at this, emitted a low but lengthened sigh, a slight sound of reluctant assent which would certainly have been amusing to an auditor. 'Then there isn't anything else?'

'I vow I don't quite see what there is.'

Maisie waited; her silence seemed to signify that she too had no alternative to suggest. But she made another appeal. 'If I come here you'll come to see me?'

'I won't lose sight of you.'

'But how often will you come?' As he hung fire she pressed him. 'Often and often?'

Still he faltered. 'My dear old woman – ' he began. Then he paused again, going on the next moment with a change of tone. 'You're too funny! Yes then,' he said; 'often and often.'

'All right!' Maisie jumped out. Mrs Beale was at home, but not in the drawing-room, and when the butler had gone for her the child suddenly broke out: 'But when I'm here what will Mrs Wix do?'

'Ah you should have thought of that sooner!' said her companion with the first faint note of asperity she had ever heard him sound.

14

MRS BEALE fairly swooped upon her, and the effect of the whole hour was to show the child how much, how quite formidably indeed, after all, she was loved. This was the more the case as her stepmother, so changed – in the very manner of her mother – that she really struck her as a new acquaintance, somehow recalled more familiarity than Maisie could feel. A rich strong expressive affection in short pounced upon her in the shape of a handsomer, ampler, older Mrs Beale. It was like making a fine friend, and they hadn't been a minute together before she felt elated at the way she had met the choice imposed on her in the cab. There was a whole future in the combination of Mrs Beale's beauty and Mrs Beale's hug. She seemed to Maisie charming to behold, and also to have no connexion at all with anybody who had once mended underclothing and had meals in the nursery. The child knew one of her father's wives was a woman of fashion, but she had always dimly made a distinction, not applying that epithet without reserve to the other. Mrs Beale had since their separation acquired a conspicuous right to it, and Maisie's first flush of response to her present delight coloured all her splendour with meanings that this time were sweet. She had told Sir Claude she was afraid of the lady in the Regent's Park; but she had confidence enough to break, on the spot, into the frankest appreciation. 'Why, aren't you beautiful? Isn't she beautiful, Sir Claude, *isn't* she?'

'The handsomest woman in London, simply,' Sir Claude gallantly replied. 'Just as sure as you're the best little girl!'

Well, the handsomest woman in London gave herself up, with tender lustrous looks and every demonstration of fondness, to a

93

happiness at last clutched again. There was almost as vivid a bloom in her maturity as in mamma's, and it took her but a short time to give her little friend an impression of positive power – an impression that seemed to begin like a long bright day. This was a perception on Maisie's part that neither mamma, nor Sir Claude, nor Mrs Wix, with their immense and so varied respective attractions, had exactly kindled, and that made an immediate difference when the talk, as it promptly did, began to turn to her father. Oh yes, Mr Farange was a complication, but she saw now that he wouldn't be one for his daughter. For Mrs Beale certainly he was an immense one – she speedily made known as much; but Mrs Beale from this moment presented herself to Maisie as a person to whom a great gift had come. The great gift was just for handling complications. Maisie felt how little she made of them when, after she had dropped to Sir Claude some recall of a previous meeting, he made answer, with a sound of consternation and yet an air of relief, that he had denied to their companion their having, since the day he came for her, seen each other till that moment.

Mrs Beale could but vaguely pity it. 'Why did you do anything so silly?'

'To protect your reputation.'

'From Maisie?' Mrs Beale was much amused. 'My reputation with Maisie is too good to suffer.'

'But you believed me, you rascal, didn't you?' Sir Claude asked of the child.

She looked at him; she smiled. 'Her reputation did suffer. I discovered you had been here.'

He was not too chagrined to laugh. 'The way, my dear, you talk of that sort of thing!'

'How should she talk,' Mrs Beale wanted to know, 'after all this wretched time with her mother?'

'It was not mamma who told me,' Maisie explained. 'It was only Mrs Wix.' She was hesitating whether to bring out before Sir Claude the source of Mrs Wix's information; but Mrs Beale, addressing the young man, showed the vanity of scruples.

'Do you know that preposterous person came to see me a day or two ago? – when I told her I had seen you repeatedly.'

Sir Claude, for once in a way, was disconcerted. 'The old cat!

She never told me. Then you thought I had lied?' he demanded of Maisie.

She was flurried by the term with which he had qualified her gentle friend, but she took the occasion for one to which she must in every manner lend herself. 'Oh I didn't mind! But Mrs Wix did,' she added with an intention benevolent to her governess.

Her intention was not very effective as regards Mrs Beale. 'Mrs Wix is too idiotic!' that lady declared.

'But to you, of all people,' Sir Claude asked, 'what had she to say?'

'Why that, like Mrs Micawber – whom she must, I think, rather resemble – she will never, never, never desert Miss Farange.'

'Oh I'll make that all right!' Sir Claude cheerfully returned.

'I'm sure I hope so, my dear man,' said Mrs Beale, while Maisie wondered just how he would proceed. Before she had time to ask Mrs Beale continued: 'That's not all she came to do, if you please. But you'll never guess the rest.'

'Shall *I* guess it?' Maisie quavered.

Mrs Beale was again amused. 'Why you're just the person! It must be quite the sort of thing you've heard at your awful mother's. Have you never seen women there crying to her to "spare" the men they love?'

Maisie, wondering, tried to remember; but Sir Claude was freshly diverted. 'Oh they don't trouble about Ida! Mrs Wix cried to you to spare *me*?'

'She regularly went down on her knees to me.'

'The darling old dear!' the young man exclaimed.

These words were a joy to Maisie – they made up for his previous description of Mrs Wix. 'And *will* you spare him?' she asked of Mrs Beale.

Her stepmother, seizing her and kissing her again, seemed charmed with the tone of her question. 'Not an inch of him! I'll pick him to the bone!'

'You mean that he'll really come often?' Maisie pressed.

Mrs Beale turned lovely eyes to Sir Claude. 'That's not for me to say – it's for him.'

He said nothing at once, however; with his hands in his pockets and vaguely humming a tune – even Maisie could see he was a

95

little nervous – he only walked to the window and looked out at the Regent's Park. 'Well, he has promised,' Maisie said. 'But how will papa like it?'

'His being in and out? Ah that's a question that, to be frank with you, my dear, hardly matters. In point of fact, however, Beale greatly enjoys the idea that Sir Claude too, poor man, has been forced to quarrel with your mother.'

Sir Claude turned round and spoke gravely and kindly. 'Don't be afraid, Maisie; you won't lose sight of me.'

'Thank you so much!' Maisie was radiant. 'But what I meant – don't you know? – was what papa would say to *me*.'

'Oh I've been having that out with him,' said Mrs Beale. 'He'll behave well enough. You see the great difficulty is that, though he changes every three days about everything else in the world, he has never changed about your mother. It's a caution, the way he hates her.'

Sir Claude gave a short laugh. 'It certainly can't beat the way she still hates *him*!'

'Well,' Mrs Beale went on obligingly, 'nothing can take the place of that feeling with either of them, and the best way they can think of to show it is for each to leave you as long as possible on the hands of the other. There's nothing, as you've seen for yourself, that makes either so furious. It isn't, asking so little as you do, that you're much of an expense or a trouble; it's only that you make each feel so well how nasty the other wants to be. Therefore Beale goes on loathing your mother too much to have any great fury left for anyone else. Besides, you know, I've squared him.'

'Oh Lord!' Sir Claude cried with a louder laugh and turning again to the window.

'*I* know how!' Maisie was prompt to proclaim. 'By letting him do what he wants on condition that he lets you also do it.'

'You're too delicious, my own pet!' – she was involved in another hug. 'How in the world have I got on so long without you? I've not been happy, love,' said Mrs Beale with her cheek to the child's.

'Be happy now!' – Maisie throbbed with shy tenderness.

'I think I shall be. You'll save me.'

'As I'm saving Sir Claude?' the little girl asked eagerly.

Mrs Beale, a trifle at a loss, appealed to her visitor. 'Is she really?'

He showed high amusement at Maisie's question. 'It's dear Mrs Wix's idea. There may be something in it.'

'He makes me his duty – he makes me his life,' Maisie set forth to her stepmother.

'Why that's what *I* want to do!' – Mrs Beale, so anticipated, turned pink with astonishment.

'Well, you can do it together. Then he'll *have* to come!'

Mrs Beale by this time had her young friend fairly in her lap and she smiled up at Sir Claude. 'Shall we do it together?'

His laughter had dropped, and for a moment he turned his handsome serious face not to his hostess, but to his stepdaughter. 'Well, it's rather more decent than some things. Upon my soul, the way things are going, it seems to me the only decency!' He had the air of arguing it out to Maisie, of presenting it, through an impulse of conscience, as a connexion in which they could honourably see her participate; though his plea of mere 'decency' might well have appeared to fall below her rosy little vision. 'If we're not good for *you*,' he exclaimed, 'I'll be hanged if I know who we shall be good for!'

Mrs Beale showed the child an intenser light. 'I daresay you *will* save us – from one thing and another.'

'Oh I know what she'll save *me* from!' Sir Claude roundly asserted. 'There'll be rows of course,' he went on.

Mrs Beale quickly took him up. 'Yes, but they'll be nothing – for you at least – to the rows your wife makes as it is. I can bear what *I* suffer – I can't bear what you go through.'

'We're doing a good deal for you, you know, young woman,' Sir Claude went on to Maisie with the same gravity.

She coloured with a sense of obligation and the eagerness of her desire it should be remarked how little was lost on her. 'Oh I know!'

'Then you must keep us all right!' This time he laughed.

'How you talk to her!' cried Mrs Beale.

'No worse than you!' he gaily answered.

'Handsome is that handsome does!' she returned in the same spirit. 'You can take off your things,' she went on, releasing Maisie.

97

The child, on her feet, was all emotion. 'Then I'm just to stop –
this way?'

'It will do as well as any other. Sir Claude, tomorrow, will
have your things brought.'

'I'll bring them myself. Upon my word I'll see them packed!'
Sir Claude promised. 'Come here and unbutton.'

He had beckoned his young companion to where he sat, and
he helped to disengage her from her coverings while Mrs Beale,
from a little distance, smiled at the hand he displayed. 'There's
a stepfather for you! I'm bound to say, you know, that he makes
up for the want of other people.'

'He makes up for the want of a nurse!' Sir Claude laughed.
'Don't you remember I told you so the very first time?'

'Remember? It was exactly what made me think so well of
you!'

'Nothing would induce me,' the young man said to Maisie, 'to
tell you what made me think so well of *her*.' Having divested the
child he kissed her gently and gave her a little pat to make her
stand off. The pat was accompanied with a vague sigh in which
his gravity of a moment before came back. 'All the same, if you
hadn't had the fatal gift of beauty – !'

'Well, what?' Maisie asked, wondering why he paused. It was
the first time she had heard of her beauty.

'Why, we shouldn't all be thinking so well of each other!'

'He isn't speaking of personal loveliness – you've not *that* vulgar beauty, my dear, at all,' Mrs Beale explained. 'He's just talking of plain dull charm of character.'

'Her character's the most extraordinary thing in all the world,'
Sir Claude stated to Mrs Beale.

'Oh I know all about that sort of thing!' – she fairly bridled
with the knowledge.

It gave Maisie somehow a sudden sense of responsibility from
which she sought refuge. 'Well, you've got it too, "that sort of
thing" – you've got the fatal gift: you both really have!' she
broke out.

'Beauty of character? My dear boy, we haven't a pennyworth!'
Sir Claude protested.

'Speak for yourself, sir!' leaped lightly from Mrs Beale. 'I'm
good and I'm clever. What more do you want? For you, I'll spare

98

your blushes and not be personal – I'll simply say that you're as handsome as you can stick together.'

'You're both very lovely; you can't get out of it!' – Maisie felt the need of carrying her point. 'And it's beautiful to see you side by side.'

Sir Claude had taken his hat and stick; he stood looking at her a moment. 'You're a comfort in trouble! But I must go home and pack you.'

'And when will you come back? – tomorrow, tomorrow?'

'You see what we're in for!' he said to Mrs Beale.

'Well, I can bear it if you can!'

Their companion gazed from one of them to the other, thinking that though she had been happy indeed between Sir Claude and Mrs Wix she should evidently be happier still between Sir Claude and Mrs Beale. But it was like being perched on a prancing horse, and she made a movement to hold on to something. 'Then, you know, shan't I bid good-bye to Mrs Wix?'

'Oh I'll make it all right with her,' said Sir Claude.

Maisie considered. 'And with mamma?'

'Ah mamma!' he sadly laughed.

Even for the child this was scarcely ambiguous; but Mrs Beale endeavoured to contribute to its clearness. 'Your mother will crow, she'll crow –'

'Like the early bird!' said Sir Claude as she looked about for a comparison.

'She'll need no consolation,' Mrs Beale went on, 'for having made your father grandly blaspheme.'

Maisie stared. 'Will he grandly blaspheme?' It was impressive, it might have been out of the Bible, and her question produced a fresh play of caresses, in which Sir Claude also engaged. She wondered meanwhile who, if Mrs Wix was disposed of, would represent in her life the element of geography and anecdote; and she presently surmounted the delicacy she felt about asking. 'Won't there be anyone to give me lessons?'

Mrs Beale was prepared with a reply that struck her as absolutely magnificent. 'You shall have such lessons as you've never had in all your life. You shall go to courses.'

'Courses?' Maisie had never heard of such things.

'At institutions – on subjects.'

Maisie continued to stare. 'Subjects?'

Mrs Beale was really splendid. 'All the most important ones. French literature – and sacred history. You'll take part in classes – with awfully smart children.'

'I'm going to look thoroughly into the whole thing, you know.' And Sir Claude, with characteristic kindness, gave her a nod of assurance accompanied by a friendly wink.

But Mrs Beale went much further. 'My dear child, you shall attend lectures.'

The horizon was suddenly vast and Maisie felt herself the smaller for it. 'All alone?'

'Oh no; I'll attend them with you,' said Sir Claude. 'They'll teach me a lot I don't know.'

'So they will me,' Mrs Beale gravely admitted. 'We'll go with her together – it will be charming. It's ages,' she confessed to Maisie, 'since I've had any time for study. That's another sweet way in which you'll be a motive to us. Oh won't the good she'll do us be immense?' she broke out uncontrollably to Sir Claude.

He weighed it; then he replied: 'That's certainly our idea.' Of this idea Maisie naturally had less of a grasp, but it inspired her with almost equal enthusiasm. If in so bright a prospect there would be nothing to long for it followed that she wouldn't long for Mrs Wix; but her consciousness of her assent to the absence of that fond figure caused a pair of words that had often sounded in her ears to ring in them again. It showed her in short what her father had always meant by calling her mother a 'low sneak' and her mother by calling her father one. She wondered if she herself shouldn't be a low sneak in learning to be so happy without Mrs Wix. What would Mrs Wix do? – where would Mrs Wix go? Before Maisie knew it, and at the door, as Sir Claude was off, these anxieties, on her lips, grew articulate and her stepfather had stopped long enough to answer them. 'Oh I'll square her!' he cried; and with this he departed.

Face to face with Mrs Beale, Maisie, giving a sigh of relief, looked round at what seemed to her the dawn of a higher order. 'Then *everyone* will be squared!' she peacefully said. On which her stepmother affectionately bent over her again.

15

It was Susan Ash who came to her with the news: 'He's down-stairs, miss, and he do look beautiful.'

In the schoolroom at her father's, which had pretty blue cur-tains, she had been making out at the piano a lovely little thing, as Mrs Beale called it, a 'Moonlight Berceuse' sent her through the post by Sir Claude, who considered that her musical education had been deplorably neglected and who, the last months at her mother's, had been on the point of making arrangements for regular lessons. She knew from him familiarly that the real thing, as he said, was shockingly dear and that anything else was a waste of money, and she therefore rejoiced the more at the sacrifice repre-sented by this composition, of which the price, five shillings, was marked on the cover and which was evidently the real thing. She was already on her feet. 'Mrs Beale has sent up for me!'

'Oh no – it's not that,' said Susan Ash. 'Mrs Beale has been out this hour.'

'Then papa!'

'Dear no – not papa. You'll do, miss, all but them wandering 'airs,' Susan went on. 'Your papa never came 'ome at all,' she added.

'Home from where?' Maisie responded a little absently and very excitedly. She gave a wild manual brush to her locks.

'Oh that, miss, I should be very sorry to tell you! I'd rather tuck away that white thing behind – though I'm blest if it's my work.'

'Do then, please. I know where papa was,' Maisie impatiently continued.

'Well, in your place I wouldn't tell.'

'He was at the club – the Chrysanthemum. So!'

'All night long? Why the flowers shut up at night, you know!' cried Susan Ash.

'Well, I don't care' – the child was at the door. 'Sir Claude asked for me *alone*?'

'The same as if you was a duchess.'

Maisie was aware on her way downstairs that she was now

quite as happy as one, and also, a moment later, as she hung round his neck, that even such a personage would scarce commit herself more grandly. There was, moreover, a hint of the duchess in the infinite point with which, as she felt, she exclaimed: 'And this is what you call coming *often*?'

Sir Claude met her delightfully and in the same fine spirit. 'My dear old man, don't make me a scene – I assure you it's what every woman I look at does. Let us have some fun -- it's a lovely day: clap on something smart and come out with me then we'll talk it over quietly.' They were on their way five minutes later to Hyde Park, and nothing that even in the good days at her mother's they had ever talked over had more of the sweetness of tranquillity than his present prompt explanations. He was at his best in such an office and with the exception of Mrs Wix the only person she had met in her life who ever explained. With him, however, the act had an authority transcending the wisdom of woman. It all came back – all the plans that always failed, all the rewards and bribes that she was perpetually paying for in advance and perpetually out of pocket by afterwards – the whole great stress to be dealt with introduced her on each occasion afresh to the question of money. Even she herself almost knew how it would have expressed the strength of his empire to say that to shuffle away her sense of being duped he had only, from under his lovely moustache, to breathe upon it. It was somehow in the nature of plans to be expensive and in the nature of the expensive to be impossible. To be 'involved' was of the essence of everybody's affairs, and also at every particular moment to be more involved than usual. This had been the case with Sir Claude's, with papa's, with mamma's, with Mrs Beale's and with Maisie's own at the particular moment, a moment of several weeks, that had elapsed since our young lady had been re-established at her father's. There wasn't 'two and tuppence' for anything or for anyone, and that was why there had been no sequel to the classes in French literature with all the smart little girls. It was devilish awkward, didn't she see? to try, without even the limited capital mentioned, to mix her up with a remote array that glittered before her after this as the children of the rich. She was to feel henceforth as if she were flattening her nose upon the hard window-pane of the sweet-shop of knowledge. If the classes, however, that were select, and accordingly the only ones, were impossibly dear, the lectures at the institutions – at least at some of them – were directly addressed to the intelligent poor, and it therefore had to be easier still to produce on the spot the reason why she had been taken to none. This reason, Sir Claude said, was that she happened to be just going to be, though they had nothing to do with that in now directing their steps to the banks of the Serpentine. Maisie's own park, in the north, had been nearer at hand, but they rolled westward in a hansom because at the end of the sweet June days this was the direction taken by everyone that anyone looked at. They cultivated for an hour, on the Row and by the Drive, this opportunity for each observer to amuse and for one of them indeed, not a little hilariously, to mystify the other, and before the hour was over Maisie had elicited, in reply to her sharpest challenge, a further account of her friend's long absence.

'Why I've broken my word to you so dreadfully – promising so solemnly and then never coming? Well, my dear, that's a question that, not seeing me day after day, you must very often have put to Mrs Beale.'

'Oh yes,' the child replied; 'again and again.'

'And what has she told you?'

'That you're as bad as you're beautiful.'

'Is that what she says?'

'Those very words.'

'Ah the dear old soul!' Sir Claude was much diverted, and his loud, clear laugh was all his explanation. Those were just the words Maisie had last heard him use about Mrs Wix. She clung to his hand, which was encased in a pearl-grey glove ornamented with the thick black lines that, at her mother's, always used to strike her as connected with the way the bestitched fists of the long ladies carried, with the elbows well out, their umbrellas upside down. The mere sense of his grasp in her own covered the ground of loss just as much as the ground of gain. His presence was like an object brought so close to her face that she couldn't see round its edges. He himself, however, remained showman of the spectacle even after they had passed out of the Park and begun, under the charm of the spot and the season, to stroll in Kensington Gardens. What they had left behind them was, as he said, only a pretty bad circus, and, through prepossessing gates and over a bridge, they had come in a quarter of an hour, as he also remarked, a hundred miles from London. A great green glade was before them, and high old trees, and under the shade of these, in the fresh turf, the crooked course of a rural footpath. 'It's the Forest of Arden,' Sir Claude had just delightfully observed, 'and I'm the banished duke, and you're – what was the young woman called? – the artless country wench. And there,' he went on, 'is the other girl – what's her name, Rosalind? – and (don't you know?) the fellow who was making up to her. Upon my word he *is* making up to her!'

His allusion was to a couple who, side by side, at the end of the glade, were moving in the same direction as themselves. These distant figures, in their slow stroll (which kept them so close together that their heads, drooping a little forward, almost touched), presented the back of a lady who looked tall, who was evidently a very fine woman, and that of a gentleman whose left hand appeared to be passed well into her arm while his right, behind him, made jerky motions with the stick that it grasped. Maisie's fancy responded for an instant to her friend's idea that the sight was idyllic; then, stopping short, she brought out with all her clearness: 'Why mercy – if it isn't mamma!'

Sir Claude paused with a stare. 'Mamma? But mamma's at Brussels.'

Maisie, with her eyes on the lady, wondered. 'At Brussels?'

'She's gone to play a match.'

'At billiards? You didn't tell me.'

'Of course I didn't!' Sir Claude ejaculated. 'There's plenty I don't tell you. She went on Wednesday.'

The couple had added to their distance, but Maisie's eyes more than kept pace with them. 'Then she has come back.'

Sir Claude watched the lady. 'It's much more likely she never went!'

'It's mamma!' the child said with decision.

They had stood still, but Sir Claude had made the most of his opportunity, and it happened that just at this moment, at the end of the vista, the others halted, and, still showing only their backs, seemed to stay talking. 'Right you are, my duck!' he exclaimed at last. 'It's my own sweet wife!'

He had spoken with a laugh, but he had changed colour,

104

and Maisie quickly looked away from him. 'Then who is it with her?'

'Blest if I know!' said Sir Claude.

'Is it Mr Perriam?'

'Oh dear no – Perriam's smashed.'

'Smashed?'

'Exposed – in the City. But there are quantities of others!' Sir Claude smiled.

Maisie appeared to count them; she studied the gentleman's back. 'Then this is Lord Eric?'

For a moment her companion made no answer, and when she turned her eyes again to him he was looking at her, she thought, rather queerly. 'What do you know about Lord Eric?'

She tried innocently to be odd in return. 'Oh I know more than you think! Is it Lord Eric?' she repeated.

'It may be. Blest if I care!'

Their friends had slightly separated and now, as Sir Claude spoke, suddenly faced round, showing all the splendour of her ladyship and all the mystery of her comrade. Maisie held her breath. 'They're coming!'

'Let them come.' And Sir Claude, pulling out his cigarettes, began to strike a light.

'We shall meet them!'

'No. They'll meet *us*.'

Maisie stood her ground. 'They see us. Just look.'

Sir Claude threw away his match. 'Come straight on.' The others, in the return, evidently startled, had half-paused again, keeping well apart. 'She's horribly surprised and wants to slope,' he continued. 'But it's too late.'

Maisie advanced beside him, making out even across the interval that her ladyship was ill at ease. 'Then what will she do?'

Sir Claude puffed his cigarette. 'She's quickly thinking.' He appeared to enjoy it.

Ida had wavered but an instant; her companion clearly gave her moral support. Maisie thought he somehow looked brave, and he had no likeness whatever to Mr Perriam. His face, thin, and rather sharp, was smooth, and it was not till they came nearer that she saw he had a remarkably fair little moustache. She could already see that his eyes were of the lightest blue. He was far nicer than

Mr Perriam. Mamma looked terrible from afar, but even under her guns the child's curiosity flickered and she appealed again to Sir Claude. 'Is it – *is* it Lord Eric?'

Sir Claude smoked composedly enough. 'I think it's the Count.'

This was a happy solution – it fitted her idea of a count. But what idea, as she now came grandly on, did mamma fit? – unless that of an actress, in some tremendous situation, sweeping down to the footlights as if she would jump them. Maisie felt really so frightened that before she knew it she passed her hand into Sir Claude's arm. Her pressure caused him to stop, and at the sight of this the other couple came equally to a stand and, beyond the diminished space, remained a moment more in talk. This, however, was the matter of an instant leaving the Count apparently to come round more circuitously – an outflanking movement, if Maisie had but known – her ladyship resumed the onset. 'What *will* she do now?' her daughter asked.

Sir Claude was at present in a position to say: 'Try to pretend it's me.'

'You?'

'Why that I'm up to something.'

In another minute poor Ida had justified this prediction, erect there before them like a figure of justice in full dress. There were parts of her face that grew whiter while Maisie looked, and other parts in which this change seemed to make other colours reign with more intensity. 'What are you doing with my daughter?' she demanded of her husband; in spite of the indignant tone of which Maisie had a greater sense than ever in her life before of not being personally noticed. It seemed to her Sir Claude also grew pale as an effect of the loud defiance with which Ida twice repeated this question. He put her, instead of answering it, an inquiry of his own: 'Who the devil have you got hold of *now*?' and at this her ladyship turned tremendously to the child, glaring at her as at an equal plotter of sin. Maisie received in petrification the full force of her mother's huge painted eyes – they were like Japanese lanterns swung under festal arches. But life came back to her from a tone suddenly and strangely softened. 'Go straight to that gentleman, my dear; I've asked him to take you a few minutes. He's charming – go. I've something to say to *this* creature.'

Maisie felt Sir Claude immediately clutch her. 'No, no – thank you: that won't do. She's mine.'

'Yours?' It was confounding to Maisie to hear her speak quite as if she had never heard of Sir Claude before.

'Mine. You've given her up. You've not another word to say about her. I have her from her father,' said Sir Claude – a statement that startled his companion, who could also measure its lively action on her mother.

There was visibly, however, an influence that made Ida consider; she glanced at the gentleman she had left, who, having strolled with his hands in his pockets to some distance, stood there with unembarrassed vagueness. She directed to him the face that was like an illuminated garden, turnstile and all, for the frequentation of which he had his season-ticket; then she looked again at Sir Claude. 'I've given her up to her father to *keep* – not to get rid of by sending about the town either with you or with anyone else. If she's not to mind me let *him* come and tell me so. I decline to take it from another person, and I like your pretending that with your humbug of "interest" you've a leg to stand on. I know your game and have something now to say to you about it.'

Sir Claude gave a squeeze of the child's arm. 'Didn't I tell you she'd have, Miss Farange?'

'You're uncommonly afraid to hear it,' Ida went on; 'but if you think she'll protect you from it you're mightily mistaken.' She gave him a moment. 'I'll give her the benefit as soon as look at you. Should you like her to know, my dear?' Maisie had a sense of her launching the question with effect; yet our young lady was also conscious of hoping that Sir Claude would declare that preference. We have already learned that she had come to like people's liking her to 'know'. Before he could reply at all, none the less, her mother opened a pair of arms of extraordinary elegance, and then she felt the loosening of his grasp. 'My own child,' Ida murmured in a voice – a voice of sudden confused tenderness – that it seemed to her she heard for the first time. She wavered but an instant, thrilled with the first direct appeal, as distinguished from the mere maternal pull, she had ever had from lips that, even in the old vociferous years, had always been sharp. The next moment she was on her mother's breast, where, amid a

107

wilderness of trinkets, she felt as if she had suddenly been thrust, with a smash of glass, into a jeweller's shop-front, but only to be as suddenly ejected with a push and the brisk injunction: 'Now go to the Captain!'

Maisie glanced at the gentleman submissively, but felt the want of more introduction. 'The Captain?'

Sir Claude broke into a laugh. 'I told her it was the Count.'

Ida stared; she rose so superior that she was colossal. 'You're too utterly loathsome,' she then declared. 'Be off!' she repeated to her daughter.

Maisie started, moved backward and, looking at Sir Claude, 'Only for a moment,' she signed to him in her bewilderment.

But he was too angry to heed her – too angry with his wife; as she turned away she heard his anger break out. 'You damned old b— !' – she couldn't quite hear all. It was enough, it was too much: she fled before it, rushing even to a stranger for the shock of such a change of tone.

16

As she met the Captain's light blue eyes the greatest marvel occurred; she felt a sudden relief at finding them reply with anxiety to the horror in her face. 'What in the world has he done?' He put it all on Sir Claude.

'He has called her a damned old brute.' She couldn't help bringing that out.

The Captain, at the same elevation as her ladyship, gaped wide; then of course, like everyone else, he was convulsed. But he instantly caught himself up, echoing her bad words. 'A damned old brute – your mother?'

Maisie was already conscious of her second movement. 'I think she tried to make him angry.'

The Captain's stupefaction was fine. 'Angry – *she*? Why she's an angel!'

On the spot, as he said this, his face won her over; it was so bright and kind, and his blue eyes had such a reflexion of some mysterious grace that, for him at least, her mother had put forth.

108

Her fund of observation enabled her as she gazed up at him to place him: he was a candid simple soldier; very grave – she came back to that – but not at all terrible. At any rate he struck a note that was new to her and that after a moment made her say: 'Do you like her very much?'

He smiled down at her, hesitating, looking pleasanter and pleasanter. 'Let me tell you about your mother.'

He put out a big military hand which she immediately took, and they turned off together to where a couple of chairs had been placed under one of the trees. 'She told me to come to you,' Maisie explained as they went and presently she was close to him in a chair, with the prettiest of pictures – the sheen of the lake through other trees – before them, and the sound of birds, the plash of boats, the play of children in the air. The Captain, inclining his military person, sat sideways to be closer and kinder, and as her hand was on the arm of her seat he put his down on it again to emphasize something he had to say that would be good for her to hear. He had already told her how her mother, from the moment of seeing her so unexpectedly with a person who was – well, not at all the right person, had promptly asked him to take charge of her while she herself tackled, as she said, the real culprit. He gave the child the sense of doing for the time what he liked with her; ten minutes before she had never seen him, but she could now sit there touching him, touched and impressed by him and thinking it nice when a gentleman was thin and brown – brown with a kind of clear depth that made his straw-coloured moustache almost white and his eyes resemble little pale flowers. The most extraordinary thing was the way she didn't appear just then to mind Sir Claude's being tackled. The Captain wasn't a bit like him, for it was an odd part of the pleasantness of mamma's friend that it resided in a manner in this friend's having a face so informally put together that the only kindness could be to call it funny. An odder part still was that it finally made our young lady, to classify him further, say to herself that, of all people in the world, he reminded her most insidiously of Mrs Wix. He had neither straighteners nor a diadem, nor, at least in the same place as the other, a button; he was sunburnt and deep-voiced and smelt of cigars, yet he marvellously had more in common with her old governess than with her young stepfather. What he had to

109

say to her that was good for her to hear was that her poor mother (didn't she know?) was the best friend he had ever had in all his life. And he added: 'She has told me ever so much about you. I'm awfully glad to know you.'

She had never, she thought, been so addressed as a young lady, not even by Sir Claude the day, so long ago, that she found him with Mrs Beale. It struck her as the way that at balls, by delightful partners, young ladies must be spoken to in the intervals of dances; and she tried to think of something that would meet it at the same high point. But this effort flurried her, and all she could produce was: 'At first, you know, I thought you were Lord Eric.'

The Captain looked vague. 'Lord Eric?'

'And then Sir Claude thought you were the Count.'

At this he laughed out. 'Why he's only five foot high and as red as a lobster!' Maisie laughed, with a certain elegance, in return – the young lady at the ball certainly would – and was on the point, as conscientiously, of pursuing the subject with an agreeable question. But before she could speak her companion challenged her. 'Who in the world's Lord Eric?'

'Don't you know him?' She judged her young lady would say that with light surprise.

'Do you mean a fat man with his mouth always open?' She had to confess that their acquaintance was so limited that she could only describe the bearer of the name as a friend of mamma's; but a light suddenly came to the Captain, who quickly spoke as knowing her man. 'What-do-you-call-him's brother, the fellow that owned Bobolink?' Then, with all his kindness, he contradicted her flat. 'Oh dear no; your mother never knew *him*.'

'But Mrs Wix said so,' the child risked.

'Mrs Wix?'

'My old governess.'

This again seemed amusing to the Captain. 'She mixed him up, your old governess. He's an awful beast. Your mother never looked at him.'

He was as positive as he was friendly, but he dropped for a minute after this into a silence that gave Maisie, confused but ingenious, a chance to redeem the mistake of pretending to know too much by the humility of inviting further correction. 'And doesn't she know the Count?'

'Oh I daresay! But he's another ass.' After which abruptly, with a different look, he put down again on the back of her own the hand he had momentarily removed. Maisie even thought he coloured a little. 'I want tremendously to speak to you. You must never believe any harm of your mother.'

'Oh I assure you I *don't*!' cried the child, blushing, herself, up to her eyes in a sudden surge of deprecation of such a thought.

The Captain, bending his head, raised her hand to his lips with a benevolence that made her wish her glove had been nicer. 'Of course you don't when you know how fond she is of *you*.'

'She's fond of me?' Maisie panted.

'Tremendously. But she thinks you don't like her. You *must* like her. She has had too much to put up with.'

'Oh yes – I know!' She rejoiced that she had never denied it.

'Of course I've no right to speak of her except as a particular friend,' the Captain went on. 'But she's a splendid woman. She has never had any sort of justice.'

'Hasn't she?' – his companion, to hear the words, felt a thrill altogether new.

'Perhaps I oughtn't to say it to you, but she has had everything to suffer.'

'Oh yes – you can *say* it to me!' Maisie hastened to profess.

The Captain was glad. 'Well, you needn't tell. It's all for *you* – do you see?'

Serious and smiling she only wanted to take it from him. 'It's between you and me! Oh there are lots of things I've never told!'

'Well, keep this with the rest. I assure you she has had the most infernal time, no matter what anyone says to the contrary. She's the cleverest woman I ever saw in all my life. She's too charming.' She had been touched already by his tone, and now she leaned back in her chair and felt something tremble within her. 'She's tremendous fun – she can do all sorts of things better than I've ever seen anyone. She has the pluck of fifty – and I know; I assure you I do. She has the nerve for a tiger-shoot – by Jove I'd *take* her! And she is awfully open and generous, don't you know? there are women that are such horrid sneaks. She'll go through anything for anyone she likes.' He appeared to watch for a moment the effect on his companion of this emphasis; then he gave a small sigh that mourned the limits of the speakable. But it

111

was almost with the note of a fresh challenge that he wound up: 'Look here, she's *true*!'

Maisie had so little desire to assert the contrary that she found herself, in the intensity of her response, throbbing with a joy still less utterable than the essence of the Captain's admiration. She was fairly hushed with the sense that he spoke of her mother as she had never heard anyone speak. It came over her as she sat silent that, after all, this admiration and this respect were quite new words, which took a distinction from the fact that nothing in the least resembling them in quality had on any occasion dropped from the lips of her father, of Mrs Beale, of Sir Claude or even of Mrs Wix. What it appeared to her to come to was that on the subject of her ladyship it was the first real kindness she had heard, so that at the touch of it something strange and deep and pitying surged up within her – a revelation that, practically and so far as she knew, her mother, apart from this, had only been disliked. Mrs Wix's original account of Sir Claude's affection seemed as empty now as the chorus in a children's game, and the husband and wife, but a little way off at that moment, were face to face in hatred and with the dreadful name he had called her still in the air. What was it the Captain on the other hand had called her? Maisie wanted to hear that again. The tears filled her eyes and rolled down her cheeks, which burned under them with the rush of a consciousness that for her too, five minutes before, the vivid towering beauty whose assault she awaited had been, a moment long, an object of pure dread. She became on the spot indifferent to her usual fear of showing what in children was notoriously most offensive – presented to her companion, soundlessly but hideously, her wet distorted face. She cried, with a pang, straight *at* him, cried as she had never cried at anyone in all her life. 'Oh do you love her?' she brought out with a gulp that was the effect of her trying not to make a noise.

It was doubtless another consequence of the thick mist through which she saw him that in reply to her question the Captain gave her such a queer blurred look. He stammered, yet in his voice there was also the ring of a great awkward insistence. 'Of course I'm tremendously fond of her – I like her better than any woman I ever saw. I don't mind in the least telling you that,' he went on, 'and I should think myself a great beast if I did.' Then to show

112

that his position was superlatively clear he made her, with a kindness that even Sir Claude had never surpassed, tremble again as she had trembled at his first outbreak. He called her by her name, and her name drove it home. 'My dear Maisie, your mother's an angel!'

It was an almost unbelievable balm – it soothed so her impression of danger and pain. She sank back in her chair, she covered her face with her hands. 'Oh mother, mother, mother!' she sobbed. She had an impression that the Captain, beside her, if more and more friendly, was by no means unembarrassed; in a minute, however, when her eyes were clearer, he was erect in front of her, very red and nervously looking about him and whacking his leg with his stick. 'Say you love her, Mr Captain; say it, say it!' she implored.

Mr Captain's blue eyes fixed themselves very hard. 'Of *course* I love her, damn it, you know!'

At this she also jumped up; she had fished out somehow her pocket-handkerchief. 'So do *I* then. I do, I do, I do!' she passionately asseverated.

'Then you will come back to her?'

Maisie, staring, stopped the tight little plug of her handkerchief on the way to her eyes. 'She won't have me.'

'Yes she will. She wants you.'

'Back at the house – with Sir Claude?'

Again he hung fire. 'No, not with him. In another place.'

They stood looking at each other with an intensity unusual as between a Captain and a little girl. 'She won't have me in any place.'

'Oh yes she will if *I* ask her!'

Maisie's intensity continued. 'Shall you be there?'

The Captain's, on the whole, did the same. 'Oh yes – some day.'

'Then you don't mean now?'

He broke into a quick smile. 'Will you come now? – go with us for an hour?'

Maisie considered. 'She wouldn't have me even now.' She could see that he had his idea, but that her tone impressed him. That disappointed her a little, though in an instant he rang out again.

113

'She will if I ask her,' he repeated. 'I'll ask her this minute.'

Maisie, turning at this, looked away to where her mother and her stepfather had stopped. At first, among the trees, nobody was visible; but the next moment she exclaimed with expression: 'It's over – here he comes!'

The Captain watched the approach of her ladyship's husband, who lounged composedly over the grass, making to Maisie with his closed fingers a little movement in the air. 'I've no desire to avoid him.'

'Well, you mustn't see him,' said Maisie.

'Oh he's in no hurry himself!' Sir Claude had stopped to light another cigarette.

She was vague as to the way it was proper he should feel; but she had a sense that the Captain's remark was rather a free reflexion on it. 'Oh he doesn't care!' she replied.

'Doesn't care for what?'

'Doesn't care who you are. He told me so. Go and ask mamma,' she added.

'If you can come with us? Very good. You really want me not to wait for him?'

'*Please* don't.' But Sir Claude was not yet near, and the Captain had with his left hand taken hold of her right, which he familiarly, sociably swung a little. 'Only first,' she continued, 'tell me this. Are you going to *live* with mamma?'

The immemorial note of mirth broke out at her seriousness. 'One of these days.'

She wondered, wholly unperturbed by his laughter. 'Then where will Sir Claude be?'

'He'll have left her, of course.'

'Does he really intend to do that?'

'You've every opportunity to ask him.'

Maisie shook her head with decision. 'He won't do it. Not first.'

Her 'first' made the captain laugh out again. 'Oh he'll be sure to be nasty! But I've said too much to you.'

'Well, you know, I'll never tell,' said Maisie.

'No, it's all for yourself. Good-bye.'

'Good-bye.' Maisie kept his hand long enough to add: 'I like you too.' And then supremely: 'You *do* love her?'

114

'My dear child – !' The Captain wanted words.

'Then don't do it only for just a little.'

'A little?'

'Like all the others.'

'All the others?' – he stood staring.

She pulled away her hand. 'Do it always!' She bounded to meet Sir Claude, and as she left the Captain she heard him ring out with apparent gaiety:

'Oh I'm in for it!'

As she joined Sir Claude she noted her mother in the distance move slowly off, and, glancing again at the Captain, saw him, swinging his stick, retreat in the same direction.

She had never seen Sir Claude look as he looked just then; flushed yet not excited – settled rather in an immovable disgust and at once very sick and very hard. His conversation with her mother had clearly drawn blood, and the child's old horror came back to her, begetting the instant moral contraction of the days when her parents had looked to her to feed their love of battle. Her greatest fear for the moment, however, was that her friend would see she had been crying. The next she became aware that he had glanced at her, and it presently occurred to her that he didn't even wish to be looked at. At this she quickly removed her gaze, while he said rather curtly: 'Well, who in the world *is* the fellow?'

She felt herself flooded with prudence. 'Oh *I* haven't found out!' This sounded as if she meant he ought to have done so himself; but she could only face doggedly the ugliness of seeming disagreeable, as she used to face it in the hours when her father, for her blankness, called her a dirty little donkey, and her mother, for her falsity, pushed her out of the room.

'Then what have you been doing all this time?'

'Oh I don't know!' It was of the essence of her method not to be silly by halves.

'Then didn't the beast say anything?' They had got down by the lake and were walking fast.

'Well, not very much.'

'He didn't speak of your mother?'

'Oh yes, a little!'

'Then what I ask you, please, is *how*?' She kept silence – so

115

long that he presently went on: 'I say, you know – don't you hear me?'

At this she produced: 'Well, I'm afraid I didn't attend to him very much.'

Sir Claude, smoking rather hard, made no immediate rejoinder; but finally he exclaimed: 'Then my dear – with such a chance – you were the perfection of a dunce!' He was so irritated – or she took him to be – that for the rest of the time they were in the Gardens he spoke no other word; and she meanwhile subtly abstained from any attempt to pacify him. That would only lead to more questions. At the gate of the Gardens he hailed a four-wheeled cab and, in silence, without meeting her eyes, put her into it, only saying 'Give him *that*' as he tossed half-a-crown upon the seat. Even when from outside he had closed the door and told the man where to go he never took her departing look. Nothing of this kind had ever yet happened to them, but it had no power to make her love him less; so she could not only bear it, she felt as she drove away – she could rejoice in it. It brought again the sweet sense of success that, ages before, she had had at a crisis when, on the stairs, returning from her father's, she had met a fierce question of her mother's with an imbecility as deep and had in consequence been dashed by Mrs Farange almost to the bottom.

17

IF for reasons of her own she could bear the sense of Sir Claude's displeasure her young endurance might have been put to a serious test. The days went by without his knocking at her father's door, and the time would have turned sadly to waste if something hadn't conspicuously happened to give it a new difference. What took place was a marked change in the attitude of Mrs Beale – a change that somehow, even in his absence, seemed to bring Sir Claude again into the house. It began practically with a conversation that occurred between them the day Maisie came home alone in the cab. Mrs Beale had by that time returned, and she was more successful than their friend in extracting from our young lady an account of the extraordinary passage with the Captain. She came back to it repeatedly, and on the very next day it grew

116

distinct to the child that she was already in full possession of what at the same moment had been enacted between her ladyship and Sir Claude. This was the real origin of her final perception that though he didn't come to the house her stepmother had some rare secret for not being quite without him. This led to some rare passages with Mrs Beale, the promptest of which had been – not on Maisie's part – a wonderful outbreak of tears. Mrs Beale was not, as she herself said, a crying creature: she hadn't cried, to Maisie's knowledge, since the lowly governess days, the grey dawn of their connexion. But she wept now with passion, professing loudly that it did her good and saying remarkable things to her charge, for whom the occasion was an equal benefit, an addition to all the fine precautionary wisdom stored away. It somehow hadn't violated that wisdom, Maisie felt, for her to have told Mrs Beale what she had not told Sir Claude, inasmuch as the greatest strain, to her sense, was between Sir Claude and Sir Claude's wife, and his wife was just what Mrs Beale was unfortunately not. He sent his stepdaughter three days after the incident in Kensington Gardens a message as frank as it was tender, and that was how Mrs Beale had had to bring out in a manner that seemed half an appeal, half a defiance: 'Well yes, hang it – I *do* see him!'

How and when and where, however, were just what Maisie was not to know – an exclusion, moreover, that she never questioned in the light of a participation large enough to make him, while she shared the ample void of Mrs Beale's rather blank independence, shine in her yearning eye like the single, the sovereign window-square of a great dim disproportioned room. As far as her father was concerned such hours had no interruption; and then it was clear between them that each was thinking of the absent and thinking the other thought, so that he was an object of conscious reference in everything they said or did. The wretched truth, Mrs Beale had to confess, was that she had hoped against hope and that in the Regent's Park it was impossible Sir Claude should really be in and out. Hadn't they at last to look the fact in the face? – it was too disgustingly evident that no one after all had been squared. Well, if no one had been squared it was because everyone had been vile. No one and everyone were of course Beale and Ida, the extent of whose power to be nasty was a thing

117

that, to a little girl, Mrs Beale simply couldn't give chapter and verse for. Therefore it was that to keep going at all, as she said, that lady had to make, as she also said, another arrangement – the arrangement in which Maisie was included only to the point of knowing it existed and wondering wistfully what it was. Conspicuously at any rate it had a side that was responsible for Mrs Beale's sudden emotion and sudden confidence – a demonstration this, however, of which the tearfulness was far from deterrent to our heroine's thought of how happy she should be if she could only make an arrangement for herself. Mrs Beale's own operated, it appeared, with regularity and frequency; for it was almost every day or two that she was able to bring Maisie a message and to take one back. It had been over the vision of what, as she called it, he did for her that she broke down; and this vision was kept in a manner before Maisie by a subsequent increase not only of the gaiety, but literally – it seemed not presumptuous to perceive – of the actual virtue of her friend. The friend was herself the first to proclaim it: he had pulled her up immensely – he had quite pulled her round. She had charming tormenting words about him: he was her good fairy, her hidden spring – above all he was just her 'higher' conscience. That was what had particularly come out with her startling tears: he had made her, dear man, think ever so much better of herself. It had been thus rather surprisingly revealed that she had been in a way to think ill, and Maisie was glad to hear of the corrective at the same time that she heard of the ailment.

She presently found herself supposing, and in spite of her envy even hoping, that whenever Mrs Beale was out of the house Sir Claude had in some manner the satisfaction of it. This was now of more frequent occurrence than ever before – so much so that she would have thought of her stepmother as almost extravagantly absent had it not been that, in the first place, her father was a superior specimen of that habit: it was the frequent remark of his present wife, as it had been, before the tribunals of their country, a prominent plea of her predecessor, that he scarce came home even to sleep. In the second place Mrs Beale, when she *was* on the spot, had now a beautiful air of longing to make up for everything. The only shadow in such bright intervals was that, as Maisie put it to herself, she could get nothing by questions. It was in the nature of things to be none of a small child's business, even when a small child had from the first been deluded into a fear that she might be only too much initiated. Things, then, were in Maisie's experience so true to their nature that questions were almost always improper; but she learned on the other hand soon to recognize how at last, sometimes, patient little silences and intelligent little looks could be rewarded by delightful little glimpses. There had been years at Beale Farange's when the monosyllable 'he' meant always, meant almost violently, the master; but all that was changed at a period at which Sir Claude's merits were of themselves so much in the air that it scarce took even two letters to name him. 'He keeps me up splendidly – he does, my own precious,' Mrs Beale would observe to her comrade; or else she would say that the situation at the other establishment had reached a point that could scarcely be believed – the point, monstrous as it sounded, of his not having laid eyes upon her for twelve days. 'She' of course at Beale Farange's had never meant anyone but Ida, and there was the difference in this case that it now meant Ida with renewed intensity. Mrs Beale – it was striking – was in a position to animadvert more and more upon her dreadfulness, the moral of all which appeared to be how abominably yet blessedly little she had to do with her husband. This flow of information came home to our two friends because, truly, Mrs Beale had not much more to do with her own; but that was one of the reflexions that Maisie could make without allowing it to break the spell of her present sympathy. How could such a spell be anything but deep when Sir Claude's influence, operating from afar, at least really determined the resumption of his stepdaughter's studies? Mrs Beale again took fire about them and was quite vivid for Maisie as to their being the greater matter to which the dear absent one kept her up.

This was the second source – I have just alluded to the first – of the child's consciousness of something that, very hopefully, she described to herself as a new phase; and it also presented in the brightest light the fresh enthusiasm with which Mrs Beale always reappeared and which really gave Maisie a happier sense than she had yet had of being very dear at least to two persons. That she had small remembrance at present of a third illustrates, I am afraid, a temporary oblivion of Mrs Wix, an accident to be explained only by a state of unnatural excitement. For what was the form taken by Mrs Beale's enthusiasm and acquiring relief in the domestic conditions still left to her but the delightful form of 'reading' with her little charge on lines directly prescribed and in works profusely supplied by Sir Claude? He had got hold of an awfully good list – 'mostly essays, don't you know?' Mrs Beale had said; a word always august to Maisie, but henceforth to be softened by hazy, in fact by quite languorous edges. There was at any rate a week in which no less than nine volumes arrived, and the impression was to be gathered from Mrs Beale that the obscure intercourse she enjoyed with Sir Claude not only involved an account and a criticism of studies, but was organized almost for the very purpose of report and consultation. It was for Maisie's education in short that, as she often repeated, she closed her door – closed it to the gentlemen who used to flock there in such numbers and whom her husband's practical desertion of her would have made it a course of the highest indelicacy to receive. Maisie was familiar from of old with the principle at least of the care that a woman, as Mrs Beale phrased it, attractive and exposed must take of her 'character', and was duly impressed with the rigour of her stepmother's scruples. There was literally no one of the other sex whom she seemed to feel at liberty to see at home, and when the child risked an inquiry about the ladies who, one by one, during her own previous period, had been made quite loudly welcome, Mrs Beale hastened to inform her that, one by one, they had, the fiends, been found out, after all, to be awful. If she wished to know more about them she was recommended to approach her father.

Maisie had, however, at the very moment of this injunction much livelier curiosities, for the dream of lectures at an institution had at last become a reality, thanks to Sir Claude's now unbounded energy in discovering what could be done. It stood out in this connexion that when you came to look into things in a spirit of earnestness an immense deal could be done for very little more than your fare in the Underground. The institution – there was a splendid one in a part of the town but little known to the child – became, in the glow of such a spirit, a thrilling place, and the walk to it from the station through Glower Street (a pronunciation for which Mrs Beale once laughed at her little friend)

120

a pathway literally strewn with 'subjects'. Maisie imagined herself to pluck them as she went, though they thickened in the great
grey rooms where the fountain of knowledge, in the form usually
of a high voice that she took at first to be angry, plashed in the
stillness of rows of faces thrust out like empty jugs. 'It *must* do us
good – it's all so hideous,' Mrs Beale had immediately declared;
manifesting a purity of resolution that made these occasions quite
the most harmonious of all the many on which the pair had
pulled together. Maisie certainly had never, in such an association, felt so uplifted, and never above all been so carried off her
feet, as at the moments of Mrs Beale's breathlessly re-entering the
house and fairly shrieking upstairs to know if they should still be
in time for a lecture. Her stepdaughter, all ready from the earliest
hours, almost leaped over the banister to respond, and they
dashed out together in quest of learning as hard as they often
dashed back to release Mrs Beale for other preoccupations. There
had been in short no bustle like these particular spasms, once
they had broken out, since that last brief flurry when Mrs Wix,
blowing as if she were grooming her, 'made up' for everything
previously lost at her father's.

These weeks as well were too few, but they were flooded with
a new emotion, part of which indeed came from the possibility
that, through the long telescope of Glower Street, or perhaps between the pillars of the institution – which impressive objects
were what Maisie thought most made it one – they should some
day spy Sir Claude. That was what Mrs Beale, under pressure,
had said – doubtless a little impatiently: 'Oh yes, oh yes, some
day!' His joining them was clearly far less of a matter of course
than was to have been gathered from his original profession of
desire to improve in their company his own mind; and this
sharpened our young lady's guess that since that occasion either
something destructive had happened or something desirable
hadn't. Mrs Beale had thrown but a partial light in telling her
how it had turned out that nobody had been squared. Maisie
wished at any rate that somebody *would* be squared. However,
though in every approach to the temple of knowledge she watched
in vain for Sir Claude, there was no doubt about the action of his
loved image as an incentive and a recompense. When the institution was most on pillars – or, as Mrs Beale put it, on stilts – when

121

the subject was deepest and the lecture longest and the listeners ugliest, then it was they both felt their patron in the background would be most pleased with them.

One day, abruptly, with a glance at this background, Mrs Beale said to her companion: 'We'll go tonight to the thingumbob at Earl's Court'; an announcement putting forth its full lustre when she had known that she referred to the great Exhibition just opened in that quarter, a collection of extraordinary foreign things in tremendous gardens, with illuminations, bands, elephants, switchbacks and side-shows, as well as crowds of people among whom they might possibly see someone they knew. Maisie flew in the same bound at the neck of her friend and at the name of Sir Claude, on which Mrs Beale confessed that – well, yes, there was just a chance that he would be able to meet them. He never of course, in his terrible position, knew what might happen from hour to hour; but he hoped to be free and he had given Mrs Beale the tip. 'Bring her there on the quiet and I'll try to turn up' – this was clear enough on what so many weeks of privation had made of his desire to see the child: it even appeared to represent on his part a yearning as constant as her own. That in turn was just puzzling enough to make Maisie express a bewilderment. She couldn't see, if they were so intensely of the same mind, why the theory on which she had come back to Mrs Beale, the general reunion, the delightful trio, should have broken down so in fact. Mrs Beale furthermore only gave her more to think about in saying that their disappointment was the result of his having got into his head a kind of idea.

'What kind of idea?'

'Oh goodness knows!' She spoke with an approach to asperity. 'He's so awfully delicate.'

'Delicate?' – that was ambiguous.

'About what he does, don't you know?' said Mrs Beale. She fumbled. 'Well, about what *we* do.'

Maisie wondered. 'You and me?'

'Me and *him*, silly!' cried Mrs Beale with, this time, a real giggle.

'But you don't do any harm – *you* don't,' said Maisie, wondering afresh and intending her emphasis as a decorous allusion to her parents.

122

'Of course we don't, you angel – that's just the ground *I* take!' her companion exultantly responded. 'He says he doesn't want you mixed up.'

'Mixed up with what?'

'That's exactly what *I* want to know: mixed up with what, and how you are any more mixed – ?' Mrs Beale paused without ending her question. She ended after an instant in a different way. 'All you can say is that it's his fancy.'

The tone of this, in spite of its expressing a resignation, the fruit of weariness, that dismissed the subject, conveyed so vividly how much such a fancy was not Mrs Beale's own that our young lady was led by the mere fact of contact to arrive at a dim apprehension of the unuttered and the unknown. The relation between her step-parents had then a mysterious residuum; this was the first time she really had reflected that except as regards herself it was not a relationship. To each other it was only what they might have happened to make it, and she gathered that this, in the event, had been something that led Sir Claude to keep away from her. Didn't he fear she would be compromised? The perception of such a scruple endeared him the more, and it flashed over her that she might simplify everything by showing him how little she made of such a danger. Hadn't she lived with her eyes on it from her third year? It was the condition most frequently discussed at the Faranges', where the word was always in the air and where at the age of five, amid rounds of applause, she could gabble it off. She knew as well in short that a person could be compromised as that a person could be slapped with a hair-brush or left alone in the dark, and it was equally familiar to her that each of these ordeals was in general held to have too little effect. But the first thing was to make absolutely sure of Mrs Beale. This was done by saying to her thoughtfully: 'Well, if you don't mind – and you really don't, do you?'

Mrs Beale, with a dawn of amusement, considered. 'Mixing you up? Not a bit. For what does it mean?'

'Whatever it means I don't in the least mind *being* mixed. Therefore if you don't and I don't,' Maisie concluded, 'don't you think that when I see him this evening I had better just tell him we don't and ask him why in the world *he* should?'

THE child, however, was not destined to enjoy much of Sir Claude at the 'thingumbob', which took for them a very different turn indeed. On the spot Mrs Beale, with hilarity, had urged her to the course proposed; but later, at the Exhibition, she withdrew this allowance, mentioning as a result of second thoughts that when a man was so sensitive anything at all frisky usually made him worse. It would have been hard indeed for Sir Claude to be 'worse', Maisie felt, as, in the gardens and the crowd, when the first dazzle had dropped, she looked for him in vain up and down. They had all their time, the couple, for frugal wistful wandering: they had partaken together at home of the light vague meal – Maisie's name for it was a 'jam-supper' – to which they were reduced when Mr Farange sought his pleasure abroad. It was abroad now entirely that Mr Farange pursued this ideal, and it was the actual impression of his daughter, derived from his wife, that he had three days before joined a friend's yacht at Cowes.

The place was full of side-shows, to which Mrs Beale could introduce the little girl only, alas, by revealing to her so attractive, so enthralling a name: the side-shows, each time, were sixpence apiece, and the fond allegiance enjoyed by the elder of our pair had been established from the earliest time in spite of a paucity of sixpences. Small coin dropped from her as half-heartedly as answers from bad children to lessons that had not been looked at. Maisie passed more slowly the great painted posters, pressing with a linked arm closer to her friend's pocket, where she hoped for the audible chink of a shilling. But the upshot of this was but to deepen her yearning: if Sir Claude would only at last come the shillings would begin to ring. The companions paused, for want of one, before the Flowers of the Forest, a large presentment of bright brown ladies – they were brown all over – in a medium suggestive of tropical luxuriance, and there Maisie dolorously expressed her belief that he would never come at all. Mrs Beale hereupon, though discernibly disappointed, reminded her that he had not been promised as a certainty – a remark that caused the child to gaze at the Flowers through a blur in which they became more magnificent, yet oddly more confused, and by which, more-over, confusion was imparted to the aspect of a gentleman who at that moment, in the company of a lady, came out of the brilliant booth. The lady was so brown that Maisie at first took her for one of the Flowers; but during the few seconds that this required – a few seconds in which she had also desolately given up Sir Claude – she heard Mrs Beale's voice, behind her, gather both wonder and pain into a single sharp little cry.

'Of all the wickedness – *Beale*!'

He had already, without distinguishing them in the mass of strollers, turned another way – it seemed at the brown lady's suggestion. Her course was marked, over heads and shoulders, by an upright scarlet plume, as to the ownership of which Maisie was instantly eager. 'Who is she? – who is she?'

But Mrs Beale for a moment only looked after them. 'The liar – the liar!'

Maisie considered. 'Because he's not – where one thought?' That was also, a month ago in Kensington Gardens, where her mother had not been. 'Perhaps he has come back,' she said.

'He never went – the hound!'

That, according to Sir Claude, had been also what her mother had not done, and Maisie could only have a sense of something that in a maturer mind would be called the way history repeats itself. 'Who *is* she?' she asked again.

Mrs Beale, fixed to the spot, seemed lost in the vision of an opportunity missed. 'If he had only seen me!' – it came from between her teeth. 'She's a brand-new one. But he must have been with her since Tuesday.'

Maisie took it in. 'She's almost black,' she then reported.

'They're always hideous,' said Mrs Beale.

This was a remark on which the child had again to reflect. 'Oh not his *wives*!' she remonstrantly exclaimed. The words at another moment would probably have set her friend 'off', but Mrs Beale was now, in her instant vigilance, too immensely 'on'. 'Did you ever in your life see such a feather?' Maisie presently continued.

This decoration appeared to have paused at some distance, and in spite of intervening groups they could both look at it. 'Oh that's the way they dress – the vulgarest of the vulgar!'

'They're coming back – they'll see us!' Maisie the next moment

125

cried; and while her companion answered that this was exactly what she wanted and the child returned 'Here they are – here they are!' the unconscious subjects of so much attention, with a change of mind about their direction, quickly retraced their steps and precipitated themselves upon their critics. Their unconsciousness gave Mrs Beale time to leap, under her breath, to a recognition which Maisie caught.

'It must be Mrs Cuddon!'

Maisie looked at Mrs Cuddon hard – her lips even echoed the name. What followed was extraordinarily rapid – a minute of livelier battle than had ever yet, in so short a span at least, been waged round our heroine. The muffled shock – lest people should notice – was violent, and it was only for her later thought that the steps fell into their order, the steps through which, in a bewilderment not so much of sound as of silence, she had come to find herself, too soon for comprehension and too strangely for fear, at the door of the Exhibition with her father. He thrust her into a hansom and got in after her, and then it was – as she drove along with him – that she recovered a little what had happened. Face to face with them in the Gardens he had seen them, and there had been a moment of checked concussion during which, in a glare of black eyes and a toss of red plumage, Mrs Cuddon had recognized them, ejaculated and vanished. There had been another moment at which she became aware of Sir Claude, also poised there in surprise, but out of her father's view, as if he had been warned off at the very moment of reaching them. It fell into its place with all the rest that she had heard Mrs Beale say to her father, but whether low or loud was now lost to her, something about his having this time a new one; on which he had growled something indistinct but apparently in the tone and of the sort that the child, from her earliest years, had associated with hearing somebody retort to somebody that somebody was 'another'. 'Oh I stick to the old!' Mrs Beale had then quite loudly pronounced; and her accent, even as the cab got away, was still in the air, Maisie's effective companion having spoken no other word from the moment of whisking her off – none at least save the indistinguishable address which, over the top of the hansom and poised on the step, he had given the driver. Reconstructing these things later Maisie theorized that she at this point would have put a question to him had not the silence into which he charmed her or scared her – she could scarcely tell which – come from his suddenly making her feel his arm about her, feel, as he drew her close, that he was agitated in a way he had never yet shown her. It struck her he trembled, trembled too much to speak, and this had the effect of making her, with an emotion which, though it had begun to throb in an instant, was by no means all dread, conform to his portentous hush. The act of possession that his pressure in a manner advertised came back to her after the longest of the long intermissions that had ever let anything come back. They drove and drove, and he kept her close; she stared straight before her, holding her breath, watching one dark street succeed another and strangely conscious that what it all meant was somehow that papa was less to be left out of everything than she had supposed. It took her but a minute to surrender to this discovery, which, in the form of his present embrace, suggested a purpose in him prodigiously reaffirmed and with that a confused confidence. She neither knew exactly what he had done nor what he was doing; she could only, altogether impressed and rather proud, vibrate with the sense that he had jumped up to do something and that she had as quickly become a part of it. It was a part of it too that here they were at a house that seemed not large, but in the fresh white front of which the street-lamp showed a smartness of flower-boxes. The child had been in thousands of stories – all Mrs Wix's and her own, to say nothing of the richest romances of French Elise – but she had never been in such a story as this. By the time he had helped her out of the cab, which drove away, and she heard in the door of the house the prompt little click of his key, the Arabian Nights had quite closed round her.

From this minute that pitch of the wondrous was in everything, particularly in such an instant 'Open Sesame' and in the departure of the cab, a rattling void filled with relinquished step-parents; it was, with the vividness, the almost blinding whiteness of the light that sprang responsive to papa's quick touch of a little brass knob on the wall, in a place that, at the top of a short soft staircase, struck her as the most beautiful she had ever seen in her life. The next thing she perceived it to be was the drawing-room of a lady – oh of a lady, she could see in a moment, and not of a gentleman, not even of one like papa himself or even like Sir

Claude – whose things were as much prettier than mamma's as it had always had to be confessed that mamma's were prettier than Mrs Beale's. In the middle of the small bright room and the presence of more curtains and cushions, more pictures and mirrors, more palm-trees drooping over brocaded and gilded nooks, more little silver boxes scattered over little crooked tables and little oval miniatures hooked upon velvet screens than Mrs Beale and her ladyship together could, in an unnatural alliance, have dreamed of mustering, the child became aware, with a sharp foretaste of compassion, of something that was strangely like a relegation to obscurity of each of those women of taste. It was a stranger operation still that her father should on the spot be presented to her as quite advantageously and even grandly at home in the dazzling scene and himself by so much the more separated from scenes inferior to it. She spent with him in it, while explanations continued to hang back, twenty minutes that, in their sudden drop of danger, affected her, though there were neither buns nor ginger-beer, like an extemporized expensive treat.

'Is she very rich?' He had begun to strike her as almost embarrassed, so shy that he might have found himself with a young lady with whom he had little in common. She was literally moved by this apprehension to offer him some tactful relief.

Beale Farange stood and smiled at his young lady, his back to the fanciful fireplace, his light overcoat – the very lightest in London – wide open, and his wonderful lustrous beard completely concealing the expanse of shirt-front. It pleased her more than ever to think that papa was handsome and, though as high aloft as mamma and almost, in his specially florid evening-dress, as splendid, of a beauty somehow less belligerent, less terrible. 'The Countess? Why do you ask me that?'

Maisie's eyes opened wider. 'Is she a Countess?'

He seemed to treat her wonder as a positive tribute. 'Oh yes, my dear, but it isn't an English title.'

Her manner appreciated this. 'Is it a French one?'

'No, nor French either. It's American.'

She conversed agreeably. 'Ah then of course she must be rich.' She took in such a combination of nationality and rank. 'I never saw anything so lovely.'

'Did you have a sight of her?' Beale asked.

'At the Exhibition?' Maisie smiled. 'She was gone too quick.'

Her father laughed. 'She did slope!' She had feared he would say something about Mrs Beale and Sir Claude, yet the way he spared them made her rather uneasy too. All he risked was, the next minute, 'She has a horror of vulgar scenes.'

This was something she needn't take up; she could still continue bland. 'But where do you suppose she went?'

'Oh I thought she'd have taken a cab and have been here by this time. But she'll turn up all right.'

'I'm sure I *hope* she will,' Maisie said; she spoke with an earnestness begotten of the impression of all the beauty about them, to which, in person, the Countess might make further contribution. 'We came awfully fast,' she added.

Her father again laughed loud. 'Yes, my dear, I made you step out!' He waited an instant, then pursued: 'I want her to see you.'

Maisie, at this, rejoiced in the attention that, for their evening out, Mrs Beale, even to the extent of personally 'doing up' her old hat, had given her appearance. Meanwhile her father went on: 'You'll like her awfully.'

'Oh I'm sure I shall!' After which, either from the effect of having said so much or from that of a sudden glimpse of the impossibility of saying more, she felt an embarrassment and sought refuge in a minor branch of the subject. 'I thought she was Mrs Cuddon.'

Beale's gaiety rather increased than diminished. 'You mean my wife did? My dear child, my wife's a damned fool!' He had the oddest air of speaking of his wife as of a person whom she might scarcely have known, so that the refuge of her scruple didn't prove particularly happy. Beale on the other hand appeared after an instant himself to feel a scruple. 'What I mean is, to speak seriously, that she doesn't really know anything about anything.' He paused, following the child's charmed eyes and tentative step or two as they brought her nearer to the pretty things on one of the tables. 'She thinks she has good things, don't you know!' He quite jeered at Mrs Beale's delusion.

Maisie felt she must confess that it *was* one; everything she had missed at the side-shows was made up to her by the Countess's luxuries. 'Yes,' she considered; 'she does think that.'

There was again a dryness in the way Beale replied that it didn't matter what she thought; but there was an increasing sweetness for his daughter in being with him so long without his doing anything worse. The whole hour of course was to remain with her, for days and weeks, ineffaceably illumined and confirmed; by the end of which she was able to read into it a hundred things that had been at the moment mere miraculous pleasantness. What they at the moment came to was simply that her companion was still in a good deal of a flutter, yet wished not to show it, and that just in proportion as he succeeded in this attempt he was able to encourage her to regard him as kind. He moved about the room after a little, showed her things, spoke to her as a person of taste, told her the name, which she remembered, of the famous French lady represented in one of the miniatures, and remarked, as if he had caught her wistful over a trinket or a trailing stuff, that he made no doubt the Countess, on coming in, would give her something jolly. He spied a pink satin box with a looking-glass let into the cover, which he raised, with a quick facetious flourish, to offer her the privilege of six rows of chocolate bonbons, cutting out thereby Sir Claude, who had never gone beyond four rows. 'I can do what I like with these,' he said, 'for I don't mind telling you I gave 'em to her myself.' The Countess had evidently appreciated the gift; there were numerous gaps, a ravage now quite unchecked, in the array. Even while they waited together Maisie had her sense, which was the mark of what their separation had become, of her having grown for him, since the last time he had, as it were, noticed her, and by increase of years and of inches if by nothing else, much more of a little person to reckon with. Yes, this was a part of the positive awkwardness that he carried off by being almost foolishly tender. There was a passage during which, on a yellow silk sofa under one of the palms, he had her on his knee, stroking her hair, playfully holding her off while he showed his shining fangs and let her, with a vague affectionate helpless pointless 'Dear old girl, dear little daughter,' inhale the fragrance of his cherished beard. She must have been sorry for him, she afterwards knew, so well could she privately follow his difficulty in being specific to her about anything. She had such possibilities of vibration, of response, that it needed nothing more than this to make up to her in fact for omissions. The tears came into her

130

eyes again as they had done when in the Park that day the Captain told her so 'splendidly' that her mother was good. What was this but splendid too – this still directer goodness of her father and this unexampled shining solitude with him, out of which everything had dropped but that he was papa and that he was magnificent? It didn't spoil it that she finally felt he must have, as he became restless, some purpose he didn't quite see his way to bring out, for in the freshness of their recovered fellowship she would have lent herself gleefully to his suggesting, or even to his pretending, that their relations were easy and graceful. There was something in him that seemed, and quite touchingly, to ask her to help him to pretend – pretend he knew enough about her life and her education, her means of subsistence and her view of himself, to give the questions he couldn't put her a natural domestic tone. She would have pretended with ecstasy if he could only have given her the cue. She waited for it while, between his big teeth, he breathed the sighs she didn't know to be stupid. And as if, though he was so stupid all through, he had let the friendly suffusion of her eyes yet tell him she was ready for anything, he floundered about, wondering what the devil he could lay hold of.

19

WHEN he had lighted a cigarette and begun to smoke in her face it was as if he had struck with the match the note of some queer clumsy ferment of old professions, old scandals, old duties, a dim perception of what he possessed in her and what, if everything had only – damn it! – been totally different, she might still be able to give him. What she was able to give him, however, as his blinking eyes seemed to make out through the smoke, would be simply what he should be able to get from her. To give something, to give here on the spot, was all her own desire. Among the old things that came back was her little instinct of keeping the peace; it made her wonder more sharply what particular thing she could do or not do, what particular word she could speak or not speak, what particular line she could take or not take, that might for everyone, even for the Countess, give a better turn to the crisis.

She was ready, in this interest, for an immense surrender, a surrender of everything but Sir Claude, of everything but Mrs Beale. The immensity didn't include *them*; but if he had an idea at the back of his head she had also one in a recess as deep, and for a time, while they sat together, there was an extraordinary mute passage between her vision of this vision of his, his vision of her vision, and her vision of his vision of her vision. What there was no effective record of indeed was the small strange pathos on the child's part of an innocence so saturated with knowledge and so directed to diplomacy. What, further, Beale finally laid hold of while he masked again with his fine presence half the flounces of the fireplace was: 'Do you know, my dear, I shall soon be off to America?' It struck his daughter both as a short cut and as the way he wouldn't have said it to his wife. But his wife figured with a bright superficial assurance in her response.

'Do you mean with Mrs Beale?'

Her father looked at her hard. 'Don't be a little ass!'

Her silence appeared to represent a concentrated effort not to be. 'Then with the Countess?'

'With her or without her, my dear; that concerns only your poor daddy. She has big interests over there, and she wants me to take a look at them.'

Maisie threw herself into them. 'Will that take very long?'

'Yes; they're in such a muddle – it may take months. Now what I want to hear, you know, is whether you'd like to come along?'

Planted once more before him in the middle of the room she felt herself turning white. 'I?' she gasped, yet feeling as soon as she had spoken that such a note of dismay was not altogether pretty. She felt it still more while her father replied, with a shake of his legs, a toss of his cigarette-ash and a fidgety look – he was for ever taking one – all the length of his waistcoat and trousers, that she needn't be quite so disgusted. It helped her in a few seconds to appear more as he would like her that she saw, in the lovely light of the Countess's splendour, exactly, however she appeared, the right answer to make. 'Dear papa, I'll go with you anywhere.'

He turned his back to her and stood with his nose at the glass of the chimney-piece while he brushed specks of ash out of his beard. Then he abruptly said: 'Do you know anything about your brute of a mother?'

It was just of her brute of a mother that the manner of the question in a remarkable degree reminded her: it had the free flight of one of Ida's fine bridgings of space. With the sense of this was kindled for Maisie at the same time an inspiration. 'Oh yes, I know everything!' and she became so radiant that her father, seeing it in the mirror, turned back to her and presently, on the sofa, had her at his knee again and was again particularly affecting. Maisie's inspiration instructed her, pressingly, that the more she should be able to say about mamma the less she would be called upon to speak of her step-parents. She kept hoping the Countess would come in before her power to protect them was exhausted; and it was now, in closer quarters with her companion, that the idea at the back of her head shifted its place to her lips. She told him she had met her mother in the Park with a gentleman who, while Sir Claude had strolled with her ladyship, had been kind and had sat and talked to her; narrating the scene with a remembrance of her pledge of secrecy to the Captain quite brushed away by the joy of seeing Beale listen without profane interruption. It was almost an amazement, but it was indeed all a joy, thus to be able to guess that papa was at last quite tired of his anger – of his anger at any rate about mamma. He was only bored with her now. That made it, however, the more imperative that his spent displeasure shouldn't be blown out again. It charmed the child to see how much she could interest him; and the charm remained even when, after asking her a dozen questions, he observed musingly and a little obscurely: 'Yes, damned if she won't!' For in this too there was a detachment, a wise weariness that made her feel safe. She had had to mention Sir Claude, though she mentioned him as little as possible and Beale only appeared to look quite over his head. It pieced itself together for her that his was the mildness of general indifference, a source of profit so great for herself personally that if the Countess was the author of it she was prepared literally to hug the Countess. She betrayed that eagerness by a restless question about her, to which her father replied:

'Oh she has a head on her shoulders. I'll back her to get out of anything!' He looked at Maisie quite as if he could trace the connexion between her inquiry and the impatience of her gratitude. 'Do you mean to say you'd really come with me?'

She felt as if he were now looking at her very hard indeed, and also as if she had grown ever so much older. 'I'll do anything in the world you ask me, papa.'

He gave again, with a laugh and with his legs apart, his proprietary glance at his waistcoat and trousers. 'That's a way, my dear, of saying, "No, thank you!" You know you don't want to go the least little mite. You can't humbug *me*!' Beale Farange laid down. 'I don't want to bully you – I never bullied you in my life; but I make you the offer, and it's to take or to leave. Your mother will never again have any more to do with you than if you were a kitchenmaid she had turned out for going wrong. Therefore of course I'm your natural protector and you've a right to get everything out of me you can. Now's your chance, you know – you won't be half-clever if you don't. You can't say I don't put it before you – you can't say I ain't kind to you or that I don't play fair. Mind you never say that, you know – it *would* bring me down on you. I know what's proper. I'll take you again, just as I *have* taken you again and again. And I'm much obliged to you for making up such a face.'

She was conscious enough that her face indeed couldn't please him if it showed any sign – just as she hoped it didn't – of her sharp impression of what he now really wanted to do. Wasn't he trying to turn the tables on her, embarrass her somehow into admitting that what would really suit her little book would be, after doing so much for good manners, to leave her wholly at liberty to arrange for herself? She began to be nervous again: it rolled over her that this was their parting, their parting for ever, and that he had brought her there for so many caresses only because it was important such an occasion should look better for him than any other. For her to spoil it by the note of discord would certainly give him ground for complaint; and the child was momentarily bewildered between her alternatives of agreeing with him about her wanting to get rid of him and displeasing him by pretending to stick to him. So she found for the moment no solution but to murmur very helplessly: 'Oh papa – oh papa!'

'I know what you're up to – don't tell *me*!' After which he came straight over and, in the most inconsequent way in the

134

world, clasped her in his arms a moment and rubbed his beard against her cheek. Then she understood as well as if he had spoken it that what he wanted, hang it, was that she should let him off with all the honours – with all the appearance of virtue and sacrifice on his side. It was exactly as if he had broken out to her: 'I say, you little booby, help me to be irreproachable, to be noble, and yet to have none of the beastly bore of it. There's only impropriety enough for one of us; so *you* must take it all. *Repudiate* your dear old daddy – in the face, mind you, of his tender supplications. He can't be rough with you – it isn't in his nature: therefore you'll have successfully chucked him because he was too generous to be as firm with you, poor man, as was, after all, his duty.' This was what he communicated in a series of tremendous pats on the back; that portion of her person had never been so thumped since Moddle thumped her when she choked. After a moment he gave her the further impression of having become sure enough of her to be able very gracefully to say out: 'You know your mother loathes you, loathes you simply. And I've been thinking over your precious man – the fellow you told me about.'

'Well,' Maisie replied with competence, 'I'm sure of *him.*'

Her father was vague for an instant. 'Do you mean sure of his liking you?'

'Oh no; of his liking *her!*'

Beale had a return of gaiety. 'There's no accounting for tastes! It's what they all say, you know.'

'I don't care – I'm sure of him!' Maisie repeated.

'Sure, you mean, that she'll bolt?'

Maisie knew all about bolting, but, decidedly, she *was* older, and there was something in her that could wince at the way her father made the ugly word – ugly enough at best – sound flat and low. It prompted her to amend his allusion, which she did by saying: 'I don't know what she'll do. But she'll be happy.'

'Let us hope so,' said Beale – almost as for edification. 'The more happy she is at any rate the less she'll want you about. That's why I press you,' he agreeably pursued, 'to consider this handsome offer – I mean seriously, you know – of your sole surviving parent.' Their eyes, at this, met again in a long and extraordinary communion which terminated in his ejaculating: 'Ah you little scoundrel!' She took it from him in the manner it seemed to her he would like best and with a success that encouraged him to go on: 'You *are* a deep little devil!' Her silence, ticking like a watch, acknowledged even this, in confirmation of which he finally brought out: 'You've settled it with the other pair!'

'Well, what if I have?' She sounded to herself most bold.

Her father, quite as in the old days, broke into a peal. 'Why, don't you know they're awful?'

She grew bolder still. 'I don't care – not a bit!'

'But they're probably the worst people in the world and the very greatest criminals,' Beale pleasantly urged. 'I'm not the man, my dear, not to let you know it.'

'Well, it doesn't prevent them from loving me. They love me tremendously.' Maisie turned crimson to hear herself.

Her companion fumbled; almost anyone – let alone a daughter – would have seen how conscientious he wanted to be. 'I daresay. But do you know why?' She braved his eyes and he added: 'You're a jolly good pretext.'

'For what?' Maisie asked.

'Why, for their game. I needn't tell you what that is.'

The child reflected. 'Well, then, that's all the more reason.'

'Reason for what, pray?'

'For their being kind to me.'

'And for your keeping in with them?' Beale roared again; it was as if his spirits rose and rose. 'Do you realize, pray, that in saying that you're a monster?'

She turned it over. 'A monster?'

'They've *made* one of you. Upon my honour it's quite awful. It shows the kind of people they are. Don't you understand,' Beale pursued, 'that when they've made you as horrid as they can – as horrid as themselves – they'll just simply chuck you?'

She had at this a flicker of passion. 'They *won't* chuck me!'

'I beg your pardon,' her father courteously insisted: 'it's my duty to put it before you. I shouldn't forgive myself if I didn't point out to you that they'll cease to require you.' He spoke as if with an appeal to her intelligence that she must be ashamed not adequately to meet, and this gave a real distinction to her superior delicacy.

It cleared the case as he had wished. 'Cease to require

136

me because they won't care?' She paused with that sketch of her idea.

'*Of course* Sir Claude won't care if his wife bolts. That's his game. It will suit him down to the ground.'

This was a proposition Maisie could perfectly embrace, but it still left a loophole for triumph. She turned it well over. 'You mean if mamma doesn't come back ever at all?' The composure with which her face was presented to that prospect would have shown a spectator the long road she had travelled. 'Well, but that won't put Mrs Beale –'

'In the same comfortable position – ?' Beale took her up with relish; he had sprung to his feet again, shaking his legs and looking at his shoes. 'Right you are, darling! Something more will be wanted for Mrs Beale.' He just paused, then he added: 'But she may not have long to wait for it.'

Maisie also for a minute looked at his shoes, though they were not the pair she most admired, the laced yellow 'uppers' and patent-leather complement. At last, with a question, she raised her eyes. 'Aren't you coming back?'

Once more he hung fire; after which he gave a small laugh that in the oddest way in the world reminded her of the unique sounds she had heard emitted by Mrs Wix. 'It may strike you as extraordinary that I should make you such an admission; and in point of fact you're not to understand that I do. But we'll put it that way to help your decision. The point is that that's the way my wife will presently be sure to put it. You'll hear her shrieking that she's deserted, so that she may just pile up her wrongs. She'll be as free as she likes – as free, you see, as your mother's muff of a husband. They won't have anything more to consider and they'll just put you into the street. Do I understand,' Beale inquired, 'that, in the face of what I press on you, you still prefer to take the risk of that?' It was the most wonderful appeal any gentleman had ever addressed to his daughter, and it had placed Maisie in the middle of the room again while her father moved slowly about her with his hands in his pockets and something in his step that seemed, more than anything else he had done, to show the habit of the place. She turned her fevered little eyes over his friend's brightnesses, as if, on her own side, to press for some help in a quandary unexampled. As if also the pressure reached him

137

he after an instant stopped short, completing the prodigy of his attitude and the pride of his loyalty by a supreme formulation of the general inducement. 'You've an eye, love! Yes, there's money. No end of money.'

This affected her at first in the manner of some great flashing dazzle in one of the pantomimes to which Sir Claude had taken her: she saw nothing in it but what it directly conveyed. 'And shall I never, never see you again – ?'

'If I do go to America?' Beale brought it out like a man. 'Never, never, never!'

Hereupon, with the utmost absurdity, she broke down; everything gave way, everything but the horror of hearing herself definitely utter such an ugliness as the acceptance of that. So she only stiffened herself and said: 'Then I can't give you up.'

She held him some seconds looking at her, showing her a strained grimace, a perfect parade of all his teeth, in which it seemed to her she could read the disgust he didn't quite like to express at this departure from the pliability she had practically promised. But before she could attenuate in any way the crudity of her collapse he gave an impatient jerk which took him to the window. She heard a vehicle stop; Beale looked out; then he freshly faced her. He still said nothing, but she knew the Countess had come back. There was a silence again between them, but with a different shade of embarrassment from that of their united arrival; and it was still without speaking that, abruptly repeating one of the embraces of which he had already been so prodigal, he whisked her back to the lemon sofa just before the door of the room was thrown open. It was thus in renewed and intimate union with him that she was presented to a person whom she instantly recognized as the brown lady.

The brown lady looked almost as astonished, though not quite as alarmed, as when, at the Exhibition, she had gasped in the face of Mrs Beale. Maisie in truth almost gasped in her own; this was with the fuller perception that she was brown indeed. She literally struck the child more as an animal than as a 'real' lady; she might have been a clever frizzled poodle in a frill or a dreadful human monkey in a spangled petticoat. She had a nose that was far too big and eyes that were far too small and a moustache that was, well, not so happy a feature as Sir Claude's. Beale jumped up to her; while, to the child's astonishment, though as if in a quick intensity of thought, the Countess advanced as gaily as if, for many a day, nothing awkward had happened for anyone. Maisie, in spite of a large acquaintance with the phenomenon, had never seen it so promptly established that nothing awkward was to be mentioned. The next minute the Countess had kissed her and exclaimed to Beale with bright tender reproach: 'Why, you never told me *half*! My dear child,' she cried, 'it was awfully nice of you to come!'

'But she hasn't come – she won't come!' Beale answered. 'I've put it to her how much you'd like it, but she declines to have anything to do with us.'

The Countess stood smiling, and after an instant that was mainly taken up with the shock of her weird aspect Maisie felt herself reminded of another smile, which was not ugly, though also interested – the kind light thrown, that day in the Park, from the clean fair face of the Captain. Papa's Captain – yes – was the Countess; but she wasn't nearly so nice as the other: it all came back, doubtless, to Maisie's minor appreciation of ladies. 'Shouldn't you like me,' said this one endearingly, 'to take you to Spa?'

'To Spa?' The child repeated the name to gain time, not to show how the Countess brought back to her a dim remembrance of a strange woman with a horrid face who once, years before, in an omnibus, bending to her from an opposite seat, had suddenly produced an orange and murmured, 'Little dearie, won't you have it?' She had felt then, for some reason, a small silly terror, though afterwards conscious that her interlocutress, unfortunately hideous, had particularly meant to be kind. This was also what the Countess meant; yet the few words she had uttered and the smile with which she had uttered them immediately cleared everything up. Oh no, she wanted to go nowhere with *her*, for her presence had already, in a few seconds, dissipated the happy impression of the room and put an end to the pleasure briefly taken in Beale's command of such elegance. There was no command of elegance in his having exposed her to the approach of the short fat wheedling whiskered person in whom she had now to recognize the only figure wholly without attraction involved in any of the intimate connexions her immediate circle had witnessed the growth of. She was abashed meanwhile, however, at having appeared to weigh in the balance the place to which she had been invited; and she added as quickly as possible: 'It isn't to America, then?' The Countess, at this, looked sharply at Beale, and Beale, airily enough, asked what the deuce it mattered when she had already given him to understand she wanted to have nothing to do with them. There followed between her companions a passage of which the sense was drowned for her in the deepening inward hum of the mere desire to get off; though she was able to guess later on that her father must have put it to his friend that it was no use talking, that she was an obstinate little pig and that, besides, she was really old enough to choose for herself. It glimmered back to her indeed that she must have failed quite dreadfully to seem ideally other than rude, inasmuch as before she knew it she had visibly given the impression that if they didn't allow her to go home she should cry. Oh if there had ever been a thing to cry about it was being so consciously and gawkily below the handsomest offers anyone could ever have received. The great pain of the thing was that she could see the Countess liked her enough to wish to be liked in return, and it was from the idea of a return she sought utterly to flee. It was the idea of a return that after a confusion of loud words had broken out between the others brought to her lips with the tremor preceding disaster: 'Can't I, please, be sent home in a cab?' Yes, the Countess wanted her and the Countess was wounded and chilled, and she couldn't help it, and it was all the more dreadful because it only made the Countess more coaxing and more impossible. The only thing that sustained either of them perhaps till the cab came – Maisie presently saw it would come – was its being in the air somehow that Beale had done what he wanted. He went out to look for a conveyance; the servants, he said, had gone to bed, but she shouldn't be kept beyond her time. The Countess left the room with him, and, alone in the possession of it, Maisie hoped she wouldn't come back. It was all the effect of her face – the child simply couldn't look at it and meet its expression half-way. All in a moment too that queer expression had leaped into the lovely things – all in a moment she had had to accept her father as liking someone whom she was sure neither her mother, nor Mrs Beale, nor Mrs Wix, nor Sir Claude, nor the Captain, nor even

140

Mr Perriam and Lord Eric could possibly have liked. Three minutes later, downstairs, with the cab at the door, it was perhaps as a final confession of not having much to boast of that, on taking leave of her, he managed to press her to his bosom without her seeing his face. For herself she was so eager to go that their parting reminded her of nothing, not even of a single one of all the 'nevers' that above, as the penalty of not cleaving to him, he had attached to the question of their meeting again. There was something in the Countess that falsified everything, even the great interests in America and yet more the first flush of that superiority to Mrs Beale and to mamma which had been expressed in Sèvres sets and silver boxes. These were still there, but perhaps there were no great interests in America. Mamma had known an American who was not a bit like this one. She was not, however, of noble rank; her name was only Mrs Tucker. Maisie's detachment would none the less have been more complete if she had not suddenly had to exclaim: 'Oh dear, I haven't any money!'

Her father's teeth, at this, were such a picture of appetite without action as to be a match for any plea of poverty. 'Make your stepmother pay.'

'Stepmothers *don't* pay!' cried the Countess. 'No stepmother ever paid in her life!' The next moment they were in the street together, and the next the child was in the cab, with the Countess, on the pavement, but close to her, quickly taking money from a purse whisked out of a pocket. Her father had vanished and there was even yet nothing in that to reawaken the pang of loss. 'Here's money,' said the brown lady: 'go!' The sound was commanding: the cab rattled off. Maisie sat there with her hand full of coin. All that for a cab? As they passed a street lamp she bent to see how much. What she saw was a cluster of sovereigns. There *must*, then, have been great interests in America. It was still at any rate the Arabian Nights.

20

THE money was far too much even for a fee in a fairy-tale, and in the absence of Mrs Beale who, though the hour was now late, had not yet returned to the Regent's Park, Susan Ash, in the hall, as loud as Maisie was low and as bold as she was bland, produced, on the exhibition offered under the dim vigil of the lamp that made the place a contrast to the child's recent scene of light, the half-crown that an unsophisticated cabman could pronounce to be the least he would take. It was apparently long before Mrs Beale would arrive, and in the interval Maisie had been induced by the prompt Susan not only to go to bed like a darling dear, but, in still richer expression of that character, to devote to the repayment of obligations general as well as particular one of the sovereigns in the ordered array that, on the dressing-table upstairs, was naturally not less dazzling to a lone orphan of a housemaid than to the subject of the manoeuvres of a quartette. This subject went to sleep with her property gathered into a knotted handkerchief, the largest that could be produced and lodged under her pillow; but the explanations that on the morrow were inevitably more complete with Mrs Beale than they had been with her humble friend found their climax in a surrender also more becomingly free. There were explanations indeed that Mrs Beale had to give as well as to ask, and the most striking of these was to the effect that it was dreadful for a little girl to take money from a woman who was simply the vilest of their sex. The sovereigns were examined with some attention, the result of which, however, was to make the author of that statement desire to know what, if one really went into the matter, they could be called but the wages of sin. Her companion went into it merely so far as the question of what then they were to do with them; on which Mrs Beale, who had by this time put them into her pocket, replied with dignity and with her hand on the place: 'We're to send them back on the spot!' Susan, the child soon afterwards learnt, had been invited to contribute to this act of restitution her one appropriated coin; but a closer clutch of the treasure showed in her private assurance to Maisie that there was a limit to the way she could be 'done'. Maisie had been open with Mrs Beale about the whole of last night's transaction; but she now found herself on the part of their indignant inferior a recipient of remarks that were so many ringing tokens of that lady's own suppressions. One of these bore upon the extraordinary hour – it was three in the morning if she really wanted to know – at which Mrs Beale had re-entered the house; another, in accents as to which Maisie's criticism was still intensely tacit, characterized her appeal as such a 'gime', such a 'shime', as one had never had to put up with; a third treated with some vigour the question of the enormous sums due below-stairs, in every department, for gratuitous labour and wasted zeal. Our young lady's consciousness was indeed mainly filled for several days with the apprehension created by the too slow subsidence of her attendant's sense of wrong. These days would become terrific like the Revolution she had learnt by heart in Histories if an outbreak in the kitchen should crown them; and to promote that prospect she had through Susan's eyes more than one glimpse of the way in which Revolutions are prepared. To listen to Susan was to gather that the spark applied to the in-flammables and already causing them to crackle would prove to have been the circumstance of one's being called a horrid low thief for refusing to part with one's own.

The redeeming point of this tension was, on the fifth day, that it actually appeared to have had to do with a breathless percep-tion in our heroine's breast that scarcely more as the centre of Sir Claude's than as that of Susan's energies she had soon after breakfast been conveyed from London to Folkestone and estab-lished at a lovely hotel. These agents, before her wondering eyes, had combined to carry through the adventure and to give it the air of having owed its success to the fact that Mrs Beale had, as Susan said, but just stepped out. When Sir Claude, watch in hand, had met this fact with the exclamation 'Then pack, Miss Farange, and come off with us!' there had ensued on the stairs a series of gymnastics of a nature to bring Miss Farange's heart into Miss Farange's mouth. She sat with Sir Claude in a four-wheeler while he still held his watch; held it longer than any doctor who had ever felt her pulse; long enough to give her a vision of something like the ecstasy of neglecting such an opportunity to show im-patience. The ecstasy had begun in the schoolroom and over the Berceuse, quite in the manner of the same foretaste on the day, a little while back, when Susan had panted up and she herself, after the hint about the duchess, had sailed down; for what harm, then, had there been in drops and disappointments if she could still have, even only a moment, the sensation of such a name 'brought up'? It had remained with her that her father had foretold her she would some day be in the street, but it clearly wouldn't be this

143

day, and she felt justified of the preference betrayed to that parent as soon as her visitor had set Susan in motion and laid his hand, while she waited with him, kindly on her own. This was what the Captain, in Kensington Gardens, had done; her present situation reminded her a little of that one and renewed the dim wonder of the fashion after which, from the first, such pats and pulls had struck her as the steps and signs of other people's business and even a little as the wriggle or the overflow of their difficulties. What had failed her and what had frightened her on the night of the Exhibition lost themselves at present alike in the impression that any 'surprise' now about to burst from Sir Claude would be too big to burst all at once. Any awe that might have sprung from his air of leaving out her stepmother was corrected by the force of a general rule, the odd truth that if Mrs Beale now never came nor went without making her think of him, it was never, to balance that, the main mark of his renewed reality to be a reference to Mrs Beale. To be with Sir Claude was to think of Sir Claude, and that law governed Maisie's mind until, through a sudden lurch of the cab, which had at last taken in Susan and ever so many bundles and almost reached Charing Cross, it popped again somehow into her dizzy head the long-lost image of Mrs Wix.

It was singular, but from this time she understood and she followed, followed with the sense of an ample filling-out of any void created by symptoms of avoidance and of flight. Her ecstasy was a thing that had yet more of a face than of a back to turn, a pair of eyes still directed to Mrs Wix even after the slight surprise of their not finding her, as the journey expanded, either at the London station or at the Folkestone hotel. It took few hours to make the child feel that if she was in neither of these places she was at least everywhere else. Maisie had known all along a great deal, but never so much as she was to know from this moment on and as she learned in particular during the couple of days that she was to hang in the air, as it were, over the sea which represented in breezy blueness and with a summer charm a crossing of more spaces than the Channel. It was granted her at this time to arrive at divinations so ample that I shall have no room for the goal if I attempt to trace the stages; as to which, therefore, I must be content to say that the fullest expression we may give to

Sir Claude's conduct is a poor and pale copy of the picture it presented to his young friend. Abruptly, that morning, he had yielded to the action of the idea pumped into him for weeks by Mrs Wix on lines of approach that she had been capable of the extraordinary art of preserving from entanglement in the fine network of his relations with Mrs Beale. The breath of her sincerity, blowing without a break, had puffed him up to the flight by which, in the degree I have indicated, Maisie too was carried off her feet. This consisted neither in more nor in less than the brave stroke of his getting off from Mrs Beale as well as from his wife – of making with the child straight for some such foreign land as would give a support to Mrs Wix's dream that she might still see his errors renounced and his delinquencies redeemed. It would all be a sacrifice – under eyes that would miss no faintest shade – to what even the strange frequenters of her ladyship's earlier period used to call the real good of the little unfortunate. Maisie's head held a suspicion of much that, during the last long interval, had confusedly, but quite candidly, come and gone in his own; a glimpse, almost awe-stricken in its gratitude, of the miracle her old governess had wrought. That functionary could not in this connexion have been more impressive, even at second hand, if she had been a prophetess with an open scroll or some ardent abbess speaking with the lips of the Church. She had clung day by day to their plastic associate, playing him with her deep, narrow passion, doing her simple utmost to convert him, and so working on him that he had at last really embraced his fine chance. That the chance was not delusive was sufficiently guaranteed by the completeness with which he could finally figure it out that, in case of his taking action, neither Ida nor Beale, whose book, on each side, it would only too well suit, would make any sort of row.

It sounds, no doubt, too penetrating, but it was not at all as an effect of Sir Claude's betrayals that Maisie was able to piece together the beauty of the special influence through which, for such stretches of time, he had refined upon propriety by keeping, so far as possible, his sentimental interests distinct. She had ever of course in her mind fewer names than conceptions, but it was only with this drawback that she now made out her companion's absences to have had for their ground that he was the lover of her stepmother and that the lover of her stepmother could scarce logically pretend to a superior right to look after her. Maisie had by this time embraced the implication of a kind of natural divergence between lovers and little girls. It was just this indeed that could throw light on the probable contents of the pencilled note deposited on the hall-table in the Regent's Park and which would greet Mrs Beale on her return. Maisie freely figured it as provisionally jocular in tone, even though to herself on this occasion Sir Claude turned a graver face than he had shown in any crisis but that of putting her into the cab when she had been horrid to him after her parting with the Captain. He might really be embarrassed, but he would be sure, to her view, to have muffled in some bravado of pleasantry the disturbance produced at her father's by the removal of a valued servant. Not that there wasn't a great deal too that wouldn't be in the note – a great deal for which a more comfortable place was Maisie's light little brain, where it hummed away hour after hour and caused the first outlook at Folkestone to swim in a softness of colour and sound. It became clear in this medium that her stepfather had really now only to take into account his entanglement with Mrs Beale. Wasn't he at last disentangled from everyone and everything else? The obstacle to the rupture pressed upon him by Mrs Wix in the interest of his virtue would be simply that he was in love, or rather, to put it more precisely, that Mrs Beale had left him no doubt of the degree in which *she* was. She was so much so as to have succeeded in making him accept for a time her infatuated grasp of him and even to some extent the idea of what they yet might do together with a little diplomacy and a good deal of patience. I may not even answer for it that Maisie was not aware of how, in this, Mrs Beale failed to share his all but insurmountable distaste for their allowing their little charge to breathe the air of their gross irregularity – his contention, in a word, that they should either cease to be irregular or cease to be parental. Their little charge, for herself, had long ago adopted the view that even Mrs Wix had at one time not thought prohibitively coarse – the view that she was after all, *as* a little charge, morally at home in atmospheres it would be appalling to analyse. If Mrs Wix, however, ultimately appalled, had now set her heart on strong measures, Maisie, as I have intimated, could also work round both to

146

the reasons for them and to the quite other reasons for that lady's not, as yet at least, appearing in them at first hand.

Oh decidedly I shall never get you to believe the number of things she saw and the number of secrets she discovered! Why in the world, for instance, couldn't Sir Claude have kept it from her – except on the hypothesis of his not caring to – that, when you came to look at it and so far as it was a question of vested interests, he had quite as much right in her as her stepmother, not to say a right that Mrs Beale was in no position to dispute? He failed at all events of any such successful ambiguity as could keep her, when once they began to look across at France, from regarding even what was least explained as most in the spirit of their old happy times, their rambles and expeditions in the easier better days of their first acquaintance. Never before had she had so the sense of giving him a lead for the sort of treatment of what was between them that would best carry it off, or of his being grateful to her for meeting him so much in the right place. She met him literally at the very point where Mrs Beale was most to be reckoned with, at the point of the jealousy that was sharp in that lady and of the need of their keeping it as long as possible obscure to her that poor Mrs Wix had still a hand. Yes, she met him too in the truth of the matter that, as her stepmother had had no one else to be jealous of, she had made up for so gross a privation by directing the sentiment to a moral influence. Sir Claude appeared absolutely to convey in a wink that a moral influence capable of pulling a string was after all a moral influence exposed to the scratching out of its eyes; and that, this being the case, there was somebody they couldn't afford to leave unprotected before they should see a little better what Mrs Beale was likely to do. Maisie, true enough, had not to put it into words to rejoin, in the coffee-room, at luncheon: 'What *can* she do but come to you if papa does take a step that will amount to legal desertion?' Neither had he then, in answer, to articulate anything but the jollity of their having found a table at a window from which, as they partook of cold beef and apollinaris – for he hinted they would have to save lots of money – they could let their eyes hover tenderly on the far-off white cliffs that so often had signalled to the embarrassed English a promise of safety. Maisie stared at them as if she might really make out after a little a queer dear figure perched on them –

147

a figure as to which she had already the subtle sense that, wherever perched, it would be the very oddest yet seen in France. But it was at least as exciting to feel where Mrs Wix wasn't as it would have been to know where she was, and if she wasn't yet at Boulogne this only thickened the plot.

If she was not to be seen that day, however, the evening was marked by an apparition before which, none the less, overstrained suspense folded on the spot its wings. Adjusting her respirations and attaching, under dropped lashes, all her thought to a smartness of frock and frill for which she could reflect that she had not appealed in vain to a loyalty in Susan Ash triumphant over the nice things their feverish flight had left behind, Maisie spent on a bench in the garden of the hotel the half-hour before dinner, that mysterious ceremony of the *table d'hôte* for which she had prepared with a punctuality of flutter. Sir Claude, beside her, was occupied with a cigarette and the afternoon papers; and though the hotel was full the garden showed the particular void that ensues upon the sound of the dressing-bell. She had almost had time to weary of the human scene; her own humanity at any rate, in the shape of a smutch on her scanty skirt, had held her so long that as soon as she raised her eyes they rested on a high fair drapery by which smutches were put to shame and which had glided towards her over the grass without her noting its rustle. She followed up its stiff sheen – up and up from the ground, where it had stopped – till at the end of a considerable journey her impression felt the shock of the fixed face which, surmounting it, seemed to offer the climax of the dressed condition. 'Why mamma!' she cried the next instant – cried in a tone that, as she sprang to her feet, brought Sir Claude to his own beside her and gave her ladyship, a few yards off, the advantage of their momentary confusion. Poor Maisie's was immense; her mother's drop had the effect of one of the iron shutters that, in evening walks with Susan Ash, she had seen suddenly, at the touch of a spring, rattle down over shining shop-fronts. The light of foreign travel was darkened at a stroke; she had a horrible sense that they were caught; and for the first time of her life in Ida's presence she so far translated an impulse into an invidious act as to clutch straight at the hand of her responsible confederate. It didn't help her that he appeared at first equally hushed with horror; a minute during which, in the

148

empty garden, with its long shadows on the lawn, its blue sea over the hedge and its startled peace in the air, both her elders remained as stiff as tall tumblers filled to the brim and held straight for fear of a spill. At last, in a tone that enriched the whole surprise by its unexpected softness, her mother said to Sir Claude: 'Do you mind at all my speaking to her?'

'Oh no; *do* you?' His reply was so long in coming that Maisie was the first to find the right note.

He laughed as he seemed to take it from her, and she felt a sufficient concession in his manner of addressing their visitor. 'How in the world did you know we were here?'

His wife, at this, came the rest of the way and sat down on the bench with a hand laid on her daughter, whom she gracefully drew to her and in whom, at her touch, the fear just kindled gave a second jump, but now in quite another direction. Sir Claude, on the further side, resumed his seat and his newspapers, so that the three grouped themselves like a family party; his connexion, in the oddest way in the world, almost cynically and in a flash acknowledged, and the mother patting the child into conformities unspeakable. Maisie could already feel how little it was Sir Claude and she who were caught. She had the positive sense of their catching their relative, catching her in the act of getting rid of her burden with a finality that showed her as unprecedentedly relaxed. Oh yes, the fear had dropped, and she had never been so irrevocably parted with as in the pressure of possession now supremely exerted by Ida's long-gloved and much bangled arm. 'I went to the Regent's Park' – this was presently her ladyship's answer to Sir Claude.

'Do you mean today?'

'This morning, just after your own call there. That's how I found you out; that's what has brought me.'

Sir Claude considered and Maisie waited. 'Whom, then, did you see?'

Ida gave a sound of indulgent mockery. 'I like your scare. I know your game. I didn't see the person I risked seeing, but I had been ready to take my chance of her.' She addressed herself to Maisie; she had encircled her more closely. 'I asked for *you*, my dear, but I saw no one but a dirty parlour-maid. She was red in the face with the great things that, as she told me, had just

149

happened in the absence of her mistress; and she luckily had the sense to have made out the place to which Sir Claude had come to take you. If he hadn't given a false scent I should find you here: that was the supposition on which I've proceeded.' Ida had never been so explicit about proceeding or supposing, and Maisie, drinking this in, noted too how Sir Claude shared her fine impression of it. 'I wanted to see you,' his wife continued, 'and now you can judge of the trouble I've taken. I had everything to do in town today, but I managed to get off.'

Maisie and her companion, for a moment, did justice to this achievement; but Maisie was the first to express it. 'I'm glad you wanted to see me, mamma.' Then after a concentration more deep and with a plunge more brave: 'A little more and you'd have been too late.' It stuck in her throat, but she brought it out: 'We're going to France.'

Ida was magnificent; Ida kissed her on the forehead. 'That's just what I thought likely; it made me decide to run down. I fancied that in spite of your scramble you'd wait to cross, and it added to the reason I have for seeing you.'

Maisie wondered intensely what the reason could be, but she knew ever so much better than to ask. She was slightly surprised indeed to perceive that Sir Claude didn't, and to hear him immediately inquire; 'What in the name of goodness can you have to say to her?'

His tone was not exactly rude, but it was impatient enough to make his wife's response a fresh specimen of the new softness. 'That, my dear man, is all my own business.'

'Do you mean,' Sir Claude asked, 'that you wish me to leave you with her?'

'Yes, if you'll be so good; that's the extraordinary request I take the liberty of making.' Her ladyship had dropped to a mildness of irony by which, for a moment, poor Maisie was mystified and charmed, puzzled with a glimpse of something that in all the years had at intervals peeped out. Ida smiled at Sir Claude with the strange air she had on such occasions of defying an interlocutor to keep it up as long; her huge eyes, her red lips, the intense marks in her face formed an *éclairage* as distinct and public as a lamp set in a window. The child seemed quite to see in it the very beacon that had lighted her path; she suddenly found herself reflecting that it was no wonder the gentlemen were guided. This must have been the way mamma had first looked at Sir Claude; it brought back the lustre of the time they had outlived. It must have been the way she looked also at Mr Perriam and Lord Eric; above all it contributed in Maisie's mind to a completer view of that satisfied state of the Captain. Our young lady grasped this idea with a quick lifting of the heart; there was a stillness during which her mother flooded her with a wealth of support to the Captain's striking tribute. This stillness remained long enough unbroken to represent that Sir Claude too might but be gasping again under the spell originally strong for him; so that Maisie quite hoped he would at least say something to show a recognition of how charming she could be.

What he presently said was: 'Are you putting up for the night?'

His wife cast grandly about. 'Not here – I've come from Dover.'

Over Maisie's head, at this, they still faced each other. 'You spent the night there?'

'Yes, I brought some things. I went to the hotel and hastily arranged; then I caught the train that whisked me on here. You see what a day I've had of it.'

The statement may surprise, but these were really as obliging if not as lucid words as, into her daughter's ears at least, Ida's lips had ever dropped; and there was a quick desire in the daughter that for the hour at any rate they should duly be welcomed as a ground of intercourse. Certainly mamma had a charm which, when turned on, became a large explanation; and the only danger now in an impulse to applaud it would be that of appearing to signalize its rarity. Maisie, however, risked the peril in the geniality of an admission that Ida had indeed had a rush; and she invited Sir Claude to expose himself by agreeing with her that the rush had been even worse than theirs. He appeared to meet this appeal by saying with detachment enough: 'You go back there tonight?'

'Oh yes – there are plenty of trains.'

Again Sir Claude hesitated; it would have been hard to say if the child, between them, more connected or divided them. Then he brought out quietly: 'It will be late for you to knock about. I'll see you over.'

'You needn't trouble, thank you. I think you won't deny that I can help myself and that it isn't the first time in my dreadful life that I've somehow managed it.' Save for this allusion to her dreadful life they talked there, Maisie noted, as if they were only rather superficial friends; a special effect that she had often wondered at before in the midst of what she supposed to be intimacies. This effect was augmented by the almost casual manner in which her ladyship went on: 'I daresay I shall go abroad.'

'From Dover do you mean, straight?'

'How straight I can't say. I'm excessively ill.'

This for a minute struck Maisie as but a part of the conversation; at the end of which time she became aware that it ought to strike her – though it apparently didn't strike Sir Claude – as a part of something graver. It helped her to twist nearer. 'Ill, mamma – really ill?'

She regretted her 'really' as soon as she had spoken it; but there couldn't be a better proof of her mother's present polish than that Ida showed no gleam of a temper to take it up. She had taken up at other times much tinier things. She only pressed Maisie's head against her bosom and said: 'Shockingly, my dear. I must go to that new place.'

'What new place?' Sir Claude inquired.

Ida thought, but couldn't recall it. 'Oh "Chose", don't you know? – where everyone goes. I want some proper treatment. It's all I've ever asked for on earth. But that's not what I came to say.'

Sir Claude, in silence, folded one by one his newspapers; then he rose and stood whacking the palm of his hand with the bundle. 'You'll stop and dine with us?'

'Dear no – I can't dine at this sort of hour. I ordered dinner at Dover.'

Her ladyship's tone in this one instance showed a certain superiority to those conditions in which her daughter had artlessly found Folkestone a paradise. It was yet not so crushing as to nip in the bud the eagerness with which the latter broke out: 'But won't you at least have a cup of tea?'

Ida kissed her again on the brow. 'Thanks, love, I had tea before coming.' She raised her eyes to Sir Claude. 'She *is* sweet!' He made no more answer than if he didn't agree; but Maisie was at ease about that and was still taken up with the joy of this happier pitch of their talk, which put more and more of a meaning into the Captain's version of her ladyship and literally kindled a conjecture that such an admirer might, over there at the other place, be waiting for her to dine. Was the same conjecture in Sir Claude's mind? He partly puzzled her, if it had risen there, by the slight perversity with which he returned to a question that his wife evidently thought she had disposed of.

He whacked his hand again with his papers. 'I had really much better take you.'

'And leave Maisie here alone?'

Mamma so clearly didn't want it that Maisie leaped at the vision of a Captain who had seen her on from Dover and who, while he waited to take her back, would be hovering just at the same distance at which, in Kensington Gardens, the companion of his walk had herself hovered. Of course, however, instead of breathing any such guess she let Sir Claude reply; all the more that his reply could contribute so much to her own present grandeur. 'She won't be alone when she has a maid in attendance.'

Maisie had never before had so much of a retinue, and she waited also to enjoy the action on her ladyship. 'You mean the woman you brought from town?' Ida considered. 'The person at the house spoke of her in a way that scarcely made her out company for my child.' Her tone was that her child had never wanted, in her hands, for prodigious company. But she as distinctly continued to decline Sir Claude's. 'Don't be an old goose,' she said charmingly. 'Let us alone.'

In front of them on the grass he looked graver than Maisie at all now thought the occasion warranted. 'I don't see why you can't say it before me.'

His wife smoothed one of her daughter's curls. 'Say what, dear?'

'Why what you came to say.'

At this Maisie at last interposed: she appealed to Sir Claude. 'Do let her say it to me.'

He looked hard for a moment at his little friend. 'How do you know what she may say?'

'She must risk it,' Ida remarked.

153

'I only want to protect you,' he continued to the child.

'You want to protect yourself – that's what you mean,' his wife replied. 'Don't be afraid. I won't touch you.'

'She won't touch you – she *won't*!' Maisie declared. She felt by this time that she could really answer for it, and something of the emotion with which she had listened to the Captain came back to her. It made her so happy and so secure that she could positively patronize mamma. She did so in the Captain's very language. 'She's good, she's good!' she proclaimed.

'Oh Lord!' – Sir Claude, at this, let himself go. He appeared to have emitted some sound of derision that was smothered, to Maisie's ears, by her being again embraced by his wife. Ida released her and held her off a little, looking at her with a very queer face. Then the child became aware that their companion had left them and that from the face in question a confirmatory remark had proceeded.

'I *am* good, love,' said her ladyship.

21

A GOOD deal of the rest of Ida's visit was devoted to explaining, as it were, so extraordinary a statement. This explanation was more copious than any she had yet indulged in, and as the summer twilight gathered and she kept the child in the garden she was conciliatory to a degree that let her need to arrange things a little perceptibly peep out. It was not merely that she explained; she almost conversed; all that was wanting to that was that she should have positively chattered a little less. It was really the occasion of Maisie's life on which her mother was to have most to say to her. That alone was an implication of generosity and virtue, and no great stretch was required to make our young lady feel that she should best meet her and soonest have it over by simply seeming struck with the propriety of her contention. They sat together while the parent's gloved hand sometimes rested sociably on the child's and sometimes gave a corrective pull to a ribbon too meagre or a tress too thick; and Maisie was conscious of the effort to keep out of her eyes the wonder with which they were occasion-

154

ally moved to blink. Oh there would have been things to blink at if one had let one's self go; and it was lucky they were alone together, without Sir Claude or Mrs Wix or even Mrs Beale to catch an imprudent glance. Though profuse and prolonged her ladyship was not exhaustively lucid, and her account of her situation, so far as it could be called descriptive, was a muddle of inconsequent things, bruised fruit of an occasion she had rather too lightly affronted. None of them were really thought out and some were even not wholly insincere. It was as if she had asked outright what better proof could have been wanted of her goodness and her greatness than just this marvellous consent to give up what she had so cherished. It was as if she had said in so many words: 'There have been things between us – between Sir Claude and me – which I needn't go into, you little nuisance, because you wouldn't understand them.' It suited her to convey that Maisie had been kept, so far as *she* was concerned or could imagine, in a holy ignorance, and that she must take for granted a supreme simplicity. She turned this way and that in the predicament she had sought and from which she could neither retreat with grace nor emerge with credit: she draped herself in the tatters of her impudence, postured to her utmost before the last little triangle of cracked glass to which so many fractures had reduced the polished plate of filial superstition. If neither Sir Claude nor Mrs Wix was there this was perhaps all the more a pity: the scene had a style of its own that would have qualified it for presentation, especially at such a moment as that of her letting it betray that she quite did think her wretched offspring better placed with Sir Claude than in her own soiled hands. There was at any rate nothing scant either in her admissions or her perversions, the mixture of her fear of what Maisie might undiscoverably think and of the support she at the same time gathered from a necessity of selfishness and a habit of brutality. This habit flushed through the merit she now made, in terms explicit, of not having come to Folkestone to kick up a vulgar row. She had not come to box any ears or to bang any doors or even to use any language: she had come at the worst to lose the thread of her argument in an occasional dumb twitch of the toggery in which Mrs Beale's low domestic had had the impudence to serve up Miss Farange. She checked all criticism, not committing herself even so far as for those missing comforts of the schoolroom on which Mrs Wix had presumed.

'I *am* good – I'm crazily, I'm criminally good. But it won't do for *you* any more, and if I've ceased to contend with him, and with you too, who have made most of the trouble between us, it's for reasons that you'll understand one of these days but too well – one of these days when I hope you'll know what it is to have lost a mother. I'm awfully ill but you mustn't ask me anything about it. If I don't get off somewhere my doctor won't answer for the consequences. He's stupefied at what I've borne – he says it has been put on me because I was formed to suffer. I'm thinking of South Africa, but that's none of your business. You must take your choice – you can't ask me questions if you're so ready to give me up. No, I won't tell you; you can find out for yourself. South Africa's wonderful, they say, and if I do go it must be to give it a fair trial. It must be either one thing or the other; if he takes you, you know, he takes you. I've struck my last blow for you; I can follow you no longer from pillar to post. I must live for myself at last, while there's still a handful left of me. I'm very, very ill; I'm very, very tired; I'm very, very determined. There you have it. Make the most of it. Your frock's too filthy; but I came to sacrifice myself.' Maisie looked at the peccant places; there were moments when it was a relief to her to drop her eyes even on anything so sordid. All her interviews, all her ordeals with her mother had, as she had grown older, seemed to have, before any other, the hard quality of duration; but longer than any, strangely, were these minutes offered to her as so pacific and so agreeably winding up the connexion. It was her anxiety that made them long, her fear of some hitch, some check of the current, one of her ladyship's famous quick jumps. She held her breath; she only wanted, by playing into her visitor's hands, to see the thing through. But her impatience itself made at instants the whole situation swim; there were things Ida said that she perhaps didn't hear, and there were things she heard that Ida perhaps didn't say. 'You're all I have, and yet I'm capable of this. Your father wishes you were dead – that, my dear, is what your father wishes. You'll have to get used to it as I've done – I mean to his wishing that *I'm* dead. At all events you see for yourself how wonderful I am to Sir Claude. He wishes me dead quite as much; and I'm sure that if making me scenes about *you* could have killed me – !' It was the mark of Ida's eloquence that she started more hares than she followed, and she gave but a glance in the direction of this one; going on to say that the very proof of her treating her husband like an angel was that he had just stolen off not to be fairly shamed. She spoke as if he had retired on tiptoe, as he might have withdrawn from a place of worship in which he was not fit to be present. 'You'll never know what I've been through about you – never, never, never. I spare you everything, as I always have; though I daresay you know things that, if I did (I mean if I knew them), would make me – well, no matter! You're old enough at any rate to know there are a lot of things I don't say that I easily might; though it would do me good, I assure you, to have spoken my mind for once in my life. I don't speak of your father's infamous wife: that may give you a notion of the way I'm letting you off. When I say "you" I mean your precious friends and backers. If you don't do justice to my forbearing, out of delicacy, to mention, just as a last word, about your stepfather, a little fact or two of the kind that really I should only *have* to mention to shine myself in comparison, and after every calumny, like pure gold: if you don't do me *that* justice you'll never do me justice at all!'

Maisie's desire to show what justice she did her had by this time become so intense as to have brought with it an inspiration. The great effect of their encounter had been to confirm her sense of being launched with Sir Claude, to make it rich and full beyond anything she had dreamed, and everything now conspired to suggest that a single soft touch of her small hand would complete the good work and set her ladyship so promptly and majestically afloat as to leave the great seaway clear for the morrow. This was the more the case as her hand had for some moments been rendered free by a marked manoeuvre of both her mother's. One of these capricious members had fumbled with visible impatience in some backward depth of drapery and had presently reappeared with a small article in its grasp. The act had a significance for a little person trained, in that relation, from an early age, to keep an eye on manual motions, and its possible bearing was not darkened by the memory of the handful of gold that Susan Ash would never, never believe Mrs Beale had sent back – 'not she; she's too

157

false and too greedy!' – to the munificent Countess. To have guessed, none the less, that her ladyship's purse might be the real figure of the object extracted from the rustling covert at her rear – this suspicion gave on the spot to the child's eyes a direction carefully distant. It added, moreover, to the optimism that for an hour could ruffle the surface of her deep diplomacy, ruffle it to the point of making her forget that she had never been safe unless she had also been stupid. She in short forgot her habitual caution in her impulse to adopt her ladyship's practical interests and show her ladyship how perfectly she understood them. She saw without looking that her mother pressed a little clasp; heard, without wanting to, the sharp click that marked the closing portemonnaie from which something had been taken. What this was she just didn't see; it was not too substantial to be locked with ease in the fold of her ladyship's fingers. Nothing was less new to Maisie than the art of not thinking singly, so that at this instant she could both bring out what was on her tongue's end and weigh, as to the object in her mother's palm, the question of its being a sovereign against the question of its being a shilling. No sooner had she begun to speak than she saw that within a few seconds this question would have been settled: she had foolishly checked the rising words of the little speech of presentation to which, under the circumstances, even such a high pride as Ida's had had to give some thought. She had checked it completely – that was the next thing she felt: the note she sounded brought into her companion's eyes a look that quickly enough seemed at variance with presentations.

'That was what the Captain said to me that day, mamma. I think it would have given you pleasure to hear the way he spoke of you.'

The pleasure, Maisie could now in consternation reflect, would have been a long time coming if it had come no faster than the response evoked by her allusion to it. Her mother gave her one of the looks that slammed the door in her face; never in a career of unsuccessful experiments had Maisie had to take such a stare. It reminded her of the way that once, at one of the lectures in Glower Street, something in a big jar that, amid an array of strange glasses and bad smells, had been promised as a beautiful yellow was produced as a beautiful black. She had been sorry on that occasion for the lecturer, but she was at this moment sorrier for herself. Oh nothing had ever made for twinges like mamma's manner of saying: 'The Captain? What Captain?'

'Why when we met you in the Gardens – the one who took me to sit with him. That was exactly what *he* said.'

Ida let it come on so far as to appear for an instant to pick up a lost thread. 'What on earth did he say?'

Maisie faltered supremely, but supremely she brought it out. 'What you say, mamma – that you're so good.'

'What "I" say?' Ida slowly rose, keeping her eyes on her child, and the hand that had busied itself in her purse conformed at her side and amid the folds of her dress to a certain stiffening of the arm. 'I say you're a precious idiot, and I won't have you put words into my mouth!' This was much more peremptory than a mere contradiction. Maisie could only feel on the spot that everything had broken short off and that their communication had abruptly ceased. That was presently proved. 'What business have you to speak to me of him?'

Her daughter turned scarlet. 'I thought you liked him.'

'Him! – the biggest cad in London!' Her ladyship towered again, and in the gathering dusk the whites of her eyes were huge.

Maisie's own, however, could by this time pretty well match them; and she had at least now, with the first flare of anger that had ever yet lighted her face for a foe, the sense of looking up quite as hard as anyone could look down. 'Well, he was kind about you then; he *was*, and it made me like him. He said things – they were beautiful, they were, they were!' She was almost capable of the violence of forcing this home, for even in the midst of her surge of passion – of which in fact it was a part – there rose in her a fear, a pain, a vision ominous, precocious, of what it might mean for her mother's fate to have forfeited such a loyalty as that. There was literally an instant in which Maisie fully saw – saw madness and desolation, saw ruin and darkness and death. 'I've thought of him often since, and I hoped it was with him – with him – !' Here, in her emotion, it failed her, the breath of her filial hope.

But Ida got it out of her. 'You hoped, you little horror – ?'

'That it was he who's at Dover, that it was he who's to take you. I mean to South Africa,' Maisie said with another drop.

Ida's stupefaction, on this, kept her silent unnaturally long, so

159

long that her daughter could not only wonder what was coming, but perfectly measure the decline of every symptom of her liberality. She loomed there in her grandeur, merely dark and dumb; her wrath was clearly still, as it had always been, a thing of resource and variety. What Maisie least expected of it was by this law what now occurred. It melted, in the summer twilight, gradually into pity, and the pity after a little found a cadence to which the renewed click of her purse gave an accent. She had put back what she had taken out. 'You're a dreadful dismal deplorable little thing,' she murmured. And with this she turned back and rustled away over the lawn.

After she had disappeared Maisie dropped upon the bench again and for some time, in the empty garden and the deeper dusk, sat and stared at the image her flight had still left standing. It had ceased to be her mother only, in the strangest way, that it might become her father, the father of whose wish that she were dead the announcement still lingered in the air. It was a presence with vague edges – it continued to front her, to cover her. But what reality that she need reckon with did it represent if Mr Farange were, on his side, also going off – going off to America with the Countess, or even only to Spa? That question had, from the house, a sudden gay answer in the great roar of a gong, and at the same moment she saw Sir Claude look out for her from the wide lighted doorway. At this she went to him and he came forward and met her on the lawn. For a minute she was with him in silence as, just before, at the last, she had been with her mother.

'She's gone?'

'She's gone.'

Nothing more, for the instant, passed between them but to move together to the house, where, in the hall, he indulged in one of those sudden pleasantries with which, to the delight of his step-daughter, his native animation overflowed. 'Will Miss Farange do me the honour to accept my arm?'

There was nothing in all her days that Miss Farange had accepted with such bliss, a bright rich element that floated them together to their feast; before they reached which, however, she uttered, in the spirit of a glad young lady taken in to her first dinner, a sociable word that made him stop short. 'She goes to South Africa.'

'To South Africa?' His face, for a moment, seemed to swing for a jump; the next it took its spring into the extreme of hilarity. 'Is that what she said?'

'Oh yes, I didn't *mistake*!' Maisie took to herself *that* credit. 'For the climate.'

Sir Claude was now looking at a young woman with black hair, a red frock and a tiny terrier tucked under her elbow. She swept past them on her way to the dining-room, leaving an impression of a strong scent which mingled, amid the clatter of the place, with the hot aroma of food. He had become a little graver; he still stopped to talk. 'I see – I see.' Other people brushed by; he was not too grave to notice them. 'Did she say anything else?'

'Oh yes, a lot more.'

On this he met her eyes again with some intensity, but only repeating: 'I see – I see.'

Maisie had still her own vision, which she brought out. 'I thought she was going to give me something.'

'What kind of a thing?'

'Some money that she took out of her purse and then put back.'

Sir Claude's amusement reappeared. 'She thought better of it. Dear thrifty soul! How much did she make by that manoeuvre?'

Maisie considered. 'I didn't see. It was very small.'

Sir Claude threw back his head. 'Do you mean very little? Sixpence?'

Maisie resented this almost as if, at dinner, she were already bandying jokes with an agreeable neighbour. 'It may have been a sovereign.'

'Or even,' Sir Claude suggested, 'a ten-pound note.' She flushed at this sudden picture of what she perhaps had lost, and he made it more vivid by adding: 'Rolled up in a tight little ball, you know – her way of treating banknotes as if they were curl-papers!' Maisie's flush deepened both with the immense plausibility of this and with a fresh wave of the consciousness that was always there to remind her of his cleverness – the consciousness of how immeasurably more after all he knew about mamma than she. She had lived with her so many times without discovering the material of her curl-papers or assisting at any other of her dealings with banknotes. The tight little ball had at any rate rolled away from her for ever – quite like one of the other balls that

161

Ida's cue used to send flying. Sir Claude gave her his arm again, and by the time she was seated at table she had perfectly made up her mind as to the amount of the sum she had forfeited. Everything about her, however – the crowded room, the bedizened banquet, the savour of dishes, the drama of figures – ministered to the joy of life. After dinner she smoked with her friend – for that was exactly what she felt she did – on a porch, a kind of terrace, where the red tips of cigars and the light dresses of ladies made, under the happy stars, a poetry that was almost intoxicating. They talked but little, and she was slightly surprised at his asking for no more news of what her mother had said; but she had no need of talk – there were a sense and a sound in everything to which words had nothing to add. They smoked and smoked, and there was a sweetness in her stepfather's silence. At last he said: 'Let us take another turn – but you must go to bed soon. Oh you know, we're going to have a system!' Their turn was back into the garden, along the dusky paths from which they could see the black masts and the red lights of boats and hear the calls and cries that evidently had to do with happy foreign travel; and their system was once more to get on beautifully in this further lounge without a definite exchange. Yet he finally spoke – he broke out as he tossed away the match from which he had taken a fresh light: 'I must go for a stroll. I'm in a fidget – I must walk it off.' She fell in with this as she fell in with everything; on which he went on: 'You go up to Miss Ash' – it was the name they had started; 'you must see she's not in mischief. Can you find your way alone?'

'Oh yes; I've been up and down seven times.' She positively enjoyed the prospect of an eighth.

Still they didn't separate; they stood smoking together under the stars. Then at last Sir Claude produced it. 'I'm free – I'm free.'

She looked up at him; it was the very spot on which a couple of hours before she had looked up at her mother. 'You're free – you're free.'

'Tomorrow we go to France.' He spoke as if he hadn't heard her; but it didn't prevent her again concurring.

'Tomorrow we go to France.'

Again he appeared not to have heard her; and after a moment –

it was an effect evidently of the depth of his reflexions and the agitation of his soul – he also spoke as if he had not spoken before. 'I'm free – I'm free!'

She repeated her form of assent. 'You're free – you're free.'

This time he did hear her; he fixed her through the darkness with a grave face. But he said nothing more; he simply stooped a little and drew her to him – simply held her a little and kissed her good night; after which, having given her a silent push upstairs to Miss Ash, he turned round again to the black masts and the red lights. Maisie mounted as if France were at the top.

22

THE next day it seemed to her indeed at the bottom – down too far, in shuddering plunges, even to leave her a sense, on the Channel boat, of the height at which Sir Claude remained and which had never in every way been so great as when, much in the wet, though in the angle of a screen of canvas, he sociably sat with his stepdaughter's head in his lap and that of Mrs Beale's housemaid fairly pillowed on his breast. Maisie was surprised to learn as they drew into port that they had had a lovely passage; but this emotion, at Boulogne, was speedily quenched in others, above all in the great ecstasy of a larger impression of life. She was 'abroad' and she gave herself up to it, responded to it, in the bright air, before the pink houses, among the bare-legged fish-wives and the red-legged soldiers, with the instant certitude of a vocation. Her vocation was to see the world and to thrill with enjoyment of the picture; she had grown older in five minutes and had by the time they reached the hotel recognized in the institutions and manners of France a multitude of affinities and messages. Literally in the course of an hour she found her initiation; a consciousness much quickened by the superior part that, as soon as they had gobbled down a French breakfast – which was indeed a high note in the concert – she observed herself to play to Susan Ash. Sir Claude, who had already bumped against people he knew and who, as he said, had business and letters, sent them out together for a walk, a walk in which the child was

163

avenged, so far as poetic justice required, not only for the loud giggles that in their London trudges used to break from her attendant, but for all the years of her tendency to produce socially that impression of an excess of the queer something which had seemed to waver so widely between innocence and guilt. On the spot, at Boulogne, though there might have been excess there was at least no wavering; she recognized, she understood, she adored and took possession; feeling herself attuned to everything and laying her hand, right and left, on what had simply been waiting for her. She explained to Susan, she laughed at Susan, she towered over Susan; and it was somehow Susan's stupidity, of which she had never yet been so sure, and Susan's bewilderment and ignorance and antagonism, that gave the liveliest rebound to her immediate perceptions and adoptions. The place and the people were all a picture together, a picture that, when they went down to the wide sands, shimmered, in a thousand tints, with the pretty organization of the *plage*, with the gaiety of spectators and bathers, with that of the language and the weather, and above all with that of our young lady's unprecedented situation. For it appeared to her that no one since the beginning of time could have had such an adventure or, in an hour, so much experience; as a sequel to which she only needed, in order to feel with conscious wonder how the past was changed, to hear Susan, inscrutably aggravated, express a preference for the Edgware Road. The past was so changed and the circle it had formed already so overstepped that on that very afternoon, in the course of another walk, she found herself inquiring of Sir Claude – and without a single scruple – if he were prepared as yet to name the moment at which they should start for Paris. His answer, it must be said, gave her the least little chill.

'Oh Paris, my dear child – I don't quite know about Paris!'

This required to be met, but it was much less to challenge him for the rich joy of her first discussion of the details of a tour that, after looking at him a minute, she replied: 'Well, isn't that the *real* thing, the thing that when one does come abroad – ?'

He had turned grave again, and she merely threw that out: it was a way of doing justice to the seriousness of their life. She couldn't, moreover, be so much older since yesterday without reflecting that if by this time she probed a little he would recognize

that she had done enough for mere patience. There was in fact
something in his eyes that suddenly, to her own, made her discretion shabby. Before she could remedy this he had answered her
last question, answered it in the way that, of all ways, she had
least expected. 'The thing it doesn't do not to do? Certainly Paris
is charming. But, my dear fellow, Paris eats your head off. I mean
it's so beastly expensive.'

That note gave her a pang – it suddenly let in a harder light.
Were they poor, then, that is, was *he* poor, really poor beyond the
pleasantry of appollinaris and cold beef? They had walked to the
end of the long jetty that enclosed the harbour and were looking
out at the dangers they had escaped, the grey horizon that was
England, the tumbled surface of the sea and the brown smacks
that bobbed upon it. Why had he chosen an embarrassed time to
make this foreign dash? unless indeed it was just the dash economic, of which she had often heard and on which, after another
look at the grey horizon and the bobbing boats, she was ready to
turn round with elation. She replied to him quite in his own
manner: 'I see, I see.' She smiled up at him. 'Our affairs are
involved.'

'That's it.' He returned her smile. 'Mine are not quite so bad
as yours; for yours are really, my dear man, in a state I can't see
through at all. But mine will do – for a mess.'

She thought this over. 'But isn't France cheaper than England?'

England, over there in the thickening gloom, looked then just
remarkably dear. 'I daresay; some parts.'

'Then can't we live in those parts?'

There was something that for an instant, in satisfaction of this,
he had the air of being about to say and yet not saying. What he
presently said was: 'This very place is one of them.'

'Then we shall live here?'

He didn't treat it quite so definitely as she liked. 'Since we've
come to save money!'

This made her press him more. 'How long shall we stay?'

'Oh three or four days.'

It took her breath away. 'You can save money in that time?'

He burst out laughing, starting to walk again and taking her
under his arm. He confessed to her on the way that she too had

put a finger on the weakest of all his weaknesses, the fact, of which he was perfectly aware, that he probably might have lived within his means if he had never done anything for thrift. 'It's the happy thoughts that do it,' he said; 'there's nothing so ruinous as putting in a cheap week.' Maisie heard afresh among the pleasant sounds of the closing day that steel click of Ida's change of mind. She thought of the ten-pound note it would have been delightful at this juncture to produce for her companion's encouragement. But the idea was dissipated by his saying irrelevantly, in presence of the next thing they stopped to admire: 'We shall stay till she arrives.'

She turned upon him. 'Mrs Beale?'

'Mrs Wix. I've had a wire,' he went on. 'She has seen your mother.'

'Seen mamma?' Maisie stared. 'Where in the world?'

'Apparently in London. They've been together.'

For an instant this looked ominous – a fear came into her eyes. 'Then she hasn't gone?'

'Your mother? – to South Africa? I give it up, dear boy,' Sir Claude said; and she seemed literally to see him give it up as he stood there and with a kind of absent gaze – absent, that is, from *her* affairs – followed the fine stride and shining limbs of a young fishwife who had just waded out of the sea with her basketful of shrimps. His thought came back to her sooner than his eyes. 'But I daresay it's all right. She wouldn't come if it wasn't, poor old thing: she knows rather well what she's about.'

This was so reassuring that Maisie, after turning it over, could make it fit into her dream. 'Well, what *is* she about?'

He finally stopped looking at the fishwife – he met his companion's inquiry. 'Oh, you know!' There was something in the way he said it that made, between them, more of an equality than she had yet imagined; but it had also more the effect of raising her up than of letting him down, and what it did with her was shown by the sound of her assent.

'Yes – I know!' What she knew, what she *could* know is by this time no secret to us: it grew and grew at any rate, the rest of that day, in the air of what he took for granted. It was better he should do that than attempt to test her knowledge; but there at the worst was the gist of the matter: it was open between them at last that their great change, as, speaking as if it had already lasted weeks, Maisie called it, was somehow built up round Mrs Wix. Before she went to bed that night she knew further that Sir Claude, since, as *he* called it, they had been on the rush, had received more telegrams than one. But they separated again without speaking of Mrs Beale.

Oh what a crossing for the straighteners and the old brown dress – which latter appurtenance the child saw thriftily revived for the possible disasters of travel! The wind got up in the night and from her little room at the inn Maisie could hear the noise of the sea. The next day it was raining and everything different: this was the case even with Susan Ash, who positively crowed over the bad weather, partly, it seemed, for relish of the time their visitor would have in the boat, and partly to point the moral of the folly of coming to such holes. In the wet, with Sir Claude, Maisie went to the Folkestone packet, on the arrival of which, with many signs of the fray, he made her wait under an umbrella by the quay; whence almost ere the vessel touched, he was to be descried, in quest of their friend, wriggling – that had been his word – through the invalids massed upon the deck. It was long till he reappeared – it was not indeed till everyone had landed; when he presented the object of his benevolence in a light that Maisie scarce knew whether to suppose the depth of prostration or the flush of triumph. The lady on his arm, still bent beneath her late ordeal, was muffled in such draperies as had never before offered so much support to so much woe. At the hotel, an hour later, this ambiguity dropped: assisting Mrs Wix in private to refresh and reinvest herself, Maisie heard from her in detail how little she could have achieved if Sir Claude hadn't put it in her power. It was a phrase that in her room she repeated in connexions indescribable: he had put it in her power to have 'changes', as she said, of the most intimate order, adapted to climates and occasions so various as to foreshadow in themselves the stages of a vast itinerary. Cheap weeks would of course be in their place after so much money spent on a governess; sums not grudged, however, by this lady's pupil, even on her feeling her own appearance give rise, through the straighteners, to an attention perceptibly mystified. Sir Claude in truth had had less time to devote to it than to Mrs Wix's; and, moreover, she would rather be in her own shoes

167

than in her friend's creaking new ones in the event of an encounter with Mrs Beale. Maisie was too lost in the idea of Mrs Beale's judgement of so much newness to pass any judgement herself. Besides, after much luncheon and many endearments, the question took quite another turn, to say nothing of the pleasure of the child's quick view that there were other eyes than Susan Ash's to open to what she could show. She couldn't show much, alas, till it stopped raining, which it declined to do that day; but this had only the effect of leaving more time for Mrs Wix's own demonstration. It came as they sat in the little white and gold salon which Maisie thought the loveliest place she had ever seen except perhaps the apartment of the Countess; it came while the hard summer storm lashed the windows and blew in such a chill that Sir Claude with his hands in his pockets and cigarette in his teeth, fidgeting, frowning, looking out and turning back, ended by causing a smoky little fire to be made in the dressy little chimney. It came in spite of something that could only be named his air of wishing to put it off; an air that had served him – oh as all his airs served him! – to the extent of his having for a couple of hours confined the conversation to gratuitous jokes and generalities, kept it on the level of the little empty coffee-cups and *petits verres* (Mrs Wix had two of each!) that struck Maisie, through the fumes of the French fire and the English tobacco, as a token more than ever that they were launched. She felt now, in close quarters and as clearly as if Mrs Wix had told her, that what this lady had come over for was not merely to be chaffed and to hear her pupil chaffed; not even to hear Sir Claude, who knew French in perfection, imitate the strange sounds emitted by the English folk at the hotel. It was perhaps half an effect of her present renovations, as if her clothes had been somebody's else: she had at any rate never produced such an impression of high colour, of a redness associated in Maisie's mind at *that* pitch either with measles or with 'habits'. Her heart was not at all in the gossip about Boulogne; and if her complexion was partly the result of the déjeuner and the *petits verres* it was also the brave signal of what she was there to say. Maisie knew when this did come how anxiously it had been awaited by the youngest member of the party. 'Her ladyship packed me off – she almost put me into the cab!' That was what Mrs Wix at last brought out.

23

SIR CLAUDE was stationed at the window; he didn't so much as turn round, and it was left to the youngest of the three to take up the remark. 'Do you mean you went to see her yesterday?'

'She came to see *me*. She knocked at my shabby door. She mounted my squalid stair. She told me she had seen you at Folkestone.'

Maisie wondered. 'She went back that evening?'

'No; yesterday morning. She drove to me straight from the station. It was most remarkable. If I had a job to get off she did nothing to make it worse – she did a great deal to make it better.' Mrs Wix hung fire, though the flame in her face burned brighter; then she became capable of saying: 'Her ladyship's kind! She did what I didn't expect.'

Maisie, on this, looked straight at her stepfather's back; it might well have been for her at that hour a monument of her ladyship's kindness. It remained, as such, monumentally still, and for a time that permitted the child to ask of their companion: 'Did she really help you?'

'Most practically.' Again Mrs Wix paused; again she quite resounded. 'She gave me a ten-pound note.'

At that, still looking out, Sir Claude, at the window, laughed loud. 'So you see, Maisie, we've not quite lost it!'

'Oh no,' Maisie responded. 'Isn't that too charming?' She smiled at Mrs Wix. 'We know all about it.' Then on her friend's showing such blankness as was compatible with such a flush she pursued: 'She does want mé to have you?'

Mrs Wix showed a final hesitation, which, however, while Sir Claude drummed on the window-pane, she presently surmounted. It came to Maisie that in spite of his drumming and of his not turning round he was really so much interested as to leave himself in a manner in her hands; which somehow suddenly seemed to her a greater proof than he could have given by interfering. 'She wants me to have *you*!' Mrs Wix declared.

Maisie answered this bang at Sir Claude. 'Then that's nice for all of us.'

Of course it was, his continued silence sufficiently admitted while Mrs Wix rose from her chair and, as if to take more of a stand, placed herself, not without majesty, before the fire. The incongruity of her smartness, the circumference of her stiff frock, presented her as really more ready for Paris than any of them. She also gazed hard at Sir Claude's back. 'Your wife was different from anything she had ever shown me. She recognizes certain proprieties.'

'Which? Do you happen to remember?' Sir Claude asked.

Mrs Wix's reply was prompt. 'The importance for Maisie of a gentlewoman, of someone who's not – well, so bad! She objects to a mere maid, and I don't in the least mind telling you what she wants me to do.' One thing was clear – Mrs Wix was now bold enough for anything. 'She wants me to persuade you to get rid of the person from Mrs Beale's.'

Maisie waited for Sir Claude to pronounce on this; then she could only understand that he on his side waited, and she felt particularly full of common sense as she met her responsibility. 'Oh I don't want Susan with *you*!' she said to Mrs Wix.

Sir Claude, always from the window, approved. 'That's quite simple. I'll take her back.'

Mrs Wix gave a positive jump; Maisie caught her look of alarm. ' "Take" her? You don't mean to go over on purpose?'

Sir Claude said nothing for a moment; after which, 'Why shouldn't I leave you here?' he inquired.

Maisie, at this, sprang up. 'Oh do, oh do, oh do!' The next moment she was interlaced with Mrs Wix, and the two, on the hearth-rug, their eyes in each other's eyes, considered the plan with intensity. Then Maisie felt the difference of what they saw in it.

'She can surely go back alone: why should you put yourself out?' Mrs Wix demanded.

'Oh she's an idiot – she's incapable. If anything should happen to her it would be awkward: it was I who brought her – without her asking. If I turn her away I ought with my own hand to place her again exactly where I found her.'

Mrs Wix's face appealed to Maisie on such folly, and her manner, as directed to their companion, had, to her pupil's surprise, an unprecedented firmness. 'Dear Sir Claude, I think

170

you're perverse. Pay her fare and give her a sovereign. She has had an experience that she never dreamed of and that will be an advantage to her through life. If she goes wrong on the way it will be simply because she wants to, and, with her expenses and her remuneration – make it even what you like! – you'll have treated her as handsomely as you always treat everyone.'

This was a new tone – as new as Mrs Wix's cap; and it could strike a young person with a sharpened sense for latent meanings as the upshot of a relation that had taken on a new character. It brought out for Maisie how much more even than she had guessed her friends were fighting side by side. At the same time it needed so definite a justification that as Sir Claude now at last did face them she at first supposed him merely resentful of excessive familiarity. She was therefore yet more puzzled to see him show his serene beauty untroubled, as well as an equal interest in a matter quite distinct from any freedom but her ladyship's. 'Did my wife come alone?' He could ask even that good-humouredly.

'When she called on me?' Mrs Wix *was* red now: his good humour wouldn't keep down her colour, which for a minute glowed there like her ugly honesty. 'No – there was someone in the cab.' The only attenuation she could think of was after a minute to add: 'But they didn't come up.'

Sir Claude broke into a laugh – Maisie herself could guess what it was at: while he now walked about, still laughing, and at the fireplace gave a gay kick to a displaced log, she felt more vague about almost everything than about the drollery of such a 'they'. She in fact could scarce have told you if it was to deepen or to cover the joke that she bethought herself to observe: 'Perhaps it was her maid.'

Mrs Wix gave her a look that at any rate deprecated the wrong tone. 'It was not her maid.'

'Do you mean there are this time two?' Sir Claude asked as if he hadn't heard.

'Two maids?' Maisie went on as if she might assume he had.

The reproach of the straighteners darkened; but Sir Claude cut across it with a sudden: 'See here; what do you mean? And what do you suppose *she* meant?'

Mrs Wix let him for a moment, in silence, understand that the answer to his question, if he didn't care, might give him more than he wanted. It was as if, with this scruple, she measured and adjusted all she gave him in at last saying: 'What she meant was to make me know that you're definitely free. To have that straight from her was a joy I of course hadn't hoped for: it made the assurance, and my delight at it, a thing I could really proceed upon. You already know now certainly I'd have started even if she hadn't pressed me; you already know what, so long, we've been looking for and what, as soon as she told me of her step taken at Folkestone, I recognized with rapture that we *have*. It's your freedom that makes me right' – she fairly bristled with her logic. 'But I don't mind telling you that it's her action that makes me happy!'

'Her action?' Sir Claude echoed. 'Why, my dear woman, her action is just a hideous crime. It happens to satisfy our sympathies in a way that's quite delicious; but that doesn't in the least alter the fact that it's the most abominable thing ever done. She has chucked our friend here overboard not a bit less than if she had shoved her, shrieking and pleading, out of that window and down two floors to the paving-stones.'

Maisie surveyed serenely the parties to the discussion. 'Oh your friend here, dear Sir Claude, doesn't plead and shriek!'

He looked at her a moment. 'Never. Never. That's one, only one, but charming so far as it goes, of about a hundred things we love her for.' Then he pursued to Mrs Wix: 'What I can't for the life of me make out is what Ida is *really* up to, what game she was playing in turning to you with that cursed cheek after the beastly way she has used you. Where – to explain her at all – does she fancy she can presently, when we least expect it, take it out of us?'

'She doesn't fancy anything, nor want anything out of anyone. Her cursed cheek, as you call it, is the best thing I've ever seen in her. I don't care a fig for the beastly way she used me – I forgive it all a thousand times over!' Mrs Wix raised her voice as she had never raised it; she quite triumphed in her lucidity. 'I understand her, I almost admire her!' she quavered. She spoke as if this might practically suffice; yet in charity to fainter lights she threw out an explanation. 'As I've said, she was different; upon my word I wouldn't have known her. She had a glimmering, she had an instinct; they brought her. It was a kind of happy thought, and if you couldn't have supposed she would ever have had such a thing, why of course I quite agree with you. But she did have it! There!'

Maisie could feel again how a certain rude rightness in this plea might have been found exasperating; but as she had often watched Sir Claude in apprehension of displeasures that didn't come, so now, instead of saying 'Oh hell!' as her father used, she observed him only to take refuge in a question that at the worst was abrupt.

'Who *is* it this time, do you know?'

Mrs Wix tried blind dignity. 'Who is what, Sir Claude?'

'The man who stands the cabs. Who was in the one that waited at your door?'

At this challenge she faltered so long that her young friend's pitying conscience gave her a hand. 'It wasn't the Captain.'

This good intention, however, only converted the excellent woman's scruple to a more ambiguous stare; besides of course making Sir Claude go off. Mrs Wix fairly appealed to him. 'Must I really tell you?'

His amusement continued. 'Did she make you promise not to?'

Mrs Wix looked at him still harder. 'I mean before Maisie.'

Sir Claude laughed again. 'Why *she* can't hurt him!'

Maisie felt herself, as it passed, brushed by the light humour of this. 'Yes, I can't hurt him.'

The straighteners again roofed her over; after which they seemed to crack with the explosion of their wearer's honesty. Amid the flying splinters Mrs Wix produced a name. 'Mr Tischbein.'

There was for an instant a silence that, under Sir Claude's influence and while he and Maisie looked at each other, suddenly pretended to be that of gravity. 'We don't know Mr Tischbein, do we, dear?'

Maisie gave the point all needful thought. 'No, I can't place Mr Tischbein.'

It was a passage that worked visibly on their friend. 'You must pardon me, Sir Claude,' she said with an austerity of which the note was real, 'if I thank God to your face that he has in his mercy – I mean his mercy to our charge – allowed me to achieve this act.' She gave out a long puff of pain. 'It was time!' Then as if still more to point the moral: 'I said just now I understood your wife. I said just now I admired her. I stand to it: I did both of

173

those things when I saw how even *she*, poor thing, saw. If you want the dots on the i's you shall have them. What she came to me for, in spite of everything, was that I'm just' – she quavered it out – 'well, just clean! What she saw for her daughter was that there must at last be a *decent* person!'

Maisie was quick enough to jump a little at the sound of this implication that such a person was what Sir Claude was not; the next instant, however, she more profoundly guessed against whom the discrimination was made. She was therefore left the more surprised at the complete candour with which he embraced the worst. 'If she's bent on decent persons why has she given her to *me*? You don't call me a decent person, and I'll do Ida the justice that *she* never did. I think I'm as decent as anyone, and that there's nothing in my behaviour that makes my wife's surrender a bit less ignoble!'

'Don't speak of your behaviour!' Mrs Wix cried. 'Don't say such horrible things; they're false and they're wicked and I forbid you! It's to *keep* you decent that I'm here and that I've done everything I have done. It's to save you – I won't say from yourself, because in yourself you're beautiful and good! It's to save you from the worst person of all. I haven't, after all, come over to be afraid to speak of her! That's the person in whose place her ladyship wants such a person as even me; and if she thought herself, as she, as good as told me, not fit for Maisie's company, it's not, as you may well suppose, that she may make room for Mrs Beale!'

Maisie watched his face as it took this outbreak, and the most she saw in it was that it turned a little white. That indeed made him look, as Susan Ash would have said, queer; and it was perhaps a part of the queerness that he intensely smiled. 'You're too hard on Mrs Beale. She has great merits of her own.'

Mrs Wix, at this, instead of immediately replying, did what Sir Claude had been doing before: she moved across to the window and stared a while into the storm. There was for a minute, to Maisie's sense, a hush that resounded with wind and rain. Sir Claude, in spite of these things, glanced about for his hat; on which Maisie spied it first and, making a dash for it, held it out to him. He took it with a gleam of a 'thank you' in his face, and then something moved her still to hold the other side of the brim;

174

so that, united by their grasp of this object, they stood some seconds looking many things at each other. By this time Mrs Wix had turned round. 'Do you mean to tell me,' she demanded, 'that you *are* going back?'

'To Mrs Beale?' Maisie surrendered his hat, and there was something that touched her in the embarrassed, almost humiliated way their companion's challenge made him turn it round and round. She had seen people do that who, she was sure, did nothing else that Sir Claude did. 'I can't just say, my dear thing. We'll see about it – we'll talk of it tomorrow. Meantime I must get some air.'

Mrs Wix, with her back to the window, threw up her head to a height that, still for a moment, had the effect of detaining him. 'All the air in France, Sir Claude, won't, I think, give you the courage to deny that you're simply afraid of her!'

Oh this time he did look queer; Maisie had no need of Susan's vocabulary to note it! It would have come to her of itself as, with his hand on the door, he turned his eyes from his stepdaughter to her governess and then back again. Resting on Maisie's, though for ever so short a time, there was something they gave up to her and tried to explain. His lips, however, explained nothing; they only surrendered to Mrs Wix. 'Yes. I'm simply afraid of her!' He opened the door and passed out.

It brought back to Maisie his confession of fear of her mother; it made her stepmother then the second lady about whom he failed of the particular virtue that was supposed most to mark a gentleman. In fact there were three of them, if she counted in Mrs Wix, before whom he had undeniably quailed. Well, his want of valour was but a deeper appeal to her tenderness. To thrill with response to it she had only to remember all the ladies she herself had, as they called it, funked.

24

IT continued to rain so hard that our young lady's private dream of explaining the Continent to their visitor had to contain a provision for some adequate treatment of the weather. At the *table*

175

d'hôte that evening she threw out a variety of lights: this was the second ceremony of the sort she had sat through, and she would have neglected her privilege and dishonoured her vocabulary – which indeed consisted mainly of the names of dishes – if she had not been proportionately ready to dazzle with interpretations. Preoccupied and overawed, Mrs Wix was apparently dim: she accepted her pupil's version of the mysteries of the *menu* in a manner that might have struck the child as the depression of a credulity conscious not so much of its needs as of its dimensions. Maisie was soon enough – though it scarce happened before bed-time – confronted again with the different sort of programme for which she reserved her criticism. They remounted together to their sitting-room while Sir Claude, who said he would join them later, remained below to smoke and to converse with the old acquaint-ances that he met wherever he turned. He had proposed his com-panions, for coffee, the enjoyment of the *salon de lecture*, but Mrs Wix had replied promptly and with something of an air that it struck her their own apartments offered them every convenience. They offered the good lady herself, Maisie could immediately observe, not only that of this rather grand reference, which, already emulous, so far as it went, of her pupil, she made as if she had spent her life in salons; but that of a stiff French sofa where she could sit and stare at the faint French lamp, in default of the French clock that had stopped, as for some account of the time Sir Claude would so markedly interpose. Her demeanour accused him so directly of hovering beyond her reach that Maisie sought to divert her by a report of Susan's quaint attitude on the matter of their conversation after lunch. Maisie had mentioned to the young woman for sympathy's sake the plan for her relief, but her disapproval of alien ways appeared, strange to say, only to prompt her to hug her gloom; so that between Mrs Wix's effect of displacing her and the visible stiffening of her back the child had the sense of a double office and enlarged play for pacific powers.

These powers played to no great purpose, it was true, in keep-ing before Mrs Wix the vision of Sir Claude's perversity, which hung there in the pauses of talk and which he himself, after unmistakable delays, finally made quite lurid by bursting in – it was near ten o'clock – with an object held up in his hand. She

176

knew before he spoke what it was; she knew at least from the underlying sense of all that, since the hour spent after the Exhibition with her father, had not sprung up to reinstate Mr Farange – she knew it meant a triumph for Mrs Beale. The mere present sight of Sir Claude's face caused her on the spot to drop straight through her last impression of Mr Farange a plummet that reached still deeper down than the security of these days of flight. She had wrapped that impression in silence – a silence that had parted with half its veil to cover also, from the hour of Sir Claude's advent, the image of Mr Farange's wife. But if the object in Sir Claude's hand revealed itself as a letter which he held up very high, so there was something in his mere motion that laid Mrs Beale again bare. 'Here we are!' he cried almost from the door, shaking his trophy at them and looking from one to the other. Then he came straight to Mrs Wix; he had pulled two papers out of the envelope and glanced at them again to see which was which. He thrust one out open to Mrs Wix. 'Read that.' She looked at him hard, as if in fear: it was impossible not to see he was excited. Then she took the letter, but it was not her face that Maisie watched while she read. Neither, for that matter, was it this countenance that Sir Claude scanned: he stood before the fire and, more calmly, now that he had acted, communed in silence with his stepdaughter.

The silence was in truth quickly broken; Mrs Wix rose to her feet with the violence of the sound she emitted. The letter had dropped from her and lay upon the floor; it had made her turn ghastly white and she was speechless with the effect of it. 'It's too abominable – it's too unspeakable!' she then cried.

'Isn't it a charming thing?' Sir Claude asked. 'It has just arrived, enclosed in a word of her own. She sends it on to me with the remark that comment's superfluous. I really think it is. That's all you can say.'

'She oughtn't to pass such a horror about,' said Mrs Wix. 'She ought to put it straight in the fire.'

'My dear woman, she's not such a fool! It's much too precious.' He had picked the letter up and he gave it again a glance of complacency which produced a light in his face. 'Such a document' – he considered, then concluded with a slight drop – 'such a document is, in fine, a basis!'

177

'A basis for what?'

'Well – for proceedings.'

'Hers?' Mrs Wix's voice had become outright the voice of derision. 'How can *she* proceed?'

Sir Claude turned it over. 'How can she get rid of him? Well – she *is* rid of him.'

'Not legally.' Mrs Wix had never looked to her pupil so much as if she knew what she was talking about.

'I daresay,' Sir Claude laughed; 'but she's not a bit less deprived than I!'

'Of the power to get a divorce? It's just your want of the power that makes the scandal of your connexion with her. Therefore it's just her want of it that makes that of hers with you. That's all I contend!' Mrs Wix concluded with an unparalleled neigh of battle. Oh she did know what she was talking about!

Maisie had meanwhile appealed mutely to Sir Claude, who judged it easier to meet what she didn't say than to meet what Mrs Wix did.

'It's a letter to Mrs Beale from your father, my dear, written from Spa and making the rupture between them perfectly irrevocable. It lets her know, and not in pretty language, that, as we technically say, he deserts her. It puts an end for ever to their relations.' He ran his eyes over it again, then appeared to make up his mind. 'In fact it concerns you, Maisie, so nearly and refers to you so particularly that I really think you ought to see the terms in which this new situation is created for you.' And he held out the letter.

Mrs Wix, at this, pounced upon it; she had grabbed it too soon even for Maisie to become aware of being rather afraid of it. Thrusting it instantly behind her she positively glared at Sir Claude. 'See it, wretched man? – the innocent child *see* such a thing? I think you must be mad, and she shall not have a glimpse of it while I'm here to prevent!'

The breadth of her action had made Sir Claude turn red – he even looked a little foolish. 'You think it's too bad, eh? But it's precisely because it's bad that it seemed to me it would have a lesson and a virtue for her.'

Maisie could do quick enough justice to his motive to be able clearly to interpose. She fairly smiled at him. 'I assure you I can quite believe how bad it is!' She thought of something, kept it back a moment, and then spoke. 'I know what's in it!'

He of course burst out laughing and, while Mrs Wix groaned an 'Oh heavens!' replied: 'You wouldn't say that, old boy, if you did! The point I make is,' he continued to Mrs Wix with a blandness now re-established – 'the point I make is simply that it sets Mrs Beale free.'

She hung fire but an instant. 'Free to live with *you*?'

'Free not to live, not to pretend to live, with her husband.'

'Ah they're mighty different things!' – a truth as to which her earnestness could now with a fine inconsequent look invite the participation of the child.

Before Maisie could commit herself, however, the ground was occupied by Sir Claude, who, as he stood before their visitor with an expression half rueful, half persuasive, rubbed his hand sharply up and down the back of his head. 'Then why the deuce do you grant so – do you, I may even say, rejoice so – that by the desertion of my own precious partner I'm free?'

Mrs Wix met this challenge first with silence, then with a demonstration the most extraordinary, the most unexpected. Maisie could scarcely believe her eyes as she saw the good lady, with whom she had associated no faintest shade of any art of provocation, actually, after an upward grimace, gave Sir Claude a great giggling insinuating naughty slap. 'You wretch – you *know* why!' And she turned away. The face that with this movement she left him to present to Maisie was to abide with his stepdaughter as the very image of stupefaction; but the pair lacked time to communicate either amusement or alarm before their admonisher was upon them again. She had begun in fact to show infinite variety and she flashed about with a still quicker change of tone. 'Have you brought me that thing as a pretext for your going over?'

Sir Claude braced himself. 'I can't, after such news, in common decency not go over. I mean, don't you know, in common courtesy and humanity. My dear lady, you can't chuck a woman that way, especially taking the moment when she has been most insulted and wronged. A fellow must behave like a gentleman, damn it, dear good Mrs Wix. We didn't come away, we two, to hang right on, you know: it was only to try our paces and just put in a few days that might prove to everyone concerned that we're in earnest. It's exactly because we're in earnest that, dash it, we needn't be so awfully particular. I mean, don't you know, we needn't be so awfully afraid.' He showed a vivacity, an intensity of argument, and if Maisie counted his words she was all the more ready to swallow after a single swift gasp those that, the next thing, she became conscious he paused for a reply to. 'We didn't come, old girl, did we,' he pleaded straight, 'to stop right away for ever and put it all in *now*?'

Maisie had never doubted she could be heroic for him. 'Oh no!' It was as if she had been shocked at the bare thought. 'We're just taking it as we find it.' She had a sudden inspiration, which she backed up with a smile. 'We're just seeing what we can afford.' She had never yet in her life made any claim for herself, but she hoped that this time, frankly, what she was doing would somehow be counted to her. Indeed she felt Sir Claude *was* counting it, though she was afraid to look at him – afraid she should show him tears. She looked at Mrs Wix; she reached her maximum. 'I don't think I ought to be bad to Mrs Beale.'

She heard, on this, a deep sound, something inarticulate and sweet, from Sir Claude; but tears were what Mrs Wix didn't scruple to show. 'Do you think you ought to be bad to *me*?' The question was the more disconcerting that Mrs Wix's emotion didn't deprive her of the advantage of her effect. 'If you see that woman again you're lost!' she declared to their companion.

Sir Claude looked at the moony globe of the lamp; he seemed to see for an instant what seeing Mrs Beale would consist of. It was also apparently from this vision that he drew strength to return: 'Her situation, by what has happened, is completely changed; and it's no use your trying to prove to me that I needn't take any account of that.'

'If you see that woman you're lost!' Mrs Wix with greater force repeated.

'Do you think she'll not let me come back to you? My dear lady, I leave you here, you and Maisie, as a hostage to fortune, and I promise you by all that's sacred that I shall be with you again at the very latest on Saturday. I provide you with funds; I install you in these lovely rooms; I arrange with the people here that you be treated with every attention and supplied with every luxury. The weather, after this, will mend; it will be sure to be

180

exquisite. You'll both be as free as air and you can roam all over the place and have tremendous larks. You shall have a carriage to drive you; the whole house shall be at your call. You'll have a magnificent position.' He paused, he looked from one of his companions to the other as to see the impression he had made. Whether or no he judged it adequate he subjoined after a moment: 'And you'll oblige me above all by not making a fuss.'

Maisie could only answer for the impression on herself, though indeed from the heart even of Mrs Wix's rigour there floated to her sense a faint fragrance of depraved concession. Maisie had her dumb word for the show such a speech could make, for the irresistible charm it could take from his dazzling sincerity; and before she could do anything but blink at excess of light she heard this very word sound on Mrs Wix's lips, just as if the poor lady had guessed it and wished, snatching it from her, to blight it like a crumpled flower. 'You're dreadful, you're terrible, for you know but too well that it's not a small thing to me that you should address me in terms that are princely!' Princely was what he stood there and looked and sounded; that was what Maisie for the occasion found herself reduced to simple worship of him for being. Yet strange to say too, as Mrs Wix went on, an echo rang within her that matched the echo she had herself just produced. 'How much you must *want* to see her to say such things as that and to be ready to do so much for the poor little likes of Maisie and me! She has a hold on you, and you know it, and you want to feel it again and – God knows, or at least *I* do, what's your motive and desire – enjoy it once more and give yourself up to it! It doesn't matter if it's one day or three: enough is as good as a feast and the lovely time you'll have with her is something you're willing to pay for! I daresay you'd like me to believe that your pay is to get her to give you up; but that's a matter on which I strongly urge you not to put down your money in advance. Give *her* up first. Then pay her what you please!'

Sir Claude took this to the end, though there were things in it that made him colour, called into his face more of the apprehension than Maisie had ever perceived there of a particular sort of shock. She had an odd sense that it was the first time she had seen anyone but Mrs Wix really and truly scandalized, and this fed her inference, which grew and grew from moment to moment, that Mrs Wix was proving more of a force to reckon with than either of them had allowed so much room for. It was true that, long before, she had obtained a 'hold' of him, as she called it, different in kind from that obtained by Mrs Beale and originally by her ladyship. But Maisie could quite feel with him now that he had really not expected this advantage to be driven so home. Oh they hadn't at all got to where Mrs Wix would stop, for the next minute she was driving harder than ever. It was the result of his saying with a certain dryness, though so kindly that what most affected Maisie in it was his patience: 'My dear friend, it's simply a matter in which I must judge for myself. You've judged *for* me, I know, a good deal, of late, in a way that I appreciate, I assure you, down to the ground. But you can't do it always; no one can do that for another, don't you see, in every case. There are exceptions, particular cases that turn up and that are awfully delicate. It would be too easy if I could shift it all off on you: it would be allowing you to incur an amount of responsibility that I should simply become quite ashamed of. You'll find, I'm sure, that you'll have quite as much as you'll enjoy if you'll be so good as to accept the situation as circumstances happen to make it for you and to stay here with our friend, till I rejoin you, on the footing of as much pleasantness and as much comfort – and I think I have a right to add, to both of you, of as much faith in *me* – as possible.'

Oh he was princely indeed: that came out more and more with every word he said and with the particular way he said it, and Maisie could feel his monitress stiffen almost with anguish against the increase of his spell and then hurl herself as a desperate defence from it into the quite confessed poorness of violence, of iteration. 'You're afraid of her – afraid, afraid, afraid! Oh dear, oh dear, oh dear!' Mrs Wix wailed it with a high quaver, then broke down into a long shudder of helplessness and woe. The next minute she had flung herself again on the lean sofa and had burst into a passion of tears.

Sir Claude stood and looked at her a moment; he shook his head slowly, altogether tenderly. 'I've already admitted it – I'm in mortal terror; so we'll let that settle the question. I think you had best go to bed,' he added; 'you've had a tremendous day and you must both be tired to death. I shall not expect you to concern yourselves in the morning with my movements. There's an early boat on; I shall have cleared out before you're up; and I shall, moreover, have dealt directly and most effectively, I assure you, with the haughty but not quite hopeless Miss Ash.' He turned to his stepdaughter as if at once to take leave of her and give her a sign of how, through all tension and friction, they were still united in such a way that she at least needn't worry. 'Maisie boy!' – he opened his arms to her. With her culpable lightness she flew into them and, while he kissed her, chose the soft method of silence to satisfy him, the silence that after battles of talk was the best balm she could offer his wounds. They held each other long enough to reaffirm intensely their vows; after which they were almost forced apart by Mrs Wix's jumping to her feet.

Her jump, either with a quick return or with a final lapse of courage, was also to supplication almost abject. 'I beseech you not to take a step so miserable and so fatal. I know her but too well, even if you jeer at me for saying it; little as I've seen her I know her, I know her. I know what she'll do – I see it as I stand here. Since you're afraid of her it's the mercy of heaven. Don't, for God's sake, be afraid to show it, to profit by it and to arrive at the very safety that it gives you. *I'm* not afraid of her, I assure you; you must already have seen for yourself that there's nothing I'm afraid of now. Let me go to her – *I'll* settle her and I'll take that woman back without a hair of her touched. Let me put in the two or three days – let me wind up the connexion. You stay here with Maisie, with the carriage and the larks and the luxury; then I'll return to you and we'll go off together – we'll live together without a cloud. Take me, take me,' she went on and on – the tide of her eloquence was high. 'Here I am; I know what I am and what I ain't; but I say boldly to the face of you both that I'll do better for you, far, than ever she'll even try to. I say it to yours, Sir Claude, even though I owe you the very dress on my back and the very shoes on my feet. I owe you everything – that's just the reason; and to pay it back, in profusion, what can that be but what I want? Here I am, here I am!' – she spread herself into an exhibition that, combined with her intensity and her decorations, appeared to suggest her for strange offices and devotions, for ridiculous replacements and substitutions. She manipulated her gown as she talked, she insisted on the items of her debt. 'I have nothing of my own, I know – no money, no clothes, no appearance, no anything, nothing but my hold of this little one truth, which is all in the world I can bribe you with: that the pair of you are more to me than all besides, and that if you'll let me help you and save you, make what you both want possible in the one way it *can* be, why, I'll work myself to the bone in your service!'

Sir Claude wavered there without an answer to this magnificent appeal; he plainly cast about for one, and in no small agitation and pain. He addressed himself in his quest, however, only to vague quarters until he met again, as he so frequently and actively met it, the more than filial gaze of his intelligent little charge. That gave him – poor plastic and dependent male – his issue. If she was still a child she was yet of the sex that could help him out. He signified as much by a renewed invitation to an embrace. She freshly sprang to him and again they inaudibly conversed. 'Be nice to her, be nice to her,' he at last distinctly articulated; 'be nice to her as you've not even been to *me*!' On which, without another look at Mrs Wix, he somehow got out of the room, leaving Maisie under the slight oppression of these words as well as of the idea that he had unmistakably once more dodged.

25

EVERY single thing he had prophesied came so true that it was after all no more than fair to expect quite as much for what he had as good as promised. His pledges they could verify to the letter, down to his very guarantee that a way would be found with Miss Ash. Roused in the summer dawn and vehemently squeezed by that interesting exile, Maisie fell back upon her couch with a renewed appreciation of his policy, a memento of which, when she rose later on to dress, glittered at her from the carpet in the shape of a sixpence that had overflowed from Susan's pride of possession. Sixpences really, for the forty-eight hours that followed, seemed to abound in her life; she fancifully computed the number of them represented by such a period of 'larks'. The number was not kept down, she presently noticed, by any scheme of revenge for Sir Claude's flight which should take on Mrs Wix's part the form of a refusal to avail herself of the facilities he had so bravely ordered. It was in fact impossible to escape them; it was in the good lady's own phrase ridiculous to go on foot when you had a carriage prancing at the door. Everything about them pranced: the very waiters even as they presented the dishes to which, from a similar sense of the absurdity of perversity, Mrs Wix helped herself with a freedom that spoke to Maisie quite as much of her depletion as of her logic. Her appetite was a sign to her companion of a great many things and testified no less on the whole to her general than to her particular condition. She had arrears of dinner to make up, and it was touching that in a dinner-less state her moral passion should have burned so clear. She partook largely as a refuge from depression, and yet the opportunity to partake was just a mark of the sinister symptoms that depressed her. The affair was in short a combat, in which the baser element triumphed, between her refusal to be bought off and her consent to be clothed and fed. It was not at any rate to be gainsaid that there was comfort for her in the developments of France; comfort so great as to leave Maisie free to take with her all the security for granted and brush all the danger aside. That was the way to carry out in detail Sir Claude's injunction to be 'nice'; that was the way, as well, to look, with her, in a survey of the pleasures of life abroad, straight over the head of any doubt.

They shrank at last, all doubts, as the weather cleared up: it had an immense effect on them and became quite as lovely as Sir Claude had engaged. This seemed to have put him so into the secret of things, and the joy of the world so waylaid the steps of his friends, that little by little the spirit of hope filled the air and finally took possession of the scene. To drive on the long cliff was splendid, but it was perhaps better still to creep in the shade – for the sun was strong – along the many-coloured and many-odoured *port* and through the streets in which, to English eyes, everything that was the same was a mystery and everything that was different a joke. Best of all was to continue the creep up the long Grand' Rue to the gate of the *haute ville* and, passing beneath it, mount to the quaint and crooked rampart, with its rows of trees, its quiet corners and friendly benches where brown old women in such white-frilled caps and such long gold ear-rings sat and knitted or snoozed, its little yellow-faced houses that looked like the homes

185

of misers or of priests and its dark château where small soldiers lounged on the bridge that stretched across an empty moat and military washing hung from the windows of towers. This was a part of the place that could lead Maisie to inquire if it didn't just meet one's idea of the middle ages; and since it was rather a satisfaction than a shock to perceive, and not for the first time, the limits in Mrs Wix's mind of the historic imagination, that only added one more to the variety of kinds of insight that she felt it her own present mission to show. They sat together on the old grey bastion; they looked down on the little new town which seemed to them quite as old, and across at the great dome and the high gilt Virgin of the church that, as they gathered, was famous and that pleased them by its unlikeness to any place in which they had worshipped. They wandered in this temple afterwards and Mrs Wix confessed that for herself she had probably made a fatal mistake early in life in not being a Catholic. Her confession in its turn caused Maisie to wonder rather interestedly what degree of lateness it was that shut the door against an escape from such an error. They went back to the rampart on the second morning – the spot on which they appeared to have come furthest in the journey that was to separate them from everything objectionable in the past: it gave them afresh the impression that had most to do with their having worked round to a confidence that on Maisie's part was determined and that she could see to be on her companion's desperate. She had had for many hours the sense of showing Mrs Wix so much that she was comparatively slow to become conscious of being at the same time the subject of a like aim. The business went the faster, however, from the moment she got her glimpse of it; it then fell into its place in her general, her habitual view of the particular phenomenon that, had she felt the need of words for it, she might have called her personal relation to her knowledge. This relation had never been so lively as during the time she waited with her old governess for Sir Claude's reappearance, and what made it so was exactly that Mrs Wix struck her as having a new suspicion of it. Mrs Wix had never yet had a suspicion – this was certain – so calculated to throw her pupil, in spite of the closer union of such adventurous hours, upon the deep defensive. Her pupil made out indeed as many marvels as she had made out on the rush to Folkestone; and if in Sir Claude's

186

company on that occasion Mrs Wix was the constant implication, so in Mrs Wix's, during these hours, Sir Claude was – and most of all through long pauses – the perpetual, the insurmountable theme. It all took them back to the first flush of his marriage and to the place he held in the schoolroom at that crisis of love and pain; only he had himself blown to a much bigger balloon the large consciousness he then filled out.

They went through it all again, and indeed while the interval dragged by the very weight of its charm they went, in spite of defences and suspicions, through everything. Their intensified clutch of the future throbbed like a clock ticking seconds; but this was a timepiece that inevitably, as well, at the best, rang occasionally a portentous hour. Oh there were several of these, and two or three of the worst on the old city-wall where everything else so made for peace. There was nothing in the world Maisie more wanted than to be as nice to Mrs Wix as Sir Claude had desired; but it was exactly because this fell in with her inveterate instinct of keeping the peace that the instinct itself was quickened. From the moment it was quickened, however, it found other work, and that was how, to begin with, she produced the very complication she most sought to avert. What she had essentially done, these days, had been to read the unspoken into the spoken; so that thus, with accumulations, it had become more definite to her that the unspoken was, unspeakably, the completeness of the sacrifice of Mrs Beale. There were times when every minute that Sir Claude stayed away was like a nail in Mrs Beale's coffin. That brought back to Maisie – it was a roundabout way – the beauty and antiquity of her connexion with the flower of the Overmores as well as that lady's own grace and charm, her peculiar prettiness and cleverness and even her peculiar tribulations. A hundred things hummed at the back of her head, but two of these were simple enough. Mrs Beale was by the way, after all, just her stepmother and her relative. She was just – and partly for that very reason – Sir Claude's greatest intimate ('lady-intimate' was Maisie's term), so that what together they were on Mrs Wix's prescription to give up and break short off with was for one of them his particular favourite and for the other her father's wife. Strangely, indescribably her perception of reasons kept pace with her sense of trouble; but there was something in her that, without

187

a supreme effort not to be shabby, couldn't take the reasons for granted. What it comes to perhaps for ourselves is that, disinherited and denuded as we have seen her, there still lingered in her life an echo of parental influence – she was still reminiscent of one of the sacred lessons of home. It was the only one she retained, but luckily she retained it with force. She enjoyed in a word an ineffaceable view of the fact that there were things papa called mamma and mamma called papa a low sneak for doing or for not doing. Now this rich memory gave her a name that she dreaded to invite to the lips of Mrs Beale: she should personally wince so just to hear it. The very sweetness of the foreign life she was steeped in added with each hour of Sir Claude's absence to the possibility of such pangs. She watched beside Mrs Wix the great golden Madonna, and one of the ear-ringed old women who had been sitting at the end of their bench got up and pottered away.

'Adieu, mesdames!' said the old woman in a little cracked civil voice – a demonstration by which our friends were so affected that they bobbed up and almost curtseyed to her. They subsided again, and it was shortly after, in a summer hum of French insects and a phase of almost somnolent reverie, that Maisie most had the vision of what it was to shut out from such a perspective so appealing a participant. It had not yet appeared so vast as at that moment, this prospect of statues shining in the blue and of courtesy in romantic forms.

'Why after all should we have to choose between you? Why shouldn't we be four?' she finally demanded.

Mrs Wix gave the jerk of a sleeper awakened or the start even of one who hears a bullet whiz at the flag of truce. Her stupefaction at such a breach of the peace delayed for a moment her answer. 'Four improprieties, do you mean? Because two of us happen to be decent people! Do I gather you to wish that I should stay on with you even if that woman *is* capable – ?'

Maisie took her up before she could further phrase Mrs Beale's capability. 'Stay on as *my* companion – yes. Stay on as just what you were at mamma's. Mrs Beale *would* let you!' the child said.

Mrs Wix had by this time fairly sprung to her arms. 'And who, I'd like to know, would let Mrs Beale? Do you mean, little unfortunate, that *you* would?'

'Why not, if now she's free?'

'Free? Are you imitating *him*? Well, if Sir Claude's old enough to know better, upon my word I think it's right to treat you as if you also were. You'll have to, at any rate – to know better – if that's the line you're proposing to take.' Mrs Wix had never been so harsh; but on the other hand Maisie could guess that she herself had never appeared so wanton. What was underlying, however, rather overawed than angered her; she felt she could still insist – not for contradiction, but for ultimate calm. Her wantonness meanwhile continued to work upon her friend, who caught again, on the rebound, the sound of deepest provocation. 'Free, free, free? If she's as free as *you* are, my dear, she's free enough, to be sure!'

'As I am?' – Maisie, after reflexion and despite whatever of portentous this seemed to convey, risked a critical echo.

'Well,' said Mrs Wix, 'nobody, you know, is free to commit a crime.'

'A crime!' The word had come out in a way that made the child sound it again.

'You'd commit as great a one as their own – and so should I – if we were to condone their immorality by our presence.'

Maisie waited a little; this seemed so fiercely conclusive. 'Why is it immorality?' she nevertheless presently inquired.

Her companion now turned upon her with a reproach softer because it was somehow deeper. 'You're too unspeakable! Do you know what we're talking about?'

In the interest of ultimate calm Maisie felt that she must be above all clear. 'Certainly; about their taking advantage of their freedom.'

'Well, to do what?'

'Why, to live with us.'

Mrs Wix's laugh, at this, was literally wild. '"Us?" Thank you!'

'Then to live with *me*.'

The words made her friend jump. 'You give me up? You break with me for ever? You turn me into the street?'

Maisie, though gasping a little, bore up under the rain of challenges. 'Those, it seems to me, are the things you do to *me*.'

Mrs Wix made little of her valour. 'I can promise you that,

189

whatever I do, I shall never let you out of my sight! You ask me why it's immorality when you've seen with your own eyes that Sir Claude has felt it to be so to that dire extent that, rather than make you face the shame of it, he has for months kept away from you altogether? Is it any more difficult to see that the first time he tries to do his duty he washes his hands of *her* – takes you straight away from her?'

Maisie turned this over, but more for apparent consideration than from any impulse to yield too easily. 'Yes, I see what you mean. But at that time they weren't free.' She felt Mrs Wix rear up again at the offensive word, but she succeeded in touching her with a remonstrant hand. 'I don't think you know how free they've become.'

'I know, I believe, at least as much as you do!'

Maisie felt a delicacy but overcame it. 'About the Countess?'

'Your father's – temptress?' Mrs Wix gave her a sidelong squint. 'Perfectly. She pays him!'

'Oh *does* she?' At this the child's countenance fell: it seemed to give a reason for papa's behaviour and place it in a more favourable light. She wished to be just. 'I don't say she's not generous. She was so to me.'

'How, to you?'

'She gave me a lot of money.'

Mrs Wix stared. 'And pray what did you do with a lot of money?'

'I gave it to Mrs Beale.'

'And what did Mrs Beale do with it?'

'She sent it back.'

'To the Countess? Gammon!' said Mrs Wix. She disposed of that plea as effectually as Susan Ash.

'Well, I don't care!' Maisie replied. 'What I mean is that you don't know about the rest.'

'The rest? What rest?'

Maisie wondered how she could best put it. 'Papa kept me there an hour.'

'I do know – Sir Claude told me. Mrs Beale had told him.'

Maisie looked incredulity. 'How could she – when I didn't speak of it?'

Mrs Wix was mystified. 'Speak of what?'

190

'Why, of her being so frightful.'

'The Countess? Of course she's frightful!' Mrs Wix returned. After a moment she added: 'That's why she pays him.'

Maisie pondered. 'It's the best thing about her, then – if she gives him as much as she gave *me*.'

'Well, it's not the best thing about *him*! Or rather perhaps it *is* too!' Mrs Wix subjoined.

'But she's awful – really and truly,' Maisie went on.

Mrs Wix arrested her. 'You needn't go into details!' It was visibly at variance with this injunction that she yet inquired: 'How does that make it any better?'

'Their living with me? Why for the Countess – and for her whiskers! – he has put me off on them. I understood him,' Maisie profoundly said.

'I hope, then, he understood you. It's more than I do!' Mrs Wix admitted.

This was a real challenge to be plainer, and our young lady immediately became so. 'I mean it isn't a crime.'

'Why, then, did Sir Claude steal you away?'

'He didn't steal – he only borrowed me. I knew it wasn't for long,' Maisie audaciously professed.

'You must allow me to reply to that,' cried Mrs Wix, 'that you knew nothing of the sort, and that you rather basely failed to back me up last night when you pretended so plump that you did! You hoped in fact, exactly as much as I did and as in my senseless passion I even hope now, that this may be the beginning of better things.'

Oh yes, Mrs Wix was indeed, for the first time, sharp; so that there at last stirred in our heroine the sense not so much of being proved disingenuous as of being precisely accused of the meanness that had brought everything down on her through her very desire to shake herself clear of it. She suddenly felt herself swell with a passion of protest. 'I never, *never* hoped I wasn't going again to see Mrs Beale! I didn't, I didn't!' she repeated. Mrs Wix bounced about with a force of rejoinder of which she also felt that she must anticipate the concussion and which, though the good lady was evidently charged to the brim, hung fire long enough to give time for an aggravation. 'She's beautiful and I love her! I love her and she's beautiful!'

'And I'm hideous and you hate *me*?' Mrs Wix fixed her a moment, then caught herself up. 'I won't embitter you by absolutely accusing you of that; though, as for my being hideous, it's hardly the first time I've been told so! I know it so well that even if I haven't whiskers – have I? – I daresay there are other ways in which the Countess is a Venus to me! My pretensions must therefore seem to you monstrous – which comes to the same thing as your not liking me. But do you mean to go so far as to tell me that you *want* to live with them in their sin?'

'You know what I want, you know what I want!' – Maisie spoke with the shudder of rising tears.

'Yes, I do; you want me to be as bad as yourself! Well, I won't. There! Mrs Beale's as bad as your father!' Mrs Wix went on.

'She's not! – she's not!' her pupil almost shrieked in retort.

'You mean because Sir Claude at least has beauty and wit and grace? But he pays just as the Countess pays!' Mrs Wix, who now rose as she spoke, fairly revealed a latent cynicism.

It raised Maisie also to her feet; her companion had walked off a few steps and paused. The two looked at each other as they had never looked, and Mrs Wix seemed to flaunt there in her finery. 'Then doesn't he pay *you* too!' her unhappy charge demanded.

At this she bounded in her place. 'Oh you incredible little waif!' She brought it out with a wail of violence; after which, with another convulsion, she marched straight away.

Maisie dropped back on the bench and burst into sobs.

26

NOTHING so dreadful of course could be final or even for many minutes prolonged: they rushed together again too soon for either to feel that either had kept it up, and though they went home in silence it was with a vivid perception for Maisie that her companion's hand had closed upon her. That hand had shown altogether, these twenty-four hours, a new capacity for closing, and one of the truths the child could least resist was that a certain greatness had now come to Mrs Wix. The case was indeed that the quality of her motive surpassed the sharpness of her angles; both the combination and the singularity of which things, when in the afternoon they used the carriage, Maisie could borrow from the contemplative hush of their grandeur the freedom to feel to the utmost. She still bore the mark of the tone in which her friend had thrown out that threat of never losing sight of her. This friend had been converted in short from feebleness to force; and it was the light of her new authority that showed from how far she had come. The threat in question, sharply exultant, might have produced defiance; but before anything so ugly could happen another process had insidiously forestalled it. The moment at which this process had begun to mature was that of Mrs Wix's breaking out with a dignity attuned to their own apartments and with an advantage now measurably gained. They had ordered coffee after luncheon, in the spirit of Sir Claude's provision, and it was served to them while they awaited their equipage in the white and gold salon. It was flanked, moreover, with a couple of liqueurs, and Maisie felt that Sir Claude could scarce have been taken more at his word had it been followed by anecdotes and cigarettes. The influence of these luxuries was at any rate in the air. It seemed to her while she tiptoed at the chimney-glass, pulling on her gloves and with a motion of her head shaking a feather into place, to have had something to do with Mrs Wix's suddenly saying: 'Haven't you really and truly *any* moral sense?'

Maisie was aware that her answer, though it brought her down to her heels, was vague even to imbecility, and that this was the first time she had appeared to practise with Mrs Wix an intellectual inaptitude to meet her – the infirmity to which she had owed so much success with papa and mamma. The appearance did her injustice, for it was not less through her candour than through her playfellow's pressure that after this the idea of a moral sense mainly coloured their intercourse. She began, the poor child, with scarcely knowing what it was; but it proved something that, with scarce an outward sign save her surrender to the swing of the carriage, she could, before they came back from their drive, strike up a sort of acquaintance with. The beauty of the day only deepened, and the splendour of the afternoon sea, and the haze of the far headlands, and the taste of the sweet air. It was the coachman indeed who, smiling and cracking his whip, turning in his place, pointing to invisible objects and uttering unintelligible sounds – all, our tourists recognized, strict features of a social order principally devoted to language: it was this polite person, I say, who made their excursion fall so much short 'that their return left them still a stretch of the long daylight and an hour that, at his obliging suggestion, they spent on foot by the shining sands. Maisie had seen the *plage* the day before with Sir Claude, but that was a reason the more for showing on the spot to Mrs Wix that it was, as she said, another of the places on her list and of the things of which she knew the French name. The bathers, so late, were absent and the tide was low; the sea-pools twinkled in the sunset and there were dry places as well, where they could sit again and admire and expatiate: a circumstance that, while they listened to the lap of the waves, gave Mrs Wix a fresh support for her challenge. 'Have you absolutely none at all?'

She had no need now, as to the question itself at least, to be specific; that on the other hand was the eventual result of their quiet conjoined apprehension of the thing that – well, yes, since they must face it – Maisie absolutely and appallingly had so little of. This marked more particularly the moment of the child's perceiving that her friend had risen to a level which might – till superseded at all events – pass almost for sublime. Nothing more remarkable had taken place in the first heat of her own departure, no act of perception less to be overtraced by our rough method, than her vision, the rest of that Boulogne day, of the manner in which she figured. I so despair of courting her noiseless mental footsteps here that I must crudely give you my word for its being from this time forward a picture literally present to her. Mrs Wix saw her as a little person knowing so extraordinarily much that, for the account to be taken of it, what she still didn't know would be ridiculous if it hadn't been embarrassing. Mrs Wix was in truth more than ever qualified to meet embarrassment; I am not sure that Maisie had not even a dim discernment of the queer law of her own life that made her educate to that sort of proficiency those elders with whom she was concerned. She promoted, as it were, their development; nothing could have been more marked, for instance, than her success in promoting Mrs Beale's. She judged that if her whole history, for Mrs Wix, had been the successive stages of her knowledge, so the very climax of the concatenation would, in the same view, be the stage at which the knowledge should overflow. As she was condemned to know more and more, how could it logically stop before she should know Most? It came to her in fact as they sat there on the sands that she was distinctly on the road to know Everything. She had not had governesses for nothing: what in the world had she ever done but learn and learn and learn? She looked at the pink sky with a placid foreboding that she soon should have learnt All. They lingered in the flushed air till at last it turned to grey and she seemed fairly to receive new information from every brush of the breeze. By the time they moved homeward it was as if this inevitability had become for Mrs Wix a long tense cord, twitched by a nervous hand, on which the valued pearls of intelligence were to be neatly strung.

In the evening upstairs they had another strange sensation, as to which Maisie couldn't afterwards have told you whether it was bang in the middle or quite at the beginning that her companion sounded with fresh emphasis the note of the moral sense. What mattered was merely that she did exclaim, and again, as at first appeared, most disconnectedly: 'God help me, it does seem to peep out!' Oh the queer confusions that had wooed it at last to such peeping! None so queer, however, as the words of woe, and it might verily be said of rage, in which the poor lady bewailed the tragic end of her own rich ignorance. There was a point at which she seized the child and hugged her as close as in the old days of partings and returns; at which she was visibly at a loss how to make up to such a victim for such contaminations: appealing, as to what she had done and was doing, in bewilderment, in explanation, in supplication, for reassurance, for pardon and even outright for pity.

'I don't know what I've said to you, my own: I don't know what I'm saying or what the turn you've given my life has rendered me, heaven forgive me, capable of saying. Have I lost all delicacy, all decency, all measure of how far and how bad? It seems to me mostly that I have, though I'm the last of whom you would ever have thought it. I've just done it for *you*, precious – not to lose you, which would have been worst of all: so that I've had to pay with my own innocence, if you do laugh! for clinging

195

to you and keeping you. Don't let me pay for nothing; don't let me have been thrust for nothing into such horrors and such shames. I never knew anything about them and I never wanted to know! Now I know too much, too much!' the poor woman lamented and groaned. 'I know so much that with hearing such talk I ask myself where I am; and with uttering it too, which is worse, say to myself that I'm far, too far, from where I started! I ask myself what I should have thought with my lost one if I had heard myself cross the line. There are lines I've crossed with *you* where I should have fancied I had come to a pretty pass – !' She gasped at the mere supposition. 'I've gone from one thing to another, and all for the real love of you; and now what would any-one say – I mean anyone but *them* – if they were to hear the way I go on? I've had to keep up with you, haven't I? – and therefore what could I do less than look to you to keep up with *me*? But it's not *them* that are the worst – by which I mean to say it's not *him*: it's your dreadfully base papa and the one person in the world whom he could have found, I do believe – and she's not the Countess, duck – wickeder than himself. While they were about it at any rate, since they *were* ruining you, they might have done it so as to spare an honest woman. Then I shouldn't have had to do whatever it is that's the worst: throw up at you the badness you haven't taken in, or find my advantage in the vileness you *have*! What I did lose patience at this morning was at how it was that without your seeming to condemn – for you didn't, you re-member! – you yet did seem to *know*. Thank God, in his mercy, at last, *if* you do!'

The night, this time, was warm and one of the windows stood open to the small balcony over the rail of which, on coming up from dinner, Maisie had hung a long time in the enjoyment of the chatter, the lights, the life of the quay made brilliant by the season and the hour. Mrs Wix's requirements had drawn her in from this posture and Mrs Wix's embrace had detained her even though midway in the outpouring her confusion and sympathy had per-mitted, or rather had positively helped, her to disengage herself. But the casement was still wide, the spectacle, the pleasure were still there, and from her place in the room, which, with its polished floor and its panels of elegance, was lighted from without more than from within, the child could still take account of them.

She appeared to watch and listen; after which she answered Mrs Wix with a question. 'If I do know – ?'

'If you do condemn.' The correction was made with some austerity.

It had the effect of causing Maisie to heave a vague sigh of oppression and then after an instant and as if under cover of this ambiguity pass out again upon the balcony. She hung again over the rail; she felt the summer night; she dropped down into the manners of France. There was a café below the hotel, before which, with little chairs and tables, people sat on a space enclosed by plants in tubs; and the impression was enriched by the flash of the white aprons of waiters and the music of a man and a woman who, from beyond the precinct, sent up the strum of a guitar and the drawl of a song about 'amour'. Maisie knew what 'amour' meant too, and wondered if Mrs Wix did: Mrs Wix remained within, as still as a mouse and perhaps not reached by the performance. After a while, but not till the musicians had ceased and begun to circulate with a little plate, her pupil came back to her. '*Is* it a crime?' Maisie then asked.

Mrs Wix was as prompt as if she had been crouching in a lair. 'Branded by the Bible.'

'Well, he won't commit a crime.'

Mrs Wix looked at her gloomily. 'He's committing one now.'

'Now?'

'In being with her.'

Maisie had it on her tongue's end to return once more: 'But now he's free.' She remembered, however, in time that one of the things she had known for the last entire hour was that this made no difference. After that, and as if to turn the right way, she was on the point of a blind dash, a weak reversion to the reminder that it might make a difference, might diminish the crime for Mrs Beale; till such a reflexion was in its order also quashed by the visibility in Mrs Wix's face of the collapse produced by her inference from her pupil's manner that after all her pains her pupil didn't even yet adequately understand. Never so much as when confronted had Maisie wanted to understand, and all her thought for a minute centred in the effort to come out with something which should be a disproof of her simplicity. 'Just *trust* me, dear; that's all!' – she came out finally with that; and it was perhaps a

197

good sign of her action that with a long impartial moan Mrs Wix floated her to bed.

There was no letter the next morning from Sir Claude – which Mrs Wix let out that she deemed the worst of omens; yet it was just for the quieter communion they so got with him that, when after the coffee and rolls which made them more foreign than ever, it came to going forth for fresh drafts upon his credit, they wandered again up the hill to the rampart instead of plunging into distraction with the crowd on the sands or into the sea with the semi-nude bathers. They gazed once more at their gilded Virgin; they sank once more upon their battered bench; they felt once more their distance from the Regent's Park. At last Mrs Wix became definite about their friend's silence. 'He *is* afraid of her! She has forbidden him to write.' The fact of his fear Maisie already knew; but her companion's mention of it had at this moment two unexpected results. The first was her wondering in dumb remonstrance how Mrs Wix, with a devotion not after all inferior to her own, could put into such an allusion such a grimness of derision; the second was that she found herself suddenly drop into a deeper view of it. She too had been afraid, as we have seen, of the people of whom Sir Claude was afraid, and by that law she had had her due measure of latent apprehension of Mrs Beale. What occurred at present, however, was that, whereas this sympathy appeared vain as for him, the ground of it loomed dimly as a reason for selfish alarm. That uneasiness had not carried her far before Mrs Wix spoke again and with an abruptness so great as almost to seem irrelevant. 'Has it never occurred to you to be jealous of her?'

It never had in the least; yet the words were scarce in the air before Maisie had jumped at them. She held them well, she looked at them hard; at last she brought out with an assurance which there was no one, alas, but herself to admire: 'Well, yes – since you ask me.' She debated, then continued: 'Lots of times!'

Mrs Wix glared askance an instant; such approval as her look expressed was not wholly unqualified. It expressed at any rate something that presumably had to do with her saying once more: 'Yes. He's afraid of her.'

Maisie heard, and it had afresh its effect on her even through the blur of the attention now required by the possibility of that idea of jealousy – a possibility created only by her feeling she had thus found the way to show she was not simple. It struck out of Mrs Wix that this lady still believed her moral sense to be interested and feigned; so what could be such a gage of her sincerity as a peep of the most restless of the passions? Such a revelation would baffle discouragement, and discouragement was in fact so baffled that, helped in some degree by the mere intensity of their need to hope, which also, according to its nature, sprang from the dark portent of the absent letter, the real pitch of their morning was reached by the note, not of mutual scrutiny, but of unprecedented frankness. There were broodings indeed and silences, and Maisie sank deeper into the vision that for her friend she was, at the most, superficial, and that also, positively, she was the more so the more she tried to appear complete. Was the sum of all knowledge only to know how little in his presence one would ever reach it? The answer to that question luckily lost itself in the brightness suffusing the scene as soon as Maisie had thrown out in regard to Mrs Beale such a remark as she had never dreamed she should live to make. 'If I thought she was unkind to him – I don't know *what* I should do!'

Mrs Wix dropped one of her squints; she even confirmed it by a wild grunt. 'I know what *I* should!'

Maisie at this felt that she lagged. 'Well, I can think of *one* thing.'

Mrs Wix more directly challenged her. 'What is it, then?'

Maisie met her expression as if it were a game with forfeits for winking. 'I'd *kill* her!' That at least, she hoped as she looked away, would guarantee her moral sense. She looked away, but her companion said nothing for so long that she at last turned her head again. Then she saw the straighteners all blurred with tears which after a little seemed to have sprung from her own eyes. There were tears in fact on both sides of the spectacles, and they were even so thick that it was presently all Maisie could do to make out through them that slowly, finally Mrs Wix put forth a hand. It was the material pressure that settled this and even at the end of some minutes more things besides. It settled in its own way one thing in particular, which, though often, between them, heaven knew, hovered round and hung over, was yet to be established without the shadow of an attenuating smile. Oh there was no gleam of levity, as little of humour as of deprecation, in the long time they now sat together or in which at some unmeasured point of it Mrs Wix became distinct enough for her own dignity and yet not loud enough for the snoozing old women.

'I adore him. I adore him.'

Maisie took it well in; so well that in a moment more she would have answered profoundly: 'So do I.' But before that moment passed something took place that brought other words to her lips; nothing more, very possibly, than the closer consciousness in her hand of the significance of Mrs Wix's. Their hands remained linked in unutterable sign of their union, and what Maisie at last said was simply and serenely: 'Oh I know!'

Their hands were so linked and their union was so confirmed that it took the far deep note of a bell, borne to them on the summer air, to call them back to a sense of hours and proprieties. They had touched bottom and melted together, but they gave a start at last: the bell was the voice of the inn and the inn was the image of luncheon. They should be late for it; they got up, and their quickened step on the return had something of the swing of confidence. When they reached the hotel the *table d'hôte* had begun; this was clear from the threshold, clear from the absence in the hall and on the stairs of the 'personnel', as Mrs Wix said – she had picked *that* up – all collected in the dining-room. They mounted to their apartments for a brush before the glass, and it was Maisie who, in passing and from a vain impulse, threw open the white and gold door. She was thus first to utter the sound that brought Mrs Wix almost on top of her, as by the other accident it would have brought her on top of Mrs Wix. It had at any rate the effect of leaving them bunched together in a strained stare at their new situation. This situation had put on in a flash the bright form of Mrs Beale: she stood there in her hat and her jacket, amid bags and shawls, smiling and holding out her arms. If she had just arrived it was a different figure from either of the two that for *their* benefit, wan and tottering and none too soon to save life, the Channel had recently disgorged. She was as lovely as the day that had brought her over, as fresh as the luck and the health that attended her: it came to Maisie on the spot that she was more beautiful than she had ever been. All this was too quick to count, but there was still time in it to give the child the sense of what had

200

kindled the light. That leaped out of the open arms, the open eyes, the open mouth; it leaped out with Mrs Beale's loud cry at her: 'I'm free, I'm free!'

27

THE greatest wonder of all was the way Mrs Beale addressed her announcement, so far as could be judged, equally to Mrs Wix, who, as if from sudden failure of strength, sank into a chair while Maisie surrendered to the visitor's embrace. As soon as the child was liberated she met with profundity Mrs Wix's stupefaction and actually was able to see that while in a manner sustaining the encounter her face yet seemed with intensity to say: 'Now, for God's sake, don't crow "I told you so!"' Maisie was somehow on the spot aware of an absence of disposition to crow; it had taken her but an extra minute to arrive at such a quick survey of the objects surrounding Mrs Beale as showed that among them was no appurtenance of Sir Claude's. She knew his dressing-bag now – oh with the fondest knowledge! – and there was an instant during which its not being there was a stroke of the worst news. She was yet to learn what it could be to recognize in some lapse of a sequence the proof of an extinction, and therefore remained unaware that this momentary pang was a foretaste of the experience of death. It of course yielded in a flash to Mrs Beale's brightness, it gasped itself away in her own instant appeal. 'You've come alone?'

'Without Sir Claude?' Strangely, Mrs Beale looked even brighter. 'Yes, in the eagerness to get at you. You abominable little villain!' – and her stepmother, laughing clear, administered to her cheek a pat that was partly a pinch. 'What were you up to and what did you take me for? But I'm glad to be abroad, and after all it's you who have shown me the way. I mightn't, without you, have been able to come – to come, that is, so soon. Well, here I am at any rate and in a moment more I should have begun to worry about you. This will do very well' – she was good-natured about the place and even presently added that it was charming. Then with a rosier glow she made again her great point: 'I'm free, I'm free!' Maisie made on her side her own: she carried back her gaze to Mrs Wix, whom amazement continued to hold; she drew afresh her old friend's attention to the superior way she didn't take that up. What she did take up the next minute was the question of Sir Claude. 'Where is he? Won't he come?'

Mrs Beale's consideration of this oscillated with a smile between the two expectancies with which she was flanked: it was conspicuous, it was extraordinary, her unblinking acceptance of Mrs Wix, a miracle of which Maisie had even now begun to read a reflexion in that lady's long visage. 'He'll come, but we must *make* him!' she gaily brought forth.

'Make him?' Maisie echoed.

'We must give him time. We must play our cards.'

'But he promised us awfully,' Maisie replied.

'My dear child, he has promised *me* awfully; I mean lots of things, and not in every case kept his promise to the letter.' Mrs Beale's good humour insisted on taking for granted Mrs Wix's, to whom her attention had suddenly grown prodigious. 'I daresay he has done the same with you, and not always come to time. But he makes it up in his own way – and it isn't as if we didn't know exactly what he is. There's one thing he is,' she went on, 'which makes everything else only a question, for us, of tact.' They scarce had time to wonder what this was before, as they might have said, it flew straight into their face. 'He's as free as I am!'

'Yes, I know,' said Maisie; as if, however, independently weighing the value of that. She really weighed also the oddity of her stepmother's treating it as news to *her*, who had been the first person literally to whom Sir Claude had mentioned it. For a few seconds, as if with the sound of it in her ears, she stood with him again, in memory and in the twilight, in the hotel garden at Folkestone.

Anything Mrs Beale overlooked was, she indeed divined, but the effect of an exaltation of high spirits, a tendency to soar that showed even when she dropped – still quite impartially – almost to the confidential. 'Well, then – we've only to wait. He can't do without us long. I'm sure, Mrs Wix, he can't do without *you*! He's devoted to you; he has told me so much about you. The extent I count on you, you know, count on you to help me – !' was an extent that even all her radiance couldn't express. What it couldn't express quite as much as what it could made at any rate every instant her presence and even her famous freedom loom larger; and it was this mighty mass that once more led her companions, bewildered and disjoined, to exchange with each other as through a thickening veil confused and ineffectual signs. They clung together at least on the common ground of unpreparedness, and Maisie watched without relief the havoc of wonder in Mrs Wix. It had reduced her to perfect impotence, and, but that gloom was black upon her, she sat as if fascinated by Mrs Beale's high style. It had plunged her into a long deep hush; for what had happened was the thing she had least allowed for and before which the particular rigour she had worked up could only grow limp and sick. Sir Claude was to have reappeared with his accomplice or without her; never, never his accomplice without *him*. Mrs Beale had gained apparently by this time an advantage she could pursue: she looked at the droll dumb figure with jesting reproach. 'You really won't shake hands with me? Never mind; you'll come round!' She put the matter to no test, going on immediately and, instead of offering her hand, raising it, with a pretty gesture that her bent head met, to a long black pin that played a part in her black hair. 'Are hats worn at luncheon? If you're as hungry as I am we must go right down.'

Mrs Wix stuck fast, but she met the question in a voice her pupil scarce recognized. 'I wear mine.'

Mrs Beale, swallowing at one glance her brand-new bravery, which she appeared at once to refer to its origin and to follow in its flights, accepted this as conclusive. 'Oh but I've not such a beauty!' Then she turned rejoicingly to Maisie. 'I've got a beauty for *you*, my dear.'

'A beauty?'

'A love of a hat – in my luggage. I remembered *that*' – she nodded at the object on her stepdaughter's head – 'and I've brought you one with a peacock's breast. It's the most gorgeous blue!'

It was too strange, this talking with her there already not about Sir Claude but about peacocks – too strange for the child to have the presence of mind to thank her. But the felicity in which she had arrived was so proof against everything that Maisie felt more and more 'the depth of the purpose that must underlie it. She had a vague sense of its being abysmal, the spirit with which Mrs Beale carried off the awkwardness, in the white and gold salon, of such a want of breath and of welcome. Mrs Wix was more breathless than ever; the embarrassment of Mrs Beale's isolation was as nothing to the embarrassment of her grace. The perception of this dilemma was the germ on the child's part of a new question altogether. What if *with* this indulgence – ? But the idea lost itself in something too frightened for hope and too conjectured for fear; and while everything went by leaps and bounds one of the waiters stood at the door to remind them that the *table d'hôte* was half over.

'Had you come up to wash hands?' Mrs Beale hereupon asked them. 'Go and do it quickly and I'll be with you: they've put my boxes in that nice room – it was Sir Claude's. Trust him,' she laughed, 'to have a nice one!' The door of a neighbouring room stood open, and now from the threshold, addressing herself again to Mrs Wix, she launched a note that gave the very key of what, as she would have said, she was up to. 'Dear lady, please attend to my daughter.'

She was up to a change of deportment so complete that it represented – oh for offices still honourably subordinate if not too explicitly menial – an absolute coercion, an interested clutch of the old woman's respectability. There was response, to Maisie's view, I may say at once, in the jump of that respectability to its feet: it was itself capable of one of the leaps, one of the bounds just mentioned, and it carried its charge, with this momentum and while Mrs Beale popped into Sir Claude's chamber, straight away to where, at the end of the passage, pupil and governess were quartered. The greatest stride of all, for that matter, was that within a few seconds the pupil had, in another relation, been converted into a daughter. Maisie's eyes were still following it when, after the rush, with the door almost slammed and no thought of soap and towels, the pair stood face to face. Mrs Wix, in this position, was the first to gasp a sound. 'Can it ever be that she has one?'

Maisie felt still more bewildered. 'One what?'

'Why, moral sense.'

They spoke as if you might have two, but Mrs Wix looked as

if it were not altogether a happy thought, and Maisie didn't see how even an affirmative from her own lips would clear up what had become most of a mystery. It was to this larger puzzle she sprang pretty straight. '*Is* she my mother now?'

It was a point as to which an horrific glimpse of the responsibility of an opinion appeared to affect Mrs Wix like a blow in the stomach. She had evidently never thought of it; but she could think and rebound. 'If she is, he's equally your father.'

Maisie, however, thought further. 'Then my father and my mother – !'

But she had already faltered and Mrs Wix had already glared back: 'Ought to live together? Don't begin it *again*!' She turned away with a groan, to reach the washing-stand, and Maisie could by this time recognize with a certain ease that that way verily madness did lie. Mrs Wix gave a great untidy splash, but the next instant had faced round. 'She has taken a new line.'

'She was nice to you,' Maisie concurred.

'What *she* thinks so – "go and dress the young lady!" But it's something!' she panted. Then she thought out the rest. 'If he won't have her, why she'll have *you*. She'll be the one.'

'The one to keep me abroad?'

'The one to give you a home.' Mrs Wix saw further; she mastered all the portents. 'Oh she's cruelly clever! It's not a moral sense.' She reached her climax: 'It's a game!'

'A game?'

'Not to lose him. She has sacrificed him – to her duty.'

'Then won't he come?' Maisie pleaded.

Mrs Wix made no answer; her vision absorbed her. 'He has fought. But she has won.'

'Then won't he come?' the child repeated.

Mrs Wix made it out. 'Yes, hang him!' She had never been so profane.

For all Maisie minded! 'Soon – tomorrow?'

'Too soon – whenever. Indecently soon.'

'But then we *shall* be together!' the child went on. It made Mrs Wix look at her as if in exasperation; but nothing had time to come before she precipitated: 'Together with *you*!' The air of criticism continued, but took voice only in her companion's bidding her wash herself and come down. The silence of quick

205

ablutions fell upon them, presently broken, however, by one of Maisie's sudden reversions. 'Mercy, isn't she handsome?'

Mrs Wix had finished; she waited. 'She'll attract attention.' They were rapid, and it would have been noticed that the shock the beauty had given them acted, incongruously, as a positive spur to their preparations for rejoining her. She had none the less, when they returned to the sitting-room, already descended; the open door of her room showed it empty and the chambermaid explained. Here again they were delayed by another sharp thought of Mrs Wix's. 'But what will she live on meanwhile?'

Maisie stopped short. 'Till Sir Claude comes?'

It was nothing to the violence with which her friend had been arrested. 'Who'll pay the bills?'

Maisie thought. 'Can't *she*?'

'She? She hasn't a penny.'

The child wondered. 'But didn't papa – ?'

'Leave her a fortune?' Mrs Wix would have appeared to speak of papa as dead had she not immediately added: 'Why he lives on other women!'

Oh yes, Maisie remembered. 'Then can't he send – ?' She faltered again; even to herself it sounded queer.

'Some of their money to his wife?' Mrs Wix gave a laugh still stranger than the weird suggestion. 'I daresay she'd take it!'

They hurried on again; yet again, on the stairs, Maisie pulled up. 'Well, if she had stopped in England – !' she threw out.

Mrs Wix considered. 'And he had come over instead?'

'Yes, as we expected.' Maisie launched her speculation. 'What, then, would she have lived on?'

Mrs Wix hung fire but an instant. 'On other men!' And she marched downstairs.

28

MRS BEALE, at table between the pair, plainly attracted the attention Mrs Wix had foretold. No other lady present was nearly so handsome, nor did the beauty of any other accommodate itself with such art to the homage it produced. She talked mainly to her other neighbour, and that left Maisie leisure both to note the manner in which eyes were riveted and nudges interchanged, and to lose herself in the meanings that, dimly as yet and disconnectedly, but with a vividness that fed apprehension, she could begin to read into her stepmother's independent move. Mrs Wix had helped her by talking of a game; it was a connexion in which the move could put on a strategic air. Her notions of diplomacy were thin, but it was a kind of cold diplomatic shoulder and an elbow of more than usual point that, temporarily at least, were presented to her by the averted inclination of Mrs Beale's head. There was a phrase familiar to Maisie, so often was it used by this lady to express the idea of one's getting what one wanted: one got it – Mrs Beale always said *she* at all events got it or proposed to get it – by 'making love'. She was at present making love, singular as it appeared, to Mrs Wix, and her young friend's mind had never moved in such freedom as on thus finding itself face to face with the question of what she wanted to get. This period of the *omelette aux rognons* and the *poulet sauté*, while her sole surviving parent, her fourth, fairly chattered to her governess, left Maisie rather wondering if her governess would hold out. It was strange, but she became on the spot quite as interested in Mrs Wix's moral sense as Mrs Wix could possibly be in hers: it had risen before her so pressingly that this was something new for Mrs Wix to resist. Resisting Mrs Beale herself promised at such a rate to become a very different business from resisting Sir Claude's view of her. More might come of what had happened – whatever it was – than Maisie felt she could have expected. She put it together with a suspicion that, had she ever in her life had a sovereign changed, would have resembled an impression, baffled by the want of arithmetic, that her change was wrong: she groped about in it that she was perhaps playing the passive part in a case of violent substitution. A victim was what she should surely be if the issue between her step-parents had been settled by Mrs Beale's saying: 'Well, if she can live with but one of us alone, with which in the world should it be but me?' That answer was far from what, for days, she had nursed herself in, and the desolation of it was deepened by the absence of anything from Sir Claude to show he had not had to take it as triumphant. Had not Mrs Beale, upstairs, as good as given out that she had quitted him with the snap of a tension, left him, dropped him in London, after some struggle as a sequel to which her own advent represented that she had practically sacrificed him? Maisie assisted in fancy at the probable episode in the Regent's Park, finding elements almost of terror in the suggestion that Sir Claude had not had fair play. They drew something, as she sat there, even from the pride of an association with such beauty as Mrs Beale's; and the child quite forgot that, though the sacrifice of Mrs Beale herself was a solution she had not invented, she would probably have seen Sir Claude embark upon it without a direct remonstrance.

What her stepmother had clearly now promised herself to wring from Mrs Wix was an assent to the great modification, the change, as smart as a juggler's trick, in the interest of which nothing so much mattered as the new convenience of Mrs Beale. Maisie could positively seize the moral that her elbow seemed to point in ribs thinly defended – the moral of its not mattering a straw which of the step-parents was the guardian. The essence of the question was that a girl wasn't a boy: if Maisie had been a mere rough trousered thing, destined at the best probably to grow up a scamp, Sir Claude would have been welcome. As the case stood he had simply tumbled out of it, and Mrs Wix would henceforth find herself in the employ of the right person. These arguments had really fallen into their place, for our young friend, at the very touch of that tone in which she had heard her new title declared. She was still, as a result of so many parents, a daughter to somebody even after papa and mamma were to all intents dead. If her father's wife and her mother's husband, by the operation of a natural or, for all she knew, a legal rule, were in the shoes of their defunct partners, then Mrs Beale's partner was exactly as defunct as Sir Claude's and her shoes the very pair to which, in 'Farange v. Farange and Others', the divorce-court had given priority. The subject of that celebrated settlement saw the rest of her day really filled out with the pomp of all that Mrs Beale assumed. The assumption rounded itself there between this lady's entertainers, flourished in a way that left them, in their bottom-less element, scarce a free pair of eyes to exchange signals. It struck Maisie even a little that there was a rope or two Mrs Wix might have thrown out if she would, a rocket or two she might have sent up. They had at any rate never been so long together without communion or telegraphy, and their companion kept them apart by simply keeping them with her. From this situation they saw the grandeur of their intenser relation to her pass and pass like an endless procession. It was a day of lively movement and of talk on Mrs Beale's part so brilliant and overflowing as to represent music and banners. She took them out with her promptly to walk and to drive, and even – towards night – sketched a plan for carrying them to the Etablissement, where, for only a franc apiece, they should listen to a concert of celebrities. It reminded Maisie, the plan, of the side-shows at Earl's Court, and the franc sounded brighter than the shillings which had at that time failed; yet this too, like the other, was a frustrated hope: the francs failed like the shillings and the side-shows had set an example to the concert. The Etablissement in short melted away, and it was little wonder that a lady who from the moment of her arrival had been so gallantly in the breach should confess herself at last done up. Maisie could appreciate her fatigue; the day had not passed without such an observer's discovering that she was excited and even mentally comparing her state to that of the breakers after a gale. It had blown hard in London, and she would take time to go down. It was of the condition known to the child by report as that of talking against time that her emphasis, her spirit, her humour, which had never dropped, now gave the impression.

She too was delighted with foreign manners; but her daughter's opportunities of explaining them to her were unexpectedly forestalled by her own tone of large acquaintance with them. One of the things that nipped in the bud all response to her volubility was Maisie's surprised retreat before the fact that Continental life was what she had been almost brought up on. It was Mrs Beale, disconcertingly, who began to explain it to her friends; it was she who, wherever they turned, was the interpreter, the historian and the guide. She was full of reference to her early travels – at the age of eighteen: she had at that period made, with a distinguished Dutch family, a stay on the Lake of Geneva. Maisie had in the old days been regaled with anecdotes of these adventures, but they had with time become phantasmal, and the heroine's quite showy exemption from bewilderment at Boulogne, her acuteness on some of the very subjects on which Maisie had been acute to

Mrs Wix, were a high note of the majesty, of the variety of advantage, with which she had alighted. It was all a part of the wind in her sails and of the weight with which her daughter was now to feel her hand. The effect of it on Maisie was to add already the burden of time to her separation from Sir Claude. This might, to her sense, have lasted for days; it was as if, with their main agitation transferred thus to France and with neither mamma now nor Mrs Beale nor Mrs Wix nor herself at his side, he must be fearfully alone in England. Hour after hour she felt as if she were waiting; yet she couldn't have said exactly for what. There were moments when Mrs Beale's flow of talk was a mere rattle to smother a knock. At no part of the crisis had the rattle so public a purpose as when, instead of letting Maisie go with Mrs Wix to prepare for dinner, she pushed her – with a push at last incontestably maternal – straight into the room inherited from Sir Claude. She titivated her little charge with her own brisk hands; then she brought out: 'I'm going to divorce your father.'

This was so different from anything Maisie had expected that it took some time to reach her mind. She was aware meanwhile that she probably looked rather wan. 'To marry Sir Claude?'

Mrs Beale rewarded her with a kiss. 'It's sweet to hear you put it so.'

This was a tribute, but it left Maisie balancing for an objection. 'How *can* you when he's married?'

'He isn't – practically. He's free, you know.'

'Free to marry?'

'Free, first, to divorce his own fiend.'

The benefit that, these last days, she had felt she owed a certain person left Maisie a moment so ill-prepared for recognizing this lurid label that she hesitated long enough to risk: 'Mamma?'

'She isn't your mamma any longer,' Mrs Beale returned. 'Sir Claude has paid her money to cease to be.' Then as if remembering how little, to the child, a pecuniary transaction must represent: 'She lets him off supporting her if he'll let her off supporting you.'

Mrs Beale appeared, however, to have done injustice to her daughter's financial grasp. 'And support me himself?' Maisie asked.

210

'Take the whole bother and burden of you and never let her hear of you again. It's a regular signed contract.'

'Why that's lovely of her!' Maisie cried.

'It's not so lovely, my dear, but that he'll get his divorce.'

Maisie was briefly silent; after which, 'No – he won't get it,' she said. Then she added still more boldly: 'And you won't get yours.'

Mrs Beale, who was at the dressing-glass, turned round with amusement and surprise. 'How do you know that?'

'Oh I know!' cried Maisie.

'From Mrs Wix?'

Maisie debated, then after an instant took her cue from Mrs Beale's absence of anger, which struck her the more as she had felt how much of her courage she needed. 'From Mrs Wix,' she admitted.

Mrs Beale, at the glass again, made play with a powder-puff. 'My own sweet, she's mistaken!' was all she said.

There was a certain force in the very amenity of this, but our young lady reflected long enough to remember that it was not the answer Sir Claude himself had made. The recollection nevertheless failed to prevent her saying: 'Do you mean, then, that he won't come till he has got it?'

Mrs Beale gave a last touch; she was ready; she stood there in all her elegance. 'I mean, my dear, that it's because he *hasn't* got it that I left him.'

This opened a view that stretched further than Maisie could reach. She turned away from it, but she spoke before they went out again. 'Do you like Mrs Wix now?'

'Why, my chick, I was just going to ask you if you think she has come at all to like poor bad me!'

Maisie thought, at this hint; but unsuccessfully. 'I haven't the least idea. But I'll find out.'

'Do!' said Mrs Beale, rustling out with her in a scented air and as if it would be a very particular favour.

The child tried promptly at bed-time, relieved now of the fear that their visitor would wish to separate her for the night from her attendant. 'Have you held out?' she began as soon as the two doors at the end of the passage were again closed on them.

Mrs Wix looked hard at the flame of the candle. 'Held out – ?'

'Why, she has been making love to you. Has she won you over?'

Mrs Wix transferred her intensity to her pupil's face. 'Over to what?'

'To *her* keeping me instead.'

'Instead of Sir Claude?' Mrs Wix was distinctly gaining time.

'Yes; who else? since it's not instead of you.'

Mrs Wix coloured at this lucidity. 'Yes, that *is* what she means.'

'Well, do you like it?' Maisie asked.

She actually had to wait, for oh her friend was embarrassed! 'My opposition to the connexion – theirs – would then naturally to some extent fall. She has treated me today as if I weren't after all quite such a worm; not that I don't know very well where she's got the pattern of her politeness. But of course,' Mrs Wix hastened to add, 'I shouldn't like her as *the* one nearly so well as him.'

'"Nearly so well!"' Maisie echoed. 'I should hope indeed not.' She spoke with a firmness under which she was herself the first to quiver. 'I thought you "adored" him.'

'I do,' Mrs Wix sturdily allowed.

'Then have you suddenly begun to adore her too?'

Mrs Wix, instead of directly answering, only blinked in support of her sturdiness. 'My dear, in what a tone you asked that! You're coming out.'

'Why shouldn't I? *You*'ve come out. Mrs Beale has come out. We each have our turn!' And Maisie threw off the most extraordinary little laugh that had ever passed her young lips.

There passed Mrs Wix's indeed the next moment a sound that more than matched it. 'You're most remarkable!' she neighed.

Her pupil, though wholly without aspirations to pertness, barely faltered. 'I think you've done a great deal to make me so.'

'Very true, I have.' She dropped to humility, as if she recalled her so recent self-arraignment.

'Would you accept her, then? That's what I ask,' said Maisie.

'As a substitute?' Mrs Wix turned it over; she met again the child's eyes. 'She has literally almost fawned upon me.'

'She hasn't fawned upon *him*. She hasn't even been kind to him.'

212

Mrs Wix looked as if she had now an advantage. 'Then do you propose to "kill" her?'

'You don't answer my question,' Maisie persisted. 'I want to know if you accept her.'

Mrs Wix continued to hedge. 'I want to know if *you* do!'

Everything in the child's person, at this, announced that it was easy to know. 'Not for a moment.'

'Not the two now?' Mrs Wix had caught on; she flushed with it. 'Only him alone?'

'Him alone or nobody.'

'Not even *me*?' cried Mrs Wix.

Maisie looked at her a moment, then began to undress. 'Oh you're nobody!'

29

HER sleep was drawn out; she instantly recognized lateness in the way her eyes opened to Mrs Wix, erect, completely dressed, more dressed than ever, and gazing at her from the centre of the room. The next thing she was sitting straight up, wide awake with the fear of the hours of 'abroad' that she might have lost. Mrs Wix looked as if the day had already made itself felt, and the process of catching up with it began for Maisie in hearing her distinctly say: 'My poor dear, he has come!'

'Sir Claude?' Maisie, clearing the little bed-rug with the width of her spring, felt the polished floor under her bare feet.

'He crossed in the night; he got in early.' Mrs Wix's head jerked stiffly backward. 'He's there.'

'And you've seen him?'

'No. He's there – he's there,' Mrs Wix repeated. Her voice came out with a queer extinction that was not a voluntary drop, and she trembled so that it added to their common emotion. Visibly pale, they gazed at each other.

'Isn't it too *beautiful*?' Maisie panted back at her; a challenge with an answer to which, however, she was not ready at once. The term Maisie had used was a flash of diplomacy – to prevent at any rate Mrs Wix's using another. To that degree it was successful; there was only an appeal, strange and mute, in the white old face, which produced the effect of a want of a decision greater than could by any stretch of optimism have been associated with her attitude towards what had happened. For Maisie herself indeed what had happened was oddly, as she could feel, less of a simple rapture than any arrival or return of the same supreme friend had ever been before. What had become over-night, what had become while she slept, of the comfortable faculty of gladness? She tried to wake it up a little wider by talking, by rejoicing, by plunging into water and into clothes, and she made out that it was ten o'clock, but also that Mrs Wix had not yet breakfasted. The day before, at nine, they had had together a *café complet* in their sitting-room. Mrs Wix on her side had evidently also a refuge to seek. She sought it in checking the precipitation of some of her pupil's present steps, in recalling to her with an approach to sternness that of such preliminaries those embodied in a thorough use of soap should be the most thorough, and in throwing even a certain reprobation on the idea of hurrying into clothes for the sake of a mere stepfather. She took her in hand with a silent insistence; she reduced the process to sequences more definite than any it had known since the days of Moddle. Whatever it might be that had now, with a difference, begun to belong to Sir Claude's presence was still after all compatible, for our young lady, with the instinct of dressing to see him with almost untidy haste. Mrs Wix meanwhile luckily was not wholly directed to repression. 'He's there – he's there!' she had said over several times. It was her answer to every invitation to mention how long she had been up and her motive for respecting so rigidly the slumber of her companion. It formed for some minutes her only account of the whereabouts of the others and her reason for not having yet seen them, as well as of the possibility of their presently being found in the salon.

'He's there – he's there!' she declared once more as she made, on the child, with an almost invidious tug, a strained undergarment 'meet'.

'Do you mean he's in the salon?' Maisie asked again.

'He's *with* her,' Mrs Wix desolately said. 'He's with her,' she reiterated.

'Do you mean in her own room?' Maisie continued.

214

She waited an instant. 'God knows!'

Maisie wondered a little why, or how, God should know; this, however, delayed but an instant her bringing out: 'Well, won't she go back?'

'Go back? Never!'

'She'll stay all the same?'

'All the more.'

'Then won't Sir Claude go?' Maisie asked.

'Go back – if *she* doesn't?' Mrs Wix appeared to give this question the benefit of a minute's thought. 'Why should he have come – only to go back?'

Maisie produced an ingenious solution. 'To *make* her go. To take her.'

Mrs Wix met it without a concession. 'If he can make her go so easily, why should he have let her come?'

Maisie considered. 'Oh just to see *me*. She has a right.'

'Yes – she has a right.'

'She's my mother!' Maisie tentatively tittered.

'Yes – she's your mother.'

'Besides,' Maisie went on, 'he didn't let her come. He doesn't like her coming, and if he doesn't like it – '

Mrs Wix took her up. 'He must lump it – that's what he must do! Your mother was right about him – I mean your real one. He has no strength. No – none at all.' She seemed more profoundly to muse. 'He might have had some even with *her* – I mean with her ladyship. He's just a poor sunk slave,' she asserted with sudden energy.

Maisie wondered again. 'A slave?'

'To his passions.'

She continued to wonder and even to be impressed; after which she went on: 'But how do you know he'll stay?'

'Because he likes us!' – and Mrs Wix, with her emphasis of the word, whirled her charge round again to deal with posterior hooks. She had positively never shaken her so.

It was as if she quite shook something out of her. 'But how will that help him if we -- in spite of his liking! – don't stay?'

'Do you mean if we go off and leave him with her?' – Mrs Wix put the question to the back of her pupil's head. 'It *won't* help him. It will be his ruin. He'll have got nothing. He'll have lost everything. It will be his utter destruction, for he's certain after a while to loathe her.'

'Then when he loathes her' – it was astonishing how she caught the idea – 'he'll just come right after us!' Maisie announced.

'Never.'

'Never?'

'She'll keep him. She'll hold him for ever.'

Maisie doubted. 'When he "loathes" her?'

'That won't matter. She won't loathe *him*. People don't!' Mrs Wix brought up.

'Some do. Mamma does,' Maisie contended.

'Mamma does *not*!' It was startling – her friend contradicted her flat. 'She loves him – she adores him. A woman knows.' Mrs Wix spoke not only as if Maisie were not a woman, but as if she would never be one. '*I* know!' she cried.

'Then why on earth has she left him?'

Mrs Wix hesitated. 'He hates *her*. Don't stoop so – lift up your hair. You know how I'm affected towards him,' she added with dignity; 'but you must also know that I see clear.'

Maisie all this time was trying hard to do likewise. 'Then if she has left him for that why shouldn't Mrs Beale leave him?'

'Because she's not such a fool!'

'Not such a fool as mamma?'

'Precisely – if you *will* have it. Does it look like her leaving him?' Mrs Wix inquired. She brooded again; then she went on with more intensity: 'Do you want to know really and truly why? So that she may be his wretchedness and his punishment.'

'His punishment?' – this was more than as yet Maisie could quite accept. 'For what?'

'For everything. That's what will happen: he'll be tied to her for ever. She won't mind in the least his hating her, and she won't hate him back. She'll only hate *us*.'

'Us?' the child faintly echoed.

'She'll hate *you*.'

'Me? Why, I brought them together!' Maisie resentfully cried.

'You brought them together.' There was a completeness in Mrs Wix's assent. 'Yes; it was a pretty job. Sit down.' She began to brush her pupil's hair and, as she took up the mass of it with some force of hand, went on with a sharp recall: 'Your mother adored him at first – it might have lasted. But he began too soon with Mrs Beale. As you say,' she pursued with a brisk application of the brush, 'you brought them together.'

'I brought them together' – Maisie was ready to reaffirm it. She felt none the less for a moment at the bottom of a hole; then she seemed to see a way out. 'But I didn't bring mamma together – ' She just faltered.

'With all those gentlemen?' – Mrs Wix pulled her up. 'No; it isn't quite so bad as that.'

'I only said to the Captain' – Maisie had the quick memory of it – 'that I hoped he at least (he was awfully nice!) would love her and keep her.'

'And even that wasn't much harm,' threw in Mrs Wix.

'It wasn't much good,' Maisie was obliged to recognize. 'She can't bear him – not even a mite. She told me at Folkestone.'

Mrs Wix suppressed a gasp; then after a bridling instant during which she might have appeared to deflect with difficulty from her odd consideration of Ida's wrongs: 'He was a nice sort of person for her to talk to you about!'

'Oh I *like* him!' Maisie promptly rejoined; and at this, with an inarticulate sound and an inconsequence still more marked, her companion bent over and dealt her on the cheek a rapid peck which had the apparent intention of a kiss.

'Well, if her ladyship doesn't agree with you, what does it only prove?' Mrs Wix demanded in conclusion. 'It proves that she's fond of Sir Claude!'

Maisie, in the light of some of the evidence, reflected on that till her hair was finished, but when she at last started up she gave a sign of no very close embrace of it. She grasped at this moment Mrs Wix's arm. 'He must have got his divorce!'

'Since the day before yesterday? Don't talk trash.'

This was spoken with an impatience which left the child nothing to reply; whereupon she sought her defence in a completely different relation to the fact. 'Well, I knew he would come!'

'So did I; but not in twenty-four hours. I gave him a few days!' Mrs Wix wailed.

Maisie, whom she had now released, looked at her with interest. 'How many did *she* give him?'

Mrs Wix faced her a moment; then as if with a bewildered

217

sniff: 'You had better ask her!' But she had no sooner uttered the words than she caught herself up. 'Lord o' mercy, how we talk!'

Maisie felt that however they talked she must see him, but she said nothing more for a time, a time during which she conscientiously finished dressing and Mrs Wix also kept silence. It was as if they each had almost too much to think of, and even as if the child had the sense that her friend was watching her and seeing if she herself were watched. At last Mrs Wix turned to the window and stood – sightlessly, as Maisie could guess – looking away. Then our young lady, before the glass, gave the supreme shake. 'Well, I'm ready. And now to *see* him!'

Mrs Wix turned round, but as if without having heard her. 'It's tremendously grave.' There were slow still tears behind the straighteners.

'It is – it is.' Maisie spoke as if she were now dressed quite up to the occasion; as if indeed with the last touch she had put on the judgement-cap. 'I must see him immediately.'

'How can you see him if he doesn't send for you?'

'Why can't I go and find him?'

'Because you don't know where he is.'

'Can't I just look in the salon?' That still seemed simple to Maisie.

Mrs Wix, however, instantly cut it off. 'I wouldn't have you look in the salon for all the world!' Then she explained a little: 'The salon isn't ours now.'

'Ours?'

'Yours and mine. It's theirs.'

'Theirs?' Maisie, with her stare, continued to echo. 'You mean they want to keep us out?'

Mrs Wix faltered; she sank into a chair and, as Maisie had often enough seen her do before, covered her face with her hands. 'They ought to, at least. The situation's too monstrous!'

Maisie stood there a moment – she looked about the room. 'I'll go to him – I'll find him.'

'*I* won't! I won't go *near* them!' cried Mrs Wix.

'Then I'll see him alone.' The child spied what she had been looking for – she possessed herself of her hat. 'Perhaps I'll take him out!' And with decision she quitted the room.

When she entered the salon it was empty, but at the sound of the opened door someone stirred on the balcony, and Sir Claude, stepping straight in, stood before her. He was in light fresh clothes and wore a straw hat with a bright ribbon; these things, besides striking her in themselves as the very promise of the grandest of grand tours, gave him a certain radiance and, as it were, a tropical ease; but such an effect only marked rather more his having stopped short and, for a longer minute than had ever at such a juncture elapsed, not opened his arms to her. His pause made her pause and enabled her to reflect that he must have been up some time, for there were no traces of breakfast; and that though it was so late he had rather markedly not caused her to be called to him. Had Mrs Wix been right about their forfeiture of the salon? Was it all his now, all his and Mrs Beale's? Such an idea, at the rate her small thoughts throbbed, could only remind her of the way in which what had been hers hitherto was what was exactly most Mrs Beale's and his. It was strange to be standing there and greeting him across a gulf, for he had by this time spoken, smiled and said: 'My dear child, my dear child!' but without coming any nearer. In a flash she saw he was different – more so than he knew or designed. The next minute indeed it was as if he caught an impression from her face: this made him hold out his hand. Then they met, he kissed her, he laughed, she thought he even blushed: something of his affection rang out as usual. 'Here I am, you see, again – as I promised you.'

It was not as he had promised them – he had not promised them Mrs Beale; but Maisie said nothing about that. What she said was simply: 'I knew you had come. Mrs Wix told me.'

'Oh yes. And where is she?'

'In her room. She got me up – she dressed me.'

Sir Claude looked at her up and down; a sweetness of mockery that she particularly loved came out in his face whenever he did that, and it was not wanting now. He raised his eyebrows and his arms to play at admiration; he was evidently after all disposed to be gay. 'Got you up? – I should think so! She has dressed you most beautifully. Isn't she coming?'

Maisie wondered if she had better tell. 'She said not.'

'Doesn't she want to see a poor devil?'

She looked about under the vibration of the way he described himself, and her eyes rested on the door of the room he had previously occupied. 'Is Mrs Beale in there?'

Sir Claude looked blankly at the same object. 'I haven't the least idea!'

'You haven't seen her?'

'Not the tip of her nose.'

Maisie thought: there settled on her, in the light of his beautiful smiling eyes, the faintest purest coldest conviction that he wasn't telling the truth. 'She hasn't welcomed you?'

'Not by a single sign.'

'Then where is she?'

Sir Claude laughed; he seemed both amused and surprised at the point she made of it. 'I give it up!'

'Doesn't she know you've come?'

He laughed again. 'Perhaps she doesn't care!'

Maisie, with an inspiration, pounced on his arm. 'Has she *gone*?'

He met her eyes and then she could see that his own were really much graver than his manner. 'Gone?' She had flown to the door, but before she could raise her hand to knock he was beside her and had caught it. 'Let her be. I don't care about her. I want to see *you*.'

Maisie fell back with him. 'Then she *hasn't* gone?'

He still looked as if it were a joke, but the more she saw of him the more she could make out that he was troubled. 'It wouldn't be like her!'

She stood wondering at him. 'Did you want her to come?'

'How can you suppose – ?' He put it to her candidly. 'We had an immense row over it.'

'Do you mean you've quarrelled?'

Sir Claude was at a loss. 'What has she told you?'

'That I'm hers as much as yours. That she represents papa.'

His gaze struck away through the open window and up to the sky; she could hear him rattle in his trouser-pockets his money or his keys. 'Yes – that's what she keeps saying.' It gave him for a moment an air that was almost helpless.

'You say you don't care about her,' Maisie went on. '*Do* you mean you've quarrelled?'

'We do nothing in life but quarrel.'

He rose before her, as he said this, so soft and fair, so rich, in spite of what might worry him, in restored familiarities, that it gave a bright blur to the meaning – to what would otherwise perhaps have been the palpable promise – of the words. 'Oh *your* quarrels!' she exclaimed with discouragement.

'I assure you hers are quite fearful!'

'I don't speak of hers. I speak of yours.'

'Ah don't do it till I've had my coffee! You're growing up clever,' he added. Then he said: 'I suppose you've breakfasted?'

'Oh no – I've had nothing.'

'Nothing in your room?' – he was all compunction. 'My dear old man! – we'll breakfast, then, together.' He had one of his happy thoughts. 'I say – we'll go out.'

'That was just what I hoped. I've brought my hat.'

'You *are* clever! We'll go to a café.' Maisie was already at the door; he glanced round the room. 'A moment – my stick.' But there appeared to be no stick. 'No matter; I left it – oh!' He remembered with an odd drop and came out.

'You left it in London?' she asked as they went downstairs.

'Yes – in London: fancy!'

'You were in such a hurry to come,' Maisie explained.

He had his arm round her. 'That must have been the reason.' Halfway down he stopped short again, slapping his leg. 'And poor Mrs Wix?'

Maisie's face just showed a shadow. 'Do you want her to come?'

'Dear no – I want to see you alone.'

'That's the way I want to see *you*!' she replied. 'Like before.'

'Like before!' he gaily echoed. 'But I mean has she had her coffee?'

'No, nothing.'

'Then I'll send it up to her. Madame!' He had already, at the foot of the stair, called out to the stout *patronne*, a lady who turned to him from the bustling, breezy hall a countenance covered with fresh matutinal powder and a bosom as capacious as the velvet shelf of a chimney-piece, over which her round white face, framed in its golden frizzle, might have figured as a showy clock. He ordered, with particular recommendations, Mrs Wix's repast, and it was a charm to hear his easy brilliant French: even

221

his companion's ignorance could measure the perfection of it. The *patronne*, rubbing her hands and breaking in with high swift notes as into a florid duet, went with him to the street, and while they talked a moment longer Maisie remembered what Mrs Wix had said about everyone's liking him. It came out enough through the morning powder, it came out enough in the heaving bosom, how the landlady liked him. He had evidently ordered something lovely for Mrs Wix. '*Et bien soigné, n'est-ce-pas?*'

'*Soyez tranquille*' – the *patronne* beamed upon him. '*Et pour Madame?*'

'*Madame?*' he echoed – it just pulled him up a little.

'*Rien encore?*'

'*Rien encore.* Come, Maisie.' She hurried along with him, but on the way to the café he said nothing.

30

AFTER they were seated there it was different: the place was not below the hotel, but farther along the quay; with wide, clear windows and a floor sprinkled with bran in a manner that gave it for Maisie something of the added charm of a circus. They had pretty much to themselves the painted spaces and the red plush benches; these were shared by a few scattered gentlemen who picked teeth, with facial contortions, behind little bare tables, and by an old personage in particular, a very old personage with a red ribbon in his button-hole, whose manner of soaking buttered rolls in coffee and then disposing of them in the little that was left of the interval between his nose and chin might at a less anxious hour have cast upon Maisie an almost envious spell. They too had their *café au lait* and their buttered rolls, determined by Sir Claude's asking her if she could with that light aid wait till the hour of déjeuner. His allusion to this meal gave her, in the shaded sprinkled coolness, the scene, as she vaguely felt, of a sort of ordered mirrored licence, the haunt of those – the irregular, like herself – who went to bed or who rose too late, something to think over while she watched the white-aproned waiter perform as nimbly with plates and saucers as a certain conjurer her friend had in London taken her to a music-hall to see. Sir Claude had presently begun to talk again, to tell her how London had looked and how long he had felt himself, on either side, to have been absent; all about Susan Ash too and the amusement as well as the difficulty he had had with her; then all about his return journey and the Channel in the night and the crowd of people coming over and the way there were always too many one knew. He spoke of other matters beside, especially of what she must tell him of the occupations, while he was away, of Mrs Wix and her pupil. Hadn't they had the good time he had promised? – had he exaggerated a bit the arrangements made for their pleasure? Maisie had something – not all there was – to say of his success and of their gratitude: she had a complication of thought that grew every minute; grew with the consciousness that she had never seen him in this particular state in which he had been given back.

Mrs Wix had once said – it was once or fifty times; once was enough for Maisie, but more was not too much – that he was wonderfully various. Well, he was certainly so, to the child's mind, on the present occasion: he was much more various than he was anything else. Besides, the fact that they were together in a shop, at a nice little intimate table as they had so often been in London, only made greater the difference of what they were together about. This difference was in his face, in his voice, in every look he gave her and every movement he made. They were not the looks and the movements he really wanted to show, and she could feel as well that they were not those she herself wanted. She had seen him nervous, she had seen everyone she had come in contact with nervous, but she had never seen him so nervous as this. Little by little it gave her a settled terror, a terror that partook of the coldness she had felt just before, at the hotel, to find herself, on his answer about Mrs Beale, disbelieve him. She seemed to see at present, to touch across the table, as if by laying her hand on it, what he had meant when he confessed on those several occasions to fear. Why was such a man so often afraid? It must have begun to come to her now that there was one thing just such a man above all could be afraid of. He could be afraid of himself. His fear at all events was there; his fear was sweet to her, beautiful and tender to her, was having coffee and buttered rolls and talk and laughter that were no talk and laughter at all with her; his fear was in his jesting postponing perverting voice; it was just in this make-believe way he had brought her out to imitate the old London playtimes, to imitate indeed a relation that had wholly changed, a relation that she had with her very eyes seen in the act of change when, the day before in the salon, Mrs Beale rose suddenly before her. She rose before her, for that matter, now, and even while their refreshment delayed Maisie arrived at the straight question for which, on their entrance, his first word had given opportunity. 'Are we going to have déjeuner with Mrs Beale?'

His reply was anything but straight. 'You and I?'

Maisie sat back in her chair. 'Mrs Wix and me.'

Sir Claude also shifted. 'That's an inquiry, my dear child, that Mrs Beale herself must answer.' Yes, he had shifted; but abruptly, after a moment during which something seemed to hang there between them and, as it heavily swayed, just fan them with the air of its motion, she felt that the whole thing was upon them. 'Do you mind,' he broke out, 'my asking you what Mrs Wix has said to you?'

'Said to me?'

'This day or two – while I was away.'

'Do you mean about you and Mrs Beale?'

Sir Claude, resting on his elbows, fixed his eyes a moment on the white marble beneath them. 'No; I think we had a good deal of that – didn't we? – before I left you. It seems to me we had it pretty well all out. I mean about yourself, about your – don't you know? – associating with us, as I might say, and staying on with us. While you were alone with our friend what did she say?'

Maisie felt the weight of the question; it kept her silent for a space during which she looked at Sir Claude, whose eyes remained bent. 'Nothing,' she returned at last.

He showed incredulity. 'Nothing?'

'Nothing,' Maisie repeated; on which an interruption descended in the form of a tray bearing the preparations for their breakfast.

These preparations were as amusing as everything else; the waiter poured their coffee from a vessel like a watering-pot and then made it froth with the curved stream of hot milk that dropped from the height of his raised arm; but the two looked across at each other through the whole play of French pleasantness with a gravity that had now ceased to dissemble. Sir Claude sent the waiter off again for something and then took up her answer. 'Hasn't she tried to affect you?'

Face to face with him thus it seemed to Maisie that she had tried so little as to be scarce worth mentioning; again therefore an instant she shut herself up. Presently she found her middle course. 'Mrs Beale likes her now; and there's one thing I've found out – a great thing. Mrs Wix enjoys her being so kind. She was tremendously kind all day yesterday.'

'I see. And what did she do?' Sir Claude asked.

Maisie was now busy with her breakfast, and her companion attacked his own; so that it was all, in form at least, even more than their old sociability. 'Everything she could think of. She was as nice to her as you are,' the child said. 'She talked to her all day.'

'And what did she say to her?'

'Oh I don't know.' Maisie was a little bewildered with his pressing her so for knowledge; it didn't fit into the degree of intimacy with Mrs Beale that Mrs Wix had so denounced and that, according to that lady, had now brought him back in bondage. Wasn't he more aware than his stepdaughter of what would be done by the person to whom he was bound? In a moment, however, she added: 'She made love to her.'

Sir Claude looked at her harder, and it was clearly something in her tone that made him quickly say: 'You don't mind my asking you, do you?'

'Not at all; only I should think you'd know better than I.'

'What Mrs Beale did yesterday?'

She thought he coloured a trifle; but almost simultaneously with that impression she found herself answering: 'Yes – if you *have* seen her.'

He broke into the loudest of laughs. 'Why, my dear boy, I told you just now I've absolutely not. I say, don't you believe me?'

There was something she was already so afraid of that it covered up other fears. 'Didn't you come back to see her?' she inquired in a moment. 'Didn't you come back because you always want to so much?'

He received her inquiry as he had received her doubt – with an extraordinary absence of resentment. 'I can imagine of course

225

why you think that. But it doesn't explain my doing what I have. It was, as I said to you just now at the inn, really and truly you I wanted to see.'

She felt an instant as she used to feel when, in the back garden at her mother's, she took from him the highest push of a swing – high, high, high – that he had had put there for her pleasure and that had finally broken down under the weight and the extravagant patronage of the cook. 'Well, that's beautiful. But to see me, you mean, and go away again?'

'My going away again is just the point. I can't tell yet – it all depends.'

'On Mrs Beale?' Maisie asked. '*She* won't go away.' He finished emptying his coffee-cup and then, when he had put it down, leaned back in his chair, where she could see that he smiled on her. This only added to her idea that he was in trouble, that he was turning somehow in his pain and trying different things. He continued to smile and she went on: 'Don't you know that?'

'Yes, I may as well confess to you that as much as that I do know. *She* won't go away. She'll stay.'

'She'll stay. She'll stay,' Maisie repeated.

'Just so. Won't you have some more coffee?'

'Yes, please.'

'And another buttered roll?'

'Yes, please.'

He signed to the hovering waiter, who arrived with the shining spout of plenty in either hand and with the friendliest interest in mademoiselle. '*Les tartines sont là.*' Their cups were replenished and, while he watched almost musingly the bubbles in the fragrant mixture, 'Just so – just so,' Sir Claude said again and again. 'It's awfully awkward!' he exclaimed when the waiter had gone.

'That she won't go?'

'Well – everything! Well, well, well!' But he pulled himself together; he began again to eat. 'I came back to ask you something. That's what I came back for.'

'I know what you want to ask me,' Maisie said.

'Are you very sure?'

'I'm *almost* very.'

226

'Well, then, risk it. You mustn't make *me* risk everything.'

She was struck with the force of this. 'You want to know if I should be happy with *them*.'

'With those two ladies only? No, no, old man: *vous n'y êtes pas*. So now – there!' Sir Claude laughed.

'Well, then, what is it?'

The next minute, instead of telling her what it was, he laid his hand across the table on her own and held her as if under the prompting of a thought. 'Mrs Wix would stay with *her*?'

'Without you? Oh yes – now.'

'On account, as you just intimated, of Mrs Beale's changed manner?'

Maisie, with her sense of responsibility, weighed both Mrs Beale's changed manner and Mrs Wix's human weakness. 'I think she talked her round.'

Sir Claude thought a moment. 'Ah poor dear!'

'Do you mean Mrs Beale?'

'Oh no – Mrs Wix.'

'She likes being talked round – treated like anyone else. Oh she likes great politeness,' Maisie expatiated. 'It affects her very much.'

Sir Claude, to her surprise, demurred a little to this. 'Very much – up to a certain point.'

'Oh up to any point!' Maisie returned with emphasis.

'Well, haven't I been polite to her?'

'Lovely – and she perfectly worships you.'

'Then, my dear child, why can't she let me alone?' – this time Sir Claude unmistakably blushed. Before Maisie, however, could answer his question, which would indeed have taken her long, he went on in another tone: 'Mrs Beale thinks she has probably quite broken her down. But she hasn't.'

Though he spoke as if he were sure, Maisie was strong in the impression she had just uttered and that she now again produced. 'She has talked her round.'

'Ah yes; round to herself, but not round to me.'

Oh she couldn't bear to hear him say that! 'To you? Don't you really believe how she loves you?'

Sir Claude examined his belief. 'Of course I know she's wonderful.'

'She's just every bit as fond of you as *I* am,' said Maisie. 'She told me so yesterday.'

'Ah then,' he promptly exclaimed, 'she *has* tried to affect you! I don't love *her*, don't you see? I do her perfect justice,' he pursued, 'but I mean I don't love her as I do you, and I'm sure you wouldn't seriously expect it. She's not my daughter – come, old chap! She's not even my mother, though I daresay it would have been better for me if she had been. I'll do for her what I'd do for my mother, but I won't do more.' His real excitement broke out in a need to explain and justify himself, though he kept trying to correct and conceal it with laughs and mouthfuls and other vain familiarities. Suddenly he broke off, wiping his moustache with sharp pulls and coming back to Mrs Beale. 'Did she try to talk *you* over?'

'No – to me she said very little. Very little indeed,' Maisie continued.

Sir Claude seemed struck with this. 'She was only sweet to Mrs Wix?'

'As sweet as sugar!' cried Maisie.

He looked amused at her comparison, but he didn't contest it; he uttered on the contrary, in an assenting way, a little inarticulate sound. 'I know what she *can* be. But much good may it have done her! Mrs Wix won't *come* "round". That's what makes it so fearfully awkward.'

Maisie knew it was fearfully awkward; she had known this now, she felt, for some time, and there was something else it more pressingly concerned her to learn. 'What is it you meant you came over to ask me?'

'Well,' said Sir Claude, 'I was just going to say. Let me tell you it will surprise you.' She had finished breakfast now and she sat back in her chair again: she waited in silence to hear. He had pushed the things before him a little way and had his elbows on the table. This time, she was convinced, she knew what was coming, and once more, for the crash, as with Mrs Wix lately in her room, she held her breath and drew together her eyelids. He was going to say she must give him up. He looked hard at her again; then he made his effort. 'Should you see your way to let her go?'

She was bewildered. 'To let who – ?'

228

'Mrs Wix simply. I put it at the worst. Should you see your way to sacrifice her? Of course I know what I'm asking.'

Maisie's eyes opened wide again; this was so different from what she had expected. 'And stay with you alone?'

He gave another push to his coffee-cup. 'With me and Mrs Beale. Of course it would be rather rum; but everything in our whole story is rather rum, you know. What's more unusual than for anyone to be given up, like you, by her parents?'

'Oh nothing is more unusual than *that*!' Maisie concurred, relieved at the contact of a proposition as to which concurrence could have lucidity.

'Of course it would be quite unconventional,' Sir Claude went on – 'I mean the little household we three should make together; but things have got beyond that, don't you see? They got beyond that long ago. We shall stay abroad at any rate – it's ever so much easier and it's our affair and nobody else's: it's no one's business but ours on all the blessed earth. I don't say that for Mrs Wix, poor dear – I do her absolute justice. I respect her; I see what she means; she has done me a lot of good. But there are the facts. There they are, simply. And here am I, and here are you. And she won't come round. She's right from her point of view. I'm talking to you in the most extraordinary way – I'm always talking to you in the most extraordinary way, ain't I? One would think you were about sixty and that I – I don't know what anyone would think *I* am. Unless a beastly cad!' he suggested. 'I've been awfully worried, and this's what it has come to. You've done us the most tremendous good, and you'll do it still and always, don't you see? We can't let you go – you're everything. There are the facts as I say. She *is* your mother now, Mrs Beale, by what has happened, and I, in the same way, I'm your father. No one can contradict that, and we can't get out of it. My idea would be a nice little place – somewhere in the South – where she and you would be together and as good as anyone else. And I should be as good too, don't you see? for I shouldn't live with you, but I should be close to you – just round the corner, and it would be just the same. My idea would be that it should all be perfectly open and frank. *Honi soit qui mal y pense*, don't you know? You're the best thing – you and what we can do for you – that either of us has ever known': he came back to that. 'When I say to her "Give her up, come," she lets me have it bang in the face: "Give her up yourself!" It's the same old vicious circle – and when I say vicious I don't mean a pun, a what-d'-ye-call-'em. Mrs Wix is the obstacle; I mean, you know, if she has affected you. She has affected *me*, and yet here I am. I never was in such a tight place: please believe it's only that that makes me put it to you as I do. My dear child, isn't that – to put it so – just the way out of it? That came to me yesterday, in London, after Mrs Beale had gone: I had the most infernal atrocious day. "Go straight over and put it to her: let her choose, freely, her own self." So I do, old girl – I put it to you. *Can* you choose freely?'

This long address, slowly and brokenly uttered, with fidgets and falterings, with lapses and recoveries, with a mottled face and embarrassed but supplicating eyes, reached the child from a quarter so close that after the shock of the first sharpness she could see intensely its direction and follow it from point to point; all the more that it came back to the point at which it had started. There was a word that had hummed all through it. 'Do you call it a "sacrifice"?'

'Of Mrs Wix? I'll call it whatever *you* call it. I won't funk it – I haven't, have I? I'll face it in all its baseness. Does it strike you it *is* base for me to get you well away from her, to smuggle you off here into a corner and bribe you with sophistries and buttered rolls to betray her?'

'To betray her?'

'Well – to part with her.'

Maisie let the question wait; the concrete image it presented was the most vivid side of it. 'If I part with her where will she go?'

'Back to London.'

'But I mean what will she do?'

'Oh as for that I won't pretend I know. I don't. We all have our difficulties.'

That, to Maisie, was at this moment more striking than it had ever been. 'Then who'll teach me?'

Sir Claude laughed out. 'What Mrs Wix teaches?'

She smiled dimly; she saw what he meant. 'It isn't so very very much.'

'It's so very very little,' he returned, 'that that's a thing we've positively to consider. We probably shouldn't give you another

230

governess. To begin with we shouldn't be able to get one – not of the only kind that would do. It wouldn't do – the kind that *would* do,' he queerly enough explained. 'I mean they wouldn't stay – heigh-ho! We'd do you ourselves. Particularly me. You see I *can* now; I haven't got to mind – what I used to. I won't fight shy as I did – she can show out *with* me. Our relation, all round, is more regular.'

It seemed wonderfully regular, the way he put it; yet none the less, while she looked at it as judiciously as she could, the picture it made persisted somehow in being a combination quite distinct – an old woman and a little girl seated in deep silence on a battered old bench by the rampart of the *haute ville*. It was just at that hour yesterday; they were hand in hand; they had melted together. 'I don't think you yet understand how she clings to you,' Maisie said at last.

'I do – I do. But for all that – !' And he gave, turning in his conscious exposure, an oppressed impatient sigh; the sigh, even his companion could recognize, of the man naturally accustomed to that argument, the man who wanted thoroughly to be reasonable, but who, if really he had to mind so many things, would be always impossibly hampered. What it came to indeed was that he understood quite perfectly. If Mrs Wix clung it was all the more reason for shaking Mrs Wix off.

This vision of what she had brought him to occupied our young lady while, to ask what he owed, he called the waiter and put down a gold piece that the man carried off for change. Sir Claude looked after him, then went on: 'How could a woman have less to reproach a fellow with? I mean as regards herself.'

Maisie entertained the question. 'Yes. How *could* she have less? So why are you so sure she'll go?'

'Surely you heard why – you heard her come out three nights ago? How can she do anything but go – after what she then said? I've done what she warned me of – she was absolutely right. So here we are. Her liking Mrs Beale, as you call it now, is a motive sufficient, with other things, to make her, for your sake, stay on without me; it's not a motive sufficient to make her, even for yours, stay on *with* me – swallow, don't you see? what she can't swallow. And when you say she's as fond of me as you are I think I can, if that's the case, challenge you a little on it. Would *you*,

231

only with those two, stay on without me?' The waiter came back with the change, and that gave her, under this appeal, a moment's respite. But when he had retreated again with the 'tip' gathered in with graceful thanks on a subtle hint from Sir Claude's forefinger, the latter, while pocketing the money, followed the appeal up. 'Would you let her make you live with Mrs Beale?'

'Without you? Never,' Maisie then answered. 'Never,' she said again.

It made him quite triumph, and she was indeed herself shaken by the mere sound of it. 'So you see you're not, like her,' he exclaimed, 'so ready to give me away!' Then he came back to his original question. '*Can* you choose? I mean can you settle it by a word yourself? Will you stay on with us without her?'

Now in truth she felt the coldness of her terror, and it seemed to her suddenly she knew, as she knew it about Sir Claude, what she was afraid of. She was afraid of herself. She looked at him in such a way that it brought, she could see, wonder into his face, a wonder held in check, however, by his frank pretension to play fair with her, not to use advantages, not to hurry nor hustle her – only to put her chance clearly and kindly before her. 'May I think?' she finally asked.

'Certainly, certainly. But how long?'

'Oh only a little while,' she said meekly.

He had for a moment the air of wishing to look at it as if it were the most cheerful prospect in the world. 'But what shall we do while you're thinking?' He spoke as if thought were compatible with almost any distraction.

There was but one thing Maisie wished to do, and after an instant she expressed it. 'Have we got to go back to the hotel?'

'Do you want to?'

'Oh no.'

'There's not the least necessity for it.' He bent his eyes on his watch; his face was now very grave. 'We can do anything else in the world.' He looked at her again almost as if he were on the point of saying that they might for instance start off for Paris. But even while she wondered if that were not coming he had a sudden drop. 'We can take a walk.'

She was all ready, but he sat there as if he had still something

232

more to say. This too, however, didn't come; so she herself spoke. 'I think I should like to see Mrs Wix first.'

'Before you decide? All right – all right.' He had put on his hat, but he had still to light a cigarette. He smoked a minute, with his head thrown back, looking at the ceiling; then he said: 'There's one thing to remember – I've a right to impress it on you: we stand absolutely in the place of your parents. It's their de-fection, their extraordinary baseness, that has made our respon-sibility. Never was a young person more directly committed and confided.' He appeared to say this over, at the ceiling, through his smoke, a little for his own illumination. It carried him after a pause somewhat further. 'Though I admit it was to each of us separately.'

He gave her so at that moment and in that attitude the sense of wanting, as it were, to be on her side – on the side of what would be in every way most right and wise and charming for her – that she felt a sudden desire to prove herself not less delicate and magnanimous, not less solicitous for his own interests. What were these but that of the 'regularity' he had just before spoken of ? 'It *was* to each of you separately,' she accordingly with much earnestness remarked. 'But don't you remember? I brought you together.'

He jumped up with a delighted laugh. 'Remember? Rather! You brought us together, you brought us together. Come!'

31

SHE remained out with him for a time of which she could take no measure save that it was too short for what she wished to make of it – an interval, a barrier indefinite, insurmountable. They walked about, they dawdled, they looked in shop windows; they did all the old things exactly as if to try to get back all the old safety, to get something out of them that they had always got before. This had come before, whatever it was, without their try-ing, and nothing came now but the intenser consciousness of their quest and their subterfuge. The strangest thing of all was what had really happened to the old safety. What had really happened was that Sir Claude was 'free' and that Mrs Beale was 'free', and yet that the new medium was somehow still more oppressive than the old. She could feel that Sir Claude concurred with her in the sense that the oppression would be worst at the inn, where, till something should be settled, they would feel the want of something – of what could they call it but a footing? The question of the settlement loomed larger to her now: it depended, she had learned, so completely on herself. Her choice, as her friend had called it, was there before her like an impossible sum on a slate, a sum that in spite of her pleas for consideration she simply got off from doing while she walked about with him. She must see Mrs Wix before she could do her sum; therefore the longer before she saw her the more distant would be the ordeal. She met at present no demand whatever of her obligation; she simply plunged, to avoid it, deeper into the company of Sir Claude. She saw nothing that she had seen hitherto – no touch in the foreign picture that had at first been always before her. The only touch was that of Sir Claude's hand, and to feel her own in it was her mute resistance to time. She went about as sightlessly as if he had been leading her blindfold. If they were afraid of themselves it was themselves they would find at the inn. She was certain now that what awaited them there would be to lunch with Mrs Beale. All her instinct was to avoid that, to draw out their walk, to find pretexts, to take him down upon the beach, to take him to the end of the pier. He said no other word to her about what they had talked of at breakfast, and she had a dim vision of how his way of not letting her see him definitely wait for anything from her would make anyone who should know of it, would make Mrs Wix, for instance, think him more than ever a gentleman. It was true that once or twice, on the jetty, on the sands, he looked at her for a minute with eyes that seemed to propose to her to come straight off with him to Paris. That, however, was not to give her a nudge about her responsibility. He evidently wanted to procrastinate quite as much as she did; he was not a bit more in a hurry to get back to the others. Maisie herself at this moment could be secretly merciless to Mrs Wix – to the extent at any rate of not caring if her continued disappearance did make that lady begin to worry about what had become of her, even begin to wonder perhaps if the truants hadn't found their remedy. Her want of mercy to Mrs Beale indeed was at least as great; for Mrs Beale's worry and wonder would be as much greater as the object at which they were directed. When at last Sir Claude, at the far end of the *plage*, which they had already, in the many-coloured crowd, once traversed, suddenly, with a look at his watch, remarked that it was time, not to get back to the *table d'hôte*, but to get over to the station and meet the Paris papers – when he did this she found herself thinking quite with intensity what Mrs Beale and Mrs Wix *would* say. On the way over to the station she had even a mental picture of the stepfather and the pupil established in a little place in the South while the governess and the stepmother, in a little place in the North, remained linked by a community of blankness and by the endless series of remarks it would give birth to. The Paris papers had come in and her companion, with a strange extravagance, purchased no fewer than eleven: it took up time while they hovered at the bookstall on the restless platform, where the little volumes in a row were all yellow and pink and one of her favourite old women in one of her favourite old caps absolutely wheedled him into the purchase of three. They had thus so much to carry home that it would have seemed simpler with such a provision for a nice straight journey through France, just to 'nip', as she phrased it to herself, into the coupé of the train that, a little farther along, stood waiting to start. She asked Sir Claude where it was going.

'To Paris. Fancy!'

She could fancy well enough. They stood there and smiled, he with all the newspapers under his arm and she with the three books, one yellow and two pink. He had told her the pink were for herself and the yellow one for Mrs Beale, implying in an interesting way that these were the natural divisions in France of literature for the young and for the old. She knew how prepared they looked to pass into the train, and she presently brought out to her companion: 'I wish we could go. Won't you take me?'

He continued to smile. 'Would you really come?'

'Oh yes, oh yes. Try.'

'Do you want me to take our tickets?'

'Yes, take them.'

'Without any luggage?'

She showed their two armfuls, smiling at him as he smiled at

235

her, but so conscious of being more frightened than she had ever been in her life that she seemed to see her whiteness as in a glass. Then she knew that what she saw was Sir Claude's whiteness: he was as frightened as herself. 'Haven't we got plenty of luggage?' she asked. 'Take the tickets – haven't you time? When does the train go?'

Sir Claude turned to a porter. 'When does the train go?'

The man looked up at the station clock. 'In two minutes. *Monsieur est placé?*'

'*Pas encore.*'

'*Et vos billets? – vous n'avez que le temps.*' Then after a look at Maisie, '*Monsieur veut-il que je les prenne?*' the man said.

Sir Claude turned back to her. '*Veux-tu bien qu'il en prenne?*'

It was the most extraordinary thing in the world: in the intensity of her excitement she not only by illumination understood all their French, but fell into it with an active perfection. She addressed herself straight to the porter. '*Prenny, prenny. Oh prenny!*'

'*Ah si mademoiselle le veut –* !' He waited there for the money.

But Sir Claude only stared – stared at her with his white face. 'You *have* chosen, then? You'll let her go?'

Maisie carried her eyes wistfully to the train, where, amid cries of '*En voiture, en voiture!*' heads were at windows and doors banging loud. The porter was pressing. '*Ah vous n'avez plus le temps!*'

'It's going – it's going!' cried Maisie.

They watched it move, they watched it start; then the man went his way with a shrug. 'It's gone!' Sir Claude said.

Maisie crept some distance up the platform; she stood there with her back to her companion, following it with her eyes, keeping down tears, nursing her pink and yellow books. She had had a real fright but had fallen back to earth. The odd thing was that in her fall her fear too had been dashed down and broken. It was gone. She looked round at last, from where she had paused, at Sir Claude's, and then saw that his wasn't. It sat there with him on the bench to which, against the wall of the station, he had retreated, and where, leaning back and, as she thought, rather queer, he still waited. She came down to him and he continued to offer his ineffectual intention of pleasantry. 'Yes, I've chosen,' she said to him. 'I'll let her go if you – if you –'

236

She faltered; he quickly took her up. 'If I, if I – ?'

'If you'll give up Mrs Beale.'

'Oh!' he exclaimed; on which she saw how much, how hopelessly he was afraid. She had supposed at the café that it was of his rebellion, of his gathering motive; but how could that be when his temptations – that temptation, for example, of the train they had just lost – were after all so slight? Mrs Wix was right. He was afraid of his weakness – of his weakness.

She couldn't have told you afterwards how they got back to the inn: she could only have told you that even from this point they had not gone straight, but once more had wandered and loitered, and, in the course of it, had found themselves on the edge of the quay where – still apparently with half an hour to spare – the boat prepared for Folkestone was drawn up. Here they hovered as they had done at the station; here they exchanged silences again, but only exchanged silences. There were punctual people on the deck, choosing places, taking the best; some of them already contented, all established and shawled, facing to England and attended by the steward, who, confined on such a day to the lighter offices, tucked up the ladies' feet or opened bottles with a pop. They looked down at these things without a word; they even picked out a good place for two that was left in the lee of a lifeboat; and if they lingered rather stupidly, neither deciding to go aboard nor deciding to come away, it was Sir Claude quite as much as she who wouldn't move. It was Sir Claude who cultivated the supreme stillness by which she knew best what he meant. He simply meant that he knew all she herself meant. But there was no pretence of pleasantry now: their faces were grave and tired. When at last they lounged off it was as if his fear, his fear of his weakness, leaned upon her heavily as they followed the harbour. In the hall of the hotel as they passed in she saw a battered old box that she recognized, an ancient receptacle with dangling labels that she knew and a big painted W, lately done over and intensely personal, that seemed to stare at her with a recognition and even with some suspicion of its own. Sir Claude caught it too, and there was agitation for both of them in the sight of this object on the move. Was Mrs Wix going and was the responsibility of giving her up lifted, at a touch, from her pupil? Her pupil and her pupil's companion, transfixed a moment, held,

237

in the presence of the omen, communication more intense than in the presence either of the Paris train or of the Channel steamer; then, and still without a word, they went straight upstairs. There, however, on the landing, out of sight of the people below, they collapsed so that they had to sink down together for support: they simply seated themselves on the uppermost step while Sir Claude grasped the hand of his stepdaughter with a pressure that at another moment would probably have made her squeal. Their books and papers were all scattered. 'She thinks you've given her up!'

'Then I must see her – I must see her,' Maisie said.

'To bid her good-bye?'

'I must see her – I must see her,' the child only repeated.

They sat a minute longer, Sir Claude, with his tight grip of her hand and looking away from her, looking straight down the stair-case to where, round the turn, electric bells rattled and the pleasant sea-draught blew. At last, loosening his grasp, he slowly got up while she did the same. They went together along the lobby, but before they reached the salon he stopped again. 'If I give up Mrs Beale – ?'

'I'll go straight out with you again and not come back till she has gone.'

He seemed to wonder. 'Till Mrs Beale – ?'

He had made it sound like a bad joke. 'I mean till Mrs Wix leaves – in that boat.'

Sir Claude looked almost foolish. 'Is she going in that boat?'

'I suppose so. I won't even bid her good-bye,' Maisie continued. 'I'll stay out till the boat has gone. I'll go up to the old rampart.'

'The old rampart?'

'I'll sit on that old bench where you see the gold Virgin.'

'The gold Virgin?' he vaguely echoed. But it brought his eyes back to her as if after an instant he could see the place and the thing she named – could see her sitting there alone. 'While I break with Mrs Beale?'

'While you break with Mrs Beale.'

He gave a long deep smothered sigh. 'I must see her first.'

'You won't do as I do? Go out and wait?'

'Wait?' – once more he appeared at a loss.

'Till they both have gone,' Maisie said.

'Giving *us* up?'

'Giving *us* up.'

Oh with what a face for an instant he wondered if that could be! But his wonder the next moment only made him go to the door and, with his hand on the knob, stand as if listening for voices. Maisie listened, but she heard none. All she heard presently was Sir Claude's saying with speculation quite choked off, but so as not to be heard in the salon: 'Mrs Beale will never go.' On this he pushed open the door and she went in with him. The salon was empty, but as an effect of their entrance the lady he had just mentioned appeared at the door of the bedroom. 'Is she going?' he then demanded.

Mrs Beale came forward, closing her door behind her. 'I've had the most extraordinary scene with her. She told me yesterday she'd stay.'

'And my arrival has altered it?'

'Oh we took that into account!' Mrs Beale was flushed, which was never quite becoming to her, and her face visibly testified to the encounter to which she alluded. Evidently, however, she had not been worsted, and she held up her head and smiled and rubbed her hands as if in sudden emulation of the *patronne*. 'She promised she'd stay even if you should come.'

'Then why has she changed?'

'Because she's a hound. The reason she herself gives is that you've been out too long.'

Sir Claude stared. 'What has that to do with it?'

'You've been out an age,' Mrs Beale continued; 'I myself couldn't imagine what had become of you. The whole morning,' she exclaimed, 'and luncheon long since over!'

Sir Claude appeared indifferent to that. 'Did Mrs Wix go down with you?' he only asked.

'Not she; she never budged!' – and Mrs Beale's flush, to Maisie's vision, deepened. 'She moped there – she didn't so much as come out to me; and when I sent to invite her simply declined to appear. She said she wanted nothing, and I went down alone. But when I came up, fortunately a little primed' – and Mrs Beale smiled a fine smile of battle – 'she *was* in the field!'

'And you had a big row?'

'We had a big row' – she assented with a frankness as large. 'And while you left me to that sort of thing I should like to know where you were!' She paused for a reply, but Sir Claude merely looked at Maisie; a movement that promptly quickened her challenge. 'Where the mischief have you been?'

'You seem to take it as hard as Mrs Wix,' Sir Claude returned.

'I take it as I choose to take it, and you don't answer my question.'

He looked again at Maisie – as if for an aid to this effort; whereupon she smiled at her stepmother and offered: 'We've been everywhere.'

Mrs Beale, however, made her no response, thereby adding to a surprise of which our young lady had already felt the light brush. She had received neither a greeting nor a glance, but perhaps this was not more remarkable than the omission, in respect to Sir Claude, parted with in London two days before, of any sign of a sense of their reunion. Most remarkable of all was Mrs Beale's announcement of the pledge given by Mrs Wix and not hitherto revealed to her pupil. Instead of heeding this witness she went on with acerbity: 'It might surely have occurred to you that something would come up.'

Sir Claude looked at his watch. 'I had no idea it was so late, nor that we had been out so long. We weren't hungry. It passed like a flash. What *has* come up?'

'Oh that she's disgusted,' said Mrs Beale.

'With whom, then?'

'With Maisie.' Even now she never looked at the child, who stood there equally associated and disconnected. 'For having no moral sense.'

'How *should* she have?' Sir Claude tried again to shine a little at the companion of his walk. 'How at any rate is it proved by her going out with me?'

'Don't ask *me*; ask that woman. She drivels when she doesn't rage,' Mrs Beale declared.

'And she leaves the child?'

'She leaves the child,' said Mrs Beale with great emphasis and looking more than ever over Maisie's head.

In this position suddenly a change came into her face, caused, as the others could the next thing see, by the reappearance of

240

Mrs Wix in the doorway which, on coming in at Sir Claude's heels, Maisie had left gaping. 'I *don't* leave the child – I don't, I don't!' she thundered from the threshold, advancing upon the opposed three but addressing herself directly to Maisie. She was girded – positively harnessed – for departure, arrayed as she had been arrayed on her advent and armed with a small fat rusty reticule which, almost in the manner of a battle-axe, she brandished in support of her words. She had clearly come straight from her room, where Maisie in an instant guessed she had directed the removal of her minor effects. 'I don't leave you till I've given you another chance. Will you come *with* me?'

Maisie turned to Sir Claude, who struck her as having been removed to a distance of about a mile. To Mrs Beale she turned no more than Mrs Beale had turned: she felt as if already their difference had been disclosed. What had come out about that in the scene between the two women? Enough came out now, at all events, as she put it practically to her stepfather. 'Will *you* come? Won't you?' she inquired as if she had not already seen that she should have to give him up. It was the last flare of her dream. By this time she was afraid of nothing.

'I should think you'd be too proud to ask!' Mrs Wix interposed. Mrs Wix was herself conspicuously too proud.

But at the child's words Mrs Beale had fairly bounded. 'Come away from *me*, Maisie?' It was a wail of dismay and reproach, in which her stepdaughter was astonished to read that she had had no hostile consciousness and that if she had been so actively grand it was not from suspicion, but from strange entanglements of modesty.

Sir Claude presented to Mrs Beale an expression positively sick. 'Don't put it to her *that* way!' There had indeed been something in Mrs Beale's tone, and for a moment our young lady was reminded of the old days in which so many of her friends had been 'compromised'.

This friend blushed; she was before Mrs Wix, and though she bridled she took the hint. 'No – it isn't the way.' Then she showed she knew the way. 'Don't be a still bigger fool, dear, but go straight to your room and wait there till I can come to you.'

Maisie made no motion to obey, but Mrs Wix raised a hand that forestalled every evasion. 'Don't move till you've heard me. *I'm* going, but I must first understand. Have you lost it again?'

Maisie surveyed – for the idea of a describable loss – the immensity of space. Then she replied lamely enough: 'I feel as if I had lost everything.'

Mrs Wix looked dark. 'Do you mean to say you *have* lost what we found together with so much difficulty two days ago?' As her pupil failed of response she continued: 'Do you mean to say you've already forgotten what we found together?'

Maisie dimly remembered. 'My moral sense?'

'Your moral sense. *Haven't* I, after all, brought it out?' She spoke as she had never spoken even in the schoolroom and with the book in her hand.

It brought back to the child's recollection how she sometimes couldn't repeat on Friday the sentence that had been glib on Wednesday, and she dealt all feebly and ruefully with the present tough passage. Sir Claude and Mrs Beale stood there like visitors at an 'exam'. She had indeed an instant a whiff of the faint flower that Mrs Wix pretended to have plucked and now with such a peremptory hand thrust at her nose. Then it left her, and, as if she were sinking with a slip from a foothold, her arms made a short jerk. What this jerk represented was the spasm within her of something still deeper than a moral sense. She looked at her examiner; she looked at the visitors; she felt the rising of the tears she had kept down at the station. They had nothing – no, distinctly nothing – to do with her moral sense. The only thing was the old flat shameful schoolroom pleas. 'I don't know – I don't know.'

'Then you've lost it.' Mrs Wix seemed to close the book as she fixed the straighteners on Sir Claude. 'You've nipped it in the bud. You've killed it when it had begun to live.'

She was a newer Mrs Wix than ever, a Mrs Wix high and great; but Sir Claude was not after all to be treated as a little boy with a missed lesson. 'I've not killed anything,' he said; 'on the contrary I think I've produced life. I don't know what to call it – I haven't even known how decently to deal with it, to approach it; but, whatever it is, it's the most beautiful thing I've ever met – it's exquisite, it's sacred.' He had his hands in his pockets and, though a trace of the sickness he had just shown perhaps lingered there, his face bent itself with extraordinary gentleness on both the friends he was about to lose. 'Do you know what I came back for?' he asked of the elder.

'I think I do!' cried Mrs Wix, surprisingly unmollified and with the heat of her late engagement with Mrs Beale still on her brow. That lady, as if a little besprinkled by such turns of the tide, uttered a loud inarticulate protest and, averting herself, stood a moment at the window.

'I came back with a proposal,' said Sir Claude.

'To me?' Mrs Wix asked.

'To Maisie. That she should give you up.'

'And does she?'

Sir Claude wavered. 'Tell her!' he then exclaimed to the child, also turning away as if to give her the chance. But Mrs Wix and her pupil stood confronted in silence, Maisie whiter than ever – more awkward, more rigid and yet more dumb. They looked at each other hard, and as nothing came from them Sir Claude faced about again. 'You won't tell her? – you can't?' Still she said nothing; whereupon, addressing Mrs Wix, he broke into a kind of ecstasy. 'She refused – she refused!'

Maisie, at this, found her voice. 'I didn't refuse. I didn't,' she repeated.

It brought Mrs Beale straight back to her. 'You accepted, angel – you accepted!' She threw herself upon the child and, before Maisie could resist, had sunk with her upon the sofa, possessed of her, encircling her. 'You've given her up already, you've given her up for ever, and you're ours and ours only now, and the sooner she's off the better!'

Maisie had shut her eyes, but at a word of Sir Claude's they opened. 'Let her go!' he said to Mrs Beale.

'Never, never, never!' cried Mrs Beale. Maisie felt herself more compressed.

'Let her go!' Sir Claude more intensely repeated. He was looking at Mrs Beale and there was something in his voice. Maisie knew from a loosening of arms that she had become conscious of what it was; she slowly rose from the sofa, and the child stood there again dropped and divided. 'You're free – you're free,' Sir Claude went on; at which Maisie's back became aware of a push that vented resentment and that placed her again in the centre of the room, the cynosure of every eye and not knowing which way to turn.

She turned with an effort to Mrs Wix. 'I didn't refuse to give you up. I said I would if *he'd* give up – !'

'Give up Mrs Beale?' burst from Mrs Wix.

'Give up Mrs Beale. What do you call that but exquisite?' Sir Claude demanded of all of them, the lady mentioned included; speaking with a relish as intense now as if some lovely work of art or of nature had suddenly been set down among them. He was rapidly recovering himself on this basis of fine appreciation. 'She made her condition – with such a sense of what it should be! She made the only right one.'

'The only right one?' – Mrs Beale returned to the charge. She had taken a moment before a snub from him, but she was not to be snubbed on this. 'How can you talk such rubbish and how can you back her up in such impertinence? What in the world have you done to her to make her think of such stuff?' She stood there in righteous wrath; she flashed her eyes round the circle. Maisie took them full in her own, knowing that here at last was the moment she had had most to reckon with. But as regards her stepdaughter Mrs Beale subdued herself to a question deeply mild. '*Have* you made, my own love, any such condition as that?'

Somehow, now that it was there, the great moment was not so bad. What helped the child was that she knew what she wanted. All her learning and learning had made her at last learn that; so that if she waited an instant to reply it was only from the desire to be nice. Bewilderment had simply gone or at any rate was going fast. Finally she answered. 'Will you give *him* up? Will you?'

'Ah leave her alone – leave her, leave her!' Sir Claude in sudden supplication murmured to Mrs Beale.

Mrs Wix at the same instant found another apostrophe. 'Isn't it enough for you, madam, to have brought her to discussing your relations?'

Mrs Beale left Sir Claude unheeded, but Mrs Wix could make her flame. 'My relations? What do you know, you hideous creature, about my relations, and what business on earth have you to speak of them? Leave this room this instant, you horrible old woman!'

'I think you had better go – you must really catch your boat,'

Sir Claude said distressfully to Mrs Wix. He was out of it now, or wanted to be; he knew the worst and had accepted it: what now concerned him was to prevent, to dissipate vulgarities. 'Won't you go – won't you just get off quickly?'

'With the child as quickly as you like. Not without her.' Mrs Wix was adamant.

'Then why did you lie to me, you fiend?' Mrs Beale almost yelled. 'Why did you tell me an hour ago that you had given her up?'

'Because I despaired of her – because I thought she had left me.' Mrs Wix turned to Maisie. 'You were *with* them – in their connexion. But now your eyes are open, and I take you!'

'No you don't!' and Mrs Beale made, with a great fierce jump, a wild snatch at her stepdaughter. She caught her by the arm and, completing an instinctive movement, whirled her round in a further leap to the door, which had been closed by Sir Claude the instant their voices had risen. She fell back against it and, even while denouncing and waving off Mrs Wix, kept it closed in an incoherence of passion. 'You don't take her, but you bundle yourself: she stays with her own people and she's rid of you! I never heard anything so monstrous!' Sir Claude had rescued Maisie and kept hold of her; he held her in front of him, resting his hands very lightly on her shoulders and facing the loud adversaries. Mrs Beale's flush had dropped; she had turned pale with a splendid wrath. She kept protesting and dismissing Mrs Wix; she glued her back to the door to prevent Maisie's flight; she drove out Mrs Wix by the window or the chimney. 'You're a nice one – "discussing relations" – with your talk of our "connexion" and your insults! What in the world's our connexion but the love of the child who's our duty and our life and who holds us together as closely as she originally brought us?'

'I know, I know!' Maisie said with a burst of eagerness. 'I did bring you.'

The strangest of laughs escaped from Sir Claude. 'You did bring us – you did!' His hands went up and down gently on her shoulders.

Mrs Wix so dominated the situation that she had something sharp for everyone. 'There you have it, you see!' she pregnantly remarked to her pupil.

'*Will* you give him up?' Maisie persisted to Mrs Beale.

'To *you*, you abominable little horror?' that lady indignantly inquired, 'and to this raving old demon who has filled your dreadful little mind with her wickedness? Have you been a hideous little hypocrite all these years that I've slaved to make you love me and deludedly believed you did?'

'I love Sir Claude – I love *him*,' Maisie replied with an awkward sense that she appeared to offer it as something that would do as well. Sir Claude had continued to pat her, and it was really an answer to his pats.

'She hates you – she hates you,' he observed with the oddest quietness to Mrs Beale.

His quietness made her blaze. 'And you back her up in it and give me up to outrage?'

'No; I only insist that she's free – she's free.'

Mrs Beale stared – Mrs Beale glared. 'Free to starve with this pauper lunatic?'

'I'll do more for her than *you* ever did!' Mrs Wix retorted. 'I'll work my fingers to the bone.'

Maisie, with Sir Claude's hands still on her shoulders, felt, just as she felt the fine surrender in them, that over her head he looked in a certain way at Mrs Wix. 'You needn't do that,' she heard him say. 'She has means.'

'Means? – Maisie?' Mrs Beale shrieked. 'Means that her vile father has stolen!'

'I'll get them back – I'll get them back. I'll look into it.' He smiled and nodded at Mrs Wix.

This had a fearful effect on his other friend. 'Haven't *I* looked into it, I should like to know, and haven't I found an abyss? It's too inconceivable – your cruelty to me!' she wildly broke out. She had hot tears in her eyes.

He spoke to her very kindly, almost coaxingly. 'We'll look into it again; we'll look into it together. It *is* an abyss, but he *can* be made – or Ida can. Think of the money they're getting now!' he laughed. 'It's all right, it's all right,' he continued. 'It wouldn't do – it wouldn't do. We *can't* work her in. It's perfectly true – she's unique. We're not good enough – oh no!' and, quite exuberantly, he laughed again.

'Not good enough, and that beast *is*?' Mrs Beale shouted.

At this moment there was a hush in the room, and in the midst of it Sir Claude replied to the question by moving with Maisie to Mrs Wix. The next thing the child knew she was at that lady's side with an arm firmly grasped. Mrs Beale still guarded the door. 'Let them pass,' said Sir Claude at last.

She remained there, however; Maisie saw the pair look at each other. Then she saw Mrs Beale turn to her. 'I'm your mother now, Maisie. And he's your father.'

'That's just where it is!' sighed Mrs Wix with an effect of irony positively detached and philosophic.

Mrs Beale continued to address her young friend, and her effort to be reasonable and tender was in its way remarkable. 'We're representative, you know, of Mr Farange and his former wife. This person represents mere illiterate presumption. We take our stand on the law.'

'Oh the law, the law!' Mrs Wix superbly jeered. 'You had better indeed let the law have a look at you!'

'Let them pass – let them pass!' Sir Claude pressed his friend hard – he pleaded.

But she fastened herself to Maisie. '*Do* you hate me, dearest?'

Maisie looked at her with new eyes, but answered as she had answered before. 'Will you give him up?'

Mrs Beale's rejoinder hung fire, but when it came it was noble. 'You shouldn't talk to me of such things!' She was shocked, she was scandalized to tears.

For Mrs Wix, however, it was her discrimination that was indelicate. 'You ought to be ashamed of yourself!' she roundly cried.

Sir Claude made a supreme appeal. 'Will you be so good as to allow these horrors to terminate?'

Mrs Beale fixed her eyes on him, and again Maisie watched them. 'You should do him justice,' Mrs Wix went on to Mrs Beale. 'We've always been devoted to him, Maisie and I – and he has shown how much he likes us. He would like to please her; he would like even, I think, to please me. But he hasn't given you up.'

They stood confronted, the step-parents, still under Maisie's observation. That observation had never sunk so deep as at this particular moment. 'Yes, my dear, I haven't given you up,' Sir Claude said to Mrs Beale at last, 'and if you'd like me to treat our friends here as solemn witnesses I don't mind giving you my word for it that I never will. There!' he dauntlessly exclaimed.

'He can't!' Mrs Wix tragically commented.

Mrs Beale, erect and alive in her defeat, jerked her handsome face about. 'He can't!' she literally mocked.

'He can't, he can't, he can't!' – Sir Claude's gay emphasis wonderfully carried it off.

Mrs Beale took it all in, yet she held her ground; on which Maisie addressed Mrs Wix. 'Shan't we lose the boat?'

'Yes, we shall lose the boat,' Mrs Wix remarked to Sir Claude.

Mrs Beale meanwhile faced full at Maisie. 'I don't know what to make of you!' she launched.

'Good-bye,' said Maisie to Sir Claude.

'Good-bye, Maisie,' Sir Claude answered.

Mrs Beale came away from the door. 'Good-bye!' she hurled at Maisie; then passed straight across the room and disappeared in the adjoining one.

Sir Claude had reached the other door and opened it. Mrs Wix was already out. On the threshold Maisie paused; she put out her hand to her stepfather. He took it and held it a moment, and their eyes met as the eyes of those who have done for each other what they can. 'Good-bye,' he repeated.

'Good-bye.' And Maisie followed Mrs Wix.

They caught the steamer, which was just putting off, and, hustled across the gulf, found themselves on the deck so breathless and so scared that they gave up half the voyage to letting their emotion sink. It sank slowly and imperfectly; but at last, in mid-channel, surrounded by the quiet sea, Mrs Wix had courage to revert. 'I didn't look back, did you?'

'Yes. He wasn't there,' said Maisie.

'Not on the balcony?'

Maisie waited a moment; then 'He wasn't there' she simply said again.

Mrs Wix was also silent a while. 'He went to *her*,' she finally observed.

'Oh I know!' the child replied.

Mrs Wix gave a sidelong look. She still had room for wonder at what Maisie knew.

The Spoils of Poynton

CHAPTER 1

MRS GERETH had said she would go with the rest to church, but suddenly it seemed to her that she should not be able to wait even till church-time for relief: breakfast, at Waterbath, was a punctual meal, and she had still nearly an hour on her hands. Knowing the church to be near, she prepared in her room for the little rural walk, and on her way down again, passing through corridors and observing imbecilities of decoration, the aesthetic misery of the big commodious house, she felt a return of the tide of last night's irritation, a renewal of everything she could secretly suffer from ugliness and stupidity. Why did she consent to such contacts, why did she so rashly expose herself? She had had, heaven knew, her reasons, but the whole experience was to be sharper than she had feared. To get away from it and out into the air, into the presence of sky and trees, flowers and birds was a necessity of every nerve. The flowers at Waterbath would probably go wrong in colour and the nightingales sing out of tune; but she remembered to have heard the place described as possessing those advantages that are usually spoken of as natural. There were advantages enough it clearly didn't possess. It was hard for her to believe that a woman could look presentable who had been kept awake for hours by the wallpaper in her room; yet none the less, as in her fresh widow's weeds she rustled across the hall, she was sustained by the consciousness, which always added to the unction of her social Sundays, that she was, as usual, the only person in the house incapable of wearing in her preparation the horrible stamp of the same exceptional smartness that would be conspicuous in a grocer's wife. She would rather have perished than have looked *endimanchée*.

She was fortunately not challenged, the hall being empty of the other women, who were engaged precisely in arraying themselves to that dire end. Once in the grounds, she recognized that, with a site, a view that struck the note, set an example to its inmates, Waterbath ought to have been charming.

How she herself, with such elements to handle, would have taken the fine hint of nature! Suddenly, at the turn of a walk, she came on a member of the party, a young lady seated on a bench in deep and lonely meditation. She had observed the girl at dinner and afterwards: she was always looking at girls with an apprehensive or speculative reference to her son. Deep in her heart was a conviction that Owen would, in spite of all her spells, marry at last a frump; and this from no evidence that she could have represented as adequate, but simply from her deep uneasiness, her belief that such a special sensibility as her own could have been inflicted on a woman only as a source of anguish. It would be her fate, her discipline, her cross, to have a frump brought hideously home to her. This girl, one of the two Vetches, had no beauty, but Mrs Gereth, scanning the dullness for a sign of life, had been straightaway able to classify such a figure as the least, for the moment, of her afflictions. Fleda Vetch was dressed with an idea, though perhaps with not much else; and that made a bond when there was none other, especially as in this case the idea was real, not imitation. Mrs Gereth had long ago generalized the truth that the temperament of the frump is amply consistent with a certain usual prettiness. There were five girls in the party, and the prettiness of this one, slim, pale, and black-haired, was less likely than that of the others ever to occasion an exchange of platitudes. The two less developed Brigstocks, daughters of the house, were in particular tiresomely 'lovely'. A second glance, this morning, at the young lady before her conveyed to Mrs Gereth the soothing assurance that she also was guiltless of looking hot and fine. They had had no talk as yet, but this was a note that would effectually introduce them if the girl should show herself in the least conscious of their community. She got up from her seat with a smile that but partly dissipated the prostration Mrs Gereth had recognized in her attitude. The elder woman drew her down again, and for a minute, as they sat together, their eyes met and sent out mutual soundings. 'Are you safe? Can I utter it?' each of them said to the other, quickly recognizing, almost proclaiming, their common need to escape. The tremendous fancy, as it came to be called, that Mrs Gereth was destined to take to Fleda Vetch virtually began with this discovery that the poor child had been moved to flight even more promptly than herself. That the poor child no less quickly perceived how far she could now go was proved by the immense friendliness with which she instantly broke out: 'Isn't it too dreadful?'

'Horrible – horrible!' cried Mrs Gereth, with a laugh, 'and it's really a comfort to be able to say it.' She had an idea, for it was her ambition, that she successfully made a secret of that awkward oddity, her proneness to be rendered unhappy by the presence of the dreadful. Her passion for the exquisite was the cause of this, but it was a passion she considered that she never advertised nor gloried in, contenting herself with letting it regulate her steps and show quietly in her life, remembering at all times that there are few things more soundless than a deep devotion. She was therefore struck with the acuteness of the little girl who had already put a finger on her hidden spring. What was dreadful now, what was horrible, was the intimate ugliness of Waterbath, and it was of that phenomenon these ladies talked while they sat in the shade and drew refreshment from the great tranquil sky, from which no blue saucers were suspended. It was an ugliness fundamental and systematic, the result of the abnormal nature of the Brigstocks, from whose composition the principle of taste had been extravagantly omitted. In the arrangement of their home some other principle, remarkably active, but uncanny and obscure, had operated instead, with consequences depressing to behold, consequences that took the form of a universal futility. The house was bad in all conscience, but it might have pased if they had only let it alone. This saving mercy was beyond them; they had smothered it with trumpery ornament and scrapbook art, with strange excrescences and bunchy draperies, with gim-cracks that might have been keepsakes for maid-servants and nondescript conveniences that might have been prizes for the blind. They had gone wildly astray over carpets and curtains; they had an infallible instinct for disaster, and were so cruelly doom-ridden that it rendered them almost tragic. Their drawing-room, Mrs Gereth lowered her voice to mention, caused her face to burn, and each of the new friends confided to the other that in her own apartment she had given way to tears. There was in the elder lady's a set of comic water-colours, a family joke by a family genius, and in the younger's a souvenir from some centennial or other Exhibition, that they shudderingly alluded to. The house was perversely full of souvenirs of places even more ugly than itself and of things it would have been a pious duty to forget. The worst horror was the acres of varnish, something advertised and smelly, with which everything was smeared; it was Fleda Vetch's conviction that the application of it, by their own hands and hilariously shoving each other, was the amusement of the Brigstocks on rainy days.

When, as criticism deepened, Fleda dropped the suggestion that some people would perhaps see something in Mona, Mrs Gereth caught her up with a groan of protest, a smothered familiar cry of 'Oh, my dear!' Mona was the eldest of the three, the one Mrs Gereth most suspected. She confided to her young friend that it was her suspicion that had brought her to Waterbath; and this was going very far, for on the spot, as a refuge, a remedy, she had clutched at the idea that something might be done with the girl before her. It was her fancied exposure at any rate that had sharpened the shock; made her ask herself with a terrible chill if fate could really be plotting to saddle her with a daughter-in-law brought up in such a place. She had seen Mona in her appropriate setting and she had seen Owen, handsome and heavy, dangle beside her; but the effect of these first hours had happily not been to darken the prospect. It was clearer to her that she could never accept Mona, but it was after all by no means certain that Owen would ask her to. He had sat by somebody else at dinner, and afterwards he had talked to Mrs Firmin, who was as dreadful as all the rest, but redeemingly married. His heaviness, which in her need of expansion she freely named, had two aspects: one of them his monstrous lack of taste, the other his exaggerated prudence. If it should come to a question of carrying Mona with a high hand there would be no need to worry, for that was rarely his manner of proceeding.

Invited by her companion, who had asked if it weren't wonderful, Mrs Gereth had begun to say a word about Poynton; but she heard a sound of voices that made her stop

254

short. The next moment she rose to her feet, and Fleda could see that her alarm was by no means quenched. Behind the place where they had been sitting the ground dropped with a certain steepness, forming a long grassy bank, up which Owen Gereth and Mona Brigstock, dressed for church but making a familiar joke of it, were in the act of scrambling and helping each other. When they had reached the even ground Fleda was able to read the meaning of the exclamation in which Mrs Gereth had expressed her reserves on the subject of Miss Brigstock's personality. Miss Brigstock had been laughing and even romping, but the circumstances hadn't contributed the ghost of an expression to her countenance. Tall, straight, and fair, long-limbed and strangely festooned, she stood there without a look in her eye or any perceptible intention of any sort in any other feature. She belonged to the type in which speech is an unaided emission of sound and the secret of being is impenetrably and incorruptibly kept. Her expression would probably have been beautiful if she had had one, but whatever she communicated she communicated, in a manner best known to herself, without signs. This was not the case with Owen Gereth, who had plenty of them, and all very simple and immediate. Robust and artless, eminently natural, yet perfectly correct, he looked pointlessly active and pleasantly dull. Like his mother and like Fleda Vetch, but not for the same reason, this young pair had come out to take a turn before church.

The meeting of the two couples was sensibly awkward, and Fleda, who was sagacious, took the measure of the shock inflicted on Mrs Gereth. There had been intimacy – oh yes, intimacy as well as puerility – in the horse-play of which they had just had a glimpse. The party began to stroll together to the house, and Fleda had again a sense of Mrs Gereth's quick management in the way the lovers, or whatever they were, found themselves separated. She strolled behind with Mona, the mother possessing herself of her son, her exchange of remarks with whom, however, remained, as they went, suggestively inaudible. That member of the party in whose intenser consciousness we shall most profitably seek a reflection of the little drama with which we are concerned received an even livelier impression of Mrs Gereth's intervention from the fact

255

that ten minutes later, on the way to church, still another pairing had been effected. Owen walked with Fleda, and it was an amusement to the girl to feel sure that this was by his mother's direction. Fleda had other amusements as well: such as noting that Mrs Gereth was now with Mona Brigstock; such as observing that she was all affability to that young woman; such as reflecting that, masterful and clever, with a great bright spirit, she was one of those who impose themselves as an influence; such as feeling finally that Owen Gereth was absolutely beautiful and delightfully dense. This young person had even from herself wonderful secrets of delicacy and pride; but she came as near distinctness as in the consideration of such matters she had ever come at all in now surrendering herself to the idea that it was of a pleasant effect and rather remarkable to be stupid without offence – of a pleasanter effect and more remarkable indeed than to be clever and horrid. Owen Gereth at any rate, with his inches, his features, and his lapses, was neither of these latter things. She herself was prepared, if she should ever marry, to contribute all the cleverness, and she liked to think that her husband would be a force grateful for direction. She was in her small way a spirit of the same family as Mrs Gereth. On that flushed and huddled Sunday a great matter occurred; her little life became aware of a singular quickening. Her meagre past fell away from her like a garment of the wrong fashion, and as she came up to town on the Monday what she stared at in the suburban fields from the train was a future full of the things she particularly loved.

CHAPTER 2

THESE were neither more nor less than the things with which she had had time to learn from Mrs Gereth that Poynton overflowed. Poynton, in the south of England, was this lady's established, or rather her disestablished home, having recently passed into the possession of her son.

The father of the boy, an only child, had died two years before, and in London, with his mother, Owen was occupying for May and June a house good-naturedly lent them by Colonel Gereth, their uncle and brother-in-law. His mother had laid her hand so engagingly on Fleda Vetch that in a very few days the girl knew it was possible they should suffer together in Cadogan Place almost as much as they had suffered together at Waterbath. The kind colonel's house was also an ordeal, but the two women, for the ensuing month, had at least the relief of their confessions. The great drawback of Mrs Gereth's situation was that, thanks to the rare perfection of Poynton, she was condemned to wince wherever she turned. She had lived for a quarter of a century in such warm closeness with the beautful that, as she frankly admitted, life had become for her a kind of fool's paradise. She couldn't leave her own house without peril of exposure. She didn't say it in so many words, but Fleda could see she held that there was nothing in England really to compare to Poynton. There were places much grander and richer, but there was no such complete work of art, nothing that would appeal so to those who were really informed. In putting such elements into her hand fortune had given her an inestimable chance; she knew how rarely well things had gone with her and that she had tasted a happiness altogether rare.

There had been in the first place the exquisite old house itself, early Jacobean, supreme in every part: it was a provocation, an inspiration, a matchless canvas for the picture. Then there had been her husband's sympathy and generosity, his knowledge and love, their perfect accord and beautiful life together, twenty-six years of planning and seeking, a long, sunny harvest of taste and curiosity. Lastly, she never denied, there had been her personal gift, the genius, the passion, the patience of the collector – a patience, an almost infernal cunning, that had enabled her to do it all with a limited command of money. There wouldn't have been money enough for anyone else, she said with pride, but there had been money enough for her. They had saved on lots of things in life, and there were lots of things they hadn't had, but they had had in every corner of Europe their swing among the Jews. It was fascinating to poor Fleda, who hadn't had a penny in the world nor anything nice at home, and whose only treasure was her subtle mind, to hear this genuine English lady, fresh and fair, young in the fifties, declare with gaiety and conviction that she was herself the greatest Jew who had ever tracked a victim. Fleda, with her mother dead, hadn't so much even as a home, and her nearest chance of one was that there was some appearance her sister would become engaged to a curate whose eldest brother was supposed to have property and would perhaps allow him something. Her father paid some of her bills, but he didn't like her to live with him; and she had lately, in Paris, with several hundred other young women, spent a year in a studio, arming herself for the battle of life by a course with an impressionist painter. She was determined to work, but her impressions, or somebody's else, were as yet her only material. Mrs Gereth had told her she liked her because she had an extraordinary *flair*; but under the circumstances a *flair* was a questionable boon: in the dry places in which she had mainly moved she could have borne a chronic catarrh. She was constantly summoned to Cadogan Place, and before the month was out was kept to stay, to pay a visit of which the end, it was agreed, should have nothing to do with the beginning. She had a sense, partly exultant and partly alarmed, of having quickly become necessary to her imperious friend, who indeed gave a reason quite sufficient for it in telling her there was nobody else who understood. From Mrs Gereth there was in these days an immense deal to understand, though it might be freely summed up in the circumstance that she was wretched. She told Fleda that she couldn't completely know why till she

258

should have seen the things at Poynton. Fleda could perfectly grasp this connexion, which was exactly one of the matters that, in their inner mystery, were a blank to everybody else.

The girl had a promise that the wonderful house should be shown her early in July, when Mrs Gereth would return to it as to her home; but even before this initiation she put her finger on the spot that in the poor lady's troubled soul ached hardest. This was the misery that haunted her, the dread of the inevitable surrender. What Fleda had to sit up to was the confirmed appearance that Owen Gereth would marry Mona Brigstock, marry her in his mother's teeth, and that such an act would have incalculable bearings. They were present to Mrs Gereth, her companion could see, with a vividness that at moments almost ceased to be that of sanity. She would have to give up Poynton, and give it up to a product of Waterbath – that was the wrong that rankled, the humiliation at which Fleda would be able adequately to shudder only when she should know the place. She did know Waterbath, and she despised it – she had that qualification for sympathy. Her sympathy was intelligent, for she read deep into the matter; she stared, aghast, as it came home to her for the first time, at the cruel English custom of the expropriation of the lonely mother. Mr Gereth had apparently been a very amiable man, but Mr Gereth had left things in a way that made the girl marvel. The house and its contents had been treated as a single splendid object; everything was to go straight to his son, and his widow was to have a maintenance and a cottage in another county. No account whatever had been taken of her relation to her treasures, of the passion with which she had waited for them, worked for them, picked them over, made them worthy of each other and the house, watched them, loved them, lived with them. He appeared to have assumed that she would settle questions with her son, that he could depend upon Owen's affection. And in truth, as poor Mrs Gereth inquired, how could he possibly have had a prevision – he who turned his eyes instinctively from everything repulsive – of anything so abnormal as a Waterbath Brigstock? He had been in ugly houses enough, but had escaped that particular nightmare.

Nothing so perverse could have been expected to happen as that the heir to the loveliest thing in England should be inspired to hand it over to a girl so exceptionally tainted. Mrs Gereth spoke of poor Mona's taint as if to mention it were almost a violation of decency, and a person who had listened without enlightenment would have wondered of what fault the girl had been or had indeed not been guilty. But Owen had from a boy never cared, had never had the least pride or pleasure in his home.

'Well, then, if he doesn't care!' – Fleda exclaimed, with some impetuosity; stopping short, however, before she completed her sentence.

Mrs Gereth looked at her rather hard. 'If he doesn't care?'

Fleda hesitated; she had not quite had a definite idea. 'Well – he'll give them up.'

'Give what up?'

'Why, those beautiful things.'

'Give them up to whom?' Mrs Gereth more boldly stared.

'To you, of course – to enjoy, to keep for yourself.'

'And leave his house as bare as your hand? There's nothing in it that isn't precious.'

Fleda considered; her friend had taken her up with a smothered ferocity by which she was slightly disconcerted. 'I don't mean of course that he should surrender everything; but he might let you pick out the things to which you're most attached.'

'I think he would if he were free,' said Mrs Gereth.

'And do you mean, as it is, that *she*'ll prevent him?' Mona Brigstock, between these ladies, was now nothing but 'she'.

'By every means in her power.'

'But surely not because she understands and appreciates them?'

'No,' Mrs Gereth replied, 'but because they belong to the house and the house belongs to Owen. If I should wish to take anything, she would simply say, with that motionless mask: "It goes with the house." And day after day, in the face of every argument, of every consideration of generosity, she would repeat, without winking, in that voice like the squeeze

260

of a doll's stomach: "It goes with the house – it goes with the house." In that attitude they'll shut themselves up.'

Fleda was struck, was even a little startled with the way Mrs Gereth had turned this over – had faced, if indeed only to recognize its futility, the notion of a battle with her only son. These words led her to make an inquiry which she had not thought it discreet to make before; she brought out the idea of the possibility, after all, of her friend's continuing to live at Poynton. Would they really wish to proceed to extremities? Was no good-humoured graceful compromise to be imagined or brought about. Couldn't the same roof cover them? Was it so very inconceivable that a married son should, for the rest of her days, share with so charming a mother the home she had devoted more than a score of years to making beautiful for him? Mrs Gereth hailed this question with a wan, compassionate smile; she replied that a common household, in such a case, was exactly so inconceivable that Fleda had only to glance over the fair face of the English land to see how few people had ever conceived it. It was always thought a wonder, a 'mistake', a piece of overstrained sentiment; and she confessed that she was as little capable of a flight of that sort as Owen himself. Even if they both had been capable, they would still have Mona's hatred to reckon with. Fleda's breath was sometimes taken away by the great bounds and elisions which, on Mrs Gereth's lips, the course of discussion could take. This was the first she had heard of Mona's hatred, though she certainly had not needed Mrs Gereth to tell her that in close quarters that young lady would prove secretly mulish. Later Fleda perceived indeed that perhaps almost any girl would hate a person who should be so markedly averse to having anything to do with her. Before this, however, in conversation with her young friend, Mrs Gereth furnished a more vivid motive for her despair by asking how she could possibly be expected to sit there with the new proprietors and accept – or call it, for a day, endure – the horrors they would perpetrate in the house. Fleda reasoned that they wouldn't after all smash things nor burn them up; and Mrs Gereth admitted when pushed that she didn't quite suppose they would. What she meant was that they would neglect them, ignore them, leave them to clumsy servants (there wasn't an object of them all but should be handled with perfect love), and in many cases probably wish to replace them by pieces answerable to some vulgar modern notion of the convenient. Above all, she saw in advance, with dilated eyes, the abominations they would inevitably mix up with them – the maddening relics of Waterbath, the little brackets and pink vases, the sweepings of bazaars, the family photographs and illuminated texts, the 'household art' and household piety of Mona's hideous home. Wasn't it enough simply to contend that Mona would approach Poynton in the spirit of a Brigstock, and that in the spirit of a Brigstock she would deal with her acquisition? Did Fleda really see *her*, Mrs Gereth demanded, spending the remainder of her days with such a creature's elbow in her eye?

Fleda had to declare that she certainly didn't, and that Waterbath had been a warning it would be frivolous to overlook. At the same time she privately reflected that they were taking a great deal for granted, and that, inasmuch as to her knowledge Owen Gereth had positively denied his betrothal, the ground of their speculations was by no means firm. It seemed to our young lady that in a difficult position Owen conducted himself with some natural art ; treating this domesticated confidant of his mother's wrongs with a simple civility that almost troubled her conscience, so deeply she felt that she might have had for him the air of siding with that lady against him. She wondered if he would ever know how little really she did this, and that she was there, since Mrs Gereth had insisted, not to betray, but essentially to confirm and protect. The fact that his mother disliked Mona Brigstock might have made him dislike the object of her preference, and it was detestable to Fleda to remember that she might have appeared to him to offer herself as an exemplary contrast. It was clear enough, however, that the happy youth had no more sense for a motive than a deaf man for a tune, a limitation by which, after all, she could gain as well as lose. He came and went very freely on the business with which London abundantly furnished him, but he found time more than once to say to her, 'It's awfully nice of you to look after poor Mummy.' As well as his quick speech, which shyness made obscure – it was usually as desperate as a 'rush' at some violent game – his child's eyes in his man's face put it to her that, you know, this really meant a good deal for him and that he hoped she would stay on. With a person in the house who, like herself, was clever, poor Mummy was conveniently occupied; and Fleda found a beauty in the candour and even in the modesty which apparently kept him from suspecting that two such wiseheads could possibly be occupied with Owen Gereth.

CHAPTER 3

THEY went at last, the wiseheads, down to Poynton, where the palpitating girl had the full revelation. '*Now* do you know how I feel?' Mrs Gereth asked when in the wonderful hall, three minutes after their arrival, her pretty associate dropped on a seat with a soft gasp and a roll of dilated eyes. The answer came clearly enough, and in the rapture of that first walk through the house Fleda took a prodigious span. She perfectly understood how Mrs Gereth felt – she had understood but meagrely before; and the two women embraced with tears over the tightening of their bond – tears which on the younger one's part were the natural and usual sign of her submission to perfect beauty. It was not the first time she had cried for the joy of admiration, but it was the first time the mistress of Poynton, often as she had shown her house, had been present at such an exhibition. She exulted in it; it quickened her own tears; she assured her companion that such an occasion made the poor old place fresh to her again and more precious than ever. Yes, nobody had ever, that way, felt what she had achieved: people were so grossly ignorant, and everybody, even the knowing ones as they thought themselves, more or less dense. What Mrs Gereth had achieved was indeed an exquisite work; and in such an art of the treasure-hunter, in selection and comparison refined to that point, there was an element of creation, of personality. She had commended Fleda's *flair*, and Fleda now gave herself up to satiety. Pre-occupations and scruples fell away from her; she had never known a greater happiness than the week she passed in this initiation.

Wandering through clear chambers where the general effect made preferences almost as impossible as if they had been shocks, pausing at open doors where vistas were long and bland, she would, even if she had not already known, have discovered for herself that Poynton was the record of a life. It was written in great syllables of colour and form, the tongues of other countries and the hands of rare artists. It was all France and Italy, with their ages composed to rest. For England you looked out of old windows – it was England that was the wide embrace. While outside, on the low terraces, she contradicted gardeners and refined on nature, Mrs Gereth left her guest to finger fondly the brasses that Louis Quinze might have thumbed, to sit with Venetian velvets just held in a loving palm, to hang over cases of enamels and pass and repass before cabinets. There were not many pictures – the panels and the stuffs were themselves the picture; and in all the great wainscoted house there was not an inch of pasted paper. What struck Fleda most in it was the high pride of her friend's taste, a fine arrogance, a sense of style which, however amused and amusing, never compromised nor stooped. She felt indeed, as this lady had intimated to her that she would, both a respect and a compassion that she had not known before; the vision of the coming surrender filled her with an equal pain. To give it all up, to die to it – that thought ached in her breast. She herself could imagine clinging there with a closeness separate from dignity. To have created such a place was to have had dignity enough; when there was a question of defending it the fiercest attitude was the right one. After so intense a taking of possession she too was to give it up; for she reflected that if Mrs Gereth's remaining there would have offered her a sort of future – stretching away in safe years on the other side of a gulf – the advent of the others could only be, by the same law, a great vague menace, the ruffling of a still water. Such were the emotions of a hungry girl whose sensibility was almost as great as her opportunities for comparison had been small. The museums had done something for her, but nature had done more.

If Owen had not come down with them nor joined them later, it was because he still found London jolly; yet the question remained of whether the jollity of London was not merely the only name his small vocabulary yielded for the jollity of Mona Brigstock. There was indeed in his conduct another ambiguity – something that required explaining so long as his motive didn't come to the surface. If he was in love, what was the matter? And what was the matter still more if he wasn't? The mystery was at last cleared up: this Fleda gathered from the tone in which, one morning at breakfast, a letter just opened made Mrs Gereth cry out. Her dismay was almost a shriek: 'Why, he's bringing her down – he wants her to see the house!' They flew, the two women, into each other's arms and, with their heads together, soon made out that the reason, the baffling reason why nothing had yet happened, was that Mona didn't know, or Owen didn't, whether Poynton would really please her. She was coming down to judge; and could anything in the world be more like poor Owen than the ponderous probity which had kept him from pressing her for a reply till she should have learned whether she approved what he had to offer her? That was a scruple it had naturally been impossible to impute. If only they might fondly hope, Mrs Gereth wailed, that the girl's expectations would be dashed! There was a fine consistency, a sincerity quite affecting, in her arguing that the better the place should happen to look and to express the conceptions to which it owed its origin, the less it would speak to an intelligence so primitive. How could a Brigstock possibility understand what it was all about? How, really, could a Brigstock logically do anything but hate it? Mrs Gereth, even as she whisked away linen shrouds, persuaded herself of the possibility on Mona's part of some bewildered blankness, some collapse of admiration that would prove disconcerting to her swain – a hope of which Fleda at least could see the absurdity and which gave the measure of the poor lady's strange, almost maniacal disposition to thrust in everywhere the question of 'things', to read all behaviour in the light of some fancied relation to them. 'Things' were of course the sum of the world; only, for Mrs Gereth, the sum of the world was rare French furniture and Oriental china. She could at a stretch imagine people's not having, but she couldn't imagine their not wanting and not missing.

The young couple were to be accompanied by Mrs Brigstock, and with a prevision of how fiercely they would be watched Fleda became conscious, before the party arrived, of an amused, diplomatic pity for them. Almost as much as Mrs Gereth's her taste was her life, but her life was somehow the larger for it. Besides, she had another care now: there was someone she wouldn't have liked to see humiliated even in the form of a young lady who would contribute to his never suspecting so much delicacy. When this young lady appeared Fleda tried, so far as the wish to efface herself allowed, to be mainly the person to take her about, show her the house, and cover up her ignorance. Owen's announcement had been that, as trains made it convenient, they would present themselves for luncheon and depart before dinner; but Mrs Gereth, true to her system of glaring civility, proposed and obtained an extension, a dining and spending of the night. She made her young friend wonder against what rebellion of fact she was sacrificing in advance so profusely to form. Fleda was appalled, after the first hour, by the rash innocence with which Mona had accepted the responsibility of observation, and indeed by the large levity with which, sitting there like a bored tourist in fine scenery, she exercised it. She felt in her nerves the effect of such a manner on her companion's, and it was this that made her want to entice the girl away, give her some merciful warning or some jocular cue. Mona met intense looks, however, with eyes that might have been blue beads, the only ones she had – eyes into which Fleda thought it strange Owen Gereth should have to plunge for his fate and his mother for a confession of whether Poynton was a success. She made no remark that helped to supply this light; her impression at any rate had nothing in common with the feeling that, as the beauty of the place throbbed out like music, had caused Fleda Vetch to burst into tears. She was as content to say nothing as if, Mrs Gereth afterwards exclaimed, she had been keeping her mouth shut in a railway tunnel. Mrs Gereth contrived at the end of an hour to convey to Fleda that it was plain she was brutally ignorant; but Fleda more subtly discovered that her ignorance was obscurely active.

She was not so stupid as not to see that something, though she scarcely knew what, was expected of her that she couldn't give; and the only mode her intelligence suggested of meeting the expectation was to plant her big feet and pull another way. Mrs Gereth wanted her to rise, somehow or somewhere, and was prepared to hate her if she didn't: very well, she couldn't, she wouldn't rise; she already moved at the altitude that suited her, and was able to see that, since she was exposed to the hatred, she might at least enjoy the calm. The smallest trouble, for a girl with no nonsense about her, was to earn what she incurred; so that, a dim instinct teaching her she would earn it best by not being effusive, and combining with the conviction that she now held Owen, and therefore the place, she had the pleasure of her honesty as well as of her security. Didn't her very honesty lead her to be belligerently blank about Poynton inasmuch as it was just Poynton that was forced upon her as a subject for effusiveness? Such subjects, to Mona Brigstock, had an air almost of indecency, and the house became uncanny to her through such an appeal – an appeal that, somewhere in the twilight of her being, as Fleda was sure, she thanked heaven she *was* the girl stiffly to draw back from. She was a person whom pressure at a given point infallibly caused to expand in the wrong place instead of, as it is usually administered in the hope of doing, the right one. Her mother, to make up for this, broke out universally, pronounced everything 'most striking', and was visibly happy that Owen's captor should be so far on the way to strike: but she jarred upon Mrs Gereth by her formula of admiration, which was that anything she looked at was 'in the style' of something else. This was to show how much she had seen, but it only showed she had seen nothing; everything at Poynton was in the style of Poynton, and poor Mrs Brigstock, who at least was determined to rise, and had brought with her a trophy of her journey, a 'lady's magazine' purchased at the station, a horrible thing with patterns for antimacassars, which, as it was quite new, the first number, and seemed so clever, she kindly offered to leave for the house, was in the style of a vulgar old woman who wore silver jewellery and tried to pass off a gross avidity as a sense of the beautiful.

By the day's end it was clear to Fleda Vetch that, however Mona judged, the day had been determinant; whether or not she felt the charm, she felt the challenge: at an early moment Owen Gereth would be able to tell his mother the worst. Nevertheless, when the elder lady, at bedtime, coming in a dressing-gown and a high fever to the younger one's room, cried out, 'She hates it; but what will she do?' Fleda pretended vagueness, played at obscurity, and assented disingenuously to the proposition that they at least had a respite. The future was dark to her, but there was a silken thread she could clutch in the gloom – she would never give Owen away. He might give himself – he even certainly would; but that was his own affair, and his blunders, his innocence, only added to the appeal he made to her. She would cover him, she would protect him, and beyond thinking her a cheerful inmate he would never guess her intention, any more than, beyond thinking her clever enough for anything, his acute mother would discover it. From this hour, with Mrs Gereth, there was a flaw in her frankness: her admirable friend continued to know everything she did; what was to remain unknown was the general motive.

From the window of her room, the next morning before breakfast, the girl saw Owen in the garden with Mona, who strolled beside him with a listening parasol, but without a visible look for the great florid picture that had been hung there by Mrs Gereth's hand. Mona kept dropping her eyes, as she walked, to catch the sheen of her patent-leather shoes, which resembled a man's and which she kicked forward a little – it gave her an odd movement – to help her see what she thought of them. When Fleda came down Mrs Gereth was in the breakfast-room; and at that moment Owen through a long window, passed in alone from the terrace and very endearingly kissed his mother. It immediately struck the girl that she was in their way, for hadn't he been borne on a wave of joy exactly to announce before the Brigstocks departed, that Mona had at last faltered out the sweet word he had been waiting for? He shook hands with his friendly violence, but Fleda contrived not to look into his face: what she liked most to see in it was not the reflection of Mona's big boot-toes. She could bear well enough that young lady herself, but she couldn't bear Owen's opinion of her. She was on the point of slipping into the garden when the movement was checked by Mrs Gereth's suddenly drawing her close, as if for the morning embrace, and then, while she kept her there with the bravery of the night's repose, breaking out: 'Well, my dear boy, what *does* your young friend there make of our odds and ends?'

'Oh, she thinks they're all right!'

Fleda immediately guessed from his tone that he had not come in to say what she supposed; there was even something in it to confirm Mrs Gereth's belief that their danger had dropped. She was sure, moreover, that his tribute to Mona's taste was a repetition of the eloquent words in which the girl had herself recorded it; she could indeed hear, with all vividness, the pretty passage between the pair. 'Don't you think it's rather jolly, the old shop?' 'Oh, it's all right!' Mona had graciously remarked; and then they had probably, with a slap on a back, run another race up or down a green bank. Fleda knew Mrs Gereth had not yet uttered a word to her son that would have shown him how much she feared; but it was impossible to feel her friend's arm round her and not become aware that this friend was now throbbing with a strange intention. Owen's reply had scarcely been of a nature to usher in a discussion of Mona's sensibilities; but Mrs Gereth went on, in a moment, with an innocence of which Fleda could measure the cold hypocrisy: 'Has she any sort of feeling for nice old things?' The question was as fresh as the morning light.

'Oh, of course she likes everything that's nice.' And Owen, who constitutionally disliked questions – an answer was almost as hateful to him as a 'trick' to a big dog – smiled kindly at Fleda and conveyed that she would understand what he meant even if his mother didn't. Fleda, however, mainly understood that Mrs Gereth, with an odd, wild laugh, held her so hard that she hurt her.

'I could give up everything without a pang, I think, to a person I could trust, I could respect.' The girl heard her voice tremble under the effort to show nothing but what she wanted to show, and felt the sincerity of her implication that the piety most real to her was to be on one's knees before one's high standard. 'The best things here, as you know, are the things your father and I collected, things all that we worked for and waited for and suffered for. Yes,' cried Mrs Gereth, with a fine freedom of fancy, 'there are things in the house that we almost starved for! They were our religion, they were our life, they were us! and now they're only me – except that they're also you, thank God, a little, you dear!' she continued, suddenly inflicting on Fleda a kiss apparently intended to knock her

270

into position. 'There isn't one of them I don't know and love – yes, as one remembers and cherishes the happiest moments of one's life. Blindfold, in the dark, with the brush of a finger, I could tell one from another. They're living things to me; they know me, they return the touch of my hand. But I could let them all go, since I have to, so strangely, to another affection, another conscience. There's a care they want, there's a sympathy that draws out their beauty. Rather than make them over to a woman ignorant and vulgar, I think I'd deface them with my own hands. Can't you see me, Fleda, and wouldn't you do it yourself?' – she appealed to her companion with glittering eyes. 'I couldn't bear the thought of such a woman here – I *couldn't*. I don't know what she'd do; she'd be sure to invent some deviltry, if it should be only to bring in her own little belongings and horrors. The world is full of cheap gimcracks, in this awful age, and they're thrust in at one at every turn. They'd be thrust in here, on top of my treasures, my own. Who would save *them* for me – I ask you who *would*?' and she turned again to Fleda with a dry, strained smile. Her handsome, high-nosed, excited face might have been that of Don Quixote tilting at a windmill. Drawn into the eddy of this outpouring, the girl, scared and embarrassed, laughed off her exposure; but only to feel herself more passionately caught up and, as it seemed to her, thrust down the fine open mouth (it showed such perfect teeth) with which poor Owen's slow cerebration gaped. '*You* would, of course – only you, in all the world, because you know, you feel, as I do myself, what's good and true and pure.' No severity of the moral law could have taken a higher tone in this implication of the young lady who had not the only virtue Mrs Gereth actively esteemed. '*You* would replace me, *you* would watch over them, *you* would keep the place right,' she austerely pursued, 'and with you here – yes, with you, I believe I might rest, at last, in my grave!' She threw herself on Fleda's neck, and before Fleda, horribly shamed, could shake her off, had burst into tears which couldn't have been explained, but which might perhaps have been understood.

CHAPTER 4

A WEEK later Owen Gereth came down to inform his mother that he had settled with Mona Brigstock; but it was not at all a joy to Fleda, conscious how much to himself it would be a surprise, that he should find her still in the house. That dreadful scene before breakfast had made her position false and odious; it had been followed, after they were left alone, by a scene of her own making with her extravagant friend. She notified Mrs Gereth of her instant departure: she couldn't possibly remain after being offered to Owen, that way, before her very face, as his mother's candidate for the honour of his hand. That was all he could have seen in such an outbreak and in the indecency of her standing there to enjoy it. Fleda had on the prior occasion dashed out of the room by the shortest course and in her confusion had fallen upon Mona in the garden. She had taken an aimless turn with her, and they had had some talk, rendered at first difficult and almost disagreeable by Mona's apparent suspicion that she had been sent out to spy, as Mrs Gereth had tried to spy, into her opinions. Fleda was saga-cious enough to treat these opinions as a mystery almost awful; which had an effect so much more than reassuring that at the end of five minutes the young lady from Waterbath suddenly and perversely said: 'Why has she never had a winter garden thrown out? If ever I have a place of my own I mean to have one.' Fleda, dismayed, could see the thing – something glazed and piped, on iron pillars, with untidy plants and cane sofas; a shiny excrescence on the noble face of Poynton. She remembered at Waterbath a conservatory where she had caught a bad cold in the company of a stuffed cockatoo fastened to a tropical bough and a waterless fountain composed of shells stuck into some hardened paste. She asked Mona if her idea would be to make something like this conservatory; to which Mona replied: 'Oh no, much finer; we haven't got a winter garden at Waterbath.' Fleda wondered if she meant to convey that it was the only grandeur they lacked, and in a moment

272

Mona went on: 'But we have got a billiard-room — that I will say for us!' There was no billiard-room at Poynton, but there would evidently be one, and it would have, hung on its walls, framed at the 'Stores', caricature-portraits of celebrities, taken from a 'society-paper'.

When the two girls had gone in to breakfast it was for Fleda to see at a glance that there had been a further passage, of some high colour, between Owen and his mother; and she had turned pale in guessing to what extremity, at her expense, Mrs Gereth had found occasion to proceed. Hadn't she, after her clumsy flight, been pressed upon Owen in still clearer terms? Mrs Gereth would practically have said to him: 'If you'll take *her*, I'll move away without a sound. But if you take anyone else, anyone I'm not sure of, as I am of her — heaven help me, I'll fight to the death!' Breakfast, this morning, at Poynton, had been a meal singularly silent, in spite of the vague little cries with which Mrs Brigstock turned up the underside of plates and the knowing but alarming raps administered by her big knuckles to porcelain cups. Someone had to respond to her, and the duty assigned itself to Fleda, who, while pretending to meet her on the ground of explanation, wondered what Owen thought of a girl still indelicately anxious, after she had been grossly hurled at him, to prove by exhibitions of her fine taste that she was really what his mother pretended. This time, at any rate, their fate was sealed: Owen, as soon as he should get out of the house, would describe to Mona that lady's extraordinary conduct, and if anything more had been wanted to 'fetch' Mona, as he would call it, the deficiency was now made up. Mrs Gereth in fact took care of that — took care of it by the way, at the last, on the threshold, she said to the younger of her departing guests, with an irony of which the sting was wholly in the sense, not at all in the sound: 'We haven't had the talk we might have had, have we? You'll feel that I've neglected you, and you'll treasure it up against me. *Don't*, because really, you know, it has been quite an accident, and I've all sorts of information at your disposal. If you should come down again (only you won't, ever — I feel that!) I should give you plenty of time to worry it out of me. Indeed there are some things I should quite insist on your learning; not permit

273

you at all, in any settled way, *not* to learn. Yes indeed, you'd put me through, and I should put you, my dear! We should have each other to reckon with, and you would see me as I really am. I'm not a bit the vague, mooning, easy creature I dare say you think. However, if you won't come, you won't; *n'en parlons plus*. It *is* stupid here after what you're accustomed to. We can only, all round, do what we can, eh? For heaven's sake, don't let your mother forget her precious publication, the female magazine, with the what-do-you-call-'em? – the grease-catchers. There!'

Mrs Gereth, delivering herself from the doorstep, had tossed the periodical higher in air than was absolutely needful – tossed it towards the carriage the retreating party was about to enter. Mona, from the force of habit, the reflex action of the custom of sport, had popped out, with a little spring, a long arm and intercepted the missile as easily as she would have caused a tennis-ball to rebound from a racket. 'Good catch!' Owen had cried, so genuinely pleased that practically no notice was taken of his mother's impressive remarks. It was to the accompaniment of romping laughter, as Mrs Gereth afterwards said, that the carriage had rolled away; but it was while that laughter was still in the air that Fleda Vetch, white and terrible, had turned upon her hostess with her scorching 'How *could* you? Great God, how *could* you?' This lady's perfect blanket was from the first a sign of her serene conscience, and the fact that till indoctrinated she didn't even know what Fleda meant by resenting her late offence to every susceptibility gave our young woman a sore, scared perception that her own value in the house was just the value, as one might say, of a good agent. Mrs Gereth was generously sorry, but she was still more surprised – surprised at Fleda's not having liked to be shown off to Owen as the right sort of wife for him. Why not, in the name of wonder, if she absolutely *was* the right sort? She had admitted on explanation that she could see what her young friend meant by having been laid, as Fleda called it, at his feet ; but it struck the girl that the admission was only made to please her, and that Mrs Gereth was secretly surprised at her not being as happy to be sacrificed to the supremacy of a high standard as she was happy to sacrifice her. She had taken a tremendous fancy to her, but that was on account of the fancy – to Poynton of course – Fleda herself had taken. Wasn't this latter fancy then so great after all? Fleda felt that she could declare it to be great indeed when really for the sake of it she could forgive what she had suffered and, after reproaches and tears, asseverations and kisses, after learning that she was cared for only as a priestess of the altar and a view of her bruised dignity which left no alternative to flight, could accept the shame with the balm, consent not to depart, take refuge in the thin comfort of at least knowing the truth. The truth was simply that all Mrs Gereth's scruples were on one side and that her ruling passion had in a manner despoiled her of her humanity. On the second day, after the tide of emotion had somewhat ebbed, she said soothingly to her companion: 'But you *would*, after all, marry him, you know, darling, wouldn't you, if that girl were not there? I mean of course if he were to ask you,' Mrs Gereth had thoughtfully added.

'Marry him if he were to ask me? Most distinctly not!'

The question had not come up with this definiteness before, and Mrs Gereth was clearly more surprised than ever. She marvelled a moment. 'Not even to have Poynton?'

'Not even to have Poynton.'

'But why on earth?' Mrs Gereth's sad eyes were fixed on her.

Fleda coloured; she hesitated. 'Because he's too stupid!' Save on one other occasion, at which we shall in time arrive, little as the reader may believe it, she never came nearer to betraying to Mrs Gereth that she was in love with Owen. She found a dim amusement in reflecting that if Mona had not been there and he had not been too stupid and he verily had asked her, she might, should she have wished to keep her secret, have found it possible to pass off the motive of her action as a mere *passion* for Poynton.

Mrs Gereth evidently thought in these days of little but things hymeneal; for she broke out with sudden rapture, in the middle of the week: 'I know what they'll do: they *will* marry, but they'll go and live at Waterbath!' There was positive joy in that form of the idea, which she embroidered and developed: it seemed so much the safest thing that could happen. 'Yes, I'll have you, but I won't go *there*!' Mona would have said with a vicious nod at the southern horizon: 'we'll leave your horrid mother alone there for life.' It would be an ideal solution, this ingress the lively pair, with their spiritual need of a warmer medium, would playfully punch in the ribs of her ancestral home; for it would not only prevent recurring panic at Poynton – it would offer them, as in one of their gimcrack baskets or other vessels of ugliness, a definite daily felicity that Poynton could never give. Owen might manage his estate just as he managed it now, and Mrs Gereth would manage everything else. When, in the hall, on the unforgettable day of his return, she had heard his voice ring out like a call to a terrier, she had still, as Fleda afterwards learned, clutched frantically at the conceit that he had come, at the worst, to announce some compromise; to tell her she would have to put up with the girl, yes, but that some way would be arrived at of leaving her in personal possession. Fleda Vetch, whom from the first hour no illusion had brushed with its wing, now held her breath, went on tiptoe, wandered in outlying parts of the house and through delicate, muffled rooms, while the mother and son faced each other below. From time to time she stopped to listen; but all was so quiet she was almost frightened: she had vaguely expected a sound of contention. It lasted longer than she would have supposed, whatever it was they were doing; and when finally, from a window, she saw Owen stroll out of the house, stop and light a cigarette and then pensively lose himself in the plantations, she found other matter for trepidation in the fact that Mrs Gereth didn't immediately come rushing up into her arms. She wondered whether she oughtn't to go down to her, and measured the gravity of what had occurred by the circumstance, which she presently ascertained, that the poor lady had retired to her room and wished not to be disturbed. This admonition had been for her maid, with whom Fleda conferred as at the door of a death-chamber; but the girl, without either fatuity or resentment, judged that, since it could render Mrs Gereth indifferent even to the ministrations of disinterested attachments, the scene had been tremendous.

She was absent from luncheon, where indeed Fleda had enough to do to look Owen in the face; there would be so much to make that hateful in their common memory of the passage in which his last visit had terminated. This had been her apprehension at least; but as soon as he stood there she was constrained to wonder at the practical simplicity of the ordeal – a simplicity which was really just his own simplicity, the particular thing that, for Fleda Vetch, some other things of course aiding, made almost any direct relation with him pleasant. He had neither wit nor tact, nor inspiration: all she could say was that when they were together the alienation these charms were usually depended on to allay didn't occur. On this occasion, for instance, he did so much better than 'carry off' an awkward remembrance: he simply didn't have it. He had clean forgotten that she was the girl his mother would have fobbed off on him; he was conscious only that she was there in a manner for service – conscious of the dumb instinct that from the first had made him regard her not as complicating his intercouse with that personage, but as simplifying it. Fleda found beautiful that this theory should have survived the incident of the other day; found exquisite that whereas she was conscious, through faint reverberations, that for her kind little circle at large, whom it didn't concern, her tendency had begun to define itself as parasitical, this strong young man, who had a right to judge and even a reason to loathe her, didn't judge and didn't loathe, let her down gently, treated her as if she pleased him, and in fact evidently liked her to be just where she was. She asked herself what he did when Mona denounced her, and the only answer to the question was that perhaps Mona didn't denounce her. If Mona was inarticulate he wasn't such a fool, then, to marry her. That he was glad Fleda was there was at any rate sufficiently shown by the domestic familiarity with which he said to her: 'I must tell you I've been having an awful row with my mother. I'm engaged to be married to Miss Brigstock.'

'Ah, really?' cried Fleda, achieving a radiance of which she was secretly proud. 'How very exciting!'

'Too exciting for poor Mummy. She won't hear of it. She has been slating her fearfully. She says she's a "barbarian".'

'Why, she's lovely!' Fleda exclaimed.

'Oh, she's all right. Mother must come round.'

'Only give her time,' said Fleda. She had advanced to the threshold of the door thus thrown open to her and, without exactly crossing it, she threw in an appreciative glance. She asked Owen when his marriage would take place, and in the light of his reply read that Mrs Gereth's wretched attitude would have no influence at all on the event, absolutely fixed when he came down, and distant by only three months. He liked Fleda's seeming to be on his side, though that was a secondary matter, for what really most concerned him now was the line his mother took about Poynton, her declared unwillingness to give it up.

'Naturally I want my own house, you know,' he said, 'and my father made every arrangement for me to have it. But she may make it devilish awkward. What in the world's a fellow to do?' This it was that Owen wanted to know, and there could be no better proof of his friendliness than his air of depending on Fleda Vetch to tell him. She questioned him, they spent an hour together, and, as he gave her the scale of the concussion from which he had rebounded, she found herself saddened and frightened by the material he seemed to offer her to deal with. It *was* devilish awkward, and it was so in part because Owen had no imagination. It had lodged itself in that empty chamber that his mother hated the surrender because she hated Mona. He didn't of course understand why she hated Mona, but this belonged to an order of mysteries that never troubled him: there were lots of things, especially in people's minds, that a fellow didn't understand. Poor Owen went through life with a frank dread of people's minds: there were explanations he would have been almost as shy of receiving as of giving. There was therefore nothing that accounted for anything, though in its way it was vivid enough, in his picture to Fleda of his mother's virtual refusal to move. That was simply what it was; for didn't she refuse to move when she as good as declared that she would move only with the furniture? It was the furniture she wouldn't give up; and what was the good of Poynton without the furniture? Besides, the furniture happened to be his, just as everything else happened to be. The furniture – the words, on his lips, had somehow, for Fleda, the sound of washing-stands and copious bedding, and she could well imagine the note it might have struck for Mrs Gereth. The girl, in this interview with him, spoke of the contents of the house only as 'the works of art'. It didn't, however, in the least matter to Owen what they were called; what did matter, she easily guessed, was that it had been laid upon him by Mona, been made in effect a condition of her consent, that he should hold his mother to the strictest accountability for them. Mona had already entered upon the enjoyment of her rights. She had made him feel that Mrs Gereth had been liberally provided for, and had asked him cogently what room there would be at Ricks for the innumerable treasures of the big house. Ricks, the sweet little place offered to the mistress of Poynton as the refuge of her declining years, had been left to the late Mr Gereth, a considerable time before his death, by an old maternal aunt, a good lady who had spent most of her life there. The house had in recent times been let, but it was amply furnished, it contained all the defunct aunt's possessions. Owen had lately inspected it, and he communicated to Fleda that he had quietly taken Mona to see it. It wasn't a place like Poynton – what dower-house ever was? – but it was an awfully jolly little place, and Mona had taken a tremendous fancy to it. If there were a few things at Poynton that were Mrs Gereth's peculiar property, of course she must take them away with her ; but one of the matters that became clear to Fleda was that this transfer would be immediately subject to Miss Brigstock's approval. The special business that she herself now became aware of being charged with was that of seeing Mrs Gereth safely and singly off the premises.

Her heart failed her, after Owen had returned to London, with the ugliness of this duty – with the ugliness, indeed, of the whole close conflict. She saw nothing of Mrs Gereth that day ; she spent it in roaming with sick sighs, in feeling, as she passed from room to room, that what was expected of her companion was really dreadful. It would have been better never to have had such a place than to have had it and lose it. It was odious to *her* to have to look for solutions: what a strange relation between mother and son when there was no fundamental tenderness out of which a solution would ir-repressibly spring! Was it Owen who was mainly responsible for that poverty? Fleda couldn't think so when she remembered that, so far as he was concerned, Mrs Gereth would still have been welcome to have her seat by the Poynton fire. The fact that from the moment one accepted his marrying one saw no very different course for Owen to take made her all the rest of that aching day find her best relief in the mercy of not having yet to face her hostess. She dodged and dreamed and romanced away the time; instead of inventing a remedy or a compromise, instead of preparing a plan by which a scandal might be averted, she gave herself, in her sentient solitude, up to a mere fairy tale, up to the very taste of the beautiful peace with which she would have filled the air if only something might have been that could never have been.

CHAPTER 5

'I'LL give up the house if they'll let me take what I require!'
That, on the morrow, was what Mrs Gereth's stifled night had
qualified her to say, with a tragic face, at breakfast. Fleda
reflected that what she 'required' was simply every object that
surrounded them. The poor woman would have admitted this
truth and accepted the conclusion to be drawn from it, the
reduction to the absurd of her attitude, the exaltation of her
revolt. The girl's dread of scandal, of spectators and critics,
diminished the more she saw how little vulgar avidity had to
do with this rigour. It was not the crude love of possession;
it was the need to be faithful to a trust and loyal to an idea.
The idea was surely noble: it was that of the beauty Mrs
Gereth had so patiently and consummately wrought. Pale but
radiant, with her back to the wall, she rose there like a heroine
guarding a treasure. To give up the ship was to flinch from her
duty; there was something in her eyes that declared she would
die at her post. If their difference should become public the
shame would be all for the others. If Waterbath thought it
could afford to expose itself, then Waterbath was welcome to
the folly. Her fanaticism gave her a new distinction, and Fleda
perceived almost with awe that she had never carried herself
so well. She trod the place like a reigning queen or a proud
usurper; full as it was of splendid pieces, it could show in
these days no ornament so effective as its menaced mistress.

Our young lady's spirit was strangely divided; she had a
tenderness for Owen which she deeply concealed, yet it left
her occasion to marvel at the way a man was made who could
care in any relation for a creature like Mona Brigstock when
he had known in any relation a creature like Adela Gereth.
With such a mother to give him the pitch, how could he take
it so low? She wondered that she didn't despise him for this,
but there was something that kept her from it. If there had been
nothing else it would have sufficed that she really found herself
from this moment the medium of communication with him.

'He'll come back to assert himself,' Mrs Gereth had said; and the following week Owen in fact reappeared. He might merely have written, Fleda could see, but he had come in person because it was at once 'nicer' for his mother and stronger for his cause. He didn't like the row, though Mona probably did; if he hadn't a sense of beauty he had after all a sense of justice; but it was inevitable he should clearly announce at Poynton the date at which he must look to find the house vacant. 'You don't think I'm rough or hard, do you?' he asked Fleda, his impatience shining in his idle eyes as the dining-hour shines in club-windows. 'The place at Ricks stands there with open arms. And then I give her lots of time. Tell her she can remove everything that belongs to her.' Fleda recognized the elements of what the newspapers call a deadlock in the circumstance that nothing at Poynton belonged to Mrs Gereth either more or less than anything else. She must either take everything or nothing, and the girl's suggestion was that it might perhaps be an inspiration to do the latter and begin again on a clean page. What, however, was the poor woman, in that case, to begin with? What was she to do at all, on her meagre income, but make the best of the *objets d'art* of Ricks, the treasures collected by Mr Gereth's maiden aunt? She had never been near the place: for long years it had been let to strangers, and after that the foreboding that it would be her doom had kept her from the abasement of it. She had felt that she should see it soon enough, but Fleda (who was careful not to betray to her that Mona had seen it and had been gratified) knew her reasons for believing that the maiden's aunt's principles had had much in common with the principles of Waterbath. The only thing, in short, that she would ever have to do with the *objets d'art* of Ricks would be to turn them out into the road. What belonged to her at Poynton, as Owen said, would conveniently mitigate the void resulting from that demonstration.

The exchange of observations between the friends had grown very direct by the time Fleda asked Mrs Gereth whether she literally meant to shut herself up and stand a siege, or whether it was her idea to expose herself, more informally, to be dragged out of the house by constables. 'Oh, I prefer the constables and the dragging!' the heroine of Poynton had answered. 'I want to make Owen and Mona do everything that will be most publicly odious.' She gave it out that it was her one thought now to force them to a line that would dishonour them and dishonour the tradition they embodied, though Fleda was privately sure that she had visions of an alternative policy. The strange thing was that, proud and fastidious all her life, she now showed so little distaste for the world's hearing of the squabble. What had taken place in her above all was that a long resentment had ripened. She hated the effacement to which English usage reduced the widowed mother: she had discoursed of it passionately to Fleda; contrasted it with the beautiful homage paid in other countries to women in that position, women no better than herself, whom she had seen acclaimed and enthroned, whom she had known and envied; made in short as little as possible a secret of the injury, the bitterness she found in it. The great wrong Owen had done her was not his 'taking up' with Mona – that was disgusting, but it was a detail, an accidental form; it was his failure from the first to understand what it was to have a mother at all, to appreciate the beauty and sanctity of the character. She was just his mother as his nose was just his nose, and he had never had the least imagination or tenderness or gallantry about her. One's mother, gracious heaven, if one were the kind of fine young man one ought to be, the only kind Mrs Gereth cared for, was a subject for poetry, for idolatry. Hadn't she often told Fleda of her friend Madame de Jaume, the wittiest of women, but a small, black, crooked person, each of whose three boys, when absent, wrote to her every day of their lives? She had the house in Paris, she had the house in Poitou, she had more than in the lifetime of her husband (to whom, in spite of her appearance, she had afforded repeated cause for jealousy), because she had to the end of her days the supreme word about everything. It was easy to see that Mrs Gereth would have given again and again her complexion, her figure, and even perhaps the spotless virtue she had still more success-fully retained, to have been the consecrated Madame de Jaume. She wasn't, alas, and this was what she had at present a mag-nificent occasion to protest against. She was of course fully aware of Owen's concession, his willingness to let her take away with her the few things she liked best ; but as yet she only declared that to meet him on this ground would be to give him a triumph, to put him impossibly in the right. 'Liked best?' There wasn't a thing in the house that she didn't like best, and what she liked better still was to be left where she was. How could Owen use such an expression without being conscious of his hypocrisy? Mrs Gereth, whose criticism was often gay, dilated with sardonic humour on the happy look a dozen objects from Poynton would wear and the charming effect they would conduce to when interspersed with the peculiar features of Ricks. What had her whole life been but an effort towards completeness and perfection? Better Waterbath at once, in its cynical unity, than the ignominy of such a mixture!

All this was of no great help to Fleda, in so far as Fleda tried to rise to her mission of finding a way out. When at the end of a fortnight Owen came down once more, it was ostensibly to tackle a farmer whose proceedings had been irregular ; the girl was sure, however, that he had really come, on the instance of Mona, to see what his mother was doing. He wished to satisfy himself that she was preparing her departure, and he wished to perform a duty, distinct but not less imperative, in regard to the question of the perquisites with which she would retreat. The tension between them was now such that he had to perpetrate these offences without meeting his adversary. Mrs Gereth was as willing as himself that he should address to Fleda Vetch whatever cruel remarks he might have to make: she only pitied her poor young friend for repeated encounters with a person as to whom she perfectly understood the girl's repulsion. Fleda thought it nice of Owen not to have expected her to write to him ; he wouldn't have wished any more than herself that she should have the air of spying on his mother in his interest. What made it comfortable to deal with him in this more familiar way was the sense that she understood so perfectly how poor Mrs Gereth suffered, and that she measured so adequately the sacrifice the other side did take rather monstrously for granted. She understood equally how Owen himself suffered, now that Mona had already begun to make him do things he didn't like. Vividly

Fleda apprehended how *she* would have first made him like anything she would have made him do ; anything even as disagreeable as this appearing there to state, virtually on Mona's behalf, that of course there must be a definite limit to the number of articles appropriated. She took a longish stroll with him in order to talk the matter over ; to say if she didn't think a dozen pieces, chosen absolutely at will, would be a handsome allowance ; and above all to consider the very delicate question of whether the advantage enjoyed by Mrs Gereth mightn't be left to her honour. To leave it so was what Owen wished ; but there was plainly a young lady at Waterbath to whom, on his side, he already had to render an account. He was as touching in his offhand annoyance as his mother was tragic in her intensity ; for if he couldn't help having a sense of propriety about the whole matter, so he could as little help hating it. It was for his hating it, Fleda reasoned, that she liked him so, and her insistence to his mother on the hatred perilously resembled on one or two occasions, a revelation of the liking. There were moments when, in conscience, that revelation pressed her ; inasmuch as it was just on the ground of her not liking him that Mrs Gereth trusted her so much. Mrs Gereth herself didn't in these days like him at all, and she was of course and always on Mrs Gereth's side. He ended really, while the preparations for his marriage went on, by quite a little custom of coming and going ; but on no one of these occasions would his mother receive him. He talked only with Fleda and strolled with Fleda ; and when he asked her, in regard to the great matter, if Mrs Gereth were really doing nothing, the girl usually replied: 'She pretends not to be, if I may say so ; but I think she's really thinking over what she'll take.' When her friend asked her what Owen was doing, she could have but one answer: 'He's waiting, dear lady, to see what *you* do!'

Mrs Gereth, a month after she had received her great shock, did something abrupt and extraordinary: she caught up her companion and went to have a look at Ricks. They had come to London first and taken a train from Liverpool Street, and the least of the sufferings they were armed against was that of passing the night. Fleda's admirable dressing-bag had been given her by her friend. 'Why, it's charming!' she exclaimed a

285

few hours later, turning back again into the small prim parlour from a friendly advance to the single plate of the window. Mrs Gereth hated such windows, the one flat glass, sliding up and down, especially when they enjoyed a view of four iron pots on pedestals, painted white and containing ugly geraniums, ranged on the edge of a gravel path and doing their best to give it the air of a terrace. Fleda had instantly averted her eyes from these ornaments, but Mrs Gereth grimly gazed, wondering of course how a place in the deepest depths of Essex and three miles from a small station could contrive to look so suburban. The room was practically a shallow box, with the junction of the walls and ceiling guiltless of curve or cornice and marked merely by the little band of crimson paper glued round the top of the other paper, a turbid grey sprigged with silver flowers. This decoration was rather new and quite fresh ; and there was in the centre of the ceiling a big square beam papered over in white, as to which Fleda hesitated about venturing to remark that it was rather picturesque. She recognized in time that this remark would be weak and that, throughout, she should be able to say nothing either for the mantlepieces or for the doors, of which she saw her companion become sensible with a soundless moan. On the subject of doors especially Mrs Gereth had the finest views: the thing in the world she most despised was the meanness of the single flap. From end to end, at Poynton, there were high double leaves. At Ricks the entrances to the rooms were like the holes of rabbit-hutches.

It was all, none the less, not so bad as Fleda had feared ; it was faded and melancholy, whereas there had been a danger that it would be contradictious and positive, cheerful and loud. The house was crowded with objects of which the aggregation somehow made a thinness and the futility a grace ; things that told her they had been gathered as slowly and as lovingly as the golden flowers of Poynton. She too, for a home, could have lived with them: they made her fond of the old maiden aunt ; they made her even wonder if it didn't work more for happiness not to have tasted, as she herself had done, of knowledge. Without resources, without a stick, as she said, of her own, Fleda was moved, after all, to some secret surprise at the pretensions of a shipwrecked woman who could hold such an asylum cheap. The more she looked about the surer she felt of the character of the maiden aunt, the sense of whose dim presence urged her to pacification: the maiden aunt had been a dear; she would have adored the maiden aunt. The poor lady had had some tender little story; she had been sensitive and ignorant and exquisite: that too was a sort of origin, a sort of atmosphere for relics and rarities, though different from the sorts most prized at Poynton. Mrs Gereth had of course more than once said that one of the deepest mysteries of life was the way that, by certain natures, hideous objects could be loved; but it wasn't a question of love, now, for these; it was only a question of a certain practical patience. Perhaps some thought of that kind had stolen over Mrs Gereth when, at the end of a brooding hour, she exclaimed, taking in the house with a strenuous sigh: 'Well, something can be done with it!' Fleda had repeated to her more than once the indulgent fancy about the maiden aunt – she was so sure she had deeply suffered. 'I'm sure I hope she did!' was, however, all that Mrs Gereth had replied.

CHAPTER 6

It was a great relief to the girl at last to perceive that the dreadful move would really be made. What might happen if it shouldn't had been from the first indefinite. It was absurd to pretend that any violence was probable – a tussle, dishevelment, shrieks; yet Fleda had an imagination of a drama, a 'great scene', a thing, somehow, of indignity and misery, of wounds inflicted and received, in which indeed, though Mrs Gereth's presence, with movements and sounds, loomed large to her, Owen remained indistinct and on the whole unaggressive. He wouldn't be there with a cigarette in his teeth, very handsome and insolently quiet: that was only the way he would be in a novel, across whose interesting page some such figure, as she half closed her eyes, seemed to her to walk. Fleda had rather, and indeed with shame, a confused, pitying vision of Mrs Gereth with her great scene left in a manner on her hands, Mrs Gereth missing her effect and having to appear merely hot and injured and in the wrong. The symptoms that she would be spared even that spectacle resided not so much, through the chambers of Poynton, in an air of concentration as in the hum of buzzing alternatives. There was no common preparation, but one day, at the turn of a corridor, she found her hostess standing very still, with the hanging hands of an invalid and the active eyes of an adventurer. These eyes appeared to Fleda to meet her own with a strange, dim bravado, and there was a silence, almost awkward, before either of the friends spoke. The girl afterwards thought of the moment as one in which her hostess mutely accused her of an accusation, meeting it however, at the same time, by a kind of defiant acceptance. Yet it was with mere melancholy candour that Mrs Gereth at last sighingly exclaimed: 'I'm thinking over what I had better take!' Fleda could have embraced her for this virtual promise of a concession, the announcement that she had finally accepted the problem of knocking together a shelter with a small salvage of the wreck.

It was true that when after their return from Ricks they tried to lighten the ship, the great embarrassment was still immutably there, the odiousness of sacrificing the exquisite things one wouldn't take to the exquisite things one would. This immediately made the things one wouldn't take the very things one ought to, and as Mrs Gereth said, condemned one, in the whole business, to an eternal vicious circle. In such a circle, for days, she had been tormentedly moving, prowling up and down, comparing incomparables. It was for that one had to cling to them and their faces of supplication. Fleda herself could judge of these faces, so conscious of their race and their danger, and she had little enough to say when her companion asked her if the whole place, perversely fair on October afternoons, looked like a place to give up. It looked, to begin with, through some effect of season and light, larger than ever, immense, and it was filled with the hush of sorrow, which in turn was all charged with memories. Everything was in the air – every history of every find, every circumstance of every struggle. Mrs Gereth had drawn back every curtain and removed every cover; she prolonged the vistas, opened wide the whole house, gave it an appearance of awaiting a royal visit. The shimmer of wrought substances spent itself in the brightness; the old golds and brasses, old ivories and bronzes, the fresh old tapestries and deep old damasks threw out a radiance in which the poor woman saw in solution all her old loves and patiences, all her old tricks and triumphs.

Fleda had a depressed sense of not, after all, helping her much: this was lightened indeed by the fact that Mrs Gereth, letting her off easily, didn't now seem to expect it. Her sympathy, her interest, her feeling for everything for which Mrs Gereth felt, were a force that really worked to prolong the deadlock. 'I only wish I bored you and my possessions bored you,' that lady, with some humour declared; 'then you'd make short work with me, bundle me off, tell me just to pile certain things into a cart and have done.' Fleda's sharpest difficulty was in having to act up to the character of thinking Owen a brute, or at least to carry off the inconsistency of seeing him when he came down. By good fortune it was her duty, her function, as well as a protection to Mrs Gereth. She thought of him perpetually, and her eyes had come to rejoice in his manly magnificence more even than they rejoiced in the royal cabinets of the red saloon. She wondered, very faintly at first, why he came so often; but of course she knew nothing about the business he had in hand, over which, with men red-faced and leather-legged, he was sometimes closeted for an hour in a room of his own that was the one monstrosity of Poynton: all tobacco-pots and bootjacks, his mother had said – such an array of arms of aggression and castigation that he himself had confessed to eighteen rifles and forty whips. He was arranging for settlements on his wife, he was doing things that would meet the views of the Brigstocks. Considering the house was his own, Fleda thought it nice of him to keep himself in the background while his mother remained; making his visits, at some cost of ingenuity about trains from town, only between meals, doing everything to let it press lightly upon her that he was there. This was rather a stoppage to her meeting Mrs Gereth on the ground of his being a brute; the most she really at last could do was not to contradict her when she repeated that he was watching – just insultingly watching. He *was* watching, no doubt; but he watched somehow with his head turned away. He knew that Fleda knew at present what he wanted of her, so that it would be gross of him to say it over and over. It existed as a confidence between them, and made him sometimes, with his wandering stare, meet her eyes as if a silence so pleasant could only unite them the more. He had no great flow of speech, certainly, and at first the girl took for granted that this was all there was to be said about the matter. Little by little she speculated as to whether, with a person who, like herself, could put him, after all, at a sort of domestic ease, it was not supposable that he would have more conversation if he were not keeping some of it back for Mona.

From the moment she suspected he might be thinking what Mona would say to his chattering so to an underhand 'companion', who was all but paid, this young lady's repressed emotion began to require still more repression. She grew impatient of her situation at Poynton; she privately pronounced it false and horrid. She said to herself that she had let Owen know that she had, to the best of her power, directed his mother in the general sense he desired; that he quite understood it and that he also understood how unworthy it was of either of them to stand over the good lady with a notebook and a lash. Wasn't this practical unanimity just practical success? Fleda became aware of a sudden desire, as well as of pressing reasons, to bring her stay at Poynton to a close. She had not, on the one hand, like a minion of the law, undertaken to see Mrs Gereth down to the train and locked, in sign of her abdication, into a compartment; neither had she on the other committed herself to hold Owen indefinitely in dalliance while his mother gained time or dug a countermine. Besides, people *were* saying that she fastened like a leech on other people – people who had houses where something was to be picked up: this revelation was frankly made by her sister, now distinctly doomed to the curate and in view of whose nuptials she had almost finished, as a present, a wonderful piece of embroidery, suggested, at Poynton, by an old Spanish altar-cloth. She would have to exert herself still further for the intended recipient of this offering, turn her out for her marriage with more than that drapery. She would go up to town, in short, to dress Maggie; and their father, in lodgings at West Kensington, would stretch a point and take them in. He, to do him justice, never reproached her with profitable devotions; so far as they existed he consciously profited by them. Mrs Gereth gave her up as heroically as if she had been a great bargain, and Fleda knew that she wouldn't at present miss any visit of Owen's for Owen was shooting at Waterbath. Owen shooting was Owen lost, and there was scant sport at Poynton.

The first news she had from Mrs Gereth was news of that lady's having accomplished, in form at least, her migration. The letter was dated from Ricks, to which place she had been transported by an impulse apparently as sudden as the inspiration she had obeyed before.

Yes, I've literally come [she wrote] with a bandbox and a kitchen-maid; I've crossed the Rubicon, I've taken possession. It has been like plumping into cold water: I saw the only thing was to do it, not to stand shivering. I shall have warmed the place a little by simply being here for a week; when I come back the ice will have been broken. I didn't write to you to meet me on my way through town, because I know how busy you are and because, besides, I'm too savage and odious to be fit company even for you. You'd say I really go too far, and there's no doubt whatever I do. I'm here, at any rate, just to look round once more, to see that certain things are done before I enter in force. I shall probably be at Poynton all next week. There's more room than I quite measured the other day, and a rather good set of old Worcester. But what are space and time, what's even old Worcester, to your wretched and affectionate A. G.?

The day after Fleda received this letter she had occasion to go into a big shop in Oxford Street – a journey that she achieved circuitously, first on foot and then by the aid of two omnibuses. The second of these vehicles put her down on the side of the street opposite her shop, and while, on the kerbstone, she humbly waited, with a parcel, an umbrella, and a tucked-up frock, to cross in security, she became aware that, close beside her, a hansom had pulled up short, in obedience to the brandished stick of a demonstrative occupant. This occupant was Owen Gereth, who had caught sight of her as he rattled along and who, with an exhibition of white teeth that, from under the hood of the cab, had almost flashed through the fog, now alighted to ask her if he couldn't give her a lift. On finding that her destination was only over the way he dismissed his vehicle and joined her, not only piloting her to the shop, but taking her in; with the assurance that his errands didn't matter, that it amused him to be concerned with hers. She told him she had come to buy a trimming for her sister's frock, and he expressed an hilarious interest in the purchase. His hilarity was almost always out of proportion to the case, but it struck her at present as more so than ever; especially when she had suggested that he might find it a good time to buy a garnishment of some sort for Mona. After wondering an instant whether he gave the full satiric meaning, such as it was, to this remark, Fleda dismissed the possibility as inconceivable. He stammered out that it was for *her* he would like to buy something, something 'ripping', and that she must give him the pleasure of telling him what would best please her: he couldn't have a better opportunity for making her a present – the present, in recognition

292

of all she had done for Mummy, that he had had in his head for weeks.

Fleda had more than one small errand in the big bazaar, and he went up and down with her, pointedly patient, pretending to be interested in questions of tape and of change. She had now not the least hesitation in wondering what Mona would think of such proceedings. But they were not her doing – they were Owen's; and Owen, inconsequent and even extravagant, was unlike anything she had ever seen him before. He broke off, he came back, he repeated questions without heeding answers, he made vague, abrupt remarks about the resemblances of shopgirls and the uses of chiffon. He unduly prolonged their business together, giving Fleda a sense that he was putting off something particular that he had to face. If she had ever dreamed of Owen Gereth as nervous she would have seen him with some such manner as this. But why should he be nervous? Even at the height of the crisis his mother hadn't made him so, and at present he was satisfied about his mother. The one idea he stuck to was that Fleda should mention something she would let him give her: there was everything in the world in the wonderful place, and he made her incongruous offers – a travelling-rug, a massive clock, a table for breakfast in bed, and above all, in a resplendent binding, a set of somebody's 'works'. His notion was a testimonial, a tribute, and the 'works' would be a graceful intimation that it was her cleverness he wished above all to commemorate. He was immensely in earnest, but the articles he pressed upon her betrayed a delicacy that went to her heart: what he would really have liked, as he saw them tumbled about, was one of the splendid stuffs for a gown – a choice proscribed by his fear of seeming to patronize her, to refer to her small means and her deficiencies. Fleda found it easy to chaff him about his exaggeration of her deserts ; she gave the just measure of them in consenting to accept a small pin-cushion, costing sixpence, in which the letter F was marked out with pins. A sense of loyalty to Mona was not needed to enforce this discretion, and after that first allusion to her she never sounded her name. She noticed on this occasion more things in Owen Gereth than she had ever noticed before, but what she noticed most was that he said no word of his intended. She asked herself what he had done, in so long a parenthesis, with his loyalty or at least his 'form', and then reflected that even if he had done something very good with them the situation in which such a question could come up was already a little strange. Of course he wasn't doing anything so vulgar as making love to her; but there was a kind of punctilio for a man who was engaged.

That punctilio didn't prevent Owen from remaining with her after they had left the shop, from hoping she had a lot more to do, and from pressing her to look with him, for a possible glimpse of something she might really let him give her, into the windows of other establishments. There was a moment when, under this pressure, she made up her mind that his tribute would be, if analysed, a tribute to her insignificance. But all the same he wanted her to come somewhere and have luncheon with him: what was that a tribute to? She must have counted very little if she didn't count too much for a romp in a restaurant. She had to get home with her trimming, and the most, in his company, she was amenable to was a retracing of her steps to the Marble Arch and then, after a discussion when they had reached it, a walk with him across the Park. She knew Mona would have considered that she ought to take the omnibus again; but she had now to think for Owen as well as for herself — she couldn't think for Mona. Even in the Park the autumn air was thick, and as they moved westward over the grass, which was what Owen preferred, the cool greyness made their words soft, made them at last rare and everything else dim. He wanted to stay with her — he wanted not to leave her: he had dropped into complete silence, but that was what his silence said. What was it he had postponed? What was it he wanted still to postpone? She grew a little scared as they strolled together and she thought. It was too confused to be believed, but it was as if somehow he felt differently. Fleda Vetch didn't suspect him at first of feeling differently to *her*, but only of feeling differently to Mona; yet she was not unconscious that this latter difference would have had something to do with his being on the grass beside her. She had read in novels about gentlemen who on the eve of marriage,

294

winding up the past, had surrendered themselves for the occasion to the influence of a former tie; and there was something in Owen's behaviour now, something in his very face, that suggested a resemblance to one of those gentlemen. But whom and what, in that case, would Fleda herself resemble? She wasn't a former tie, she wasn't any tie at all; she was only a deep little person for whom happiness was a kind of pearl-diving plunge. It was down at the very bottom of all that had lately happened; for all that had lately happened was that Owen Gereth had come and gone at Poynton. That was the small sum of her experience, and what it had made for her was her own affair, quite consistent with her not having dreamed it had made a tie – at least what *she* called one – for Owen. The old one, at any rate, was Mona – Mona who he had known so very much longer.

They walked far, to the south-west corner of the great Gardens, where, by the old round pond and the old red palace, when she had put out her hand to him in farewell, declaring that from the gate she must positively take a conveyance, it seemed suddenly to rise between them that this was a real separation. She was on his mother's side, she belonged to his mother's life, and his mother, in the future, would never come to Poynton. After what had passed she wouldn't even be at his wedding, and it was not possible now that Mrs Gereth should mention that ceremony to the girl, much less express a wish that the girl should be present at it. Mona, from decorum and with reference less to the bridegroom than to the bridegroom's mother, would of course not invite any such girl as Fleda. Everything therefore was ended; they would go their different ways; this was the last time they would stand face to face. They looked at each other with the fuller sense of it and, on Owen's part, with an expression of dumb trouble, the intensification of his usual appeal to any interlocutor to add the right thing to what he said. To Fleda, at this moment, it appeared that the right thing might easily be the wrong. He only said, at any rate: 'I want you to understand, you know – I want you to understand.'

What did he want her to understand? He seemed unable to bring it out, and this understanding was moreover exactly what she wished not to arrive at. Bewildered as she was, she had already taken in as much as she should know what to do with; the blood also was rushing into her face. He liked her — it was stupefying — more than he really ought: that was what was the matter with him and what he desired her to assimilate; so that she was suddenly as frightened as some thoughtless girl who finds herself the object of an overture from a married man.

'Good-bye, Mr Gereth — I *must* get on!' she declared with a cheerfulness that she felt to be an unnatural grimace. She broke away from him sharply, smiling, backing across the grass and then turning altogether and moving as fast as she could. 'Good-bye, good-bye!' she threw off again as she went, wondering if he would overtake her before she reached the gate; conscious with a red disgust that her movement was almost a run; conscious too of just the confused, handsome face with which he would look after her. She felt as if she had answered a kindness with a great flouncing snub, but at any rate she had got away, though the distance to the gate, her ugly gallop down the Broad Walk, every graceless jerk of which hurt her, seemed endless. She signed from afar to a cab on the stand in the Kensington Road and scrambled into it, glad of the encompassment of the four-wheeler that had officiously obeyed her summons and that, at the end of the twenty yards, when she had violently pulled up a glass, permitted her to recognize the fact that she was on the point of bursting into tears.

CHAPTER 7

As soon as her sister was married she went down to Mrs
Gereth at Ricks – a promise to this effect having been promptly
exacted and given; and her inner vision was much more
fixed on the alterations there, complete now, as she understood, than on the success of her plotting and pinching for
Maggie's happiness. Her imagination, in the interval, had
indeed had plently to do and numerous scenes to visit; for
when on the summons just mentioned it had taken a flight
from West Kensington to Ricks, it had hung but an hour over
the terrace of painted pots and then yielded to a current of the
upper air that swept it straight off to Poynton and to Waterbath. Not a sound had reached her of any supreme clash, and
Mrs Gereth had communicated next to nothing; giving out
that, as was easily conceivable, she was too busy, too bitter,
and too tired for vain civilities. All she had written was that
she had got the new place well in hand and that Fleda would
be surprised at the way it was turning out. Everything was
even yet upside down; nevertheless, in the sense of having
passed the threshold of Poynton for the last time, the amputa-
tion, as she called it, had been performed. Her leg had come
off – she had now begun to stump along with the lovely
wooden substitute; she would stump for life, and what her
young friend was to come and admire was the beauty of her
movement and the noise she made about the house. The reserve
of Poynton and Waterbath had been matched by the austerity
of Fleda's own secret, under the discipline of which she had
repeated to herself a hundred times a day that she rejoiced at
having cares that excluded all thought of it. She had lavished
herself, in act, on Maggie and the curate, and had opposed to
her father's selfishness a sweetness quite ecstatic. The young
couple wondered why they had waited so long, since everything was after all so easy. She had thought of everything,
even to how the 'quietness' of the wedding should be relieved
by champagne and her father kept brilliant on a single bottle.

Fleda knew, in short, and liked the knowledge, that for several weeks she had appeared exemplary in every relation of life.

She had been perfectly prepared to be surprised at Ricks, for Mrs Gereth was a wonder-working wizard, with a command, when all was said, of good material; but the impression in wait for her on the threshold made her catch her breath and falter. Dusk had fallen when she arrived, and in the plain square hall, one of the few good features, the glow of a Venetian lamp just showed, on either wall, the richness of an admirable tapestry. This instant perception that the place had been dressed at the expense of Poynton was a shock: it was as if she had abruptly seen herself in the light of an accomplice. The next moment, folded in Mrs Gereth's arms, her eyes were diverted; but she had already had, in a flash, the vision of the great gaps in the other house. The two tapestries, not the largest, but those most splendidly toned by time, had been on the whole its most uplifted pride. When she could really see again she was on a sofa in the drawing-room, staring with intensity at an object soon distinct as the great Italian cabinet that, at Poynton, had been in the red saloon. Without looking, she was sure the room was occupied with other objects like it, stuffed with as many as it could hold of the trophies of her friend's struggle. By this time the very fingers of her glove, resting on the seat of the sofa, had thrilled at the touch of an old velvet brocade, a wondrous texture that she could recognize, would have recognized among a thousand, without dropping her eyes on it. They stuck to the cabinet with a kind of dissimulated dread, while she painfully asked herself whether she should notice it, notice everything, or just pretend not to be affected. How could she pretend not to be affected, with the very pendants of the lustres tinkling at her and with Mrs Gereth, beside her and staring at her even as she herself stared at the cabinet, hunching up a back like Atlas under his globe? She was appalled at this image of what Mrs Gereth had on her shoulders. That lady was waiting and watching her, bracing herself, and preparing the same face of confession and defiance she had shown the day, at Poynton, she had been surprised in the corridor. It was farcical not to speak; and yet to exclaim, to participate, would give one a bad sense of being mixed up with a theft. This ugly word sounded, for herself, in Fleda's silence, and the very violence of it jarred her into a scared glance, as of a creature detected, to right and left. But what again the full picture most showed her was the far-away empty sockets, a scandal of nakedness in high, bare walls. She at last uttered something formal and incoherent – she didn't know what: it had no relation to either house. Then she felt Mrs Gereth's hand once more on her arm. 'I've arranged a charming room for you – it's really lovely. You'll be very happy there.' This was spoken with extraordinary sweetness and with a smile that meant, 'Oh, I know what you're thinking; but what does it matter when you're so loyally on my side?' It had come indeed to a question of 'sides', Fleda thought, for the whole place was in battle array. In the soft lamplight, with one fine feature after another looming up into sombre richness, it defied her not to pronounce it a triumph of taste. Her passion for beauty leaped back into life; and was not what now most appealed to it a certain gorgeous audacity? Mrs Gereth's high hand was, as mere great effect, the climax of the impression.

'It's too wonderful, what you've done with the house!' – the visitor met her friend's eyes. They lighted up with joy – that friend herself so pleased with what she had done. This was not at all, in its accidental air of enthusiasm, what Fleda wanted to have said: it offered her as stupidly announcing from the first minute on whose side she was. Such was clearly the way Mrs Gereth took it: she threw herself upon the delightful girl and tenderly embraced her again; so that Fleda soon went on, with a studied difference and a cooler inspection: 'Why, you brought away absolutely everything!'

'Oh no, not everything; I saw how little I could get into this scrap of a house. I only brought away what I required.'

Fleda had got up; she took a turn round the room. 'You "required" the very best pieces – the *morceaux de musée*, the individual gems!'

'I certainly didn't want the rubbish, if that's what you mean.' Mrs Gereth, on the sofa, followed the direction of her companion's eyes; with the light of her satisfaction still in her face, she slowly rubbed her large, handsome hands.

299

Wherever she was, she was herself the great piece in the gallery. It was the first Fleda had heard of there being 'rubbish' at Poynton, but she didn't for the moment take up this insincerity; she only, from where she stood in the room, called out, one after the other, as if she had had a list in her hand, the pieces that in the great house had been scattered and that now, if they had a fault, were too much like a minuet danced on a hearth-rug. She knew them each, in every chink and charm – knew them by the personal name their distinctive sign or story had given them; and a second time she felt how, against her intention, this uttered knowledge struck her hostess as so much free approval. Mrs Gereth was never indifferent to approval, and there was nothing she could so love you for as for doing justice to her deep morality. There was a particular gleam in her eyes when Fleda exclaimed at last, dazzled by the display: 'And even the Maltese cross!' That description, though technically incorrect, had always been applied, at Poynton, to a small but marvellous crucifix of ivory, a masterpiece of delicacy, of expression, and of the great Spanish period, the existence and precarious accessibility of which she had heard of at Malta, years before, by an odd and romantic chance – a clue followed through mazes of secrecy till the treasure was at last unearthed.

'"Even" the Maltese cross?' Mrs Gereth rose as she sharply echoed the words. 'My dear child, you don't suppose I'd have sacrificed *that*! For what in the world would you have taken me?'

'A *bibelot* the more or the less,' Fleda said, 'could have made little difference in this grand general view of you. I take you simply for the greatest of all conjurers. You've operated with a quickness – and with a quietness!' Her voice trembled a little as she spoke, for the plain meaning of her words was that what her friend had achieved belonged to the class of operation essentially involving the protection of darkness. Fleda felt she really could say nothing at all if she couldn't say that she knew what the danger had been. She completed her thought by a resolute and perfectly candid question: 'How in the world did you get off with them?'

Mrs Gereth confessed to the fact of danger with a cynicism

300

that surprised the girl. 'By calculating, by choosing my time.
I *was* quiet, and I *was* quick. I manoeuvred; then at the last
rushed!' Fleda drew a long breath: she saw in the poor woman
something much better than sophistical ease, a crude elation
that was a comparatively simple state to deal with. Her elation,
it was true, was not so much from what she had done as from
the way she had done it – by as brilliant a stroke as any com-
memorated in the annals of crime. 'I succeeded because I had
thought it all out and left nothing to chance: the whole process
was organized in advance, so that the mere carrying it into
effect took but a few hours. It was largely a matter of money:
oh, I was horribly extravagant – I had to turn on so many people. But they were all to be had – a little army of workers, the
packers, the porters, the helpers of every sort, the men with the
mighty vans. It was a question of arranging in Tottenham
Court Road and of paying the price. I haven't paid it yet;
there'll be a horrid bill; but at least the thing's done! Expedi-
tion pure and simple was the essence of the bargain. "I can
give you two days," I said; "I can't give you another second."
They undertook the job, and the two days saw them through.
The people came down on a Tuesday morning; they were off
on the Thursday. I admit that some of them worked all Wednesday night. I had thought it all out; I stood over them; I
showed them how. Yes, I coaxed them, I made love to them.
Oh, I was inspired – they found me wonderful. I neither ate nor
slept, but I was as calm as I am now. I didn't know what was
in me ; it was worth finding out. I'm very remarkable, my dear:
I lifted tons with my own arms. I'm tired, very, very tired; but
there's neither a scratch nor a nick, there isn't a teacup missing.'
Magnificent both in her exhaustion and in her triumph, Mrs
Gereth sank on the sofa again, the sweep of her eyes a
rich synthesis and the restless friction of her hands a clear
betrayal. 'Upon my word,' she laughed, 'they really look better
here!'

Fleda had listened in awe. 'And no one at Poynton said
anything? There was no alarm?'

'What alarm should there have been? Owen left me almost
defiantly alone: I had taken a time that I had reason to believe
was safe from a descent.' Fleda had another wonder, which she

301

hesitated to express: it would scarcely do to ask Mrs Gereth if she hadn't stood in fear of her servants. She knew, moreover, some of the secrets of her humorous household rule, all made up of shocks to shyness and provocations to curiosity – a diplomacy so artful that several of the maids quite yearned to accompany her to Ricks. Mrs Gereth, reading sharply the whole of her visitor's thought, caught it up with fine frankness. 'You mean that I was watched – that he had his myrmidons, pledged to wire him if they should see what I was "up to"? Precisely. I know the three persons you have in mind: I had them in mind myself. Well, I took a line with them – I settled them.'

Fleda had had no one in particular in mind; she had never believed in the myrmidons; but the tone in which Mrs Gereth spoke added to her suspense. 'What did you do to them?'

'I took hold of them hard – I put them in the forefront. I made them work.'

'To move the furniture?'

'To help, and to help so as to please me. That was the way to take them ; it was what they had least expected. I marched up to them and looked each straight in the eye, giving him the chance to choose if he'd gratify me or gratify my son. He gratified *me*. They were too stupid!'

Mrs Gereth massed herself there more and more as an immoral woman, but Fleda had to recognize that she too would have been stupid and she too would have gratified her. 'And when did all this take place?'

'Only last week; it seems a hundred years. We've worked here as fast as we worked there, but I'm not settled yet: you'll see in the rest of the house. However, the worst is over.'

'Do you really think so?' Fleda presently inquired. 'I mean, does he, after the fact, as it were, accept it?'

'Owen – what I've done? I haven't the least idea,' said Mrs Gereth.

'Does Mona?'

'You mean that she'll be the soul of the row?'

'I hardly see Mona as the "soul" of anything,' the girl replied. 'But have they made no sound? Have you heard nothing at all?'

'Not a whisper, not a step, in all the eight days. Perhaps they don't know. Perhaps they're crouching for a leap.'

'But wouldn't they have gone down as soon as you left?'

'They may not have known of my leaving.' Fleda wondered afresh; it struck her as scarcely supposable that some sign shouldn't have flashed from Poynton to London. If the storm was taking this term of silence to gather, even in Mona's breast, it would probably discharge itself in some startling form. The great hush of everyone concerned was strange; but when she pressed Mrs Gereth for some explanation of it, that lady only replied, with her brave irony: 'Oh, I took their breath away!' She had no illusions, however; she was still prepared to fight. What indeed was her spoliation of Poynton but the first engagement of a campaign?

All this was exciting, but Fleda's spirit dropped, at bedtime, in the chamber embellished for her pleasure, where she found several of the objects that in her earlier room she had most admired. These had been reinforced by other pieces from other rooms, so that the quiet air of it was a harmony without a break, the finished picture of a maiden's bower. It was the sweetest Louis Seize, all assorted and combined – old chastened, figured, faded France. Fleda was impressed anew with her friend's genius for composition. She could say to herself that no girl in England, that night, went to rest with so picked a guard; but there was no joy for her in her privilege, no sleep even for the tired hours that made the place, in the embers of the fire and the winter dawn, look grey somehow, and loveless. She couldn't care for such things when they came to her in such ways; there was a wrong about them all that turned them to ugliness. In the watches of the night she saw Poynton dishonoured; she had cared for it as a happy whole, she reasoned, and the parts of it now around her seemed to suffer like chopped limbs. Before going to bed she had walked about with Mrs Gereth and seen at whose expense the whole house had been furnished. At poor Owen's from top to bottom – there wasn't a chair he hadn't sat upon. The maiden aunt had been exterminated – no trace of her to tell her tale. Fleda tried to think of some of the things at Poynton still unappropriated, but her memory was a blank about them, and in trying to focus the old combinations she saw again nothing but gaps and scars, a vacancy that gathered at moments into something worse. This concrete image was her greatest trouble, for it was Owen Gereth's face, his sad, strange eyes, fixed upon her now as they had never been. They stared at her out of the darkness, and their expression was more than she could bear: it seemed to say that he was in pain and that it was somehow her fault. He had looked to her to help him, and this was what her help had been. He had done her the honour to ask her to exert herself in his interest, confiding to her a task of difficulty, but of the highest delicacy. Hadn't that been exactly the sort of service she longed to render him? Well, her way of rendering it had been simply to betray him and hand him over to his enemy. Shame, pity, resentment oppressed her in turn; in the last of these feelings the others were quickly submerged. Mrs Gereth had imprisoned her in that torment of taste; but it was clear to her for an hour at least that she might hate Mrs Gereth.

Something else, however, when morning came, was even more intensely definite: the most odious thing in the world for her would be ever again to meet Owen. She took on the spot a resolve to neglect no precaution that could lead to her going through life without that accident. After this, while she dressed, she took still another. Her position had become, in a few hours, intolerably false; in as few more hours as possible she would therefore put an end to it. The way to put an end to it would be to inform Mrs Gereth that, to her great regret, she couldn't be with her now, couldn't cleave to her to the point that everything about her so plainly urged. She dressed with a sort of violence, a symbol of the manner in which this purpose was precipitated. The more they parted company the less likely she was to come across Owen; for Owen would be drawn closer to his mother now by the very necessity of bringing her down. Fleda, in the inconsequence of distress, wished to have nothing to do with her fall; she had had too much to do with everything. She was well aware of the importance, before breakfast and in view of any light they might shed on the question of motive, of not suffering her invidious expression of a difference to be accompanied by the traces of tears; but it none the less came to pass, downstairs, that after she had subtly put her back to the window, to make a mystery of the state of her eyes, she stupidly let a rich sob escape her before she could properly meet the consequences of being asked if she wasn't delighted with her room. This accident struck her on the spot as so grave that she felt the only refuge to be instant hypocrisy, some graceful impulse that would charge her emotion to the quickened sense of her friend's generosity – a demonstration entailing a flutter round the table and a renewed embrace, and not so successfully improvised but that Fleda fancied Mrs Gereth to have been only half reassured. She had been startled, at any rate, and she might remain suspicious: this reflection interposed by the time, after breakfast, the girl had recovered sufficiently to say what was in her heart. She accordingly didn't say it that morning at all: she had absurdly veered about; she had encountered the shock of the fear that Mrs Gereth, with sharpened eyes, might wonder why the deuce (she often wondered in that phrase) she had grown so warm about Owen's rights. She would doubtless, at a pinch, be able to defend them on abstract grounds, but that would involve a discussion, and the idea of a discussion made her nervous for her secret. Until in some way Poynton should return the blow and give her a cue, she must keep nervousness down; and she called herself a fool for having forgotten, however briefly, that her one safety was in silence.

Directly after luncheon Mrs Gereth took her into the garden for a glimpse of the revolution – or at least, said the mistress of Ricks, of the great row – that had been decreed there; but the ladies had scarcely placed themselves for this view before the younger one found herself embracing a prospect that opened in quite another quarter. Her attention was called to it, oddly, by the streamers of the parlourmaid's cap, which, flying straight behind the neat young woman who unexpectedly burst from the house and showed a long red face as she ambled over the grass, seemed to articulate in their flutter the name that Fleda lived at present only to catch. 'Poynton – Poynton!' said the morsels of muslin; so that the parlour-maid became on the instant an actress in the drama, and Fleda, assuming pusillanimously that she herself was only a spectator, looked across the footlights at the exponent of the principal part. The manner in which this artist returned her look showed that she was equally preoccupied. Both were haunted alike by possibilities, but the apprehension of neither, before the announcement was made, took the form of the arrival at Ricks, in the flesh, of Mrs Gereth's victim. When the messenger informed them that Mr Gereth was in the drawing-room, the blank 'Oh!' emitted by Fleda was quite as precipitate as the sound of her hostess's lips, besides being, as she felt, much less pertinent. 'I thought it would be somebody,' that lady afterwards said ; 'but I expected on the whole a solicitor's clerk.' Fleda didn't mention that she herself had expected on the whole a pair of constables. She was surprised by Mrs Gereth's question to the parlour-maid.

'For whom did he ask?'

'Why, for *you,* of course, dearest friend!' Fleda interjected, falling instinctively into the address that embodied the intensest pressure. She wanted to put Mrs Gereth between her and her danger.

'He asked for Miss Vetch, mum,' the girl replied, with a face that brought startlingly to Fleda's ear the muffled chorus of the kitchen.

'Quite proper,' said Mrs Gereth austerely. Then to Fleda: 'Please go to him.'

'But what to do?'

'What you always do – to see what he wants.' Mrs Gereth dismissed the maid. 'Tell him Miss Vetch will come.' Fleda saw that nothing was in the mother's imagination at this moment but the desire not to meet her son. She had completely broken with him, and there was little in what had just happened to repair the rupture. It would now take more to do so than his presenting himself uninvited at her door. 'He's right in asking for you – he's aware that you're still our communicator ; nothing has occurred to alter that. To what he wishes to transmit through you I'm ready, as I've been ready before, to listen. As far as *I*'m concerned, if I couldn't meet him a month ago, how am I to meet him today? If he has come to say, "My dear mother, you're here, in the hovel into which I've flung you, with consolations that give me pleasure," I'll listen to him ; but on no other footing. That's what you're to ascertain,

306

please. You'll oblige me as you've obliged me before. There!'
Mrs Gereth turned her back and, with a fine imitation of
superiority, began to redress the miseries immediately before
her. Fleda meanwhile hesitated, lingered for some minutes
where she had been left, feeling secretly that her fate still had
her in hand. It had put her face to face with Owen Gereth, and
it evidently meant to keep her so. She was reminded afresh of
two things: one of which was that, though she judged her
friend's rigour, she had never really had the story of the scene
enacted in the great awestricken house between the mother and
the son weeks before – the day the former took to her bed in
her overthrow; the other was, that at Ricks as at Poynton, it
was before all things her place to accept thankfully a usefulness
not, she must remember, universally asknowledged. What
determined her at the last, while Mrs Gereth disappeared in
the shrubbery, was that, though she was at a distance from
the house and the drawing-room was turned the other way, she
could absolutely see the young man alone there with the
sources of his pain. She saw his simple stare at his tapestries,
heard his heavy tread on his carpets and the hard breath of
his sense of unfairness. At this she went to him fast.

CHAPTER 8

'I ASKED for you,' he said when she stood there, 'because I heard from the flyman who drove me from the station to the inn that he had brought you here yesterday. We had some talk, and he mentioned it.'

'You didn't know I was here?'

'No. I knew only that you had had, in London, all that you told me, that day, to do; and it was Mona's idea that after your sister's marriage you were staying on with your father. So I thought you were with him still.'

'I am,' Fleda replied, idealizing a little the fact. 'I'm here only for a moment. But do you mean,' she went on, 'that if you had known I was with your mother you wouldn't have come down?'

The way Owen hung fire at this question made it sound more playful than she had intended. She had, in fact, no consciousness of any intention but that of confining herself rigidly to her function. She could already see that, in whatever he had now braced himself for, she was an element he had not reckoned with. His preparation had been of a different sort — the sort congruous with his having been careful to go first and lunch solidly at the inn. He had not been forced to ask for her, but she became aware, in his presence, of a particular desire to make him feel that no harm could really come to him. She might upset him, as people called it, but she would take no advantage of having done so. She had never seen a person with whom she wished more to be light and easy, to be exceptionally human. The account he presently gave of the matter was that he indeed wouldn't have come if he had known she was on the spot; because then, didn't she see? he could have written to her. He would have had her there to let fly at his mother.

'That would have saved me — well, it would have saved me a lot. Of course I would rather see you than her,' he somewhat awkwardly added. 'When the fellow spoke of you, I assure you I quite jumped at you. In fact I've no real desire to see Mummy at all. If she thinks I *like* it – ! ' he sighed disgustedly. 'I only came down because it seemed better than any other way. I didn't want her to be able to say I hadn't been all right. I dare say you know she has taken everything; or if not quite everything, why, a lot more than one ever dreamed. You can see for yourself – she has got half the place down. She has got them crammed – you can see for yourself! ' He had his old trick of artless repetition, his helpless iteration of the obvious; but he was sensibly different, for Fleda, if only by the difference of his clear face, mottled over and almost disfigured by little points of pain. He might have been a fine young man with a bad toothache; with the first even of his life. What ailed him above all, she felt was that trouble was new to him: he had never known a difficulty; he had taken all his fences, his world wholly the world of the personally possible, rounded indeed by a grey suburb into which he had never had occasion to stray. In this vulgar and ill-lighted region he had evidently now lost himself. 'We left it quite to her honour, you know,' he said ruefully.

'Perhaps you've a right to say that you left it a little to mine.' Mixed up with the spoils there, rising before him as if she were in a manner their keeper, she felt that she must absolutely dissociate herself. Mrs Gereth had made it impossible to do anything but give her away. 'I can only tell you that, on my side, I left it to her. I never dreamed either that she would pick out so many things.'

'And you don't really think it's fair, do you? You *don't*! ' He spoke very quickly; he really seemed to plead.

Fleda faltered a moment. 'I think she has gone too far.' Then she added: 'I shall immediately tell her that I've said that to you.'

He appeared puzzled by this statement, but he presently rejoined: 'You haven't then said to mamma what you think?'

'Not yet; remember that I only got here last night.' She appeared to herself ignobly weak. 'I had had no idea what she was doing; I was taken completely by surprise. She managed it wonderfully.'

'It's the sharpest thing I ever saw in *my* life! ' They looked at each other with intelligence, in appreciation of the sharpness, and Owen quickly broke into a loud laugh. The laugh was in itself natural, but the occasion of it strange; and stranger still, to Fleda, so that she too almost laughed, the inconsequent charity with which he added: 'Poor dear old Mummy! That's one of the reasons I asked for you,' he went on – 'to see if you'd back her up.'

Whatever he said or did, she somehow liked him the better for it. 'How can I back her up, Mr Gereth, when I think, as I tell you, that she has made a great mistake?'

'A great mistake! That's all right.' He spoke – it wasn't clear to her why – as if this declaration were a great point gained.

'Of course there are many things she hasn't taken,' Fleda continued.

'Oh yes, a lot of things. But you wouldn't know the place, all the same.' He looked about the room with his discoloured, swindled face, which deepened Fleda's compassion for him, conjuring away any smile at so candid an image of the dupe. 'You'd know this one soon enough, wouldn't you? These are just the things she ought to have left. Is the whole house full of them?'

'The whole house,' said Fleda uncompromisingly. She thought of her lovely room.

'I never knew how much I cared for them. They're awfully valuable, aren't they?' Owen's manner mystified her; she was conscious of a return of the agitation he had produced in her on that last bewildering day, and she reminded herself that, now she was warned, it would be inexcusable of her to allow him to justify the fear that had dropped on her. 'Mother thinks I never took any notice, but I assure you I was awfully proud of everything. Upon my honour, I *was* proud, Miss Vetch.'

There was an oddity in his helplessness; he appeared to wish to persuade her and to satisfy himself that she sincerely felt how worthy he really was to treat what had happened as an injury. She could only exclaim, almost as helplessly as himself: 'Of course you did justice! It's all most painful. I shall instantly let your mother know,' she again declared, 'the way I've

310

spoken of her to you.' She clung to that idea as to the sign of her straightness.

'You'll tell her what you think she ought to do?' he asked with some eagerness.

'What she ought to do?'

'*Don't* you think it – I mean that she ought to give them up?'

'To give them up?' Fleda hesitated again.

'To send them back – to keep it quiet.' The girl had not felt the impulse to ask him to sit down among the monuments of his wrong, so that, nervously, awkwardly, he fidgeted about the room with his hands in his pockets and an effect of returning a little into possession through the formulation of his view. 'To have them packed and dispatched again, since she knows so well how. She does it beautifully' – he looked close at two or three precious pieces. 'What's sauce for the goose is sauce for the gander!'

He had laughed at his way of putting it, but Fleda remained grave. 'Is that what you came to say to her?'

'Not exactly those words. But I did come to say' – he stammered, then brought it out – 'I did come to say we must have them right back.'

'And did you think your mother would see you?'

'I wasn't sure, but I thought it right to try – to put it to her kindly, don't you see? If she won't see me, then she has herself to thank. The only other way would have been to set the lawyers at her.'

'I'm glad you didn't do that.'

'I'm dashed if I want to!' Owen honestly declared. 'But what's a fellow to do if she won't meet a fellow?'

'What do you call meeting a fellow?' Fleda asked, with a smile.

'Why, letting *me* tell her a dozen things she can have.'

This was a transaction that Fleda, after a moment, had to give up trying to represent to herself. 'If she won't do that – ?' she went on.

'I'll leave it all to my solicitor. *He* won't let her off: by Jove, I know the fellow!'

'That's horrible!' said Fleda, looking at him in woe.

'It's utterly beastly!'

His want of logic as well as his vehemence startled her; and with her eyes still on his she considered before asking him the question these things suggested. At last she asked it. 'Is Mona very angry?'

'Oh dear, yes!' said Owen.

She had perceived that he wouldn't speak of Mona without her beginning. After waiting fruitlessly now for him to say more, she continued: 'She has been there again? She has seen the state of the house?'

'Oh dear, yes!' Owen repeated.

Fleda disliked to appear not to take account of his brevity, but it was just because she was struck by it that she felt the pressure of the desire to know more. What it suggested was simply what her intelligence supplied, for he was incapable of any art of insinuation. Wasn't it at all events the rule of communication with him to say for him what he couldn't say? This truth was present to the girl as she inquired if Mona greatly resented what Mrs Gereth had done. He satisfied her promptly; he was standing before the fire, his back to it, his long legs apart, his hands, behind him, rather violently jiggling his gloves. 'She hates it awfully. In fact, she refuses to put up with it at all. Don't you see? – she saw the place with all the things.'

'So that of course she misses them.'

'Misses them – rather! She was awfully sweet on them.' Fleda remembered how sweet Mona had been, and reflected that if that was the sort of plea he had prepared it was indeed as well he shouldn't see his mother. This was not all she wanted to know, but it came over her that it was all she needed. 'You see it puts me in the position of not carrying out what I promised,' Owen said. 'As she says herself' – he hesitated an instant – 'it's just as if I had obtained her under false pretences.' Just before, when he spoke with more drollery than he knew, it had left Fleda serious; but now his own clear gravity had the effect of exciting her mirth. She laughed out, and he looked surprised, but went on: 'She regards it as a regular sell.'

Fleda was silent; but finally, as he added nothing, she exclaimed: 'Of course it makes a great difference!' She knew all she needed, but none the less she risked, after another pause,

312

an interrogative remark. 'I forgot when it is that your marriage takes place?'

Owen came away from the fire and, apparently at a loss where to turn, ended by directing himself to one of the windows. 'It's a little uncertain ; the date isn't quite fixed.'

'Oh, I thought I remembered that at Poynton you had told me a day, and that it was near at hand.'

'I dare say I did ; it was for the 19th. But we've altered that – she wants to shift it.' He looked out of the window ; then he said : 'In fact, it won't come off till Mummy has come round.'

'Come round?'

'Put the place as it was.' In his offhand way he added : 'You know what I mean!'

He spoke not impatiently, but with a kind of intimate familiarity, the sweetness of which made her feel a pang for having forced him to tell her what was embarrassing to him, what was even humiliating. Yes, indeed, she knew all she needed : all she needed was that Mona had proved apt at putting down that wonderful patent-leather foot. Her type was misleading only to the superficial, and no one in the world was less superficial than Fleda. She had guessed the truth at Waterbath and she had suffered from it at Poynton ; at Ricks the only thing she could do was to accept it with the dumb exaltation that she felt rising. Mona had been prompt with her exercise of the member in question, for it might be called prompt to do that sort of thing before marriage. That she had indeed been premature who should say save those who should have read the matter in the full light of results? Neither at Waterbath nor at Poynton had even Fleda's thoroughness discovered all that there was – or rather, all that there was not – in Owen Gereth. 'Of course it makes all the difference!' she said in answer to his last words. She pursued, after considering : 'What you wish me to say from you then to your mother is that you demand immediate and practically complete restitution?'

'Yes, please. It's tremendously good of you.'

'Very well, then. Will you wait?'

'For Mummy's answer?' Owen stared and looked perplexed ; he was more and more fevered with so much vivid expression of his case. 'Don't you think that if I'm here she may hate it worse – think I may want to make her reply bang off?'

Fleda thought. 'You don't then?'

'I want to take her in the right way, don't you know? – treat her as if I gave her more than just an hour or two.'

'I see,' said Fleda. 'Then, if you don't wait – good-bye.'

This again seemed not what he wanted. 'Must *you* do it bang off?'

'I'm only thinking she'll be impatient – I mean, you know, to learn what will have passed between us.'

'I see,' said Owen, looking at his gloves. 'I can give her a day or two, you know. Of course I didn't come down to sleep,' he went on. 'The inn seems a horrid hole. I know all about the trains – having no idea you were here.' Almost as soon as his interlocutress he was struck with the absence of the visible, in this, as between effect and cause. 'I mean because in that case I should have felt I could stop over. I should have felt I could talk with you a blessed sight longer than with Mummy.'

'We've already talked a long time,' smiled Fleda.

'Awfully, haven't we?' He spoke with the stupidity she didn't object to. Inarticulate as he was, he had more to say; he lingered perhaps because he was vaguely aware of the want of sincerity in her encouragement to him to go. 'There's one thing, please,' he mentioned, as if there might be a great many others too. 'Please don't say anything about Mona.'

She didn't understand. 'About Mona?'

'About its being *her* that thinks she has gone too far.' This was still slightly obscure, but now Fleda understood. 'It mustn't seem to come from *her* at all, don't you know? That would only make Mummy worse.'

Fleda knew exactly how much worse, but she felt a delicacy about explicitly assenting. She was already immersed moreover in the deep consideration of what might make 'Mummy' better. She couldn't see as yet at all; she could only clutch at the hope of some inspiration after he should go. Oh, there was a remedy, to be sure, but it was out of the question; in spite of which, in the strong light of Owen's troubled presence, of his anxious face and restless step, it hung there before her for

314

some minutes. She felt that, remarkably, beneath the decent rigour of his errand, the poor young man, for reasons, for weariness, for disgust, would have been ready not to insist. His fitness to fight his mother had left him – he wasn't in fighting trim. He had no natural avidity and even no special wrath ; he had none that had not been taught him, and it was doing his best to learn the lesson that had made him so sick. He had his delicacies, but he hid them away like presents before Christmas. He was hollow, perfunctory, pathetic ; he had been guided by another hand. That hand had naturally been Mona's, and it was heavy even now on his strong, broad back. Why then had he originally rejoiced so in its touch? Fleda dashed aside this question, for it had nothing to do with her problem. Her problem was to help him to live as a gentleman and carry through what he had undertaken ; her problem was to reinstate him in his rights. It was quite irrelevant that Mona had no intelligence of what she had lost – quite irrelevant that she was moved not by the privation, but by the insult : she had every reason to be moved, though she was so much more movable, in the vindictive way, at any rate, than one might have supposed – assuredly more than Owen himself had imagined.

'Certainly I shall not mention Mona,' Fleda said, 'and there won't be the slightest necessity for it. The wrong's quite sufficiently yours, and the demand you make is perfectly justified by it.'

'I can't tell you what it is to me to feel you on my side!' Owen exclaimed.

'Up to this time,' said Fleda, after a pause, 'your mother has had no doubt of my being on hers.'

'Then of course she won't like your changing.'

'I dare say she won't like it at all.'

'Do you mean to say you'll have a regular kick-up with her?'

'I don't exactly know what you mean by a regular kick-up. We shall naturally have a great deal of discussion – if she consents to discuss the matter at all. That's why you must decidedly give her two or three days.'

'I see you think she *may* refuse to discuss it at all,' said Owen.

'I'm only trying to be prepared for the worst. You must remember that to have to withdraw from the ground she has taken, to make a public surrender of what she has publicly appropriated, will go uncommonly hard with her pride.'

Owen considered; his face seemed to broaden, but not into a smile. 'I suppose she's tremendously proud, isn't she?' This might have been the first time it had occurred to him.

'You know better than I,' said Fleda, speaking with high extravagance.

'I don't know anything in the world half so well as you. If I were as clever as you I might hope to get round her.' Owen hesitated; then he went on: 'In fact I don't quite see what even you can say or do that will really fetch her.'

'Neither do I, as yet. I must think – I must pray!' the girl pursued, smiling. 'I can only say to you that I'll try. I *want* to try, you know – I want to help you.' He stood looking at her so long on this that she added with much distinctness: 'So you must leave me, please, quite alone with her. You must go straight back.'

'Back to the inn?'

'Oh no, back to town. I'll write to you tomorrow.'

He turned about vaguely for his hat.

'There's a chance, of course, that she may be afraid.'

'Afraid, you mean, of the legal steps you may take?'

'I've got a perfect case – I could have her up. The Brigstocks say it's simple stealing.'

'I can easily fancy what the Brigstocks say!' Fleda permitted herself to remark without solemnity.

'It's none of their business, is it?' was Owen's unexpected rejoinder. Fleda had already noted that no one so slow could ever have had such rapid transitions.

She showed her amusement. 'They've a much better right to say it's none of mine.'

'Well, at any rate, you don't call her names.'

Fleda wondered whether Mona did; and this made it all the finer of her to exclaim in a moment: 'You don't know what I shall call her if she holds out!'

Owen gave her a gloomy glance; then he blew a speck off the crown of his hat. 'But if you do have a set-to with her?'

He paused so long for a reply that Fleda said: 'I don't think I know what you mean by a set-to.'

'Well, if she calls *you* names.'

'I don't think she'll do that.'

'What I mean to say is, if she's angry at your backing me up – what will you do then? She can't possibly like it, you know.'

'She may very well not like it; but everything depends. I must see what I shall do. You mustn't worry about me.'

She spoke with decision, but Owen seemed still unsatisfied. 'You won't go away, I hope?'

'Go away?'

'If she does take it ill of you.'

Fleda moved to the door and opened it. 'I'm not prepared to say. You must have patience and see.'

'Of course I must,' said Owen – 'of course, of course.' But he took no more advantage of the open door than to say: 'You want me to be off, and I'm off in a minute. Only, before I go, please answer me a question. If you *should* leave my mother, where would you go?'

Fleda smiled again. 'I haven't the least idea.'

'I suppose you'd go back to London.'

'I haven't the least idea,' Fleda repeated.

'You don't – a – live anywhere in particular, do you?' the young man went on. He looked conscious as soon as he had spoken; she could see that he felt himself to have alluded more grossly than he meant to the circumstances of her having, if one were plain about it, no home of her own. He had meant it as an illusion of a tender sort to all that she would sacrifice in the case of a quarrel with his mother; but there was indeed no graceful way of touching on that. One just couldn't be plain about it.

Fleda, wound up as she was, shrank from any treatment at all of the matter, and she made no answer to his question. 'I *won't* leave your mother,' she said. 'I'll produce an effect on her; I'll convince her absolutely.'

'I believe you will, if you look at her like that!'

She was wound up to such a height that there might well be a light in her pale, fine little face – a light that, while, for all return, at first, she simply shone back at him, was intensely

reflected in his own. 'I'll make her see it – I'll make her see it!'
She rang out like a silver bell. She had at that moment a perfect faith that she should succeed; but it passed into something
else when, the next instant, she became aware that Owen,
quickly getting between her and the door she had opened, was
sharply closing it, as might be said, in her face. He had done
this before she could stop him, and he stood there with his
hand on the knob and smiled at her strangely. Clearer than he
could have spoken it was the sense of those seconds of silence.

'When I got into this I didn't know you, and now that I
know you how can I tell you the difference? And *she's* so
different, so ugly and vulgar, in the light of this squabble. No,
like *you* I've never known one. It's another thing, it's a new
thing altogether. Listen to me a little: can't something be
done?' It was what had been in the air in those moments at
Kensington, and it only wanted words to be a committed act.
The more reason, to the girl's excited mind, why it shouldn't
have words; her one thought was not to hear, to keep the act
uncommitted. She would do this if she had to be horrid.

'Please let me out, Mr Gereth,' she said; on which he opened
the door with an hesitation so very brief that in thinking of
these things afterwards – for she was to think of them for ever
– she wondered in what tone she could have spoken. They went
into the hall, where she encountered the parlour-maid of
whom she inquired whether Mrs Gereth had come in.

'No miss; and I think she has left the garden. She has gone
up the back road.' In other words, they had the whole place to
themselves. It would have been a pleasure, in a different mood
to converse with that parlour-maid.

'Please open the house-door,' said Fleda.

Owen, as if in quest of his umbrella, looked vaguely about
the hall – looked even wistfully up the staircase – while the
neat young woman complied with Fleda's request. Owen's
eyes then wandered out of the open door. 'I think it's awfully
nice here,' he observed; 'I assure you I could do with it myself.'

'I should think you might, with half your things here! It's
Poynton itself – almost. Good-bye, Mr Gereth,' Fleda added.
Her intention had naturally been that the neat young woman,
opening the front door, should remain to close it on the

departing guest. That functionary, however, had acutely vanished behind a stiff flap of green baize which Mrs Gereth had not yet had time to abolish. Fleda put out her hand, but Owen turned away – he couldn't find his umbrella. She passed into the open air – she was determined to get him out ; and in a moment he joined her in the little plastered portico which had small resemblance to any feature of Poynton. It was, as Mrs Gereth had said, like the portico of a house in Brompton.

'Oh, I don't mean with all the things here,' he explained in regard to the opinion he had just expressed. 'I mean I could put up with it just as it was ; it had a lot of good things, don't you think? I mean if everything was back at Poynton, if everything was all right.' He brought out these last words with a sort of smothered sigh. Fleda didn't understand his explanation unless it had reference to another and more wonderful exchange – the restoration to the great house not only of its tables and chairs, but of its alienated mistress. This would imply the installation of his own life at Ricks, and obviously that of another person. Such another person could scarcely be Mona Brigstock. He put out his hand now ; and once more she heard his unsounded words: 'With everything patched up at the other place, I could live here with *you*. Don't you see what I mean?'

Fleda saw perfectly, and, with a face in which she flattered herself that nothing of this vision appeared, gave him her hand and said: 'Good-bye, good-bye.'

Owen held her hand very firmly and kept it even after an effort made by her to recover it – an effort not repeated, as she felt it best not to show she was flurried. That solution – of her living with him at Ricks – disposed of him beautifully, and disposed not less so of herself ; it disposed admirably too of Mrs Gereth. Fleda could only vainly wonder how it provided for poor Mona. While he looked at her, grasping her hand, she felt that now indeed she was paying for his mother's extravagance at Poynton – the vividness of that lady's public plea that little Fleda Vetch was the person to insure the general peace. It was to that vividness poor Owen had come back, and if Mrs Gereth had had more discretion little Fleda Vetch wouldn't have been in a predicament. She saw that Owen had at this moment his sharpest necessity of speech, and so long as he didn't release her hand she could only submit to him. Her defence would be perhaps to look blank and hard; so she looked as blank and as hard as she could, with the reward of an immediate sense that this was not a bit what he wanted. It even made him hang fire, as if he were suddenly ashamed of himself, were recalled to some idea of duty and of honour. Yet he none the less brought it out. 'There's one thing I dare say I ought to tell you, if you're going so kindly to act for me; though of course you'll see for yourself it's a thing it won't do to tell *her*.' What was it? He made her wait for it again, and while she waited, under firm coercion, she had the extraordinary impression that Owen's simplicity was in eclipse. His natural honesty was like the scent of a flower, and she felt at this moment as if her nose had been brushed by the bloom without the odour. The allusion was undoubtedly to his mother; and was not what he meant about the matter in question the opposite of what he said – that it just *would* do to tell her? It would have been the first time he had said the opposite of what he meant, and there was certainly a fascination in the phenomenon, as well as a challenge to suspense in the ambiguity. 'It's just that I understand from Mona, you know,' he stammered; 'it's just that she has made no bones about bringing home to me – ' He tried to laugh, and in the effort he faltered again.

'About bringing home to you?' – Fleda encouraged him.

He was sensible of it, he achieved his performance. 'Why, that if I don't get the things back – every blessed one of them except a few *she'll* pick out – she won't have anything more to say to me.'

Fleda, after an instant, encouraged him again. 'To say to you?'

'Why, she simply won't marry me, don't you see?'

Owen's legs, not to mention his voice, had wavered while he spoke, and she felt his possession of her hand loosen so that she was free again. Her stare of perception broke into a lively laugh. 'Oh, you're all right, for you *will* get them. You will; you're quite safe; don't worry!' She fell back into the house with her hand on the door. 'Good-bye, good-bye.' She repeated it several times, laughing bravely, quite waving him away and,

320

as he didn't move and save that he was on the other side of it, closing the door in his face quite as he had closed that of the drawing-room in hers. Never had a face, never at least had such a handsome one, been so presented to that offence. She even held the door a minute, lest he should try to come in again. At last, as she heard nothing, she made a dash for the stairs and ran up.

CHAPTER 9

IN knowing a while before all she needed, Fleda had been far from knowing as much as that; so that once upstairs, where, in her room, with her sense of danger and trouble, the age of Louis-Seize suddenly struck her as wanting in taste and point, she felt that she now for the first time knew her temptation. Owen had put it before her with an art beyond his own dream. Mona would cast him off if he didn't proceed to extremities; if his negotiation with his mother should fail he would be completely free. That negotiation depended on a young lady to whom he had pressingly suggested the condition of his freedom; and as if to aggravate the young lady's predicament designing fate had sent Mrs Gereth, as the parlour-maid said, 'up the back roads'. This would give the young lady more time to make up her mind that nothing should come of the negotiation. There would be different ways of putting the question to Mrs Gereth, and Fleda might profitably devote the moments before her return to a selection of the way that would most surely be tantamount to failure. This selection indeed required no great adroitness; it was so conspicuous that failure would be the reward of an effective introduction of Mona. If that abhorred name should be properly invoked Mrs Gereth would resist to the death, and before envenomed resistance Owen would certainly retire. His retirement would be into single life, and Fleda reflected that he had now gone away conscious of having practically told her so. She could only say, as she waited for the back road to disgorge, that she hoped it was a consciousness he enjoyed. There was something *she* enjoyed; but that was a very different matter. To know that she had become to him an object of desire gave her wings that she felt herself flutter in the air: it was like the rush of a flood into her own accumulations. These stored depths had been fathomless and still, but now, for half an hour, in the empty house, they spread till they overflowed. He seemed to have made it right for her to confess to herself her secret. Strange

322

then there should be for him in return nothing that such a confession could make right! How could it make right that he should give up Mona for another woman? His attitude was a sorry appeal to Fleda to legitimate that. But he didn't believe it himself, and he had none of the courage of his suggestion. She could easily see how wrong everything must be when a man so made to be manly was wanting in courage. She had upset him, as people called it, and he had spoken out from the force of the jar of finding her there. He had upset her too, heaven knew, but she was one of those who could pick themselves up. She had the real advantage, she considered, of having kept him from seeing that she had been overthrown.

She had moreover at present completely recovered her feet, though there was in the intensity of the effort required to do so a vibration which throbbed away into an immense allowance for the young man. How could she after all know what, in the disturbance wrought by his mother, Mona's relations with him might have become? If he had been able to keep his wits, such as they were, more about him he would probably have felt – as sharply as she felt on his behalf – that so long as those relations were not ended he had no right to say even the little he had said. He had no right to appear to wish to draw in another girl to help him to an escape. If he was in a plight he must get out of the plight himself, he must get out of it first, and anything he should have to say to anyone else must be deferred and detached. She herself, at any rate – it was her own case that was in question – couldn't dream of assisting him save in the sense of their common honour. She could never be the girl to be drawn in, she could never lift her finger against Mona. There was something in her that would make it a shame to her for ever to have owed her happiness to an interference. It would seem intolerably vulgar to her to have 'ousted' the daughter of the Brigstocks; and merely to have abstained even wouldn't assure her that she had been straight. Nothing was really straight but to justify her little pensioned presence by her use; and now, won over as she was to heroism, she could see her use only as some high and delicate deed. She couldn't do anything at all, in short, unless she could do it with a kind of pride, and there would be nothing to be proud of in having arranged for poor Owen to get off easily. Nobody had a right to get off easily from pledges so deep, so sacred. How could Fleda doubt they had been tremendous when she knew so well what any pledge of her own would be? If Mona was so formed that she could hold such vows light, that was Mona's peculiar business. To have loved Owen apparently, and yet to have loved him only so much, only to the extent of a few tables and chairs, was not a thing she could so much as try to grasp. Of a different way of loving him she was herself ready to give an instance, an instance of which the beauty indeed would not be generally known. It would not perhaps if revealed be generally understood, inasmuch as the effect of the particular pressure she proposed to exercise would be, should success attend it, to keep him tied to an affection that had died a sudden and violent death. Even in the ardour of her meditation Fleda remained in sight of the truth that it would be an odd result of her magnanimity to prevent her friend's shaking off a woman he disliked. If he didn't dislike Mona, what was the matter with him? And if he did, Fleda asked, what was the matter with her own silly self?

Our young lady met this branch of the temptation it pleased her frankly to recognize by declaring that to encourage any such cruelty would be tortuous and base. She had nothing to do with his dislikes; she had only to do with his good nature and his good name. She had joy of him just as he was, but it was of these things she had the greatest. The worst aversion and the liveliest reaction moreover wouldn't alter the fact – since one was facing facts – that but the other day his strong arms must have clasped a remarkably handsome girl as close as she had permitted. Fleda's emotion at this time was a wonderous mixture, in which Mona's permissions and Mona's beauty figured powerfully as aids to reflection. She herself had no beauty, and *her* permissions were the stony stares she had just practised in the drawing-room – a consciousness of a kind appreciably to add to the particular sense of triumph that made her generous. I may not perhaps too much diminish the merit of that generosity if I mention that it could take the flight we are considering just because really, with the telescope of her long thought, Fleda saw what might bring her out of

324

the wood. Mona herself would bring her out; at the least Mona possibly might. Deep down plunged the idea that even should she achieve what she had promised Owen, there was still the contingency of Mona's independent action. She might by that time, under stress of temper or of whatever it was that was now moving her, have said or done the things there is no patching up. If the rupture should come from Waterbath they might all be happy yet. This was a calculation that Fleda wouldn't have committed to paper, but it affected the total of her sentiments. She was meanwhile so remarkably constituted that while she refused to profit by Owen's mistake, even while she judged it and hastened to cover it up, she could drink a sweetness from it that consorted little with her wishing it mightn't have been made. There was no harm done, because he had instinctively known, poor dear, with whom to make it, and it was a compensation for seeing him worried that he hadn't made it with some horrid mean girl who would immediately have dished him by making a still bigger one. Their protected error (for she indulged a fancy that it was hers too) was like some dangerous, lovely living thing that she had caught and could keep – keep vivid and helpless in the cage of her own passion and look at and talk to all day long. She had got it well locked up there by the time that, from an upper window, she saw Mrs Gereth again in the garden. At this she went down to meet her.

CHAPTER 10

FLEDA'S line had been taken, her word was quite ready; on the terrace of the painted pots she broke out before her interlocutress could put a question. 'His errand was perfectly simple: he came to demand that you shall pack everything straight up again and send it back as fast as the railway will carry it.'

The back road had apparently been fatiguing to Mrs Gereth; she rose there rather white and wan with her walk. A certain sharp thinness was in her ejaculation of 'Oh!' — after which she glanced about her for a place to sit down. The movement was a criticism of the order of events that offered such a piece of news to a lady coming in tired; but Fleda could see that in turning over the possibilities this particular peril was the one that during the last hour her friend had turned up oftenest. At the end of the short, grey day, which had been moist and mild, the sun was out; the terrace looked to the south, and a bench, formed as to legs and arms of iron representing knotted boughs, stood against the warmest wall of the house. The mistress of Ricks sank upon it and presented to her companion the handsome face she had composed to hear everything. Strangely enough, it was just this fine vessel of her attention that made the girl most nervous about what she must drop in. 'Quite a "demand", dear, is it?' asked Mrs Gereth, drawing in her cloak.

'Oh, that's what I should call it!' Fleda laughed, to her own surprise.

'I mean with the threat of enforcement and that sort of thing.'

'Distinctly with the threat of enforcement — what would be called, I suppose, coercion.'

'What sort of coercion?' said Mrs Gereth.

'Why, legal, don't you know? — what he calls setting the lawyers at you.'

'Is that what he calls it?' She seemed to speak with disinterested curiosity.

'That's what he calls it,' said Fleda.

Mrs Gereth considered an instant. 'Oh, the lawyers!' she exclaimed lightly. Seated there almost cosily in the reddening winter sunset, only with her shoulders raised a little and her mantle tightened as if from a slight chill, she had never yet looked to Fleda so much in possession nor so far from meeting unsuspectedness half-way. 'Is he going to send them down here?'

'I dare say he thinks it may come to that.'

'The lawyers can scarcely do the packing,' Mrs Gereth humorously remarked.

'I suppose he means them – in the first place, at least – to try to talk you over.'

'In the first place, eh? And what does he mean in the second?'

Fleda hesitated; she had not foreseen that so simple an inquiry could disconcert her. 'I'm afraid I don't know.'

'Didn't you ask?' Mrs Gereth spoke as if she might have said, 'What then were you doing all the while?'

'I didn't ask very much,' said her companion. 'He has been gone some time. The great thing seemed to be to understand clearly that he wouldn't be content with anything less than what he mentioned.'

'My just giving everything back?'

'Your just giving everything back.'

'Well, darling, what did you tell him?' Mrs Gereth blandly inquired.

Fleda faltered again, wincing at the term of endearment, at what the words took for granted, charged with the confidence she had now committed herself to betray. 'I told him I would tell you!' She smiled, but she felt that her smile was rather hollow and even that Mrs Gereth had begun to look at her with some fixedness.

'Did he seem very angry?'

'He seemed very sad. He takes it very hard,' Fleda added.

'And how does *she* take it?'

'Ah, that – that I felt a delicacy about asking.'

'So you didn't ask?' The words had the note of surprise.

Fleda was embarrassed; she had not made up her mind definitely to lie. 'I didn't think you'd care.' That small untruth she would risk.

'Well – I don't!' Mrs Gereth declared; and Fleda felt less guilty to hear her, for the statement was as inexact as her own. 'Didn't you say anything in return?' Mrs Gereth presently continued.

'Do you mean in the way of justifying you?'

'I didn't mean to trouble you to do that. My justification,' said Mrs Gereth, sitting there warmly and, in the lucidity of her thought, which nevertheless hung back a little, dropping her eyes on the gravel – 'my justification was all the past. My justification was the cruelty – ' But at this, with a short, sharp gesture, she checked herself. 'It's too good of me to talk – now.' She produced these sentences with a cold patience, as if addressing Fleda in the girl's virtual and actual character of Owen's representative. Our young lady crept to and fro before the bench, combating the sense that it was occupied by a judge, looking at her boot-toes, reminding herself in doing so of Mona, and lightly crunching the pebbles as she walked. She moved about because she was afraid, putting off from moment to moment the exercise of the courage she had been sure she possessed. That courage would all come to her if she could only be equally sure that what she should be called upon to do for Owen would be to suffer. She had wondered, while Mrs Gereth spoke, how that lady would describe her justification. She had described it as if to be irreproachably fair, give her adversary the benefit of every doubt, and then dismiss the question for ever. 'Of course,' Mrs Gereth went on, 'if we didn't succeed in showing him at Poynton the ground we took, it's simply that he shuts his eyes. What I supposed was that you would have given him your opinion that if I was the woman so signally to assert myself, I'm also the woman to rest upon it imperturbably enough.'

Fleda stopped in front of her hostess. 'I gave him my opinion that you're very logical, very obstinate, and very proud.'

'Quite right, my dear: I'm a rank bigot – about that sort of thing!' and Mrs Gereth jerked her head at the contents of the house. 'I've never denied it. I'd kidnap – to save them, to convert them – the children of heretics. When I know I'm right I go to the stake. Oh, he may burn me alive!' she cried with a happy face. 'Did he abuse me?' she then demanded.

Fleda had remained there, gathering in her purpose. 'How little you know him!'

Mrs Gereth stared, then broke into a laugh that her companion had not expected. 'Ah, my dear, certainly not so well as you!' The girl, at this, turned away again – she felt she looked too conscious; and she was aware that, during a pause, Mrs Gereth's eyes watched her as she went. She faced about afresh to meet them, but what she met was a question that reinforced them. 'Why had you a "delicacy" as to speaking of Mona?'

She stopped again before the bench, and an inspiration came to her. 'I should think *you* would know,' she said with proper dignity.

Blankness was for a moment on Mrs Gereth's brow; then light broke – she visibly remembered the scene in the breakfast-room after Mona's night at Poynton. 'Because I contrasted you – told him *you* were the one?' Her eyes looked deep. 'You were – you are still!'

Fleda gave a bold dramatic laugh. 'Thank you, my love – with all the best things at Ricks!'

Mrs Gereth considered, trying to penetrate, as it seemed; but at last she brought out roundly: 'For you, you know, I'd send them back!'

The girl's heart gave a tremendous bound; the right way dawned upon her in a flash. Obscurity indeed the next moment engulfed this course, but for a few thrilled seconds she had understood. To send the things back 'for her' meant of course to send them back if there were even a dim chance that she might become mistress of them. Fleda's palpitation was not allayed as she asked herself what portent Mrs Gereth had suddenly perceived of such a chance: that perception could only from a sudden suspicion of her secret. This suspicion, in turn, was a tolerably straight consequence of that implied view of the propriety of surrender from which, she was well aware, she could say nothing to dissociate herself. What she first felt was that if she wished to rescue the spoils she wished also to rescue her secret. So she looked as innocent as she could and said as quickly as possible: 'For me? Why in the world for me?'

'Because you're so awfully keen.'

'Am I? Do I strike you so? You know I hate him,' Fleda went on.

She had the sense for a while of Mrs Gereth's regarding her with the detachment of some stern, clever stranger. 'Then what's the matter with you? Why do you want me to give in?'

Fleda hesitated; she felt herself reddening. 'I've only said your son wants it. I haven't said I do.'

'Then say it and have done with it!'

This was more peremptory than any word her friend, though often speaking in her presence with much point, had ever yet directly addressed to her. It affected her like the crack of a whip, but she confined herself, with an effort, to taking it as a reminder that she must keep her head. 'I know he has his engagement to carry out.'

'His engagement to marry? Why, it's just that engagement we loathe!'

'Why should I loathe it?' Fleda asked with a strained smile. Then, before Mrs Gereth could reply, she pursued: 'I'm thinking of his general undertaking – to give her the house as she originally saw it.'

'To give her the house!' Mrs Gereth brought up the words from the depth of the unspeakable. The effort was like the moan of an autumn wind; it was in the power of such an image to make her turn pale.

'I'm thinking,' Fleda continued, 'of the simple question of his keeping faith on an important clause of his contract: it doesn't matter whether it's with a stupid girl or with a monster of cleverness. I'm thinking of his honour and his good name.'

'The honour and good name of a man you hate?'

'Certainly,' the girl resolutely answered. 'I don't see why you should talk as if one had a petty mind. You don't think so.

330

It's not on that assumption you've ever dealt with me. I can do your son justice, as he put his case to me.'

'Ah, then he did put his case to you!' Mrs Gereth exclaimed, with an accent of triumph. 'You seemed to speak just now as if really nothing of any consequence had passed between you.'

'Something always passes when one has a little imagination,' our young lady declared.

'I take it you don't mean that Owen has any!' Mrs Gereth cried with her large laugh.

Fleda was silent a moment. 'No, I don't mean that Owen has any,' she returned at last.

'Why is it you hate him so?' her hostess abruptly inquired.

'Should I love him for all he has made you suffer?'

Mrs Gereth slowly rose at this and, coming across the walk, took her young friend in her arms and kissed her. She then passed into one of Fleda's an arm perversely and imperiously sociable. 'Let us move a little,' she said, holding her close and giving a slight shiver. They strolled along the terrace, and she brought out another question. 'He *was* eloquent, then, poor dear – he poured forth the story of his wrongs?'

Fleda smiled down at her companion, who, cloaked and perceptibly bowed, leaned on her heavily and gave her an odd, unwonted sense of age and cunning. She took refuge in an evasion. 'He couldn't tell me anything that I didn't know pretty well already.'

'It's very true that you know everything. No, dear, you haven't a petty mind; you've a lovely imagination and you're the nicest creature in the world. If you were inane, like most girls – like everyone, in fact – I would have insulted you, I would have outraged you, and then you would have fled from me in terror. No, now that I think of it,' Mrs Gereth went on, 'you wouldn't have fled from me; nothing, on the contrary, would have made you budge. You would have cuddled into your warm corner, but you would have been wounded and weeping and martyrized, and you would have taken every opportunity to tell people I'm a brute – as indeed I should have been!' They went to and fro, and she would not allow Fleda, who laughed and protested, to attenuate with any light civility this spirited picture. She praised her cleverness and her

331

patience; then she said it was getting cold and dark and they must go in to tea. She delayed quitting the place, however, and reverted instead to Owen's ultimatum, about which she asked another question or two; in particular whether it had struck Fleda that he really believed she would comply with such a summons.

'I think he really believes that if I try hard enough I can make you': after uttering which words our young lady stopped short and emulated the embrace she had received a few moments before.

'And you've promised to try: I see. You didn't tell me that, either,' Mrs Gereth added as they went on. 'But you're rascal enough for anything!' While Fleda was occupied in thinking in what terms she could explain why she had indeed been rascal enough for the reticence thus denounced, her companion broke out with an inquiry somewhat irrelevant and even in form somewhat profane. 'Why the devil, at any rate, doesn't it come off?'

Fleda hesitated. 'You mean their marriage?'

'Of course I mean their marriage!'

Fleda hesitated again. 'I haven't the least idea.'

'You didn't ask him?'

'Oh, how in the world can you fancy?' She spoke in a shocked tone.

'Fancy your putting a question so indelicate? *I* should have put it – I mean in your place; but I'm quite coarse, thank God!' Fleda felt privately that she herself was coarse, or at any rate would presently have to be; and Mrs Gereth, with a purpose that struck the girl as increasing, continued: 'What, then, *was* the day to be? Wasn't it just one of these?'

'I'm sure I don't remember.'

It was part of the great rupture and an effect of Mrs Gereth's character that up to this moment she had been completely and haughtily indifferent to that detail. Now, however, she had a visible reason for being clear about it. She bethought herself and she broke out – 'Isn't the day past?' Then, stopping short, she added: 'Upon my word, they must have put it off!' As Fleda made no answer to this she sharply went on: '*Have* they put it off?'

'I haven't the least idea,' said the girl.

Her hostess was looking at her hard again. 'Didn't he tell you – didn't he say anything about it?'

Fleda, meanwhile, had had time to make her reflections, which were moreover the continued throb of those that had occupied the interval between Owen's departure and his mother's return. If she should now repeat his words, this wouldn't at all play the game of her definite vow; it would only play the game of her little gagged and blinded desire. She could calculate well enough the effect of telling Mrs Gereth how she had had it from Owen's troubled lips that Mona was only waiting for the restitution and would do nothing without it. The thing was to obtain the restitution without imparting that knowledge. The only way, also, not to impart it was not to tell any truth at all about it; and the only way to meet this last condition was to reply to her companion, as she presently did: 'He told me nothing whatever: he didn't touch on the subject.'

'Not in any way?'

'Not in any way.'

Mrs Gereth watched Fleda and considered. 'You haven't any idea if they are waiting for the things?'

'How should I have? I'm not in their counsels.'

'I dare say they are – or that Mona is.' Mrs Gereth reflected again; she had a bright idea. 'If I don't give in, I'll be hanged if she'll not break off.'

'She'll never, never break off!' said Fleda.

'Are you sure?'

'I can't be sure, but it's my belief.'

'Derived from him?'

The girl hung fire a few seconds. 'Derived from him.'

Mrs Gereth gave her a long last look, then turned abruptly away. 'It's an awful bore you didn't really get it out of him! Well, come to tea,' she added rather dryly, passing straight into the house.

CHAPTER 11

THE sense of her adversary's dryness, which was ominous of something she couldn't read, made Fleda, before complying, linger a little on the terrace; she felt the need moreover of taking breath after such a flight into the cold air of denial. When at last she rejoined Mrs Gereth she found her erect before the drawing-room fire. Their tea had been set out in the same quarter, and the mistress of the house, for whom the preparation of it was in general a high and undelegated function, was in an attitude to which the hissing urn made no appeal. This omission, for Fleda, was such a further sign of something to come that, to disguise her apprehension, she immediately and without an apology took the duty in hand; only, however, to be promptly reminded that she was performing it confusedly and not counting the journeys of the little silver shovel she emptied into the pot. 'Not *five,* my dear – the usual three,' said her hostess, with the same dryness; watching her then in silence while she clumsily corrected her mistake. The tea took some minutes to draw, and Mrs Gereth availed herself of them suddenly to exclaim: 'You haven't yet told me, you know, how it is you propose to "make" me!'

'Give everything back?' Felda looked into the pot again and uttered her question with a briskness that she felt to be a little overdone. 'Why, by putting the question well before you; by being so eloquent that I shall persuade you, shall act upon you; by making you sorry for having gone so far,' she said boldly; 'by simply and earnestly asking it of you, in short; and by reminding you at the same time that it's the first thing I ever have so asked. Oh, you've done things for me – endless and beautiful things,' she exclaimed; 'but you've done them all from your own generous impulse. I've never so much as hinted to you to lend me a postage stamp.'

'Give me a cup of tea,' said Mrs Gereth. A moment later, taking the cup, she replied: 'No, you've never asked me for a postage stamp.'

'That gives me a pull!' Fleda returned, smiling.

'Puts you in the situation of expecting that I shall do this thing just simply to oblige you?'

The girl hesitated. 'You said a while ago that for me you *would* do it.'

'For you, but not for your eloquence. Do you understand what I mean by the difference?' Mrs Gereth asked as she stood stirring her tea.

Fleda, to postpone answering, looked round, while she drank it, at the beautiful room. 'I don't in the least like, you know, your having taken so much. It was a great shock to me, on my arrival here, to find you had done so.'

'Give me some more tea,' said Mrs Gereth ; and there was a moment's silence as Fleda poured out another cup. 'If you were shocked, my dear, I'm bound to say you concealed your shock.'

'I know I did. I was afraid to show it.'

Mrs Gereth drank off her second cup. 'And you're not afraid now?'

'No, I'm not afraid now.'

'What has made the difference?'

'I've pulled myself together' Fleda paused ; then she added : 'and I've seen Mr Owen.'

'You've seen Mr Owen' – Mrs Gereth concurred. She put down her cup and sank into a chair, in which she leaned back, resting her head and gazing at her young friend. 'Yes, I did tell you a while ago that for you I'd do it. But you haven't told me yet what you'll do in return.'

Fleda thought an instant. 'Anything in the wide world you may require.'

'Oh, "anything" is nothing at all! That's too easily said.' Mrs Gereth, reclining more completely, closed her eyes with an air of disgust, an air indeed of inviting slumber.

Fleda looked at her quiet face, which the appearance of slumber always made particularly handsome ; she noted how much the ordeal of the last few weeks had added to its indications of age. 'Well then, try me with something. What is it you demand?'

At this, opening her eyes, Mrs Gereth sprang straight up. 'Get him away from her!'

Fleda marvelled: her companion had in an instant become young again. 'Away from Mona? How in the world – ?'

'By not looking like a fool!' cried Mrs Gereth very sharply. She kissed her, however, on the spot, to make up for this roughness, and summarily took off her hat, which, on coming into the house, our young lady had not removed. She applied a friendly touch to the girl's hair and gave a businesslike pull to her jacket. 'I say don't look like an idiot, because you happen not to be one, not the least bit. *I'm* idiotic; I've been so, I've just discovered, ever since our first days together. I've been a precious donkey; but that's another affair.'

Fleda, as if she humbly assented, went through no form of controverting this; she simply stood passive to her companion's sudden refreshment of her appearance. 'How *can* I get him away from her?' she presently demanded.

'By letting yourself go.'

'By letting myself go?' She spoke mechanically, still more like an idiot, and felt as if her face flamed out the insincerity of her question. It was vividly back again, the vision of the real way to act upon Mrs Gereth. This lady's movements were now rapid; she turned off from her as quickly as she had seized her, and Fleda sat down to steady herself for full responsibility.

Her hostess, without taking up her ejaculation, gave a violent poke at the fire and then faced her again. 'You've done two things, then, today – haven't you? – that you've never done before. One has been asking me the service, or favour, or concession – whatever you call it – that you just mentioned; the other has been telling me – certainly too for the first time – an immense little fib.'

'An immense little fib?' Fleda felt weak; she was glad of the support of her seat.

'An immense big one, then!' said Mrs Gereth irritatedly. 'You don't in the least "hate" Owen, my darling. You care for him very much. In fact, my own, you're in love with him – there! Don't tell me any more lies!' cried Mrs Gereth with a voice and a face in the presence of which Fleda recognized that there was nothing for her but to hold herself and take them. When once the truth was out, it was out, and she could

336

see more and more every instant that it would be the only way. She accepted therefore what had to come; she leaned back her head and closed her eyes as her companion had done just before. She would have covered her face with her hands but for the still greater shame. 'Oh, you're a wonder, a wonder,' said Mrs Gereth; 'you're magnificent, and I was right, as soon as I saw you, to pick you out and trust you!' Fleda closed her eyes tighter at this last word, but her friend kept it up. 'I never dreamed of it till a while ago, when, after he had come and gone, we were face to face. Then something stuck out of you; it strongly impressed me, and I didn't know at first quite what to make of it. It was that you had just been with him and that you were not natural. Not natural to *me*,' she added with a smile. 'I pricked up my ears, and all that this might mean dawned upon me when you said you had asked nothing about Mona. It put me on the scent, but I didn't show you, did I? I felt it was *in* you, deep down, and that I must draw it out. Well, I *have* drawn it, and it's a blessing. Yesterday, when you shed tears at breakfast, I was awfully puzzled. What has been the matter with you all the while? Why, Fleda, it isn't a crime, don't you know that?' cried the delighted woman. 'When I was a girl I was always in love, and not always with such nice people as Owen. I didn't behave as well as you; compared with you I think I must have been horrid. But if you're proud and reserved, it's your own affair; I'm proud too, though I'm not reserved — that's what spoils it. I'm stupid, above all — that's what I am; so dense that I really blush for it. However, no one but you could have deceived me. If I trusted you, moreover, it was exactly to be cleverer than myself. You must be so now more than ever!' Suddenly Fleda felt her hands grasped: Mrs Gereth had plumped down at her feet and was leaning on her knees. 'Save him — save him: you *can*!' she passionately pleaded. 'How could you *not* like him, when he's such a dear? He *is* a dear, darling; there's no harm in my own boy! You can do what you will with him — you know you can! What else does he give us all this time for? Get him away from her; it's as if he besought you to, poor wretch! Don't abandon him to such a fate, and I'll never abandon *you*. Think of him with that

337

creature, that future! If you'll take him I'll give up everything. There, it's a solemn promise, the most sacred of my life! Get the better of her, and he shall have every stick I removed. Give me your word, and I'll accept it. I'll write for the packers tonight!'

Fleda, before this, had fallen forward on her companion's neck, and the two women, clinging together, had got up while the younger wailed on the other's bosom. 'You smooth it down because you see more in it than there can ever be ; but after my hideous double game how will you be able to believe in me again?'

'I see in it simply what *must* be, if you've a single spark of pity. Where on earth was the double game, when you've behaved like such a saint? You've been beautiful, you've been exquisite, and all our trouble is over.'

Fleda, drying her eyes, shook her head ever so sadly. 'No, Mrs Gereth, it isn't over. I can't do what you ask — I can't meet your condition.'

Mrs Gereth stared ; the cloud gathered in her face again. 'Why, in the name of goodness, when you adore him? I know what you see in him,' she declared in another tone. 'You're right!'

Fleda gave a faint, stubborn smile. 'He cares for her too much.'

'Then why doesn't he marry her? He's giving you an extra-ordinary chance.'

'He doesn't dream I've ever thought of him,' said Fleda. 'Why should he, if you didn't?'

'It wasn't with me you were in love, my duck.' Then Mrs Gereth added: 'I'll go and tell him.'

'If you do any such thing, you shall never see me again, — absolutely, literally never!'

Mrs Gereth looked hard at her young friend, showing she saw she must believe her. 'Then you're perverse, you're wicked. Will you swear he doesn't know?'

'Of course he doesn't know!' cried Fleda indignantly.

Her interlocutress was silent a little. 'And that he has no feeling on *his* side?'

'For me?' Fleda stared. 'Before he has even married her?'

Mrs Gereth gave a sharp laugh at this. 'He ought at least to appreciate your wit. Oh, my dear, you *are* a treasure! Doesn't he appreciate anything? Has he given you absolutely no symptom – not looked a look, not breathed a sigh?'

'The case,' said Fleda coldly, 'is as I've had the honour to state it.'

'Then he's as big a donkey as his mother! But you know you must account for their delay,' Mrs Gereth remarked.

'Why must I?' Fleda asked after a moment.

'Because you were closeted with him here so long. You can't pretend at present, you know, not to have any art.'

The girl hesitated an instant; she was conscious that she must choose between two risks. She had had a secret and the secret was gone. Owen had one, which was still unbruised, and the greater risk now was that his mother should lay her formidable hand upon it. All Fleda's tenderness for him moved her to protect it; so she faced the smaller peril. 'Their delay,' she brought herself to reply, 'may perhaps be Mona's doing. I mean because he has lost her the things.'

Mrs Gereth jumped at this. 'So that she'll break altogether if I keep them?'

Fleda winced. 'I've told you what I believe about that. She'll make scenes and conditions; she'll worry him. But she'll hold him fast; she'll never give him up.'

Mrs Gereth turned it over. 'Well, I'll keep them, to try her,' she finally pronounced; at which Fleda felt quite sick, as if she had given everything and got nothing.

CHAPTER 12

'I MUST in common decency let him know that I've talked of the matter with you,' she said to her hostess that evening. 'What answer do you wish me to write to him?'

'Write to him that you must see him again,' said Mrs Gereth.

Fleda looked very blank. 'What on earth am I to see him for?'

'For anything you like.'

The girl would have been struck with the levity of this had she not already, in an hour, felt the extent of the change suddenly wrought in her commerce with her friend – wrought above all, to that friend's view, in her relation to the great issue. The effect of what had followed Owen's visit was to make that relation the very key of the crisis. Pressed upon her, goodness knew, the crisis had been, but it now seemed to put forth big, encircling arms – arms that squeezed till they hurt and she must cry out. It was as if everything at Ricks had been poured into a common receptacle, a public ferment of emotion and zeal, out of which it was ladled up to be tasted and talked about ; everything at least but the one little treasure of knowledge that she kept back. She ought to have liked this, she reflected, because it meant sympathy, meant a closer union with the source of so much in her life that had been beautiful and renovating ; but there were fine instincts in her that stood off. She had had – and it was not merely at this time – to recognize that there were things for which Mrs Gereth's *flair* was not so happy as for bargains and 'marks'. It wouldn't be happy now as to the best action on the knowledge she had just gained ; yet as from this moment they were still more intimately together, so a person deeply in her debt would simply have to stand and meet what was to come. There were ways in which she could sharply incommode such a person, and not only with the best conscience in the world, but with a sort of brutality of good intentions. One of the straightest of these

340

strokes, Fleda saw, would be the dance of delight over the mystery Mrs Gereth had laid bare – the loud, lawful, tactless joy of the explorer leaping upon the strand. Like any other lucky discoverer, she would take possession of the fortunate island. She was nothing if not practical: almost the only thing she took account of in her young friend's soft secret was the excellent use she could make of it – a use so much to her taste that she refused to feel a hindrance in the quality of the material. Fleda put into Mrs Gereth's answer to her question a good deal more meaning than it would have occurred to her a few hours before that she was prepared to put, but she had on the spot a foreboding that even so broad a hint would live to be bettered.

'Do you suggest that I shall propose to him to come down here again?' she presently inquired.

'Dear, no; say that you'll go up to town and meet him.' It *was* bettered, the broad hint; and Fleda felt this to be still more the case when, returning to the subject before they went to bed, her companion said: 'I make him over to you wholly, you know – to do what you please with. Deal with him in your own clever way – I ask no questions. All I ask is that you succeed.'

'That's charming,' Fleda replied, 'but it doesn't tell me a bit, you'll be so good as to consider, in what terms to write to him. It's not an answer from you to the message I was to give you.'

'The answer to his message is perfectly distinct: he shall have everything in the place the minute he'll say he'll marry you.'

'You really pretend,' Fleda asked, 'to think me capable of transmitting him that news?'

'What else can I really pretend when you threaten so to cast me off if I speak the word myself?'

'Oh, if *you* speak the word!' the girl murmured very gravely, but happy at least to know that in this direction Mrs Gereth confessed herself warned and helpless. Then she added: 'How can I go on living with you on a footing of which I so deeply disapprove? Thinking as I do that you've despoiled him far more than is just or merciful – for if I expected you to take something, I didn't in the least expect you to take everything

– how can I stay here without a sense that I'm backing you up in your cruelty and participating in your ill-gotten gains?' Fleda was determined that if she had the chill of her exposed and investigated state she would also have the convenience of it, and that if Mrs Gereth popped in and out of the chamber of her soul she would at least return the freedom. 'I shall quite hate, you know, in a day or two, every object that surrounds you – become blind to all the beauty and rarity that I formerly delighted in. Don't think me harsh; there's no use in my not being frank now. If I leave you, everything's at an end.'

Mrs Gereth, however, was imperturbable: Fleda had to recognize that her advantage had become too real. 'It's too beautiful, the way you care for him; it's music in my ears. Nothing else but such a passion could make you say such things ; that's the way I should have been too, my dear. Why didn't you tell me sooner? I'd have gone right in for you ; I never would have moved a candlestick. Don't stay with me if it torments you ; don't, if you suffer, be where you see the old rubbish. Go up to town – go back for a little to your father's. It need be only for a little: two or three weeks will see us through. Your father will take you and be glad, if you only will make him understand what it's a question of – of your getting yourself off his hands for ever. *I*'ll make him understand, you know, if you feel shy. I'd take you up myself, I'd go with you, to spare your being bored; we'd put up at an hotel and we might amuse ourselves a bit. We haven't had much pleasure since we met, have we? But of course that wouldn't suit our book. I should be a bugaboo to Owen – I should be fatally in the way. Your chance is there – your chance is to be alone ; for God's sake, use it to the right end. If you're in want of money I've a little I can give you. But I ask no questions – not a question as small as your shoe!'

She asked no questions, but she took the most extraordinary things for granted. Fleda felt this still more at the end of a couple of days. On the second of these our young lady wrote to Owen ; her emotion had to a certain degree cleared itself – there was something she could say briefly. If she had given everything to Mrs Gereth and as yet got nothing, so she had on the other hand quickly reacted – it took but a night – against

342

the discouragement of her first check. Her desire to serve him was too passionate, the sense that he counted upon her too sweet: these things caught her up again and gave her a new patience and a new subtlety. It shouldn't really be for nothing that she had given so much; deep within her burned again the resolve to get something back. So what she wrote to Owen was simply that she had had a great scene with his mother, but that he must be patient and give her time. It was difficult, as they both had expected, but she was working her hardest for him. She had made an impression – she would do everything to follow it up. Meanwhile he must keep intensely quiet and take no other steps; he must only trust her and pray for her and believe in her perfect loyalty. She made no allusion whatever to Mona's attitude, nor to his not being, as regarded that young lady, master of the situation; but she said in a postscript, in reference to his mother, 'Of course she wonders a good deal why your marriage doesn't take place.' After the letter had gone she regretted having used the word 'loyalty', there were two or three milder terms which she might as well have employed. The answer she immediately received from Owen was a little note of which she met all the deficiencies by describing it to herself as pathetically simple, but which, to prove that Mrs Gereth might ask as many questions as she liked, she at once made his mother read. He had no art with his pen, he had not even a good hand, and his letter, a short profession of friendly confidence, consisted of but a few familiar and colourless words of acknowledgement and assent. The gist of it was that he would certainly, since Miss Vetch recommended it, not hurry mamma too much. He would not for the present cause her to be approached by anyone else, but he would nevertheless continue to hope that she would see she *must* come round. 'Of course, you know,' he added, 'she can't keep me waiting indefinitely. Please give her my love and tell her that. If it can be done peaceably I know you're just the one to do it.'

Fleda had awaited his rejoinder in deep suspense; such was her imagination of the possibility of his having, as she tacitly phrased it, let himself go on paper that when it arrived she was at first almost afraid to open it. There was indeed a distinct danger, for if he should take it into his head to write her love-letters the whole chance of aiding him would drop: she would have to return them, she would have to decline all further communication with him: it would be quite the end of the business. This imagination of Fleda's was a faculty that easily embraced all the heights and depths and extremities of things; that made a single mouthful, in particular, of any tragic or desperate necessity. She was perhaps at first just a trifle disappointed not to find in the note in question a syllable that strayed from the text; but the next moment she had risen to a point of view from which its presented itself as a production almost inspired in its simplicity. It was simple even for Owen, and she wondered what had given him the cue to be more so than usual. Then she saw how natures that are right just do the things that are right. He wasn't clever – his manner of writing showed it; but the cleverest man in England couldn't have had more the instinct that, under the circumstances, was the supremely happy one, the instinct of giving her something that would do beautifully to be shown to Mrs Gereth. This was a kind of divination, for naturally he couldn't know the line Mrs Gereth was taking. It was furthermore explained – and that was the most touching part of all – by his wish that she herself should notice how awfully well he was behaving. His very bareness called her attention to his virtue; and these were the exact fruits of her beautiful and terrible admonition. He was cleaving to Mona; he was doing his duty; he was making tremendously sure he should be without reproach.

If Fleda handed this communication to her friend as a triumphant gage of the innocence of the young man's heart, her elation lived but a moment after Mrs Gereth had pounced upon the tell-tale spot in it. 'Why in the world, then,' that lady cried, 'does he still not breathe a breath about the day, the *day*, the DAY?' She repeated the word with a crescendo of superior acuteness; she proclaimed that nothing could be more marked than its absence – and absence that simply spoke volumes. What did it prove in fine but that she was producing the effect she had toiled for – that she had settled or was rapidly settling Mona?

Such a challenge Fleda was obliged in some manner to take up. 'You may be settling Mona,' she returned with a smile, 'but I can hardly regard it as sufficient evidence that you're settling Mona's lover.'

'Why not, with such a studied omission on his part to gloss over in any manner the painful tension existing between them – the painful tension that, under providence, I've been the means of bringing about? He gives you by his silence clear notice that his marriage is practically off.'

'He speaks to me of the only thing that concerns me. He gives me clear notice that he abates not one jot of his demand.'

'Well, then, let him take the only way to get it satisfied.'

Fleda had no need to ask again what such a way might be, nor was her support removed by the fine assurance with which Mrs Gereth could make her argument wait upon her wish. These days, which dragged their length into a strange, uncomfortable fortnight, had already borne more testimony to that element than all the other time the two women had passed together. Our young lady had been at first far from measuring the whole of a feature that Owen himself would probably have described as her companion's 'cheek'. She lived now in a kind of bath of boldness, felt as if a fierce light poured in upon her from windows open wide; and the singular part of the ordeal was that she couldn't protest against it fully without incurring, even to her own mind, some reproach of ingratitude, some charge of smallness. If Mrs Gereth's apparent determination to hustle her into Owen's arms was accompanied with an air of holding her dignity rather cheap, this was after all only as a consequence of her being held in respect to some other attributes rather dear. It was a new version of the old story of being kicked upstairs. The wonderful woman was the same woman who, in the summer, at Poynton, had been so puzzled to conceive why a good-natured girl shouldn't have contributed more to the personal rout of the Brigstocks – shouldn't have been grateful even for the handsome puff of Fleda Vetch. Only her passion was keener now and her scruple more absent; the fight made a demand upon her, and her pugnacity had become one with her constant habit of using such weapons as she could pick up. She had no imagination about anybody's life save on the side she bumped against. Fleda was quite aware that she would have otherwise been a rare creature; but a rare creature was originally just what she had struck her as being. Mrs Gereth had really no perception of anybody's nature – had only one question about persons: were they clever or stupid? To be clever meant to know the marks. Fleda knew them by direct inspiration, and a warm recognition of this had been her friend's tribute to her character. The girl had hours, now, of sombre wishing that she might never see anything good again: that kind of experience was evidently not an infallible source of peace. She would be more at peace in some vulgar little place that should owe its *cachet* to Tottenham Court Road. There were nice strong horrors in West Kensington; it was as if they beckoned her and wooed her back to them. She had a relaxed recollection of Waterbath; and of her reasons for staying on at Ricks the force was rapidly ebbing. One of these was her pledge to Owen – her vow to press his mother close; the other was the fact that of the two discomforts, that of being prodded by Mrs Gereth and that of appearing to run after somebody else, the former remained for a while the more endurable.

As the days passed, however, it became plainer to Fleda that her only chance of success would be in lending herself to this low appearance. Then, moreover, at last, her nerves settling the question, the choice was simply imposed by the violence done to her taste – to whatever was left of that high principle, at least, after the free and reckless meeting, for months, of great drafts and appeals. It was all very well to try to evade discussion: Owen Gereth was looking to her for a struggle, and it wasn't a bit of a struggle to be disgusted and dumb. She was on too strange a footing – that of having presented an ultimatum and having had it torn up in her face. In such a case as that the envoy always departed; he never sat gaping and dawdling before the city. Mrs Gereth, every morning, looked publicly into the *Morning Post*, the only newspaper she received; and every morning she treated the blankness of that journal as fresh evidence that everything was 'off'. What did the *Post* exist for but to tell you your children were wretchedly married? – so that if such a source of misery was dry, what could you do but infer that for once you had miraculously escaped? She almost taunted Fleda with supineness in not getting something out of somebody – in the same breath indeed in which she drenched her with a kind of appreciation more onerous to the girl than blame. Mrs Gereth herself had of course washed her hands of the matter; but Fleda knew people who knew Mona and would be sure to be in her confidence – inconceivable people who admired her and had the privilege of Waterbath. What was the use therefore of being the most natural and the easiest of letter-writers, if no sort of side-light – in some pretext for correspondence – was, by a brilliant creature, to be got out of such barbarians? Fleda was not only a brilliant creature, but she heard herself commended in these days for new and strange attractions; she figured suddenly, in the queer conversations of Ricks, as a distinguished, almost as a dangerous beauty. That retouching of her hair and dress in which her friend had impulsively indulged on a first glimpse of her secret was by implication very frequently repeated. She had the sense not only of being advertised and offered, but of being counselled and enlightened in ways that she scarcely understood – arts obscure even to a poor girl who had had, in good society and motherless poverty, to look straight at realities and fill out blanks.

These arts, when Mrs Gereth's spirits were high, were handled with a brave and cynical humour with which Fleda's fancy could keep no step: they left our young lady wondering what on earth her companion wanted her to do. 'I want you to cut in!' – that was Mrs Gereth's familiar and comprehensive phrase for the course she prescribed. She challenged again and again Fleda's picture, as she called it (though the sketch was too slight to deserve the name), of the indifference to which a prior attachment had committed the proprietor of Poynton. 'Do you mean to say that, Mona or no Mona, he could see you that way, day after day, and not have the ordinary feelings of a man?' This was the sort of interrogation to which Fleda was fitfully and irrelevantly treated. She had grown almost used to the refrain. 'Do you mean to say that when, the other day, one had quite made you over to him, the great gawk, and he was, on this very spot, utterly alone with you – ' The poor girl at this point never left any doubt of what she meant to say, but Mrs Gereth could be trusted to break out in another place and at another time. At last Fleda wrote to her father that he must take her in for a while; and when, to her companion's delight, she returned to London, that lady went with her to the station and wafted her on her way. The *Morning Post* had been delivered as they left the house, and Mrs Gereth had brought it with her for the traveller, who never spent a penny on a newspaper. On the platform, however, when this young person was ticketed, labelled, and seated, she opened it at the window of the carriage, exclaiming as usual, after looking into it a moment: 'Nothing – nothing – nothing: don't tell *me*!' Every day that there was nothing was a nail in the coffin of the marriage. An instant later the train was off, but, moving quickly beside it, while Fleda leaned inscrutably forth, Mrs Gereth grasped her friend's hand and looked up with wonderful eyes. 'Only let yourself go, darling – only let yourself go!'

CHAPTER 13

THAT she desired to ask no questions Mrs Gereth conscientiously proved by closing her lips tight after Fleda had gone to London. No letter from Ricks arrived at West Kensington, and Fleda, with nothing to communicate that could be to the taste of either party, forbore to open a correspondence. If her heart had been less heavy she might have been amused to perceive how much rope this reticence of Ricks seemed to signify to her that she could take. She had at all events no good news for her friend save in the sense that her silence was not bad news. She was not yet in a position to write that she had 'cut in'; but neither, on the other hand, had she gathered material for announcing that Mona was undisseverable from her prey. She had made no use of the pen so glorified by Mrs Gereth to wake up the echoes of Waterbath; she had sedulously abstained from inquiring what in any quarter, far or near, was said or suggested or supposed. She only spent a matutinal penny on the *Morning Post*; she only saw, on each occasion, that that inspired sheet had as little to say about the imminence as about the abandonment of certain nuptials. It was at the same time obvious that Mrs Gereth triumphed on these occasions much more than she trembled, and that with a few such triumphs repeated she would cease to tremble at all. What was most manifest, however, was that she had had a rare preconception of the circumstances that would have ministered, had Fleda been disposed, to the girl's cutting in. It was brought home to Fleda that these circumstances would have particularly favoured intervention ; she was quickly forced to do them a secret justice. One of the effects of her intimacy with Mrs Gereth was that she had quite lost all sense of intimacy with anyone else. The lady of Ricks had made a desert around her, possessing and absorbing her so utterly that other partakers had fallen away. Hadn't she been admonished, months before, that people considered they had lost her and were reconciled on the whole to the privation? Her present position in the great unconscious town defined itself as obscure: she regarded it at any rate with eyes suspicious of that lesson. She neither wrote notes nor received them; she indulged in no reminders nor knocked at any doors; she wandered vaguely in the western wilderness or cultivated shy forms of that 'household art' for which she had had a respect before tasting the bitter tree of knowledge. Her only plan was to be as quiet as a mouse, and when she failed in the attempt to lose herself in the flat suburb she felt like a lonely fly crawling over a dusty chart.

How had Mrs Gereth known in advance that if she had chosen to be 'vile' (that was what Fleda called it) everything would happen to help her? — especially the way her poor father, after breakfast, doddered off to his club, showing seventy when he was really fifty-seven, and leaving her richly alone for the day. He came back about midnight, looking at her very hard and not risking long words – only making her feel by inimitable touches that the presence of his family compelled him to alter all his hours. She had in their common sitting-room the company of the objects he was fond of saying that he had collected – objects, shabby and battered, of a sort that appealed little to his daughter: old brandy-flasks and matchboxes, old calendars and hand-books, intermixed with an assortment of pen-wipers and ashtrays, a harvest he had gathered in from penny bazaars. He was blandly unconscious of that side of Fleda's nature which had endeared her to Mrs Gereth, and she had often heard him wish to goodness there was something striking she cared for. Why didn't she try collecting something? – it didn't matter what. She would find it gave an interest to life, and there was no end of little curiosities one could easily pick up. He was conscious of having a taste for fine things which his children had unfortunately not inherited. This indicated the limits of their acquaintance with him – limits which, as Fleda was now sharply aware, could only leave him to wonder what the mischief she was there for. As she herself echoed this question to the letter she was not in a position to clear up the mystery. She couldn't have given a name to her errand in town or explained it save by saying that she had had to get away from Ricks. It was intensely provisional, but what was to come next? Nothing could come

350

next but a deeper anxiety. She had neither a home nor an outlook – nothing in all the wide world but a feeling of suspense.

Of course she had her duty – her duty to Owen – a definite undertaking, reaffirmed, after his visit to Ricks, under her hand and seal ; but there was no sense of possession attached to that ; there was only a horrible sense of privation. She had quite moved from under Mrs Gereth's wide wing ; and now that she was really among the penwipers and ashtrays she was swept, at the thought of all the beauty she had forsworn, by short wild gusts of despair. If her friend should really keep the spoils she would never return to her. If that friend should on the other hand part with them, what on earth would there be to return to? The chill struck deep as Fleda thought of the mistress of Ricks reduced, in vulgar parlance, to what she had on her back: There was nothing to which she could compare such an image but her idea of Marie Antoinette in the Conciergerie, or perhaps the vision of some tropical birds, the creature of hot, dense forests, dropped on a frozen moor to pick up a living. The mind's eye could see Mrs Gereth, indeed, only in her thick, coloured air ; it took all the light of her treasures to make her concrete and distinct. She loomed for a moment, in any mere house, gaunt and unnatural ; then she vanished as if she had suddenly sunk into a quicksand. Fleda lost herself in the rich fancy of how, if *she* were mistress of Poynton, a whole province, as an abode, should be assigned there to the august queenmother. She would have returned from her campaign with her baggage-train and her loot, and the palace would unbar its shutters and the morning flash back from its halls. In the event of a surrender the poor woman would never again be able to begin to collect: She was now too old and too moneyless, and times were altered and good things impossibly dear. A surrender, furthermore, to any daughter-in-law save an oddity like Mona needn't at all be an abdication in fact ; any other fairly nice girl whom Owen should have taken it into his head to marry would have been positively glad to have, for the museum, a custodian who was a walking catalogue and who understood beyond anyone in England the hygiene and temperament of rare pieces. A fairly nice girl would somehow be away a good deal and would at such times count it a blessing to feel Mrs Gereth at her post.

Fleda had fully recognized, the first days, that, quite apart from any question of letting Owen know where she was; it would be a charity to give him some sign: it would be weak, it would be ugly, to be diverted from that kindness by the fact that Mrs Gereth had attached a tinkling bell to it. A frank relation with him was only superficially discredited: she ought for his own sake to send him a word of cheer. So she repeatedly reasoned, but she as repeatedly delayed performance: if her general plan had been to be as still as a mouse, an interview like the interview at Ricks would be an odd contribution to that ideal. Therefore with a confused preference of practice to theory she let the days go by; she felt that nothing was so imperative as the gain of precious time. She shouldn't be able to stay with her father forever, but she might now reap the benefit of having married her sister. Maggie's union had been built up round a small spare room. Concealed in this apartment she might try to paint again, and abetted by the grateful Maggie – for Maggie at least was grateful – she might try to dispose of her work. She had not indeed struggled with a brush since her visit to Waterbath, where the sight of the family splotches had put her immensely on her guard. Poynton moreover had been an impossible place for producing; no active art could flourish there but a Buddhistic contemplation. It had stripped its mistress clean of all feeble accomplishments; her hands were imbrued neither with ink nor with water-colour. Close to Fleda's present abode was the little shop of a man who mounted and framed pictures and desolately dealt in artists' materials. She sometimes paused before it to look at a couple of shy experiments for which its dull window constituted publicity, small studies placed there for sale and full of warning to a young lady without fortune and without talent. Some such young lady had brought them forth in sorrow; some such young lady, to see if they had been snapped up, had passed and repassed as helplessly as she herself was doing. They never had been, they never would be, snapped up; yet they were quite above the actual attainment of some other young ladies. It was a matter of discipline with Fleda to take an occasional

352

lesson from them; besides which, when she now quitted the house, she had to look for reasons after she was out. The only place to find them was in the shop-windows. They made her feel like a servant girl taking her 'afternoon', but that didn't signify: perhaps some day she would resemble such a person still more closely. This continued a fortnight, at the end of which the feeling was suddenly dissipated. She had stopped as usual in the presence of the little pictures; then, as she turned away, she had found herself face to face with Owen Gereth.

At the sight of him two fresh waves passed quickly across her heart, one at the heels of the other. The first was an instant perception that this encounter was not an accident; the second a consciousness as prompt that the best place for it was the street. She knew before he told her that he had been to see her, and the next thing she knew was that he had had information from his mother. Her mind grasped these things while he said with a smile: 'I saw only your back, but I was sure. I was over the way. I've been at your house.'

'How came you to know my house?' Fleda asked.

'I like that!' he laughed. 'How came you not to let me know that you were there?'

Fleda, at this, thought it best also to laugh. 'Since I didn't let you know, why did you come?'

'Oh, I say!' cried Owen. 'Don't add insult to injury. Why in the world didn't you let me know? I came because I want awfully to see you.' He hesitated, then he added: 'I got the tip from mother: she has written to me – fancy!'

They still stood where they had met. Fleda's instinct was to keep him there; the more so that she could already see him take for granted that they would immediately proceed together to her door. He rose before her with a different air: he looked less ruffled and bruised than he had done at Ricks, he showed a recovered freshness. Perhaps, however, this was only because she had scarcely seen him at all as yet in London form, as he would have called it – 'turned out' as he was turned out in town. In the country, heated with the chase and splashed with the mire, he had always reminded her of a picturesque peasant in national costume. This costume, as Owen wore it, varied from day to day; it was as copious as the wardrobe of an actor ; but it never failed of suggestions of the earth and the weather, the hedges and the ditches, the beasts and the birds. There had been days when it struck her as all nature in one pair of boots. It didn't make him now another person that he was delicately dressed, shining and splendid – that he had a higher hat and light gloves with black seams, and a spear-like umbrella ; but it made him, she soon decided, really hand-somer, and that in turn gave him – for she never could think of him, or indeed of some other things, without the aid of his vo-cabulary – a tremendous pull. Yes, this was for the moment, as he looked at her, the great fact of their situation – his pull was tremendous. She tried to keep the acknowledgement of it from trembling in her voice as she said to him with more surprise than she really felt: 'You've then reopened relations with her?'

'It's she who has reopened them with me. I got her letter this morning. She told me you were here and that she wished me to know it. She didn't say much ; she just gave me your address. I wrote her back, you know, "Thanks no end. Shall go today." So we *are* in correspondence again, aren't we? She means of course that you've something to tell me from her, eh? But if you have, why haven't you let a fellow know?' He waited for no answer to this, he had so much to say. 'At your house, just now, they told me how long you've been here. Haven't you known all the while that I'm counting the hours ; I left a word for you – that I would be back at six ; but I'm awfully glad to have caught you so much sooner. You don't mean to say you're not going home!' he exclaimed in dismay. 'The young woman there told me you went out early.'

'I've been out a very short time,' said Fleda, who had hung back with the general purpose of making things difficult for him. The street would make them difficult ; she could trust the street. She reflected in time, however, that to betray to him she was afraid to admit him would give him more a feeling of facility than of anything else. She moved on with him after a moment, letting him direct their course to her door, which was only round a corner: she considered as they went that it might not prove such a stroke to have been in London so long and yet not to have called him. She desired he should feel she was perfectly simple with him, and there was no simplicity in that.

None the less, on the steps of the house, though she had a key, she rang the bell; and while they waited together and she averted her face she looked straight into the depths of what Mrs Gereth had meant by giving him the 'tip'. This had been perfidious, had been monstrous of Mrs Gereth, and Fleda wondered if her letter had contained only what Owen repeated.

CHAPTER 14

WHEN Owen and Fleda were in her father's little place and, among the brandy-flasks and pen-wipers, still more disconcerted and divided, the girl – to do something, though it would make him stay – had ordered tea, he put the letter before her quite as if he had guessed her thought. 'She's still a bit nasty – fancy!' He handed her the scrap of a note which he had pulled out of his pocket and from its envelope. 'Fleda Vetch,' it ran, 'is at 10 Raphael Road, West Kensington. Go to see her, and try, for God's sake, to cultivate a glimmer of intelligence.' When in handing it back to him she took in his face she saw that its heightened colour was the effect of his watching her read such an allusion to his want of wit. Fleda knew what it was an allusion to, and his pathetic air of having received this buffet, tall and fine and kind as he stood there, made her conscious of not quite concealing her knowledge. For a minute she was kept silent by an angered sense of the trick that had been played her. It was a trick because Fleda considered there had been a covenant; and the trick consisted of Mrs Gereth's having broken the spirit of their agreement while conforming in a fashion to the letter. Under the girl's menace of a complete rupture she had been afraid to make of her secret the use she itched to make; but in the course of these days of separation she had gathered pluck to hazard an indirect betrayal. Fleda measured her hesitations and the impulse which she had finally obeyed and which the continued procrastination of Waterbath had encouraged, had at last made irresistible. If in her high-handed manner of playing their game she had not named the thing hidden, she had named the hiding-place. It was over the sense of this wrong that Fleda's lips closed tight: she was afraid of aggravating her case by some ejaculation that would make Owen prick up his ears. A great, quick effort, however, helped her to avoid the danger; with her constant idea of keeping cool and repressing a visible flutter, she found herself able to choose her words. Meanwhile he had exclaimed with his

356

uncomfortable laugh: 'That's a good one for me, Miss Vetch, isn't it?'

'Of course you know by this time that your mother's very sharp,' said Fleda.

'I think I can understand well enough when I know what's to be understood,' the young man asserted. 'But I hope you won't mind my saying that you've kept me pretty well in the dark about that. I've been waiting, waiting, waiting; so much has depended on your news. If you've been working for me I'm afraid it has been a thankless job. Can't she say what she'll do, one way or the other? I can't tell in the least where I am, you know. I haven't really learnt from you, since I saw you there, where *she* is. You wrote me to be patient, and upon my soul I have been. But I'm afraid you don't quite realize what I'm to be patient with. At Waterbath, don't you know? I've simply to account and answer for the damned things. Mona looks at me and waits, and I, hang it, I look at you and do the same.' Fleda had gathered fuller confidence as he continued; so plain was it that she had succeeded in not dropping into his mind the spark that might produce the glimmer invoked by his mother. But even this fine assurance gave a start when, after an appealing pause, he went on: 'I hope, you know, that after all you're not keeping anything back from me.'

In the full face of what she was keeping back such a hope could only make her wince; but she was prompt with her explanations in proportion as she felt they failed to meet him. The smutty maid came in with tea-things, and Fleda, moving several objects, eagerly accepted the diversion of arranging a place for them on one of the tables. 'I've been trying to break your mother down because it has seemed there may be some chance of it. That's why I've let you go on expecting it. She's too proud to veer round all at once, but I think I speak correctly in saying that I've made an impression.'

In spite of ordering tea she had not invited him to sit down; she herself made a point of standing. He hovered by the window that looked into Raphael Road; she kept at the other side of the room; the stunted slavey, gazing wide-eyed at the beautiful gentleman and either stupidly or cunningly bringing

357

but one thing at a time, came and went between the tea-tray and the open door.

'You pegged at her so hard?' Owen asked.

'I explained to her fully your position and put before her much more strongly than she liked what seemed to me her absolute duty.'

Owen waited a little. 'And having done that, you departed?'

Fleda felt the full need of giving a reason for her departure; but at first she only said with cheerful frankness: 'I departed.'

Her companion again looked at her in silence. 'I thought you had gone to her for several months.'

'Well,' Fleda replied, 'I couldn't stay. I didn't like it. I didn't like it at all — I couldn't bear it,' she went on. 'In the midst of those trophies of Poynton, living with them, touching them, using them, I felt as if I were backing her up. As I was not a bit of an accomplice, as I hate what she has done, I didn't want to be, even to the extent of the mere look of it — what is it you call such people? — an accessory after the fact.' There was something she kept back so rigidly that the joy of uttering the rest was double. She felt the sharpest need of giving him all the other truth. There was a matter as to which she had deceived him, and there was a matter as to which she had deceived Mrs Gereth, but her lack of pleasure in deception as such came home to her now. She busied herself with the tea and, to extend the occupation, cleared the table still more, spreading out the coarse cups and saucers and the vulgar little plates. She was aware that she produced more confusion than symmetry, but she was also aware that she was violently nervous. Owen tried to help her with something: this made rather for disorder. 'My reason for not writing to you,' she pursued, 'was simply that I was hoping to hear more from Ricks. I've waited from day to day for that.'

'But you've heard nothing?'

'Not a word.'

'Then what I understand,' said Owen, 'is that, practically, you and Mummy have quarrelled. And you've done it — I mean you personally — for *me*.'

'Oh no, we haven't quarrelled a bit!' Then with a smile: 'We've only diverged.'

'You've diverged uncommonly far!' – Owen laughed back. Fleda, with her hideous crockery and her father's collections, could conceive that these objects, to her visitor's perception even more strongly than to her own, measured the length of the swing from Poynton and Ricks; she was aware too that her high standards figured vividly enough even to Owen's simplicity to make him reflect that West Kensington was a tremendous fall. If she had fallen it was because she had acted for him. She was all the more content he should thus see she *had* acted, as the cost of it, in his eyes, was none of her own showing. 'What seems to have happened,' he exclaimed, 'is that you've had a row with her and yet not moved her!'

Fleda considered a moment; she was full of the impression that, notwithstanding her scant help, he saw his way clearer than he had seen it at Ricks. He might mean many things; and what if the many should mean in their turn only one? 'The difficulty is, you understand, that she doesn't really see into your situation.' She hesitated. 'She doesn't comprehend why your marriage hasn't yet taken place.'

Owen stared. 'Why, for the reason I told you: that Mona won't take another step till mother has given full satisfaction. Everything must be there. You see, everything *was* there the day of that fatal visit.'

'Yes, that's what I understood from you at Ricks,' said Fleda ; 'but I haven't repeated it to your mother.' She had hated, at Ricks, to talk with him about Mona, but now that scruple was swept away. If he could speak of Mona's visit as fatal, she need at least not pretend not to notice it. It made all the difference that she had tried to assist him and had failed: to give him any faith in her service she must give him all her reasons but one. She must give him, in other words, with a corresponding omission, all Mrs Gereth's. 'You can easily see that, as she dislikes your marriage, anything that may seem to make it less certain works in her favour. Without my telling her, she has suspicions and views that are simply suggested by your delay. Therefore it didn't seem to me right to make them worse. By holding off long enough, she thinks she may put an end to your engagement. If Mona's waiting, she believes she

359

may at last tire Mona out.' That, in all conscience, Fleda felt was lucid enough.

So the young man, following her attentively, appeared equally to feel. 'So far as that goes,' he promptly declared, 'she *has* at last tired Mona out.' He uttered the words with a strange approach to hilarity.

Fleda's surprise at this aberration left her a moment looking at him. 'Do you mean your marriage is off?'

Owen answered with a kind of gay despair. 'God knows, Miss Vetch, where or when or what my marriage is! If it isn't "off", it certainly, at the point things have reached, isn't *on*. I haven't seen Mona for ten days, and for a week I haven't heard from her. She used to write me every week, don't you know? She won't budge from Waterbath, and I haven't budged from town.' Then he suddenly broke out: 'If she *does* chuck me, will mother come round?'

Fleda, at this, felt that her heroism had come to its real test – felt that in telling him the truth she should effectively raise a hand to push his impediment out of the way. Was the knowledge that such a motion would probably dispose forever of Mona capable of yielding to the conception of still giving her every chance she was entitled to? That conception was heroic, but at the same moment it reminded Fleda of the place it had held in her plan, she was also reminded of the not less urgent claim of the truth. Ah, the truth – there was a limit to the impunity with which one could juggle with it! Wasn't what she had most to remember the fact that Owen had a right to his property and that he had also her vow to stand by him in the effort to recover it? How did she stand by him if she hid from him the single way to recover it of which she was quite sure? For an instant that seemed to her the fullest of her life she debated. 'Yes,' she said at last, 'if your marriage is really abandoned, she will give up everything she has taken.'

'That's just what makes Mona hesitate!' Owen honestly exclaimed. 'I mean the idea that I shall get back the things only if she gives me up.'

Fleda thought an instant. 'You mean makes her hesitate to keep you – not hesitate to renounce you?'

Owen looked a trifle bewildered. 'She doesn't see the use of

360

hanging on, as I haven't even yet put the matter into legal hands. She's awfully keen about that, and awfully disgusted that I don't. She says it's the only real way, and she thinks I'm afraid to take it. She has given me time and then has given me again more. She says I give Mummy too much. She says I'm a muff to go pottering on. That's why she's drawing off so hard, don't you see?'

'I don't see very clearly. Of course you must give her what you offered her ; of course you must keep your word. There must be no mistake about *that*! ' the girl declared.

Owen's bewilderment visibly increased. 'You think, then, as she does, that I *must* send down the police?'

The mixture of reluctance and dependence in this made her feel how much she was failing him. She had the sense of 'chucking' him too. 'No, no, not yet! ' she said, though she had really no other and no better course to prescribe. 'Doesn't it occur to you,' she asked in a moment, 'that if Mona is, as you say, drawing away, she may have, in doing so, a very high motive? She knows the immense value of all the objects detained by your mother, and to restore the spoils of Poynton, she is ready – is that it! – to make a sacrifice. The sacrifice is that of an engagement she had entered upon with joy.'

Owen had been blank a moment before, but he followed this argument with success – a success so immediate that it enabled him to produce with decision: 'Ah, she's not that sort! She wants them herself,' he added ; 'she wants to feel they're hers ; she doesn't care whether I have them or not! And if she can't get them she doesn't want *me*. If she can't get them she doesn't want anything at all.'

This was categoric ; Fleda drank it in. 'She takes such an interest in them?'

'So it appears.'

'So much that they're *all*, and that she can let everything else absolutely depend upon them?'

Owen weighed her question as if he felt the responsibility of his answer. But that answer came in a moment, and, as Fleda could see, out of a wealth of memory. 'She never wanted them particularly till they seemed to be in danger. Now she has an idea about them ; and when she gets hold of an idea – Oh dear me!' He broke off, pausing and looking away as with a sense of the futility of expression: it was the first time Fleda had ever heard him explain a matter so pointedly or embark at all on a generalization. It was striking, it was touching to her, as he faltered, that he appeared but half capable of floating his generalization to the end. The girl, however, was so far competent to fill up his blank as that she had divined, on the occasion of Mona's visit to Poynton, what would happen in the event of the accident at which he glanced. She had there with her own eyes seen Owen's betrothed get hold of an idea. 'I say, you know, *do* give me some tea!' he went on irrelevantly and familiarly.

Her profuse preparations had all this time had no sequel, and, with a laugh that she felt to be awkward, she hastily complied with his request. 'It's sure to be horrid,' she said ; 'we don't have at all good things.' She offered him also bread and butter, of which he partook, holding his cup and saucer in his other hand and moving slowly about the room. She poured herself a cup, but not to take it ; after which, without wanting it, she began to eat a small stale biscuit. She was struck with the extinction of the unwillingness she had felt at Ricks to contribute to the bandying between them of poor Mona's name ; and under this influence she presently resumed: 'Am I to understand that she engaged herself to marry you without caring for you?'

Owen looked out into Raphael Road. 'She *did* care for me awfully. But she can't stand the strain.'

'The strain of what?'

'Why of the whole wretched thing.'

'The whole thing has indeed been wretched, and I can easily conceive its effect upon her,' Fleda said.

Her visitor turned sharp round. 'You *can*?' There was a light in his strong stare. 'You can understand it's spoiling her temper and making her come down on *me*? She behaves as if I were of no use to her at all!'

Fleda hesitated. 'She's rankling under the sense of her wrong.'

'Well, was it *I*, pray, who perpetrated the wrong? Ain't I doing what I can to get the thing arranged?'

362

The ring of his question made his anger at Mona almost resemble for a minute an anger at Fleda ; and this resemblance in turn caused our young lady to observe how handsome he looked when he spoke, for the first time in her hearing, with that degree of heat, and used, also for the first time, such a term as 'perpetrated'. In addition, his challenge rendered still more vivid to her the mere flimsiness of her own aid. 'Yes, you've been perfect,' she said. 'You've had a most difficult part. You've *had* to show tact and patience, as well as firmness, with your mother, and you've strikingly shown them. It's I who, quite unintentionally, have deceived you. I haven't helped you at all to your remedy.'

'Well, you wouldn't at all events have ceased to like me, would you?' Owen demanded. It evidently mattered to him to know if she really justified Mona. 'I mean of course if you *had* liked me – like me as *she* liked me,' he explained.

Fleda looked this inquiry in the face only long enough to recognize that, in her embarrassment, she must take instant refuge in a superior one. 'I can answer that better if I know how kind to her you've been. *Have* you been kind to her?' she asked as simply as she could.

'Why, rather, Miss Vetch!' Owen declared. 'I've done every blessed thing she wished. I rushed down to Ricks, as you saw, with fire and sword, and the day after that I went to see her at Waterbath.' At this point he checked himself, though it was just the point at which her interest deepened. A different look had come into his face as he put down his empty teacup. 'But why should I tell you such things, for any good it does me? I gather that you've no suggestion to make me now except that I shall request my solicitor to act. *Shall* I request him to act?'

Fleda scarcely heard his words ; something new had suddenly come into her mind. 'When you went to Waterbath after seeing me,' she asked, 'did you tell her all about that?'

Owen looked conscious. 'All about it?'

'That you had had a long talk with me, without seeing your mother at all?'

'Oh yes, I told her exactly, and that you had been most awfully kind, and that I had placed the whole thing in your hands.'

Fleda was silent a moment. 'Perhaps that displeased her,' she at last suggested.

'It displeased her fearfully,' said Owen, looking very queer.

'Fearfully?' broke from the girl. Somehow, at the word, she was startled.

'She wanted to know what right you had to meddle. She said you were not honest.'

'Oh!' Fleda cried, with a long wail. Then she controlled herself. 'I see.'

'She abused you, and I defended you. She denounced you –'

She checked him with a gesture. 'Don't tell me what she did!' She had coloured up to her eyes, where, as with the effect of a blow in the face, she quickly felt the tears gathering. It was a sudden drop in her great flight, a shock to her attempt to watch over what Mona was entitled to. While she had been straining her very soul in this attempt, the object of her magnanimity had been pronouncing her 'not honest'. She took it all in, however, and after an instant was able to smile. She would not have been surprised to learn, indeed, that her smile was strange. 'You said a while ago that your mother and I quarrelled about you. It's much more true that you and Mona have quarrelled about *me*.'

Owen hesitated, but at last he brought it out. 'What I mean to say is, don't you know, that Mona, if you don't mind my saying so, has taken it into her head to be jealous.'

'I see,' said Fleda. 'Well, I dare say our conferences have looked very odd.'

'They've looked very beautiful, and they've been very beautiful. Oh, I've told her the sort you are!' the young man pursued.

'That of course hasn't made her love me better.'

'No, nor love me,' said Owen. 'Of course, you know, she says she loves me.'

'And do you say you love her?'

'I say nothing else – I say it all the while. I said it the other day a dozen times.' Fleda made no immediate rejoinder to this, and before she could choose one he repeated his question of a moment before. '*Am* I to tell my solicitor to act?'

She had at that moment turned away from this solution,

precisely because she saw in it the great chance of her secret. If she should determine him to adopt it she might put out her hand and take him. It would shut in Mrs Gereth's face the open door of surrender: she would flare up and fight, flying the flag of a passionate, an heroic defence. The case would obviously go against her, but the proceedings would last longer than Mona's patience or Owen's propriety. With a formal rupture he would be at large; and she had only to tighten her fingers round the string that would raise the curtain on that scene. 'You tell me you "say" you love her, but is there nothing more in it than your saying so? You wouldn't say so, would you, if it's not true? What in the world has become, in so short a time, of the affection that led to your engagement?'

'The deuce knows what has become of it, Miss Vetch!' Owen cried. 'It seemed all to go to pot as this horrid struggle came on.' He was close to her now, and, with his face lighted again by the relief of it, he looked all his helpless history into her eyes. 'As I saw you and noticed you more, as I knew you better and better, I felt less and less – I couldn't help it – about anything or anyone else. I wished I had known you sooner – I knew I should have liked you better than anyone in the world. But it wasn't you who made the difference,' he eagerly continued, 'and I was awfully determined to stick to Mona to the death. It was she herself who made it, upon my soul, by the state she got into, the way she sulked, the way she took things, and the way she let me have it! She destroyed our prospects and our happiness, upon my honour. She made just the same smash of them as if she had kicked over that tea-table. She wanted to know all the while what was passing between us, between you and me; and she wouldn't take my solemn assurance that nothing was passing but what might have directly passed between me and old Mummy. She said a pretty girl like you was a nice old Mummy for me, and, if you'll believe it, she never called you anything else but that. I'll be hanged if I haven't been good, haven't I? I haven't breathed a breath of any sort to you, have I? You'd have been down on me hard if I had, wouldn't you? You're down on me pretty hard as it is, I think, aren't you? But I don't care what you say now, or what Mona says, either, or a single rap what anyone says: she has

365

given me at last, by her confounded behaviour, a right to speak out, to utter the way I feel about it. The way I feel about it, don't you know, is that it had all better come to an end. You ask me if I don't love her, and I suppose it's natural enough you should. But you ask it at the very moment I'm half mad to say to you that there's only one person on the whole earth I *really* love, and that that person – ' Here Owen pulled up short, and Fleda wondered if it was from the effect of his perceiving, through the closed door, the sound of steps and voices on the landing of the stairs. She had caught this sound herself with surprise and a vague uneasiness: it was not an hour at which her father ever came in, and there was no present reason why she should have a visitor. She had a fear, which after a few seconds deepened: a visitor was at hand ; the visitor would be simply Mrs Gereth. That lady wished for a near view of the consequence of her note to Owen. Fleda straightened herself with the instant thought that if this was what Mrs Gereth desired Mrs Gereth should have it in a form not to be mistaken. Owen's pause was the matter of a moment, but during that moment our young couple stood with their eyes holding each other's eyes and their ears catching the suggestion, still through the door, of a murmured conference in the hall. Fleda had begun to make the movement to cut it short when Owen stopped her with a grasp of her arm. 'You're surely able to guess,' he said, with his voice dropped and her arm pressed as she had never known such a drop or such a pressure – 'you're surely able to guess the one person on earth I love?'

The handle of the door turned, and Fleda had only time to jerk at him: 'Your mother!'

The door opened, and the smutty maid, edging in, announced 'Mrs Brigstock!'

CHAPTER 15

MRS BRIGSTOCK, in the doorway, stood looking from one of
the occupants of the room to the other ; then they saw her
eyes attach themselves to a small object that had lain hitherto
unnoticed on the carpet. This was the biscuit of which, on
giving Owen his tea, Fleda had taken a perfunctory nibble:
she had immediately laid it on the table, and that subsequently, in some precipitate movement, she should have
brushed it off was doubtless a sign of the agitation that
possessed her. For Mrs Brigstock there was apparently more
in it than met the eye. Owen at any rate picked it up, and
Fleda felt as if he were removing the traces of some scene that
the newspapers would have characterized as lively. Mrs Brigstock clearly took in also the sprawling tea-things and the
mark as of high water in the full faces of her young friends.
These elements made the little place a vivid picture of
intimacy. A minute was filled by Fleda's relief at finding her
visitor not to be Mrs Gereth, and a longer space by the
ensuing sense of what was really more compromising in the
actual apparition. It dimly occurred to her that the lady of
Ricks had also written to Waterbath. Not only had Mrs Brigstock never paid her a call, but Fleda would have been unable
to figure her so employed. A year before the girl had spent
a day under her roof, but never feeling that Mrs Brigstock
regarded this as constituting a bond. She had never stayed in
any house but Poynton where the imagination of a bond, one
way or the other, prevailed. After the first astonishment she
dashed gayly at her guest, emphasizing her welcome and wondering how her whereabouts had become known at Waterbath.
Had not Mrs Brigstock quitted that residence for the very
purpose of laying her hand on the associate of Mrs Gereth's
misconduct? The spirit in which this hand was to be laid our
young lady was yet to ascertain ; but she was a person who
could think ten thoughts at once – a circumstance which, even
putting her present plight at its worst, gave her a great

advantage over a person who required easy conditions for dealing even with one. The very vibration of the air, however, told her that whatever Mrs Brigstock's spirit might originally have been, it had been sharply affected by the sight of Owen. He was essentially a surprise: she had reckoned with everything that concerned him but his presence. With that, in awkward silence, she was reckoning now, as Fleda could see, while she effected with friendly aid an embarrassed transit to the sofa. Owen would be useless, would be deplorable: that aspect of the case Fleda had taken in as well. Another aspect was that he would admire her, adore her, exactly in proportion as she herself should rise gracefully superior. Fleda felt for the first time free to let herself 'go', as Mrs Gereth had said, and she was full of the sense that to 'go' meant now to aim straight at the effect of moving Owen to rapture at her simplicity and tact. It was her impression that he had no positive dislike of Mona's mother; but she couldn't entertain that notion without a glimpse of the implication that he had a positive dislike of Mrs Brigstock's daughter. Mona's mother declined tea, declined a better seat, declined a cushion, declined to remove her boa: Fleda guessed that she had not come on purpose to be dry, but that the voice of the invaded room had itself given her the hint.

'I just came on the mere chance,' she said. 'Mona found yesterday, somewhere, the card of invitation to your sister's marriage that you sent us, or your father sent us, some time ago. We couldn't be present – it was impossible; but as it had this address on it I said to myself that I might find you here.'

'I'm very glad to be at home,' Fleda responded.

'Yes, that doesn't happen very often, does it?' Mrs Brigstock looked round afresh at Fleda's home.

'Oh, I came back from Ricks last week. I shall be here now till I don't know when.'

'We thought it very likely you would have come back. We knew of course of your having been at Ricks. If I didn't find you I thought I might perhaps find Mr Vetch,' Mrs Brigstock went on.

'I'm sorry he's out. He's always out – all day long.'

Mrs Brigstock's round eyes grew rounder. 'All day long?'

'All day long,' Fleda smiled.

'Leaving you quite to yourself?'

'A good deal to myself, but a little, today, as you see, to Mr Gereth — ' and the girl looked at Owen to draw him into their sociability. For Mrs Brigstock he had immediately sat down; but the movement had not corrected the sombre stiffness taking possession of him at the sight of her. Before he found a response to the appeal addressed to him Fleda turned again to her other visitor. 'Is there any purpose for which you would like my father to call on you?'

Mrs Brigstock received this question as if it were not to be unguardedly answered; upon which Owen intervened with pale irrelevance: 'I wrote to Mona this morning of Miss Vetch's being in town; but of course the letter hadn't arrived when you left home.'

'No, it hadn't arrived. I came up for the night — I've several matters to attend to.' Then looking with an intention of fixedness from one of her companions to the other, 'I'm afraid I've interrupted your conversation,' Mrs Brigstock said. She spoke without effectual point, had the air of merely announcing the fact. Fleda had not yet been confronted with the question of the sort of person Mrs Brigstock was; she had only been confronted with the question of the sort of person Mrs Gereth scorned her for being. She was really, somehow, no sort of person at all, and it came home to Fleda that if Mrs Gereth could see her at this moment she would scorn her more than ever. She had a face of which it was impossible to say anything but that it was pink, and a mind that it would be possible to describe only if one had been able to mark it in a similar fashion. As nature had made this organ neither green nor blue nor yellow, there was nothing to know it by: it strayed and bleated like an unbranded sheep. Fleda felt for it at this moment much of the kindness of compassion, since Mrs Brigstock had brought it with her to do something for her that she regarded as delicate. Fleda was quite prepared to help it to perform, if she should be able to gather what it wanted to do. What she gathered, however, more and more, was that it wanted to do something different from what it had wanted to do in leaving Waterbath. There was still

369

nothing to enlighten her more specifically in the way her visitor continued: 'You must be very much taken up. I believe you quite espouse his dreadful quarrel.'

Fleda vaguely demurred. 'His dreadful quarrel?'

'About the contents of the house. Aren't you looking after them for him?'

'She knows how awfully kind you've been to me,' Owen said. He showed such discomfiture that he really gave away their situation; and Fleda found herself divided between the hope that he would take leave and the wish that he should see the whole of what the occasion might enable her to bring to pass for him.

She explained to Mrs Brigstock. 'Mrs Gereth, at Ricks, the other day, asked me particularly to see him for her.'

'And did she ask you also particularly to see him here in town?' Mrs Brigstock's hideous bonnet seemed to argue for the unsophisticated truth; and it was on Fleda's lips to reply that such had indeed been Mrs Gereth's request. But she checked herself, and before she could say anything else Owen had addressed their companion.

'I made a point of letting Mona know that I should be here, don't you see? That's exactly what I wrote her this morning.'

'She would have had no doubt you would be here, if you had a chance,' Mrs Brigstock returned. 'If your letter had arrived it might have prepared me for finding you here at tea. In that case I certainly wouldn't have come.'

'I'm glad, then, it didn't arrive. Shouldn't you like him to go?' Fleda asked.

Mrs Brigstock looked at Owen and considered: nothing showed in her face but that it turned a deeper pink. 'I should like him to go with *me*.' There was no menace in her tone, but she evidently knew what she wanted. As Owen made no response to this Fleda glanced at him to invite him to assent; then, for fear that he wouldn't, and would thereby make his case worse, she took upon herself to declare that she was sure he would be very glad to meet such a wish. She had no sooner spoken than she felt that the words had a bad effect of intimacy: she had answered for him as if she had been his wife. Mrs Brigstock continued to regard him as if she had observed nothing, and she continued to address Fleda: 'I've not seen him for a long time – I've particular things to say to him.'

'So have I things to say to you, Mrs Brigstock!' Owen interjected. With this he took up his hat as if for an immediate departure.

The other visitor meanwhile turned to Fleda. 'What is Mrs Gereth going to do?'

'Is that what you came to ask me?' Fleda demanded.

'That and several other things.'

'Then you had much better let Mr Gereth go, and stay by yourself and make me a pleasant visit. You can talk with him when you like, but it is the first time you've been to see me.'

This appeal had evidently a certain effect; Mrs Brigstock visibly wavered. 'I can't talk with him whenever I like,' she returned ; 'he hasn't been near us since I don't know when. But there are things that have brought me here.'

'They are not things of any importance,' Owen, to Fleda's surprise, suddenly asserted. He had not at first taken up Mrs Brigstock's expression of a wish to carry him off : Fleda, could see that the instinct at the bottom of this was that of standing by her, of seeming not to abandon her. But abruptly, all his soreness working within him, it had struck him that he should abandon her still more if he should leave her to be dealt with by her other visitor. 'You must allow me to say, you know, Mrs Brigstock, that I don't think you should come down on Miss Vetch about anything. It's very good of her to take the smallest interest in us and our horrid little squabble. If you want to talk about it, talk about it with *me*.' He was flushed with the idea of protecting Fleda, of exhibiting his consideration for her. 'I don't like your cross-questioning her, don't you see? She's as straight as a die: *I*'ll tell you all about her!' he declared with an excited laugh. 'Please come off with me and let her alone.'

Mrs Brigstock, at this, became vivid at once ; Fleda thought she looked most peculiar. She stood straight up, with a queer distention of her whole person and of everything in her face but her mouth, which she gathered into a small, tight orifice.

371

Fleda was painfully divided ; her joy was deep within, but it was more relevant to the situation that she should not appear to associate herself with the tone of familiarity in which Owen addressed a lady who had been, and was perhaps still, about to become his mother-in-law. She laid on Mrs Brigstock's arm a repressive hand. Mrs Brigstock, however, had already exclaimed on her having so wonderful a defender. 'He speaks, upon my word, as if I had come here to be rude to you!'

At this, grasping her hard, Fleda laughed ; then she achieved the exploit of delicately kissing her. 'I'm not in the least afraid to be alone with you, or of your tearing me to pieces. I'll answer any question that you can possibly dream of putting to me.'

'I'm the proper person to answer Mrs Brigstock's questions,' Owen broke in again, 'and I'm not a bit less ready to meet them than you are.' He was firmer than she had ever seen him: it was as if she had not known he could be so firm.

'But she'll only have been here a few minutes. What sort of a visit is that? ' Fleda cried.

'It has lasted long enough for my purpose. There was something I wanted to know, but I think I know it now.'

'Anything you don't know I dare say I can tell you!' Owen observed as he impatiently smoothed his hat with the cuff of his coat.

Fleda by this time desired immensely to keep his companion, but she saw she could do so only at the cost of provoking on his part a further exhibition of the sheltering attitude, which he exaggerated precisely because it was the first thing, since he had begun to 'like' her, that he had been able frankly to do for her. It was not in her interest that Mrs Brigstock should be more struck than she already was with that benevolence. 'There may be things you know that I don't,' she presently said to her, with a smile. 'But I've a sort of sense that you're labouring under some great mistake.'

Mrs Brigstock, at this, looked into her eyes more deeply and yearningly than she had supposed Mrs Brigstock could look ; it was the flicker of a certain willingness to give her a chance. Owen, however, quickly spoiled everything. 'Nothing is more probable than that Mrs Brigstock is doing what you say; but there's no one in the world to whom you owe an explanation. I may owe somebody one – I dare say I do; but not you, no!'

'But what if there's one that it's no difficulty at all for me to give?' Fleda inquired. 'I'm sure that's the only one Mrs Brigstock came to ask, if she came to ask any at all.'

Again the good lady looked hard at her young hostess. 'I came, I believe, Fleda, just, you know, to plead with you.'

Fleda, with a bright face, hesitated a moment. 'As if I were one of those bad women in a play?'

The remark was disastrous. Mrs Brigstock, on whom her brightness was lost, evidently thought it singularly free. She turned away, as from a presence that had really defined itself as objectionable, and Fleda had a vain sense that her good humour, in which there was an idea, was taken for impertinence, or at least for levity. Her allusion was improper, even if she herself wasn't; Mrs Brigstock's emotion simplified: it came to the same thing. 'I'm quite ready,' that lady said to Owen rather mildly and woundedly. 'I do want to speak to you very much.'

'I'm completely at your service.' Owen held out his hand to Fleda. 'Good-bye, Miss Vetch. I hope to see you again tomorrow.' He opened the door for Mrs Brigstock, who passed before the girl with an oblique, averted salutation. Owen and Fleda, while he stood at the door, then faced each other darkly and without speaking. Their eyes met once more for a long moment, and she was conscious there was something in hers that the darkness didn't quench, that he had never seen before and that he was perhaps never to see again. He stayed long enough to take it – to take it with a sombre stare that just showed the dawn of wonder; then he followed Mrs Brigstock out of the house.

CHAPTER 16

HE had uttered the hope that he should see her the next day, but Fleda could easily reflect that he wouldn't see her if she were not there to be seen. If there was a thing in the world she desired at that moment, it was that the next day should have no point of resemblance with the day that had just elapsed. She accordingly aspired to an absence: she would go immediately down to Maggie. She ran out that evening and telegraphed to her sister, and in the morning she quitted London by an early train. She required for this step no reason but the sense of necessity. It was a strong personal need ; she wished to interpose something, and there was nothing she could interpose but distance, but time. If Mrs Brigstock had to deal with Owen she would allow Mrs Brigstock the chance. To be there, to be in the midst of it, was the reverse of what she craved : she had already been more in the midst of it than had ever entered into her plan. At any rate she had renounced her plan ; she had no plan now but the plan of separation. This was to abandon Owen, to give up the fine office of helping him back to his own ; but when she had undertaken that office she had not foreseen that Mrs Gereth would defeat it by a manoeuvre so simple. The scene at her father's rooms had extinguished all offices, and the scene at her father's rooms was of Mrs Gereth's producing. Owen, at all events, must now act for himself : he had obligations to meet, he had satisfactions to give, and Fleda fairly ached with the wish that he might be equal to them. She never knew the extent of her tenderness for him till she became conscious of the present force of her desire that he should be superior, be perhaps even sublime. She obscurely made out that superiority, that sublimity, mightn't after all be fatal. She closed her eyes and lived for a day or two in the mere beauty of confidence. It was with her on the short journey ; it was with her at Maggie's ; it glorified the mean little house in the stupid little town. Owen had grown larger to her : he would do, like a man, whatever

374

he should have to do. He wouldn't be weak – not as she was: she herself was weak exceedingly.

Arranging her few possessions in Maggie's fewer receptacles, she caught a glimpse of the bright side of the fact that her old things were not such a problem as Mrs Gereth's. Picking her way with Maggie through the local puddles, diving with her into smelly cottages and supporting her, at smellier shops, in firmness over the weight of joints and the taste of cheese, it was still her own secret that was universally interwoven. In the puddles, the cottages, the shops she was comfortably alone with it ; that comfort prevailed even while, at the evening meal, her brother-in-law invited her attention to a diagram, drawn with a fork on too soiled a tablecloth, of the scandalous drains of the Convalescent Home. To be alone with it she had come away from Ricks ; and now she knew that to be alone with it she had come away from London. This advantage was of course menaced, but not immediately destroyed, by the arrival, on the second day, of the note she had been sure she should receive from Owen. He had gone to West Kensington and found her flown, but he had got her address from the little maid and then hurried to a club and written to her. 'Why have you left me just when I want you most?' he demanded. The next words, it was true, were more reassuring on the question of his steadiness.

I don't know what your reason may be [they went on] nor why you've not left a line for me; but I don't think you can feel that I did anything yesterday that it wasn't right for me to do. As regards Mrs Brigstock, certainly I just felt what was right and I did it. She had no business whatever to attack you that way, and I should have been ashamed if I had left her there to worry you. I won't have you worried by anyone; no one shall be disagreeable to you but me. I didn't mean to be so yesterday, and I don't today; but I'm perfectly free now to want you, and I want you much more than you've allowed me to explain. You'll see if I'm not all right, if you'll let me come to you. Don't be afraid – I'll not hurt you nor trouble you. I give you my honour I'll not hurt anyone. Only I *must* see you, on what I had to say to Mrs B. She was nastier than I thought she could be, but I'm behaving like an angel. I assure you I'm all right – that's exactly what I want you to see. You owe me something, you know, for what you said you would

375

do and haven't done; what your departure without a word gives me to understand – doesn't it? – that you definitely can't do. Don't simply forsake me. See me, if you only see me once. I sha'n't wait for any leave – I shall come down tomorrow. I've been looking into trains and find there's something that will bring me down just after lunch and something very good for getting me back. I won't stop long. For God's sake, be there.

This communication arrived in the morning, but Fleda would still have had time to wire a protest. She debated on that alternative; then she read the note over and found in one phrase an exact statement of her duty. Owen's simplicity had expressed it, and her subtlety had nothing to answer. She owed him something for her obvious failure, and what she owed him was to receive him. If indeed she had known he would make this attempt she might have been held to have gained nothing by her flight. Well, she had gained what she had gained – she had gained the interval. She had no compunction for the greater trouble she should give the young man; it was now doubtless right that he should have as much trouble as possible. Maggie, who thought she was in her confidence, but was immensely not, had reproached her for having left Mrs Gereth, and Maggie was just in this proportion gratified to hear of the visitor with whom, early in the afternoon, she would have to ask to be left alone. Maggie liked to see far, and now she could sit upstairs and rake the whole future. She had known that, as she familiarly said, there was something the matter with Fleda, and the value of that knowledge was augmented by the fact that there was apparently also something the matter with Mr Gereth.

Fleda, downstairs, learned soon enough what this was. It was simply that, as he announced the moment he stood before her, he was now all right. When she asked him what he meant by that state he replied that he meant he could practically regard himself henceforth as a free man: he had had at West Kensington, as soon as they got into the street, such a horrid scene with Mrs Brigstock.

'I knew what she wanted to say to me: that's why I was determined to get her off. I knew I shouldn't like it, but I was perfectly prepared,' said Owen. 'She brought it out as soon as

376

we got round the corner; she asked me point-blank if I was in love with you.'

'And what did you say to that?'

'That it was none of her business.'

'Ah,' said Fleda, 'I'm not so sure!'

'Well, *I* am, and I'm the person most concerned. Of course I didn't use just those words: I was perfectly civil, quite as civil as she. But I told her I didn't consider she had a right to put me any such question. I said I wasn't sure that even Mona had, with the extraordinary line, you know, that Mona has taken. At any rate the whole thing, the way *I* put it, was between Mona and me; and between Mona and me, if she didn't mind, it would just have to remain.'

Fleda was silent a little. 'All that didn't answer her question.'

'Then you think I ought to have told her?'

Again our young lady reflected. 'I think I'm rather glad you didn't.'

'I knew what I was about,' said Owen. 'It didn't strike me that she had the least right to come down on us that way and ask for explanations.'

Fleda looked very grave, weighing the whole matter. 'I dare say that when she started, when she arrived, she didn't mean to "come down".'

'What then did she mean to do?'

'What she said to me just before she went: she meant to plead with me.'

'Oh, I heard her!' said Owen. 'But plead with you for what?'

'For you, of course – to entreat me to give you up. She thinks me awfully designing – that I've taken some sort of possession of you.'

Owen stared. 'You haven't lifted a finger! It's I who have taken possession.'

'Very true, you've done it all yourself.' Fleda spoke gravely and gently, without a breath of coquetry. 'But those are shades between which she's probably not obliged to distinguish. It's enough for her that we're singularly intimate.'

'I am, but you're not!' Owen exclaimed.

Fleda gave a dim smile. 'You make me at least feel that

I'm learning to know you very well when I hear you say such a thing as that. Mrs Brigstock came to get round me, to supplicate me,' she went on ; 'but to find you there, looking so much at home, paying me a friendly call and shoving the tea-things about – that was too much for her patience. She doesn't know, you see, that I'm after all a decent girl. She simply made up her mind on the spot that I'm a very bad case.'

'I couldn't stand the way she treated you, and that was what I had to say to her,' Owen returned.

'She's simple and slow, but she's not a fool: I think she treated me, on the whole, very well.' Fleda remembered how Mrs Gereth had treated Mona when the Brigstocks came down to Poynton.

Owen evidently thought her painfully perverse. 'It was you who carried it off ; you behaved like a brick. And so did I, I consider. If you only knew the difficulty I had! I told her you were the noblest and straightest of women.'

'That can hardly have removed her impression that there are things I put you up to.'

'It didn't,' Owen replied with candour. 'She said our relation, yours and mine, isn't innocent.'

'What did she mean by that?'

'As you may suppose, I particularly inquired. Do you know what she had the cheek to tell me?' Owen asked. 'She didn't better it much: she said she meant that it's excessively unnatural.'

Fleda considered afresh. 'Well, it is!' she brought out at last.

'Then, upon my honour, it's only you who make it so!' Her perversity was distinctly too much for him. 'I mean you make it so by the way you keep me off.'

'Have I kept you off today?' Fleda sadly shook her head, raising her arms a little and dropping them.

Her gesture of resignation gave him a pretext for catching at her hand, but before he could take it she had put it behind her. They had been seated together on Maggie's single sofa, and her movement brought her to her feet, while Owen, looking at her reproachfully, leaned back in discouragement.

'What good does it do me to be here when I find you only a stone?'

She met his eyes with all the tenderness she had not yet uttered, and she had not known till this moment how great was the accumulation. 'Perhaps, after all,' she risked, 'there may be even in a stone still some little help for you.'

Owen sat there a minute staring at her. 'Ah, you're beautiful, more beautiful than anyone,' he broke out, 'but I'll be hanged if I can ever understand you! On Tuesday, at your father's, you were beautiful – as beautiful, just before I left, as you are at this instant. But the next day, when I went back, I found it had apparently meant nothing ; and now, again, that you let me come here and you shine at me like an angel, it doesn't bring you an inch nearer to saying what I want you to say.' He remained a moment longer in the same position ; then he jerked himself up. 'What I want you to say is that you like me – what I want you to say is that you pity me.' He sprang up and came to her. 'What I want you to say is that you'll *save* me!'

Fleda hesitated. 'Why do you need saving, when you announced to me just now that you're a free man?'

He too hesitated, but he was not checked. 'It's just for the reason that I'm free. Don't you know what I mean, Miss Vetch? I want you to marry me.'

Fleda, at this, put out her hand in charity ; she held his own, which quickly grasped it a moment, and if he had described her as shining at him it may be assumed that she shone all the more in her deep, still smile. 'Let me hear a little more about your freedom first,' she said. 'I gather that Mrs Brigstock was not wholly satisfied with the way you disposed of her question.'

'I dare say she wasn't. But the less she's satisfied the more I'm free.'

'What bearing have *her* feelings, pray?' Fleda asked.

'Why, Mona's much worse than her mother. She wants much more to give me up.'

'Then why doesn't she do it?'

'She will, as soon as her mother gets home and tells her.'

'Tells her what?' Fleda inquired.

'Why, that I'm in love with *you*!'

Fleda debated. 'Are you so very sure she will?'

'Certainly I'm sure, with all the evidence I already have. That will finish her!' Owen declared.

This made his companion thoughtful again. 'Can you take such pleasure in her being "finished" – a poor girl you've once loved?'

Owen waited long enough to take in the question; then with a serenity startling even to her knowledge of his nature, 'I don't think I can have *really* loved her, you know,' he replied.

Fleda broke into a laugh which gave him a surprise as visible as the emotion it testified to. 'Then how am I to know that you "really" love – anybody else?'

'Oh, I'll show you that!' said Owen.

'I must take it on trust,' the girl pursued. 'And what if Mona doesn't give you up?' she added.

Owen was baffled but a few seconds; he had thought of everything. 'Why, that's just where you come in.'

'To save you? I see. You mean I must get rid of her for you.' His blankness showed for a little that he felt the chill of her cold logic; but as she waited for his rejoinder she knew to which of them it cost most. He gasped a minute, and that gave her time to say: 'You see, Mr Owen, how impossible it is to talk of such things yet!'

Like lightning he had grasped her arm. 'You mean you *will* talk of them?' Then as he began to take the flood of assent from her eyes: 'You *will* listen to me? Oh, you dear, you dear – when, when?'

'Ah, when it isn't mere misery!' The words had broken from her in a sudden loud cry, and what next happened was that the very sound of her pain upset her. She heard her own true note; she turned short away from him; in a moment she had burst into sobs; in another his arms were round her; the next she had let herself go so far that even Mrs Gereth might have seen it. He clasped her, and she gave herself – she poured out her tears on his breast; something prisoned and pent throbbed and gushed; something deep and sweet surged up – something that came from far within and far off, that had begun with the sight of him in his indifference and had

380

never had rest since then. The surrender was short, but the relief was long: she felt his lips upon her face and his arms tightened with his full divination. What she did, what she *had* done, she scarcely knew: she only was aware, as she broke from him again, of what had taken place in his own quick breast. What had taken place was that, with the click of a spring, he saw. He had cleared the high wall at a bound ; they were together without a veil. She had not a shred of a secret left ; it was as if a whirlwind had come and gone, laying low the great false front that she had built up stone by stone. The strangest thing of all was the momentary sense of desolation.

'Ah, all the while you *cared*?' Owen read the truth with a wonder so great that it was visibly almost a sadness, a terror caused by his sudden perception of where the impossibility was not. That made it all perhaps elsewhere.

'I cared, I cared, I cared!' Fleda moaned it as defiantly as if she were confessing a misdeed. 'How couldn't I care? But you mustn't, you must never, never ask! It isn't for us to talk about! ' she insisted. 'Don't speak of it, don't speak! '

It was easy indeed not to speak when the difficulty was to find words. He clasped his hands before her as he might have clasped them at an altar ; his pressed palms shook together while he held his breath and while she stilled herself in the effort to come round again to the real and the right. He helped this effort, soothing her into a seat with a touch as light as if she had really been something sacred. She sank into a chair and he dropped before her on his knees; she fell back with closed eyes and he buried his face in her lap. There was no way to thank her but this act of prostration, which lasted, in silence, till she laid consenting hands on him, touched his head and stroked it, held it in her tenderness till he acknowledged his long density. He made the avowal seem only his – made her, when she rose again, raise him at last, softly, as if from the abasement of shame. If in each other's eyes now, however, they saw the truth, this truth, to Fleda, looked harder even than before – all the harder that when, at the very moment she recognized it, he murmured to her ecstatically, in fresh possession of her hands, which he drew up to his breast, holding them tight there with both his own: 'I'm saved, I'm saved – I *am*! I'm ready for anything. I have your word. Come!' he cried, as if from the sight of a response slower than he needed, and in the tone he so often had of a great boy at a great game.

She had once more disengaged herself, with the private vow that he shouldn't yet touch her again. It was all too horribly soon – her sense of this was rapidly surging back. 'We mustn't talk, we mustn't talk; we must *wait*!' she intensely insisted. 'I don't know what you mean by your freedom; I don't see it. I don't feel it. Where is it yet, where, your freedom? If it's real there's plenty of time, and if it isn't there's more than enough. I hate myself,' she protested, 'for having anything to say about her: it's like waiting for dead men's shoes! What business is it of mine what she does? She has her own trouble and her own plan. It's too hideous to watch her and count on her!'

Owen's face, at this, showed a reviving dread, the fear of some darksome process of her mind. 'If you speak for yourself I can understand, but why is it hideous for *me*?'

'Oh, I mean for myself!' Fleda said impatiently.

'*I* watch her, *I* count on her: how can I do anything else? If I count on her to let me definitely know how we stand, I do nothing in life but what she herself has led straight up to. I never thought of asking you to "get rid of her" for me, and I never would have spoken to you if I hadn't held that I *am* rid of her, that she has backed out of the whole thing. Didn't she do so from the moment she began to put it off? I had already applied for the licence; the very invitations were half addressed. Who but she, all of a sudden, demanded an unnatural wait? It was none of *my* doing; I had never dreamed of anything but coming up to the scratch.' Owen grew more and more lucid, and more confident of the effect of his lucidity. 'She called it "taking a stand", to see what mother would do. I told her mother would do what I would make her do; and to that she replied that she would like to see me make her first. I said I would arrange that everything should be all right, and she said she really preferred to arrange it herself. It was a flat refusal to trust me in the smallest degree. Why then had she pretended so tremendously to care for me? And of course, at present,' said Owen, 'she trusts me, if possible, still less.'

Fleda paid this statement the homage of a minute's muteness. 'As to that, naturally, she has reason.'

'Why on earth has she reason?' Then, as his companion, moving away, simply threw up her hands, 'I never looked at you – not to call looking – till she had regularly driven me to it,' he went on. 'I know what I'm about. I do assure you I'm all right!'

'You're not all right – you're all wrong!' Fleda cried in despair. 'You mustn't stay here, you mustn't!' she repeated with clear decision. 'You make me say dreadful things, and I feel as if I made *you* say them.' But before he could reply she took it up in another tone. 'Why in the world, if everything had changed, didn't you break off?'

'I? – ' The inquiry seemed to have moved him to stupefaction. 'Can you ask me that question when I only wanted to please you? Didn't you seem to show me, in your wonderful way, that that was exactly how? I didn't break off just on purpose to leave it to *her*. I didn't break off so that there shouldn't be a thing to be said against me.'

The instant after her challenge Fleda had faced him again in self-reproof. 'There *isn't* a thing to be said against you, and I don't know what nonsense you make me talk! You *have* pleased me, and you've been right and good, and it's the only comfort, and you must go. Everything must come from Mona, and if it doesn't come we've said entirely too much. You must leave me alone – for ever.'

'For ever?' Owen gasped.

'I mean unless everything is different.'

'Everything *is* different – when I *know*!'

Fleda winced at what he knew; she made a wild gesture which seemed to whirl it out of the room. The mere allusion was like another embrace. 'You know nothing – and you must go and wait! You mustn't break down at this point.'

He looked about him and took up his hat: it was as if, in spite of frustration, he had got the essence of what he wanted and could afford to agree with her to the extent of keeping up the forms. He covered her with his fine, simple smile, but made no other approach. 'Oh, I'm so awfully happy!' he exclaimed.

She hesitated: she would only be impeccable even though she should have to be sententious. 'You'll be happy if you're perfect!' she risked.

He laughed out at this, and she wondered if, with a newborn acuteness, he saw the absurdity of her speech, and that no one was happy just because no one could be what she so lightly prescribed. 'I don't pretend to be perfect, but I shall find a letter tonight!'

'So much the better, if it's the kind of one you desire.' That was the most she could say, and having made it sound as dry as possible she lapsed into a silence so pointed as to deprive him of all pretext for not leaving her. Still, nevertheless, he stood there, playing with his hat and filling the long pause with a strained and anxious smile. He wished to obey her thoroughly, to appear not to presume on any advantage he had won from her; but there was clearly something he longed for beside. While he showed this by hanging on she thought of two other things. One of these was that his countenance, after all, failed to bear out his description of his bliss. As for the other, it had no sooner come into her head than she found it seated, in spite of her resolution, on her lips. It took the form of an inconsequent question. 'When did you say Mrs Brigstock was to have gone back?'

Owen stared. 'To Waterbath? She was to have spent the night in town, don't you know? But when she left me, after our talk, I said to myself that she would take an evening train. I know I made her want to get home.'

'Where did you separate?' Fleda asked.

'At the West Kensington station – she was going to Victoria. I had walked with her there, and our talk was all on the way.'

Fleda pondered a moment. 'If she did go back that night you would have heard from Waterbath by this time.'

'I don't know,' said Owen. 'I thought I might hear this morning.'

'She can't have gone back,' Fleda declared. 'Mona would have written on the spot.'

'Oh yes, she *will* have written bang off!' Owen cheerfully conceded.

Fleda thought again. 'Then, even in the event of her mother's not having got home till the morning, you would have had your letter at the latest today. You see she has had plenty of time.'

Owen hesitated; then, 'Oh, she's all right!' he laughed. 'I go by Mrs Brigstock's certain effect on her – the effect of the temper the old lady showed when we parted. Do you know what she asked me?' he sociably continued. 'She asked me in a kind of nasty manner if I supposed you "really" cared anything about me. Of course I told her I supposed you didn't – not a solitary rap. How could I suppose you *do*, with your extraordinary ways? It doesn't matter; I could see she thought I lied.'

'You should have told her, you know, that I had seen you in town only that one time,' Fleda observed.

'By Jove, I did – for *you*! It was only for you.'

Something in this touched the girl so that for a moment she could not trust herself to speak. 'You're an honest man,' she said at last. She had gone to the door and opened it. 'Good-bye.'

Even yet, however, he hung back; and she remembered how, at the end of his hour at Ricks, she had been put to it to get him out of the house. He had in general a sort of cheerful slowness which helped him at such times, though she could now see his strong fist crumple his big, stiff gloves as if they had been paper. 'But even if there's no letter – ' he began. He began, but there he left it.

'You mean, even if she doesn't let you off? Ah, you ask me too much!' Fleda spoke from the tiny hall, where she had taken refuge between the old barometer and the old mackintosh. 'There are things too utterly for yourselves alone. How can I tell? What do I know? Good-bye, good-bye! If she doesn't let you off, it will be because she *is* attached to you.'

'She's not, she's not: there's nothing in it! Doesn't a fellow know? – except with *you*!' Owen ruefully added. With this he came out of the room, lowering his voice to secret supplication, pleading with her really to meet him on the ground of

385

the negation of Mona. It was this betrayal of his need of support and sanction that made her retreat — harden herself in the effort to save what might remain of all she had given, given probably for nothing. The very vision of him as he thus morally clung to her was the vision of a weakness somewhere in the core of his bloom, a blessed manly weakness of which, if she had only the valid right, it would be all a sweetness to take care. She faintly sickened, however, with the sense that there was as yet no valid right poor Owen could give. 'You can take it from my honour, you know,' he whispered, 'that she loathes me.'

Fleda had stood clutching the knob of Maggie's little painted stair-rail ; she took, on the stairs, a step backward. 'Why then doesn't she prove it in the only clear way?'

'She *has* proved it. Will you believe it if you see the letter?'

'I don't want to see any letter,' said Fleda. 'You'll miss your train.'

Facing him, waving him away, she had taken another upward step ; but he sprang to the side of the stairs and brought his hand, above the banister, down hard on her wrist. 'Do you mean to tell me that I must marry a woman I hate?'

From her step she looked down into his raised face. 'Ah, you see it's not true that you're free! ' She seemed almost to exult. 'It's not true — it's not true! '

He only, at this, like a buffeting swimmer, gave a shake of his head and repeated his question. 'Do you mean to tell me I must marry such a woman?'

Fleda hesitated ; he held her fast. 'No. Anything is better than that.'

'Then, in God's name, what must I do?'

'You must settle that with her. You mustn't break faith. Anything is better than that. You must at any rate be utterly sure. She *must* love you — how can she help it? *I* wouldn't give you up! ' said Fleda. She spoke in broken bits panting out her words. 'The great thing is to keep faith. Where *is* a man if he doesn't? If he doesn't he may be so cruel. So cruel, so cruel, so cruel! ' Fleda repeated. 'I couldn't have a hand in *that*, you know: that's my position — that's mine. You offered her marriage: it's a tremendous thing for her.' Then looking at him another moment, '*I* wouldn't give you up!' she said again. He still had hold of her arm; she took in his blank alarm. With a quick dip of her face she reached his hand with her lips, pressing them to the back of it with a force of her words. 'Never, never, never!' she cried; and before he could succeed in seizing her she had turned and, scrambling up the stairs, got away from him even faster than she had got away from him at Ricks.

CHAPTER 17

TEN days after his visit she received a communication from Mrs Gereth – a telegram of eight words, exclusive of signature and date. 'Come up immediately and stay with me here' – it was characteristically sharp, as Maggie said; but, as Maggie added, it was also characteristically kind. 'Here' was an hotel in London, and Maggie had embraced a condition of life which already began to produce in her some yearning for hotels in London. She would have responded in an instant, and she was surprised that her sister seemed to hesitate. Fleda's hesitation, which lasted but an hour, was expressed in that young lady's own mind by the reflection that in obeying her friend's summons she shouldn't know what she should be 'in for'. Her friend's summons, however, was but another name for her friend's appeal; and Mrs Gereth's bounty had laid her under obligations more sensible than any reluctance. In the event – that is at the end of her hour – she testified to her gratitude by taking the train and to her mistrust by leaving her luggage. She went as if she had gone up for the day. In the train, however, she had another thoughtful hour, during which it was her mistrust that mainly deepened. She felt as if for ten days she had sat in darkness, looking to the east for a dawn that had not yet glimmered. Her mind had lately been less occupied with Mrs Gereth; it had been so exceptionally occupied with Mona. If the sequel was to justify Owen's prevision of Mrs Brigstock's action upon her daughter, this action was at the end of a week as much a mystery as ever. The stillness, all round, had been exactly what Fleda desired, but it gave her for the time a deep sense of failure, the sense of a sudden drop from a height at which she had all things beneath her. She had nothing beneath her now; she herself was at the bottom of the heap. No sign had reached her from Owen – poor Owen, who had clearly no news to give about his precious letter from Waterbath. If Mrs Brigstock had hurried back to obtain that this letter should be written, Mrs

Brigstock might then have spared herself so great an inconvenience. Owen had been silent for the best of all reasons – the reason that he had had nothing in life to say. If the letter had not been written he would simply have had to introduce some large qualification into his account of his freedom. He had left his young friend under her refusal to listen to him until he should be able, on the contrary, to extend that picture ; and his present submission was all in keeping with the rigid honesty that his young friend had prescribed.

It was this that formed the element through which Mona loomed large ; Fleda had enough imagination, a fine enough feeling for life, to be impressed with such an image of successful immobility. The massive maiden at Waterbath *was* successful from the moment she could entertain her resentments as if they had been poor relations who needn't put her to expense. She was a magnificent dead weight ; there was something positive and portentous in her quietude. 'What game are they all playing?' poor Fleda could only ask ; for she had an intimate conviction that Owen was now under the roof of his betrothed. That was stupefying if he really hated Mona ; and if he didn't really hate her what had brought him to Raphael Road and to Maggie's? Fleda had no real light, but she felt that to account for the absence of any result of their last meeting would take a supposition of the full sacrifice to charity that she had held up before him. If he had gone to Waterbath it had been simply because he had to go. She had as good as told him that he would have to go ; that this was an inevitable incident of his keeping perfect faith – faith so literal that the smallest subterfuge would always be a reproach to him. When she tried to remember that it was for herself he was taking his risk, she felt how weak a way that was of expressing Mona's supremacy. There would be no need of keeping him up if there were nothing to keep him up to. Her eyes grew wan as she discerned in the impenetrable air that Mona's thick outline never wavered an inch. She wondered fitfully what Mrs Gereth had by this time made of it, and reflected with a strange elation that the sand on which the mistress of Ricks had built a momentary triumph was quaking beneath the surface. As the *Morning Post* still held its peace, she would be, of course, more confident ;

but the hour was at hand at which Owen would have absolutely to do either one thing or the other. To keep perfect faith was to inform against his mother, and to hear the police at her door would be Mrs Gereth's awakening. How much she was beguiled Fleda could see from her having been for a whole month quite as deep and dark as Mona. She had let her young friend alone because of the certitude, cultivated at Ricks, that Owen had done the opposite. He had done the opposite indeed, but much good had that brought forth! To have sent for her now, Fleda felt, was from this point of view wholly natural: she had sent for her to show at last how much she had scored. If, however, Owen was really at Waterbath the refutation of that boast was easy.

Fleda found Mrs Gereth in modest apartments and with an air of fatigue in her distinguished face – a sign, as she privately remarked, of the strain of that effort to be discreet of which she herself had been having the benefit. It was a constant feature of their relation that this lady could make Fleda blench a little, and that the effect proceeded from the intense pressure of her confidence. If the confidence had been heavy even when the girl, in the early flush of devotion, had been able to feel herself most responsive, it drew her heart into her mouth now that she had reserves and conditions, now that she couldn't simplify with the same bold hand as her protectress. In the very brightening of the tired look, and at the moment of their embrace, Fleda felt on her shoulders the return of the load, so that her spirit frankly quailed as she asked herself what she had brought up from her trusted seclusion to support it. Mrs Gereth's free manner always made a joke of weakness, and there was in such a welcome a richness, a kind of familiar nobleness, that suggested shame to a harried conscience. Something had happened, she could see, and she could also see, in the bravery that seemed to announce it had changed everything, a formidable assumption that what had happened was that a healthy young woman must like. The absence of luggage had made this young woman feel meagre even before her companion, taking in the bareness at a second glance, exclaimed upon it and roundly rebuked her. Of course she had expected her to stay.

Fleda thought best to show bravery too, and to show it from

390

the first. 'What you expected, dear Mrs Gereth, is exactly what I came up to ascertain. It struck me as right to do that first. I mean to ascertain without making preparations.'

'Then you'll be so good as to make them on the spot!' Mrs Gereth was most emphatic. 'You're going abroad with me.'

Fleda wondered, but she also smiled. 'Tonight – tomorrow?'

'In as few days as possible. That's all that's left for me now.' Fleda's heart, at this, gave a bound; she wondered to what particular difference in Mrs Gereth's situation as last known to her it was an allusion. 'I've made my plan,' her friend continued: 'I go for at least a year. We shall go straight to Florence; we can manage there. I of course don't look to you, however,' she added, 'to stay with me all that time. That will require to be settled. Owen will have to join us as soon as possible; he may not be quite ready to get off with us. But I'm convinced it's quite the right thing to go. It will make a good change; it will put in a decent interval.'

Fleda listened; she was deeply mystified. 'How kind you are to me!' she presently said. The picture suggested so many questions that she scarcely knew which to ask first. She took one at a venture. 'You really have it from Mr Gereth that he'll give us his company?'

If Mr Gereth's mother smiled in response to this, Fleda knew that her smile was a tacit criticism of such a form of reference to her son. Fleda habitually spoke of him as Mr Owen, and it was a part of her present vigilance to appear to have relinquished that right. Mrs Gereth's manner confirmed a certain impression of her pretending to more than she felt; her very first words had conveyed it, and it reminded Fleda of the conscious courage with which, weeks before, the lady had met her visitor's first startled stare at the clustered spoils of Poynton. It was her practice to take immensely for granted whatever she wished. 'Oh, if you'll answer for him, it will do quite as well!' she said. Then she put her hands on the girl's shoulders and held them at arm's length, as if to shake them a little, while in the depths of her shining eyes Fleda discovered something obscure and unquiet. 'You bad, false thing, why didn't you tell me?' Her tone softened her harshness, and her visitor had never had such a sense of her indulgence. Mrs

Gereth could show patience; it was a part of the general bribe, but it was also like the handing in of a heavy bill before which Fleda could only fumble in a penniless pocket. 'You must perfectly have known at Ricks, and yet you practically denied it. That's why I call you bad and false!' It was apparently also why she again almost roughly kissed her.

'I think that before I answer you I had better know what you're talking about,' Fleda said.

Mrs Gereth looked at her with a slight increase of hardness. 'You've done everything you need for modesty, my dear! If he's sick with love of you, you haven't had to wait for me to inform you.'

Fleda hesitated. 'Has he informed *you*, dear Mrs Gereth?'

Dear Mrs Gereth smiled sweetly. 'How could he, when our situation is such that he communicates with me only through you, and that you are so tortuous you conceal everything?'

'Didn't he answer the note in which you let him know that I was in town?' Fleda asked.

'He answered it sufficiently by rushing off on the spot to see you.'

Mrs Gereth met that allusion with a prompt firmness that made almost insolently light of any ground of complaint, and Fleda's own sense of responsibility was now so vivid that all resentments turned comparatively pale. She had no heart to produce a grievance; she could only, left as she was with the little mystery on her hands, produce, after a moment, a question. 'How then do you come to know that your son has ever thought – '

'That he would give his ears to get you?' Mrs Gereth broke in. 'I had a visit from Mrs Brigstock.'

Fleda opened her eyes. 'She went down to Ricks?'

'The day after she had found Owen at your feet. She knows everything.'

Fleda shook her head sadly; she was more startled than she cared to show. This odd journey of Mrs Brigstock's, which, with a simplicity equal for once to Owen's, she had not divined, now struck her as having produced the hush of the last ten days. 'There are things she doesn't know!' she presently exclaimed.

392

'She knows he would do anything to marry you.'

'He hasn't told her so,' Fleda said.

'No, but he has told you. That's better still!' laughed Mrs Gereth. 'My dear child,' she went on with an air that affected the girl as a sort of blind profanity, 'don't try to make yourself out better than you are. *I* know what you are. I haven't lived with you so much for nothing. You're not quite a saint in heaven yet. Lord, what a creature you'd have thought me in my good time! But you do like it, fortunately, you idiot. You're pale with your passion, you sweet thing. That's exactly what I wanted to see. I can't for the life of me think where the shame comes in.' Then with a finer significance, a look that seemed to Fleda strange, she added: 'It's all right.'

'I've seen him but twice,' said Fleda.

'But twice?' Mrs Gereth still smiled.

'On the occasion, at papa's, that Mrs Brigstock told you of, and one day, since then, down at Maggie's.'

'Well, those things are between yourselves, and you seem to me both poor creatures at best.' Mrs Gereth spoke with a rich humour which tipped with light for an instant a real conviction. 'I don't know what you've got in your veins: you absurdly exaggerated the difficulties. But enough is as good as a feast, and when once I get you abroad together – !' She checked herself as if from excess of meaning; what might happen when she should get them abroad together was to be gathered only from the way she slowly rubbed her hands.

The gesture, however, made the promise so definite that for a moment her companion was almost beguiled. But there was nothing to account, as yet, for the wealth of Mrs Gereth's certitude: the visit of the lady of Waterbath appeared but half to explain it. 'Is it permitted to be surprised,' Fleda deferentially asked, 'at Mrs Brigstock's thinking it would help her to see you?'

'It's never permitted to be surprised at the aberrations of born fools,' said Mrs Gereth. 'If a cow should try to calculate, that's the kind of happy thought she'd have. Mrs Brigstock came down to plead with me.'

Fleda mused a moment. 'That's what she came to do with *me*,' she then honestly returned. 'But what did she expect to get of you, with your opposition so marked from the first?'

'She didn't know I want *you*, my dear. It's a wonder, with all my violence – the gross publicity I've given my desires. But she's as stupid as an owl – she doesn't feel your charm.'

Fleda felt herself flush slightly, but she tried to smile. 'Did you tell her all about it? Did you make her understand you want me?'

'For what do you take me? I wasn't such a donkey.'

'So as not to aggravate Mona?' Fleda suggested.

'So as not to aggravate Mona, naturally. We've had a narrow course to steer, but thank God we're at last in the open!'

'What do you call the open, Mrs Gereth?' Fleda demanded. Then as the other faltered: 'Do you know where Mr Owen is today?'

Mrs Gereth stared. 'Do you mean he's at Waterbath? Well, that's your own affair. I can bear it if *you* can.'

'Wherever he is, I can bear it,' Fleda said. 'But I haven't the least idea where he is.'

'Then you ought to be ashamed of yourself!' Mrs Gereth broke out with a change of note that showed how deep a passion underlay everything she had said. The poor woman, catching her companion's hand, however, the next moment, as if to retract something of this harshness, spoke more patiently. 'Don't you understand, Fleda, how immensely, how devotedly, I've trusted you?' Her tone was indeed a supplication.

Fleda was infinitely shaken; she was silent a little. 'Yes, I understand. Did she go to you to complain of me?'

'She came to see what she could do. She had been tremendously upset, the day before, by what had taken place at your father's, and she had posted down to Ricks on the inspiration of the moment. She hadn't meant it on leaving home; it was the sight of you closeted there with Owen that had suddenly determined her. The whole story, she said, was written in your two faces: she spoke as if she had never seen such an exhibition. Owen was on the brink, but there might still be time to save him, and it was with this idea she had bearded me in my den. "What won't a mother do, you know?" – that was one of the things she said. What wouldn't a mother do indeed? I thought I had sufficiently shown her what! She tried to break me down by an appeal to my good nature, as she called it, and from the moment she opened on *you*, from the moment she denounced Owen's falsity, I was as good-natured as she could wish. I understood that it was a plea for mere mercy, that you and he between you were killing her child. Of course I was delighted that Mona should be killed, but I was studiously kind to Mrs Brigstock. At the same time I was honest. I didn't pretend to anything I couldn't feel. I asked her why the marriage hadn't taken place months ago, when Owen was perfectly ready; and I showed her how completely that fatuous mistake on Mona's part cleared his responsibility. It was she who had killed *him* – it was she who had destroyed his affection, his illusions. Did she want him now when he was estranged, when he was disgusted, when he had a sore grievance? She reminded me that Mona had a sore grievance too, but she admitted that she hadn't come to me to speak of that. What she had come to me for was not to get the old things back, but simply to get Owen. What she wanted was that I would, in simple pity, see fair play. Owen had been awfully bedevilled – she didn't call it that, she called it "misled" – but it was simply you who had bedevilled him. He would be all right still if I would see that you were out of the way. She asked me point-blank if it was possible I could want him to marry you.'

Fleda had listened in unbearable pain and growing terror, as if her interlocutress, stone by stone, were piling some fatal mass upon her breast. She had the sense of being buried alive, smothered in the mere expansion of another will; and now there was but one gap left to the air. A single word, she felt, might close it, and with the question that came to her lips as Mrs Gereth paused she seemed to herself to ask, in cold dread, for her doom. 'What did you say to that?' she inquired.

'I was embarrassed, for I saw my danger – the danger of her going home and saying to Mona that I was backing you up. It had been a bliss to learn that Owen had really turned to you, but my joy didn't put me off my guard. I reflected intensely for a few seconds; then I saw my issue.'

'Your issue?' Fleda murmured.

'I remembered how you had tied my hands about saying a word to Owen.'

Fleda wondered. 'And did you remember the little letter that, with your hands tied, you still succeeded in writing to him?'

'Perfectly; my little letter was a model of reticence. What I remembered was all that in those few words I forbade myself to say. I had been an angel of delicacy – I had effaced myself like a saint. It was not for me to have done all that and then figure to such a woman as having done the opposite. Besides, it was none of her business.'

'Is that what you said to her?' Fleda asked.

'I said to her that her question revealed a total misconception of the nature of my present relations with my son. I said to her that I had no relations with him at all, and that nothing had passed between us for months. I said to her that my hands were spotlessly clean of any attempt to make him make up to you. I said to her that I had taken from Poynton what I had a right to take, but had done nothing else in the world. I was determined that if I had bit my tongue off to oblige you I would at least have the righteousness that my sacrifice gave me.'

'And was Mrs Brigstock satisfied with your answer?'

'She was visibly relieved.'

'It was fortunate for you,' said Fleda, 'that she's apparently not aware of the manner in which, almost under her nose, you advertised me to him at Poynton.'

Mrs Gereth appeared to recall that scene; she smiled with a serenity remarkably effective as showing how cheerfully used she had grown to invidious allusions to it. 'How should she be aware of it?'

'She would if Owen had described your outbreak to Mona.'

'Yes, but he didn't describe it. All his instinct was to conceal it from Mona. He wasn't conscious, but he was already in love with you!' Mrs Gereth declared.

Fleda shook her head wearily. 'No – I was only in love with him!'

Here was a faint illumination with which Mrs Gereth instantly mingled her fire. 'You dear old wretch!' she exclaimed; and she again, with ferocity, embraced her young friend.

Fleda submitted like a sick animal: she would submit to everything now. 'Then what further passed?'

'Only that she left me thinking she had got something.'

'And what had she got?'

'Nothing but her luncheon. But *I* got everything!'

'Everything?' Fleda quavered.

Mrs Gereth, struck apparently by something in her tone, looked at her from a tremendous height. 'Don't fail me now!'

It sounded so like a menace that, with a full divination at last, the poor girl fell weakly into a chair. 'What on earth have you done?'

Mrs Gereth stood there in all the glory of a great stroke. 'I've settled you.' She filled the room, to Fleda's scared vision, with the glare of her magnificence. 'I've sent everything back.'

'Everything?' Fleda gasped.

'To the smallest snuff-box. The last load went yesterday. The same people did it. Poor little Ricks is empty.' Then as if, for a crowning splendour, to check all deprecation: 'They're yours, you goose!' Mrs Gereth concluded, holding up her handsome head and rubbing her white hands. Fleda saw that there were tears in her deep eyes.

CHAPTER 18

SHE was slow to take in the announcement, but when she had done so she felt it to be more than her cup of bitterness would hold. Her bitterness was her anxiety, the taste of which suddenly sickened her. What had she become, on the spot, but a traitress to her friend? The treachery increased with the view of the friend's motive, a motive magnificent as a tribute to her value. Mrs Gereth had wished to make sure of her and had reasoned that there would be no such way as by a large appeal to her honour. If it be true, as men have declared, that the sense of honour is weak in women, some of the bearings of this stroke might have thrown a light on the question. What was now, at all events, put before Fleda was that she had been made sure of, for the greatness of the surrender imposed an obligation as great. There was an expression she had heard used by young men with whom she danced: the only word to fit Mrs Gereth's intention was that Mrs Gereth had designed to 'fetch' her. It was a calculated, it was a crushing bribe ; it looked her in the eyes and said simply: 'That's what I do for you! ' What Fleda was to do in return required no pointing out. The sense, at present, of how little she had done made her almost cry aloud with pain ; but her first endeavour, in the face of the fact, was to keep such a cry from reaching her companion. How little she had done Mrs Gereth didn't yet know, and possibly there would be still some way of turning round before the discovery. On her own side too Fleda had almost made one: she had known she was wanted, but she had not after all conceived how magnificently much. She had been treated by. her friend's act as a conscious prize, but what made her a conscious prize was only the power the act itself imputed to her. As high, bold diplomacy it dazzled and carried her off her feet. She admired the noble risk of it, a risk Mrs Gereth had faced for the utterly poor creature that the girl now felt herself. The change it instantly wrought in her was, moreover, extraordinary: it transformed at a touch her emotion on the subject of concessions. A few weeks earlier she had jumped at the duty of pleading for them, practically quarrelling with the lady of Ricks for her refusal to restore what she had taken. She had been sore with the wrong to Owen, she had bled with the wounds of Poynton; now however, as she heard of the replenishment of the void that had so haunted her, she came as near sounding an alarm as if from the deck of a ship she had seen a person she loved jump into the sea. Mrs Gereth had become in a flash the victim; poor little Ricks had been laid bare in a night. If Fleda's feeling about the old things had taken precipitate form the form would have been a frantic command. It was indeed for mere want of breath that she didn't shout: 'Oh, stop them – it's no use ; bring them back – it's too late!' And what most kept her breathless was her companion's very grandeur. Fleda distinguished as never before the purity of such a passion; it made Mrs Gereth august and almost sublime. It was absolutely unselfish – she cared nothing for mere possession. She thought solely and incorruptibly of what was best for the things ; she had surrendered them to the presumptive care of the one person of her acquaintance who felt about them as she felt herself, and whose long lease of the future would be the nearest approach that could be compassed to committing them to a museum. Now it was indeed that Fleda knew what rested on her ; now it was also that she measured as if for the first time Mrs Gereth's view of the natural influence of a fine acquisition. She had adopted the idea of blowing away the last doubt of what her young friend would gain, of making good still more than she was obliged to make it the promise of weeks before. It was one thing for the girl to have heard that in a certain event restitution would be made; it was another for her to see the condition, with a noble trust, treated in advance as performed, and to be able to feel that she should have only to open a door to find every old piece in every old corner. To have played such a card was therefore, practically, for Mrs Gereth, to have won the game. Fleda had certainly to recognize that, so far as the theory of the matter went, the game had been won. Oh, she had been made sure of!

She couldn't, however, succeed for so many minutes in deferring her exposure. 'Why didn't you wait, dearest? Ah, why didn't you wait?' – if that inconsequent appeal kept rising to her lips to be cut short before it was spoken, this was only because at first the humility of gratitude helped her to gain time, enabled her to present herself very honestly as too over-come to be clear. She kissed her companion's hands, she did homage at her feet, she murmured soft snatches of praise, and yet in the midst of it all was conscious that what she really showed most was the wan despair at her heart. She saw Mrs Gereth's glimpse of this despair suddenly widen, heard the quick chill of her voice pierce through the false courage of endearments. 'Do you mean to tell me at such an hour as this that you've really lost him?'

The tone of the question made the idea a possibility for which Fleda had nothing from this moment but terror. 'I don't know, Mrs Gereth; how can I say?' she asked. 'I've not seen him for so long; as I told you just now, I don't even know where he is. That's by no fault of his,' she hurried on: 'he would have been with me every day if I had consented. But I made him understand, the last time, that I'll receive him again only when he's able to show me that his release has been com-plete and definite. Oh, he can't yet, don't you see, and that's why he hasn't been back. It's far better than his coming only that we should both be miserable. When he does come he'll be in a better position. He'll be tremendously moved by the splen-did thing you've done. I know you wish me to feel that you've done it as much for me as for Owen, but your having done it for me is just what will delight him most! When he hears of it,' said Fleda, in desperate optimism, 'when he hears of it – '
There indeed, regretting her advance, she quite broke down. She was wholly powerless to say what Owen would do when he heard of it. 'I don't know what he won't make of you and how he won't hug you!' she had to content herself with lamely declaring. She had drawn Mrs Gereth to a sofa with a vague instinct of pacifying her and still, after all, gaining time ; but it was a position in which her great duped benefactress, por-tentously patient again during this demonstration, looked far from inviting a 'hug'. Fleda found herself tricking out the situation with artificial flowers, trying to talk even herself into the fancy that Owen, whose name she now made simple and

400

sweet, might come in upon them at any moment. She felt an immense need to be understood and justified; she averted her face in dread from all that she might have to be forgiven. She pressed on her companion's arm as if to keep her quiet till she should really know, and then, after a minute, she poured out the clear essence of what in happier days had been her 'secret'. 'You mustn't think I don't adore him when I've told him so to his face. I love him so that I'd die for him – I love him so that it's horrible. Don't look at me therefore as if I had not been kind, as if I had not been as tender as if he were dying and my tenderness were what would save him. Look at me as if you believe me, as if you feel what I've been through. Darling Mrs Gereth, I could kiss the ground he walks on. I haven't a rag of pride ; I used to have, but it's gone. I used to have a secret, but everyone knows it now, and anyone who looks at me can say, I think, what's the matter with me. It's not so very fine, my secret, and the less one really says about it the better ; but I want you to have it from me because I was stiff before. I want you to see for yourself that I've been brought as low as a girl can very well be. It serves me right,' Fleda laughed, 'if I was ever proud and horrid to you! I don't know what you wanted me, in those days at Ricks, to do, but I don't think you can have wanted much more than what I've done. The other day at Maggie's I did things that made me, afterwards, think of you! I don't know what girls may do ; but if he doesn't know that there isn't an inch of me that isn't his – ! ' Fleda sighed as if she couldn't express it ; she piled it up, as she would have said ; holding Mrs Gereth with dilated eyes, she seemed to sound her for the effect of these words. 'It's idiotic,' she wearily smiled ; 'it's so strange that I'm almost angry for it, and the strangest part of all is that it isn't even happiness. It's anguish – it was from the first; from the first there was a bitterness and a kind of dread. But I owe you every word of the truth. You don't do him justice, either: he's a dear, I assure you he's a dear. I'd trust him to the last breath ; I don't think you really know him. He's ever so much cleverer than he makes a show of ; he's remarkable in his own shy way. You told me at Ricks that you wanted me to let myself go, and I've "gone" quite far enough to discover as much as that, as well as all sorts of other delightful things about him. You'll tell me I make myself out worse than I am,' said the girl, feeling more and more in her companion's attitude a quality that treated her speech as a desperate rigmarole and even perhaps as a piece of cold immodesty. She wanted to make herself out 'bad' – it was a part of her justification ; but it suddenly occured to her that such a picture of her extravagance imputed a want of gallantry to the young man. 'I don't care for anything you think,' she declared, 'because Owen, don't you know, sees me as I am. He's so kind that it makes up for everything!'

This attempt at gaiety was futile ; the silence with which, for a minute, her adversary greeted her troubled plea brought home to her afresh that she was on the bare defensive. 'Is it a part of his kindness never to come near you?' Mrs Gereth inquired at last. 'Is it a part of his kindness to leave you without an inkling of where he is?' She rose again from where Fleda had kept her down ; she seemed to tower there in the majesty of her gathered wrong. 'Is it a part of his kindness that, after I've toiled as I've done for six days, and with my own weak hands, which I haven't spared, to denude myself, in your interest, to that point that I've nothing left, as I may say, but what I have on my back – it is a part of his kindness that you're not even able to produce him for me?'

There was a high contempt in this which was for Owen quite as much, and in the light of which Fleda felt that her effort at plausibility had been mere grovelling. She rose from the sofa with an humiliated sense of rising from ineffectual knees. That discomfort, however, lived but an instant: it was swept away in a rush of loyalty to the absent. She herself could bear his mother's scorn ; but to avert it from his sweet innocence she broke out with a quickness that was like the raising of an arm. 'Don't blame him – don't blame him: he'd do anything on earth for me! It was I,' said Fleda, eagerly, 'who sent him back to her ; I made him go ; I pushed him out of the house ; I declined to have anything to say to him except on another footing.'

Mrs Gereth stared as at some gross material ravage. 'Another footing? What other footing?'

'The one I've already made so clear to you: my having it in

black and white, as you may say, from her that she freely gives him up.'

'Then you think he lies when he tells you that he has recovered his liberty?'

Fleda hesitated a moment; after which she exclaimed with a certain hard pride: 'He's enough in love with me for anything!'

'For anything, apparently, except to act like a man and impose his reason and his will on your incredible folly. For anything except to put an end, as any man worthy of the name, would have put it, to your systematic, to your idiotic perversity. What are you, after all, my dear, I should like to know, that a gentleman who offers you what Owen offers should have to meet such wonderful exactions, to take such extraordinary precautions about your sweet little scruples?' Her resentment rose to a strange insolence which Fleda took full in the face and which, for the moment at least, had the horrible force to present to her vengefully a showy side of the truth. It gave her a blinding glimpse of lost alternatives. 'I don't know what to think of him,' Mrs Gereth went on; 'I don't know what to call him: I'm so ashamed of him that I can scarcely speak of him even to *you*. But indeed I'm so ashamed of you both together that I scarcely know in common decency where to look.' She paused to give Fleda the full benefit of this remarkable statement; then she exclaimed: 'Anyone but a jackass would have tucked you under his arm and marched you off to the Registrar!'

Fleda wondered; with her free imagination she could wonder even while her cheek stung from a slap. 'To the Registrar?'

'That would have been the sane, sound, immediate course to adopt. With a grain of gumption you'd both instantly have felt it. *I* should have found a way to take you, you know, if I'd been what Owen's supposed to be. *I* should have got the business over first; the rest could come when you liked! Good God, girl, your place was to stand before me as a woman honestly married. One doesn't know what one has hold of in touching you, and you must excuse my saying that you're literally unpleasant to me to meet as you are. Then at least we could have talked, and Owen, if he had the ghost of a sense

403

of humour, could have snapped his fingers at your refinements.'

This stirring speech affected our young lady as if it had been the shake of a tambourine borne towards her from a gypsy dance: her head seemed to go round and she felt a sudden passion in her feet. The emotion, however, was but meagrely expressed in the flatness with which she heard herself presently say: 'I'll go to the Registrar now.'

'Now?' Magnificent was the sound Mrs Gereth threw into this monosyllable. 'And pray who's to take you?' Fleda gave a colourless smile, and her companion continued: 'Do you literally mean that you can't put your hand upon him?' Fleda's wan grimace appeared to irritate her ; she made a short, imperious gesture. 'Find him for me, you fool – *find* him for me !'

'What do you want of him,' Fleda sadly asked, 'feeling as you do to both of us?'

'Never mind how I feel, and never mind what I say when I'm furious!' Mrs Gereth still more incisively added. 'Of course I cling to you, you wretches, or I shouldn't suffer as I do. What I want of him is to see that he takes you ; what I want of him is to go with you myself to the place.' She looked round the room as if, in feverish haste, for a mantle to catch up ; she bustled to the window as if to spy out a cab: she would allow half an hour for the job. Already in her bonnet, she had snatched from the sofa a garment for the street: she jerked it on as she came back. 'Find him, find him,' she repeated ; 'come straight out with me, to try, at least, to get at him !'

'How can I get at him? He'll come when he's ready,' Fleda replied.

Mrs Gereth turned on her sharply. 'Ready for what? Ready to see me ruined without a reason or a reward?'

Fleda was silent ; the worst of it all was that there was something unspoken between them. Neither of them dared to utter it, but the influence of it was in the girl's tone when she returned at last, with great gentleness: 'Don't be harsh to me – I'm very unhappy.' The words produced a visible impression on Mrs Gereth, who held her face averted and sent off through the window a gaze that kept pace with the long caravan of her treasures. Fleda knew she was watching it wind up the avenue of Poynton – Fleda participated indeed fully in the vision ; so that after a little the most consoling thing seemed to her to add: 'I don't see why in the world you take so for granted that he's, as you say, "lost".'

Mrs Gereth continued to stare out of the window, and her stillness denoted some success in controlling herself. 'If he's not lost, why are you unhappy?'

'I'm unhappy because I torment you, and you don't understand me.'

'No, Fleda, I don't understand you,' said Mrs Gereth, finally facing her again. 'I don't understand you at all, and it's as if you and Owen were of quite another race and another flesh. You make me feel very old-fashioned and simple and bad. But you must take me as I am, since you take so much else *with* me!' She spoke now with the drop of her resentment, with a dry and weary calm. 'It would have been better for me if I had never known you,' she pursued, 'and certainly better if I hadn't taken such an extraordinary fancy to you. But that too was inevitable: everything, I suppose, is inevitable. It was all my own doing — you didn't run after me: I pounced on you and caught you up. You're a stiff little beggar, in spite of your pretty manners: yes, you're hideously misleading. I hope you feel how handsome it is of me to recognize the independence of your character. It was your clever sympathy that did it — your extraordinary feeling for those accursed vanities. You were sharper about them than anyone I had ever known, and that was a thing I simply couldn't resist. Well,' the poor lady concluded after a pause, 'you see where it has landed us!'

'If you'll go for him yourself, I'll wait here,' said Fleda.

Mrs Gereth, holding her mantle together, appeared for a while to consider.

'To his club, do you mean?'

'Isn't it there, when he's in town, that he has a room? He has at present no other London address,' Fleda said: 'It's there one writes to him.'

'How do *I* know, with my wretched relations with him?' Mrs Gereth asked.

'Mine have not been quite so bad as that,' Fleda desperately smiled. Then she added: 'His silence, *her* silence, our hearing

405

nothing at all – what are these but the very things on which, at Poynton and at Ricks, you rested your assurance that everything is at an end between them?'

Mrs Gereth looked dark and void. 'Yes, but I hadn't heard from you then that you could invent nothing better than, as you call it, to send him back to her.'

'Ah, but, on the other hand, you've learned from them what you didn't know – you've learned by Mrs Brigstock's visit that he cares for me.' Fleda found herself in the position of availing herself of optimistic arguments that she formerly had repudiated ; her refutation of her companion had completely changed its ground.

She was in a fever of ingenuity and painfully conscious, on behalf of her success, that her fever was visible. She could herself see the reflection of it glitter in Mrs Gereth's sombre eyes.

'You plunge me in stupefaction,' that lady answered, 'and at the same time you terrify me. Your account of Owen is inconceivable, and yet I don't know what to hold on by. He cares for you, it does appear, and yet in the same breath you inform me that nothing is more possible than that he's spending these days at Waterbath. Excuse me if I'm so dull as not to see my way in such darkness. If he's at Waterbath he doesn't care for you. If he cares for you he's not at Waterbath.'

'Then where is he?' poor Fleda helplessly wailed. She caught herself up, however ; she did her best to be brave and clear. Before Mrs Gereth could reply, with due obviousness, that this was a question for her not to ask, but to answer, she found an air of assurance to say: 'You simplify far too much. You always did and you always will. The tangle of life is much more intricate than you've ever, I think, felt it to be. You slash into it,' cried Fleda finely, 'with a great pair of shears, you nip at it as if you were one of the Fates! If Owen's at Waterbath he's there to wind everything up.'

Mrs Gereth shook her head with slow austerity. 'You don't believe a word you're saying. I've frightened you, as you've frightened me: you're whistling in the dark to keep up our courage. I do simplify, doubtless, if to simplify is to fail to comprehend the insanity of a passion that bewilders a young blockhead with bugaboo barriers, with hideous and monstrous

406

sacrifices. I can only repeat that you're beyond me. Your perversity's a thing to howl over. However,' the poor woman continued with a break in her voice, a long hesitation, and then the dry triumph of her will, 'I'll never mention it to you again! Owen I can just make out ; for Owen *is* a blockhead. Owen's a blockhead,' she repeated with a quiet, tragic finality, looking straight into Fleda's eyes. 'I don't know why you dress up so the fact that he's disgustingly weak.'

Fleda hesitated ; at last, before her companion's, she lowered her look. 'Because I love him. It's because he's weak that he needs me,' she added.

'That was why his father, whom he exactly resembles, needed me. And I didn't fail his father,' said Mrs Gereth. She gave Fleda a moment to appreciate the remark ; after which she pursued: 'Mona Brigstock isn't weak ; she's stronger than you!'

'I never thought she was weak,' Fleda answered. She looked vaguely round the room with a new purpose: she had lost sight of her umbrella.

'I did tell you to let yourself go, but it's clear enough that you really haven't,' Mrs Gereth declared. 'If Mona has got him – '

Fleda had accomplished her search ; her interlocutress paused. 'If Mona has got him?' the girl inquired, tightening the umbrella.

'Well,' said Mrs Gereth profoundly, 'it will be clear enough that Mona *has*.'

'Has let herself go?'

'Has let herself go.' Mrs Gereth spoke as if she saw it in every detail.

Fleda felt the tone and finished her preparation ; then she went and opened the door. 'We'll look for him together,' she said to her friend, who stood a moment taking in her face. 'They may know something about him at the Colonel's.'

'We'll go there.' Mrs Gereth had picked up her gloves and her purse. 'But the first thing,' she went on, 'will be to wire to Poynton.'

'Why not to Waterbath at once?' Fleda asked.

Her companion hesitated. 'In *your* name?'

'In my name. I noticed a place at the corner.'

While Fleda held the door open Mrs Gereth drew on her gloves. 'Forgive me,' she presently said. 'Kiss me,' she added.

Fleda, on the threshold, kissed her ; then they went out.

CHAPTER 19

IN the place at the corner, on the chance of its saving time, Fleda wrote her telegram – wrote it in silence under Mrs Gereth's eye and then in silence handed it to her. 'I send this to Waterbath, on the possibility of your being there, to ask you to come to me.' Mrs Gereth held it a moment, read it more than once ; then keeping it, and with her eyes on her companion, seemed to consider. There was the dawn of a kindness in her look ; Fleda perceived in it, as if as the reward of complete submission, a slight relaxation of her rigour.

'Wouldn't it perhaps after all be better,' she asked, 'before doing this, to see if we can make his whereabouts certain?'

'Why so? It will be always so much done,' said Fleda. 'Though I'm poor,' she added with a smile, 'I don't mind the shilling.'

'The shilling's *my* shilling,' said Mrs Gereth.

Fleda stayed her hand. 'No, no – I'm superstitious.'

'Superstitious?'

'To succeed, it must be all me!'

'Well, if that will make it succeed!' Mrs Gereth took back her shilling, but she still kept the telegram. 'As he's most probably not there – '

'If he shouldn't be there,' Fleda interrupted, 'there will be no harm done.'

'If he "shouldn't be" there!' Mrs Gereth ejaculated. 'Heaven help us, how you assume it!'

'I'm only prepared for the worst. The Brigstocks will simply send any telegram on.'

'Where will they send it?'

'Presumably to Poynton.'

'They'll read it first,' said Mrs Gereth.

'Read it?'

'Yes, Mona will. She'll open it under the pretext of having it repeated ; and then she'll probably do nothing. She'll keep it as a proof of your immodesty.'

'What of that?' asked Fleda.

'You don't mind her seeing it?'

Rather musingly and absently Fleda shook her head. 'I don't mind anything.'

'Well, then, that's all right,' said Mrs Gereth as if she had only wanted to feel that she had been irreproachably considerate. After this she was gentler still, but she had another point to clear up. 'Why have you given, for a reply, your sister's address?'

'Because if he *does* come to me he must come to me there. If that telegram goes,' said Fleda, 'I return to Maggie's tonight.'

Mrs Gereth seemed to wonder at this. 'You won't receive him here with me?'

'No, I won't receive him here with you. Only where I received him last – only there again.' She showed her companion that as to that she was firm.

But Mrs Gereth had obviously now had some practice in following queer movements prompted by queer feelings. She resigned herself, though she fingered the paper a moment longer. She appeared to hesitate; then she brought out: 'You couldn't then, if I release you, make your message a little stronger?'

Fleda gave her a faint smile. 'He'll come if he can.'

Mrs Gereth met fully what this conveyed; with decision she pushed in the telegram. But she laid her hand quickly upon another form and with still greater decision wrote another message. 'From *me*, this,' she said to Fleda when she had finished, 'to catch him possibly at Poynton. Will you read it?'

Fleda turned away. 'Thank you.'

'It's stronger than yours.'

'I don't care,' said Fleda, moving to the door. Mrs Gereth, having paid for the second missive, rejoined her, and they drove together to Owen's club, where the elder lady alone got out. Fleda, from the hansom, watched through the glass doors her brief conversation with the hall-porter and then met in silence her return with the news that he had not seen Owen for a fortnight and was keeping his letters till called for. These had been the last orders; there were a dozen letters lying there. He had no more information to give, but they would see what they could find at Colonel Gereth's. To any connexion with this inquiry, however, Fleda now roused herself to object, and her friend had indeed to recognize that on second thoughts it couldn't be quite to the taste of either of them to advertise in the remoter reaches of the family that they had forfeited the confidence of the master of Poynton. The letters lying at the club proved effectively that he was not in London, and this was the question that immediately concerned them. Nothing could concern them further till the answers to their telegrams should have had time to arrive. Mrs Gereth had got back into the cab, and, still at the door of the club, they sat staring at their need of patience. Fleda's eyes rested, in the great hard street, on passing figures that struck her as puppets pulled by strings. After a little the driver challenged them through the hole in the top. 'Anywhere in particular, ladies?'

Fleda decided. 'Drive to Euston, please.'

'You won't wait for what we may hear?' Mrs Gereth asked.

'Whatever we hear, I must go.' As the cab went on she added: 'But I needn't drag *you* to the station.'

Mrs Gereth was silent a moment; then 'Nonsense!' she sharply replied.

In spite of this sharpness they were now almost equally and almost tremulously mild; though their mildness took mainly the form of an inevitable sense of nothing left to say. It was the unsaid that occupied them – the thing that for more than an hour had been going round and round without naming it. Much too early for Fleda's train, they encountered at the station a long half-hour to wait. Fleda made no further allusion to Mrs Gereth's leaving her; their dumbness, with the elapsing minutes, grew to be in itself a reconstituted bond. They slowly paced the great grey platform, and presently Mrs Gereth took the girl's arm and leaned on it with a hard demand for support. It seemed to Fleda not difficult for each to know of what the other was thinking – to know indeed that they had in common two alternating visions, one of which, at moments, brought them as by a common impulse to a pause.

411

This was the one that was fixed; the other filled at times the whole space and then was shouldered away. Owen and Mona glared together out of the gloom and disappeared, but the replenishment of Poynton made a shining, steady light. The old splendour was there again, the old things were in their places. Our friends looked at them with an equal yearning; face to face, on the platform, they counted them in each other's eyes. Fleda had come back to them by a road as strange as the road they themselves had followed. The wonder of their great journeys, the prodigy of this second one, was the question that made her occasionally stop. Several times she uttered it, asked how this and that difficulty had been met. Mrs Gereth replied with pale lucidity – was naturally the person most familiar with the truth that what she undertook was always somehow achieved. To do it was to do it – she had more than one kind of magnificence. She confessed there, audaciously enough, to a sort of arrogance of energy, and Fleda, going on again, her inquiry more than answered and her arm rendering service, flushed in her diminished identity, with the sense that such a woman was great.

'You do mean literally everything, to the last little miniature on the last little screen?'

'I mean literally everything. Go over them with the catalogue!'

Fleda went over them while they walked again; she had no need of the catalogue. At last she spoke once more: 'Even the Maltese cross?'

'Even the Maltese cross. Why not that as well as everything else? – especially as I remembered how you like it.'

Finally, after an interval, the girl exclaimed: 'But the mere fatigue of it, the exhaustion of such a feat! I drag you to and fro here while you must be ready to drop.'

'I'm very, very tired.' Mrs Gereth's slow head-shake was tragic. 'I couldn't do it again.'

'I doubt if they'd bear it again!'

'That's another matter: they'd bear it if I could. There won't have been, this time either, a shake or a scratch. But I'm too tired – I very nearly don't care.'

412

'You must sit down, then, till I go,' said Fleda. 'We must find a bench.'

'No. I'm tired of *them*: I'm not tired of you. This is the way for you to feel most how much I rest on you.' Fleda had a compunction, wondering as they continued to stroll whether it was right after all to leave her. She believed, however, that if the flame might for the moment burn low, it was far from dying out ; an impression presently confirmed by the way Mrs Gereth went on: 'But one's fatigue is nothing. The idea under which one worked kept one up. For you I *could* – I can still. Nothing will have mattered if *she's* not there.'

There was a question that this imposed, but Fleda at first found no voice to utter it: it was the thing that, between them, since her arrival, had been so consciously and vividly unsaid. Finally she was able to breathe: 'And if she *is* there – if she's there already?'

Mrs Gereth's rejoinder too hung back ; then when it came – from sad eyes as well as from lips barely moved – it was unexpectedly merciful. 'It will be very hard.' That was all, now ; and it was poignantly simple. The train Fleda was to take had drawn up ; the girl kissed her as if in farewell. Mrs Gereth submitted, then after a little brought out: 'If we *have* lost – '

'If we have lost?' Fleda repeated as she paused again.

'You'll all the same come abroad with me?'

'It will seem very strange to me if you want me. But whatever you ask, whatever you need, that I will always do.'

'I shall need your company,' said Mrs Gereth. Fleda wondered an instant if this were not practically a demand for penal submission – for a surrender that, in its complete humility, would be a long expiation. But there was none of the latent chill of the vindictive in the way Mrs Gereth pursued: 'We can always, as time goes on, talk of them together.'

'Of the old things?' Fleda had selected a third-class compartment: she stood a moment looking into it and at a fat woman with a basket who had already taken possession. 'Always?' she said, turning again to her companion. 'Never!'

she exclaimed. She got into the carriage, and two men with bags and boxes immediately followed, blocking up door and window so long that when she was able to look out again Mrs Gereth had gone.

CHAPTER 20

THERE came to her at her sister's no telegram in answer to
her own: the rest of that day and the whole of the next
elapsed without a word either from Owen or from his mother.
She was free, however, to her infinite relief, from any direct
dealing with suspense, and conscious, to her surprise, of
nothing that could show her, or could show Maggie and her
brother-in-law, that she was excited. Her excitement was
composed of pulses as swift and fine as the revolutions of a
spinning top: she supposed she was going round, but she went
round so fast that she couldn't even feel herself move. Her
emotion occupied some quarter of her soul that had closed its
doors for the day and shut out even her own sense of it ; she
might perhaps have heard something if she had pressed her
ear to a partition. Instead of that she sat with her patience
in a cold, still chamber from which she could look out in
quite another direction. This was to have achieved an equilib-
rium to which she couldn't have given a name: indifference,
resignation, despair were the terms of a forgotten tongue. The
time even seemed not long, for the stages of the journey were
the items of Mrs Gereth's surrender. The detail of that performance, which filled the scene, was what Fleda had now
before her eyes. The part of her loss that she could think of
was the reconstituted splendour of Poynton. It was the beauty
she was most touched by that, in tons, she had lost – the
beauty that, charged upon big wagons, had safely crept back
to its home. But the loss was a gain to memory and love ; it
was to her too, at last, that, in condonation of her treachery,
the old things had crept back. She greeted them with open
arms ; she thought of them hour after hour ; they made a
company with which solitude was warm and a picture that,
at this crisis, overlaid poor Maggie's scant mahogany. It was
really her obliterated passion that had revived, and with it an
immense assent to Mrs Gereth's early judgement of her. She
too, she felt, was of the religion, and like any other of the

415

passionately pious she could worship now even in the desert. Yes, it was all for her; far round as she had gone she had been strong enough: her love had gathered in the spoils. She wanted indeed no catalogue to count them over; the array of them, miles away, was complete; each piece, in its turn, was perfect to her; she could have drawn up a catalogue from memory. Thus again she lived with them, and she thought of them without a question of any personal right. That they might have been, that they might still be hers, that they were perhaps already another's, were ideas that had too little to say to her. They were nobody's at all – too proud, unlike base animals and humans, to be reducible to anything so narrow. It was Poynton that was theirs; they had simply recovered their own. The joy of that for them was the source of the strange peace in which the girl found herself floating.

It was broken on the third day by a telegram from Mrs Gereth. 'Shall be with you at 11.30 – don't meet me at station.' Fleda turned this over, but was sufficiently expert not to disobey the injunction. She had only an hour to take in its meaning, but that hour was longer than all the previous time. If Maggie had studied her convenience the day Owen came, Maggie was also at the present juncture a miracle of refinement. Increasingly and resentfully mystified, in spite of all reassurance, by the impression that Fleda suffered more than she gained from the grandeur of the Gereths, she had it at heart to exemplify the perhaps truer distinction of nature that characterized the house of Vetch. She was not, like poor Fleda, at everyone's beck, and the visitor was to see no more of her than what the arrangement of luncheon might tantaliz-ingly show. Maggie described herself to her sister as intending for a just provocation even the understanding she had had with her husband that he also should remain invisible. Fleda accordingly awaited alone the subject of so many manoeuvres – a period that was slightly prolonged even after the drawing-room door, at 11.30, was thrown open. Mrs Gereth stood there with a face that spoke plain, but no sound fell from her till the withdrawal of the maid, whose attention had immediately attached itself to the rearrangement of a window-blind and who seemed, while she bustled at it, to contribute to the pregnant silence; before the duration of which, however, she retreated with a sudden stare.

'He has done it,' said Mrs Gereth, turning her eyes avoidingly but not unperceivingly about her and in spite of herself dropping an opinion upon the few objects in the room. Fleda, on her side, in her silence, observed how characteristically she looked at Maggie's possessions before looking at Maggie's sister. The girl understood and at first had nothing to say; she was still dumb while Mrs Gereth selected, with hesitation, a seat less distasteful than the one that happened to be nearest. On the sofa near the window the poor woman finally showed what the two past days had done for the age of her face. Her eyes at last met Fleda's. 'It's the end.'

'They're married?'

'They're married.'

Fleda came to the sofa in obedience to the impulse to sit down by her; then paused before her while Mrs Gereth turned up a dead grey mask. A tired old woman sat there with empty hands in her lap. 'I've heard nothing,' said Fleda. 'No answer came.'

'That's the only answer. It's the answer to everything.' So Fleda saw; for a minute she looked over her companion's head and far away. 'He wasn't at Waterbath; Mrs Brigstock must have read your telegram and kept it. But mine, the one to Poynton, brought something. "We are here – what do you want?"' Mrs Gereth stopped as if with a failure of voice; on which Fleda sank upon the sofa and made a movement to take her hand. It met no response; there could be no attenuation. Fleda waited; they sat facing each other like strangers. 'I wanted to go down,' Mrs Gereth presently continued. 'Well, I went.'

All the girl's effort tended for the time to a single aim – that of taking the thing with outward detachment, speaking of it as having happened to Owen and to his mother and not in any degree to herself. Something at least of this was in the encouraging way she said: 'Yesterday morning?'

'Yesterday morning. I saw him.'

Fleda hesitated. 'Did you see *her*?'

'Thank God, no!'

417

Fleda laid on her arm a hand of vague comfort, of which Mrs Gereth took no notice. 'You've been capable, just to tell me, of this wretched journey, of this consideration that I don't deserve?'

'We're together, we're together,' said Mrs Gereth. She looked helpless as she sat there, her eyes, unseeingly enough, on a tall Dutch clock, old but rather poor, that Maggie had had as a wedding-gift and that eked out the bareness of the room.

To Fleda, in the face of the event, it appeared that this was exactly what they were not: the last inch of common ground, the ground of their past intercourse, had fallen from under them. Yet what was still there was the grand style of her companion's treatment of her. Mrs Gereth couldn't stand upon small questions, couldn't, in conduct, make small differences. 'You're magnificent!' her young friend exclaimed. 'There's a rare greatness in your generosity.'

'We're together, we're together,' Mrs Gereth lifelessly repeated. 'That's all we *are* now; it's all we have.' The words brought to Fleda a sudden vision of the empty little house at Ricks; such a vision might also have been what her companion found in the face of the stopped Dutch clock. Yet with this it was clear that she would now show no bitterness: she had done with that, had given the last drop to those horrible hours in London. No passion even was left to her, and her forbearance only added to the force with which she represented the final vanity of everything.

Fleda was so far from a wish to triumph that she was absolutely ashamed of having anything to say for herself ; but there was one thing, all the same, that not to say was impossible. 'That he has done it, that he couldn't *not* do it, shows how right I was.' It settled forever her attitude, and she spoke as if for her own mind; then after a little she added very gently, for Mrs Gereth's: 'That's to say, it shows that he was bound to her by an obligation that, however much he may have wanted to, he couldn't in any sort of honour break.'

Blanched and bleak, Mrs Gereth looked at her. 'What sort of an obligation do you call that? No such obligation exists for an hour between any man and any woman who have

418

hatred on one side. He had ended by hating her, and now he hates her more than ever.'

'Did he tell you so?' Fleda asked.

'No. He told me nothing but the great gawk of a fact. I saw him but for three minutes.' She was silent again, and Fleda, as before some lurid image of this interview, sat without speaking. 'Do you wish to appear as if you don't care?' Mrs Gereth presently demanded.

'I'm trying not to think of myself.'

'Then if you're thinking of Owen, how can you *bear* to think?'

Sadly and submissively Fleda shook her head; the slow tears had come into her eyes. 'I can't. I don't understand — I don't understand!' she broke out.

'*I* do, then.' Mrs Gereth looked hard at the floor. 'There was no obligation at the time you saw him last — when you sent him, hating her as he did, back to her.'

'If he went,' Fleda asked, 'doesn't that exactly prove that he recognized one?'

'He recognized rot! You know what *I* think of him.' Fleda knew; she had no wish to challenge a fresh statement. Mrs Gereth made one — it was her sole, faint flicker of passion — to the extent of declaring that he was too abjectly weak to deserve the name of a man. For all Fleda cared! — it was his weakness she loved in him. 'He took strange ways of pleasing you!' her friend went on. 'There was no obligation till suddenly, the other day, the situation changed.'

Fleda wondered. 'The other day?'

'It came to Mona's knowledge — I can't tell you how, but it came — that the things I was sending back had begun to arrive at Poynton. I had sent them for you, but it was *her* I touched.' Mrs Gereth paused; Fleda was too absorbed in her explanation to do anything but take blankly the full, cold breath of this. 'They were there, and that determined her.'

'Determined her to what?'

'To act, to take means.'

'To take means?' Fleda repeated.

'I can't tell you what they were, but they were powerful. She knew how,' said Mrs Gereth.

Fleda received with the same stoicism the quiet immensity of this allusion to the person who had not known how. But it made her think a little, and the thought found utterance, with unconscious irony, in the simple interrogation: 'Mona?'

'Why not? She's a brute.'

'But if he knew that so well, what chance was there in it for her?'

'How can I tell you? How can I talk of such horrors? I can only give you, of the situation, what I see. He knew it, yes. But as she couldn't make him forget it, she tried to make him like it. She tried and she succeeded: that's what she did. She's after all so much less of a fool than he. And what *else* had he originally liked?' Mrs Gereth shrugged her shoulders. 'She did what you wouldn't!' Fleda's face had grown dark with her wonder, but her friend's empty hands offered no balm to the pain in it. 'It was that if it was anything. Nothing else meets the misery of it. Then there was quick work. Before he could turn round he was married.'

Fleda, as if she had been holding her breath, gave the sigh of a listening child. 'At that place you spoke of in town?'

'At the Registrar's, like a pair of low atheists.'

The girl hesitated. 'What do people say of that? I mean the "world".'

'Nothing, because nobody knows. They're to be married on the 17th, at Waterbath church. If anything else comes out, everybody is a little prepared. It will pass for some stroke of diplomacy, some move in the game, some outwitting of *me*. It's known there has been a row with me.'

Fleda was mystified. 'People surely knew at Poynton,' she objected, 'if, as you say, she's there.'

'She was there, day before yesterday, only for a few hours. She met him in London and went down to see the things.'

Fleda remembered that she had seen them only once. 'Did *you* see them?' she then ventured to ask.

'Everything.'

'Are they right?'

'Quite right. There's nothing like them,' said Mrs Gereth. At this her companion took up one of her hands again and kissed it as she had done in London. 'Mona went back that night; she was not there yesterday. Owen stayed on,' she added.

Fleda stared. 'Then she's not to live there?'

'Rather! But not till after the public marriage.' Mrs Gereth seemed to muse; then she brought out: 'She'll live there alone.'

'Alone?'

'She'll have it to herself.'

'He won't live with her?'

'Never! But she's none the less his wife, and you're not,' said Mrs Gereth, getting up. 'Our only chance is the chance she may die.'

Fleda appeared to consider: she appreciated her visitor's magnanimous use of the plural. 'Mona won't die,' she replied.

'Well, *I* shall, thank God! Till then' – and with this, for the first time, Mrs Gereth put out her hand – 'don't desert me.'

Fleda took her hand, and her clasp of it was a reiteration of a promise already given. She said nothing, but her silence was an acceptance as responsible as the vow of a nun. The next moment something occurred to her. 'I musn't put myself in your son's way.'

Mrs Gereth gave a dry, flat laugh. 'You're prodigious! But how shall you possibly be more out of it? Owen and I – ' She didn't finish her sentence.

'That's your great feeling about *him*,' Fleda said: 'but how, after what has happened, can it be his about you?'

Mrs Gereth hesitated. 'How *do* you know what has happened? You don't know what I said to him.'

'Yesterday?'

'Yesterday.'

They looked at each other with a long, deep gaze. Then as Mrs Gereth seemed again about to speak, the girl, closing her eyes, made a gesture of strong prohibition. 'Don't tell me!'

'Merciful powers, how you worship him!' Mrs Gereth wonderingly moaned. It was, for Fleda, the shake that made the cup overflow. She had a pause, that of the child who takes time to know that he responds to an accident with pain; then,

421

dropping again on the sofa, she broke into tears. They were beyond control, they came in long sobs, which for a moment Mrs Gereth, almost with an air of indifference, stood hearing and watching. At last Mrs Gereth too sank down again. Mrs Gereth soundlessly, wearily wept.

CHAPTER 21

'IT looks just like Waterbath; but, after all, we bore *that* together': these words formed part of a letter in which, before the 17th, Mrs Gereth, writing from disfigured Ricks, named to Fleda the day on which she would be expected to arrive there on a second visit. 'I sha'n't, for a long time to come,' the missive continued, 'be able to receive anyone who may *like* it, who would try to smooth it down, and me with it ; but there are always things you and I can comfortably hate together, for you're the only person who comfortably understands. You don't understand quite everything, but of all my acquaintance you're far away the least stupid. For action you're no good at all; but action is over, for me, for ever, and you will have the great merit of knowing, when I'm brutally silent, what I shall be thinking about. Without setting myself up for your equal, I dare say I shall also know what are your own thoughts. Moreover, with nothing else but my four walls, you'll at any rate be a bit of furniture. For that, you know, a little, I've always taken you – quite one of my best finds. So come, if possible, on the 15th.'

The position of a bit of furniture was one that Fleda could conscientiously accept, and she by no means insisted on so high a place in the list. This communication made her easier, if only by its acknowledgement that her friend had something left: it still implied recognition of the principle of property. Something to hate, and to hate 'comfortably', was at least not the utter destitution to which, after their last interview, she had helplessly seemed to see Mrs Gereth go forth. She remembered indeed that, in the state in which they first saw it, she herself had 'liked' the blessed refuge of Ricks ; and she now wondered if the tact for which she was commended had then operated to make her keep her kindness out of sight. She was at present ashamed of such obliquity, and made up her mind that if this happy impression, quenched in the spoils of Poynton, should revive on the spot, she would utter it to her companion without reserve. Yes, she was capable of as much 'action' as that: all the more that the spirit of her hostess seemed, for the time at least, wholly to have failed. Mrs Gereth's three minutes with Owen had been a blow to all talk of travel, and after her woeful hour at Maggie's she had, like some great moaning, wounded bird, made her way, with wings of anguish, back to the nest she knew she should find empty. Fleda, on that dire day, could neither keep her nor give her up; she had pressingly offered to return with her, but Mrs Gereth, in spite of the theory that their common grief was a bond, had even declined all escort to the station, conscious apparently of something abject in her collapse and almost fiercely eager, as with a personal shame, to be unwatched. All she had said to Fleda was that she would go back to Ricks that night, and the girl had lived for days after with a dreadful image of her position and her misery there. She had had a vision of her now lying prone on some unmade bed, now pacing a bare floor like a lioness deprived of her cubs. There had been moments when her mind's ear was strained to listen for some sound of grief wild enough to be wafted from afar. But the first sound, at the end of a week, had been a note announcing, without reflections, that the plan of going abroad had been abandoned. 'It has come to me indirectly, but with much appearance of truth, that *they* are going – for an indefinite time. That quite settles it; I shall stay where I am, and as soon as I've turned round again I shall look for you.' The second letter had come a week later, and on the 15th Fleda was on her way to Ricks.

Her arrival took the form of a surprise very nearly as violent as that of the other time. The elements were different, but the effect, like the other, arrested her on the threshold: she stood there stupified and delighted at the magic of a passion of which such a picture represented the low-water mark. Wound up but sincere, and passing quickly from room to room, Fleda broke out before she even sat down. 'If you turn me out of the house for it, my dear, there isn't a woman in England for whom it wouldn't be a privilege to live here.' Mrs Gereth was as honestly bewildered as she had of old been falsely calm. She looked about at the few sticks that, as she

424

afterwards phrased it, she had gathered in, and then hard at her guest, as if to protect herself against a joke sufficiently cruel. The girl's heart gave a leap, for this stare was the sign of an opportunity. Mrs Gereth was all unwitting ; she didn't in the least know what she had done, and as Fleda could tell her Fleda suddenly became the one who knew most. That counted for the moment as a magnificent position ; it almost made all the difference. Yet what contradicted it was the vivid presence of the artist's idea. 'Where on earth did you put your hand on such beautiful things?'

'Beautiful things?' Mrs Gereth turned again to the little worn, bleached stuffs and the sweet spindle-legs. 'They're the wretched things that were here — that stupid starved old woman's.'

'The maiden aunt's, the nicest, the dearest old woman that ever lived? I thought you had got rid of the maiden aunt.'

'She was stored in an empty barn — stuck away for a sale ; a matter that, fortunately, I've had neither time nor freedom of mind to arrange. I've simply, in my extremity, fished her out again.'

'You've simply, in your extremity, made a delight of her.' Fleda took the highest line and the upper hand, and as Mrs Gereth challenging her cheerfulness turned again a lustreless eye over the contents of the place, she broke into a rapture that was unforced but that she was conscious of an advantage in being able to feel. She moved, as she had done on the previous occasion, from one piece to another, with looks of recognition and hands that lightly lingered, but she was as feverishly jubilant now as she had formerly been anxious and mute. 'Ah, the little melancholy, tender, tell-tale things : how can they *not* speak to you and find a way to your heart? It's not the great chorus of Poynton ; but you're not, I'm sure, either so proud or so broken as to be reached by nothing but that. This is a voice so gentle, so human, so feminine — a faint, far-away voice with the little quaver of a heart-break. You've listened to it unawares ; for the arrangement and effect of everything — when I compare them with what we found the first day we came down — shows, even if mechanically and disdainfully exercised, your admirable, infallible hand. It's

425

your extraordinary genius; you make things "compose" in spite of yourself. You've only to be a day or two in a place with four sticks for something to come of it!'

'Then if anything has come of it here, it has come precisely of just four. That's literally, by the inventory, all there are!' said Mrs Gereth.

'If there were more there would be too many to convey the impression in which half the beauty resides – the impression, somehow, of something dreamed and missed, something reduced, relinquished, resigned: the poetry, as it were, of something sensibly *gone*.' Fleda ingeniously and triumphantly worked it out. 'Ah, there's something here that will never be in the inventory!'

'Does it happen to be in your power to give it a name?' Mrs Gereth's face showed the dim dawn of an amusement at finding herself seated at the feet of her pupil.

'I can give it a dozen. It's a kind of fourth dimension. It's a presence, a perfume, a touch. It's a soul, a story, a life. There's ever so much more here than you and I. We're in fact just three!'

'Oh, if you count the ghosts!'

'Of course I count the ghosts. It seems to me ghosts count double – for what they were and for what they are. Somehow there were no ghosts at Poynton,' Fleda went on. 'That was the only fault.'

Mrs Gereth, considering, appeared to fall in with the girl's fine humour. 'Poynton was too splendidly happy.'

'Poynton was too splendidly happy,' Fleda promptly echoed.

'But it's cured of that now,' her companion added.

'Yes, henceforth there'll be a ghost or two.'

Mrs Gereth thought again: she found her young friend suggestive. 'Only *she* won't see them.'

'No, "she" won't see them.' Then Fleda said, 'What I mean is, for this dear one of ours, that if she had (as I *know* she did; it's in the very taste of the air!) a great accepted pain –'

She had paused an instant, and Mrs Gereth took her up. 'Well, if she had?'

Fleda still hesitated. 'Why, it was worse than yours.'

Mrs Gereth reflected. 'Very likely.' Then she too hesitated. 'The question is if it was worse than yours.'

'Mine?' Fleda looked vague.

'Precisely. Yours.'

At this our young lady smiled. 'Yes, because it was a disappointment. She had been so sure.'

'I see. And you were never sure.'

'Never. Besides, I'm happy,' said Fleda.

Mrs Gereth met her eyes awhile. 'Goose!' she quietly remarked as she turned away. There was a curtness in it; nevertheless it represented a considerable part of the basis of their new life.

On the 18th the *Morning Post* had at last its clear message, a brief account of the marriage, from the residence of the bride's mother, of Mr Owen Gereth of Poynton Park to Miss Mona Brigstock of Waterbath. There were two ecclesiastics and six bridesmaids and, as Mrs Gereth subsequently said, a hundred frumps, as well as a special train from town: the scale of the affair sufficiently showed that the preparations had been complete for weeks. The happy pair were described as having taken their departure for Mr Gereth's own seat, famous for its unique collection of artistic curiosities. The newspapers and letters, the fruits of the first London post, had been brought to the mistress of Ricks in the garden; and she lingered there alone a long time after receiving them. Fleda kept at a distance; she knew what must have happened, for from one of the windows she saw her rigid in a chair, her eyes strange and fixed, the newspaper open on the ground and the letters untouched in her lap. Before the morning's end she had disappeared, and the rest of that day she remained in her room: it recalled to Fleda, who had picked up the newspaper, the day, months before, on which Owen had come down to Poynton to make his engagement known. The hush of the house was at least the same, and the girl's own waiting, her soft wandering, through the hours: there was a difference indeed sufficiently great, of which her companion's absence might in some degree have represented a considerate recognition. That was at any rate the meaning Fleda, devoutly glad to be alone, attached to her opportunity. Mrs Gereth's sole allusion, the next day, to

427

the subject of their thoughts, has already been mentioned: it was a dazzled glance at the fact that Mona's quiet pace had really never slackened.

Fleda fully assented. 'I said of our disembodied friend here that she had suffered in proportion as she had been sure. But that's not always a source of suffering. It's Mona who must have been sure!'

'She was sure of *you*!' Mrs Gereth returned. But this didn't diminish the satisfaction taken by Fleda in showing how serenely and lucidly she could talk.

CHAPTER 22

HER relation with her wonderful friend had, however, in becoming a new one, begun to shape itself almost wholly on breaches and omission. Something had dropped out altogether, and the question between them, which time would answer, was whether the change had made them strangers or yokefellows. It was as if at last, for better or worse, they were, in a clearer, cruder air, really to know each other. Fleda wondered how Mrs Gereth had escaped hating her: there were hours when it seemed that such a feat might leave after all a scant margin for future accidents. The thing indeed that now came out in its simplicity was that even in her shrunken state the lady of Ricks was larger than her wrongs. As for the girl herself, she had made up her mind that her feelings had no connexion with the case. It was her pretension that they had never yet emerged from the seclusion into which, after her friend's visit to her at her sister's, we saw them precipitately retire: if she should suddenly meet them in straggling procession on the road it would be time enough to deal with them. They were all bundled there together, likes with dislikes and memories with fears; and she had for not thinking of them the excellent reason that she was too occupied with the actual. The actual was not that Owen Gereth had seen his necessity where she had pointed it out; it was that his mother's bare spaces demanded all the tapestry that the recipient of her bounty could furnish. There were moments during the month that followed when Mrs Gereth struck her as still older and feebler, and as likely to become quite easily amused.

At the end of it, one day, the London paper had another piece of news: 'Mr and Mrs Owen Gereth, who arrived in town last week, proceed this morning to Paris.' They exchanged no word about it till the evening, and none indeed would then have been uttered had not Mrs Gereth irrelevantly broken out: 'I dare say you wonder why I declared the other day with such assurance that he wouldn't live with her. He apparently *is* living with her.'

'Surely it's the only proper thing for him to do.'

'They're beyond me – I give it up,' said Mrs Gereth.

'I don't give it up – I never did,' Fleda returned.

'Then what do you make of his aversion to her?'

'Oh, she has dispelled it.'

Mrs Gereth said nothing for a minute. 'You're prodigious in your choice of terms!' she then simply ejaculated.

But Fleda went luminously on; she once more enjoyed her great command of her subject: 'I think that when you came to see me at Maggie's you saw too many things, you had too many ideas.'

'You had none,' said Mrs Gereth: 'you were completely bewildered.'

'Yes, I didn't quite understand – but I think I understand now. The case is simple and logical enough. She's a person who's upset by failure and who blooms and expands with success. There was something she had set her heart upon, set her teeth about – the house exactly as she had seen it.'

'She never saw it at all, she never looked at it!' cried Mrs Gereth.

'She doesn't look with her eyes; she looks with her ears. In her own way she had taken it in; she knew, she felt when it had been touched. That probably made her take an attitude that was extremely disagreeable. But the attitude lasted only while the reason for it lasted.'

'Go on – I can bear it now,' said Mrs Gereth. Her companion had just perceptibly paused.

'I know you can, or I shouldn't dream of speaking. When the pressure was removed she came up again. From the moment the house was once more what it had to be, her natural charm reasserted itself.'

'Her natural charm!' Mrs Gereth could barely articulate.

'It's very great; everybody thinks so; there must be something in it. It operated as it had operated before. There's no need of imagining anything very monstrous. Her restored good humour, her splendid beauty, and Mr Owen's impressibility

430

and generosity sufficiently cover the ground. His great bright sun came out!'

'And his great bright passion for another person went in. Your explanation would doubtless be perfection if he didn't love you.'

Fleda was silent a little. 'What do you know about his "loving me?"'

'I know what Mrs Brigstock herself told me.'

'You never in your life took her word for any other matter.'

'Then won't yours do?' Mrs Gereth demanded. 'Haven't I had it from your own mouth that he cares for you?'

Fleda turned pale, but she faced her companion and smiled. 'You confound, Mrs Gereth, you mix things up. You've only had it from my own mouth that I care for *him*!'

It was doubtless in contradictious allusion to this (which at the time had made her simply drop her head as in a strange, vain reverie) that Mrs Gereth, a day or two later, said to Fleda: 'Don't think I shall be a bit affected if I'm here to see it when he comes again to make up to you.'

'He won't do that,' the girl replied. Then she added, smiling: 'But if he should be guilty of such bad taste, it wouldn't be nice of you not to be disgusted.'

'I'm not talking of disgust; I'm talking of its opposite,' said Mrs Gereth.

'Of its opposite?'

'Why, of any reviving pleasure that one might feel in such an exhibition. I shall feel none at all. You may personally take it as you like; but what conceivable good will it do?'

Fleda wondered. 'To me, do you mean?'

'Deuce take you, no! To what we don't, you know, by your wish, ever talk about.'

'The old things?' Fleda considered again. 'It will do no good of any sort to anything or anyone. That's another question I would rather we shouldn't discuss, please,' she gently added.

Mrs Gereth shrugged her shoulders.

'It certainly isn't worth it!'

Something in her manner prompted her companion, with a certain inconsequence, to speak again. 'That was partly why I came back to you, you know – that there should be the less possibility of anything painful.'

'Painful?' Mrs Gereth stared. 'What pain can I ever feel again?'

'I meant painful to myself,' Fleda, with a slight impatience, explained.

'Oh, I see.' Her friend was silent a minute. 'You use sometimes such odd expressions. Well, I shall last a little, but I sha'n't last forever.'

'You'll last quite as long – ' Here Fleda suddenly hesitated.

Mrs Gereth took her up with a cold smile that seemed the warning of experience against hyperbole. 'As long as what, please?'

The girl thought an instant ; then met the difficulty by adopting, as an amendment, the same tone. 'As any danger of the ridiculous.'

That did for the time, and she had moreover, as the months went on, the protection of suspended allusions. This protection was marked when, in the following November, she received a letter directed in a hand at which a quick glance sufficed to make her hesitate to open it. She said nothing, then or afterwards ; but she opened it, for reasons that had come to her, on the morrow. It consisted of a page and a half from Owen Gereth, dated from Florence, but with no other preliminary. She knew that during the summer he had returned to England with his wife, and that after a couple of months they had again gone abroad. She also knew, without communication, that Mrs Gereth, round whom Ricks had grown submissively and indescribably sweet, had her own interpretation of her daughter-in-law's share in this second migration. It was a piece of calculated insolence – a stroke odiously directed at showing whom it might concern that now she had Poynton fast she was perfectly indifferent to living there. The *Morning Post*, at Ricks, had again been a resource: it was stated in that journal that Mr and Mrs Owen Gereth proposed to spend the winter in India. There was a person to whom it was clear that she led her wretched husband by the nose. Such was the light in which contemporary history was offered to Fleda until, in her own room, late at night, she broke the seal of her letter.

432

I want you, inexpressibly, to have, as a remembrance, something of mine – something of real value. Something from Poynton is what I mean and what I should prefer. You know everything there, and far better than I what's best and what isn't. There are a lot of differences, but aren't some of the smaller things the most remark- able? I mean for judges, and for what they'd bring. What I want you to take from me, and to chose for yourself, is the thing in the whole house that's most beautiful and precious, I mean the "gem of the collection", don't you know? If it happens to be of such a sort that you can take immediate possession of it – carry it right away with you – so much the better. You're to have it on the spot, what- ever it is. I humbly beg of you to go down there and see. The people have complete instructions: they'll act for you in every possible way and put the whole place at your service. There's a thing mamma used to call the Maltese cross and that I think I've heard her say is very wonderful. Is *that* the gem of the collection? Per- haps you would take it, or anything equally convenient. Only I do want you awfully to let it be the very pick of the place. Let me feel that I can trust you for this. You won't refuse if you will think a little what it must be that makes me ask.

Fleda read that last sentence over more times even than the rest ; she was baffled – she couldn't think at all of what it might be. This was indeed because it might be one of so many things. She made for the present no answer ; she merely, little by little, fashioned for herself the form that her answer should event- ually wear. There was only one form that was possible – the form of doing, at her time, what he wished. She would go down to Poynton as a pilgrim might go to a shrine, and as to this she must look out for her chance. She lived with her letter, before any chance came, a month, and even after a month it had mysteries for her that she couldn't meet. What did it mean, what did it represent, to what did it correspond in his imagina- tion or his soul? What was behind it, what was beyond it, what was in the deepest depth, within it? She said to herself that with these questions she was under no obligation to deal. There was an explanation of them that, for practical purposes, would do as well as another: he had found in his marriage a happiness so much greater than, in the distress of his dilemma, he had been able to take heart to believe, that he now felt he owed her a token of gratitude for having kept him in the straight path. That explanation, I say, she could throw off; but no explanation in the least mattered: what determined her was the simple strength of her impulse to respond. The passion for which what had happened had made no difference, the passion that had taken this into account before as well as after, found here an issue that there was nothing whatever to choke. It found even a relief to which her imagination immensely contributed. Would she act upon his offer? She would act with secret rapture. To have as her own something splendid that he had given her, of which the gift had been his signed desire, would be a greater joy than the greatest she had supposed to be left to her, and she felt that till the sense of this came home she had even herself not known what burned in her successful stillness. It was an hour to dream of and watch for; to be patient was to draw out the sweetness. She was capable of feeling it as an hour of triumph, the triumph of everything in her recent life that had not held up its head. She moved there in thought – in the great rooms she knew ; she should be able to say to herself that, for once at least, her possesion was as complete as that of either of the others whom it had filled only with bitterness. And a thousand times yes – her choice should know no scruple: the thing she should go down to take would be up to the height of her privilege. The whole place was in her eyes, and she spent for weeks her private hours in a luxury of comparison and debate. It should be one of the smallest things because it should be one she could have close to her ; and it should be one of the finest because it was in the finest he saw his symbol. She said to herself that of what it would symbolize she was content to know nothing more than just what her having it would tell her. At bottom she inclined to the Maltese cross – with the added reason that he had named it. But she would look again and judge afresh ; she would on the spot so handle and ponder that there shouldn't be the shade of a mistake.

Before Christmas she had a natural opportunity to go to London ; there was her periodical call upon her father to pay as well as a promise to Maggie to redeem. She spent her first night in West Kensington, with the idea of carrying out on the morrow the purpose that had most of a motive. Her father's affection was not inquisitive, but when she mentioned to him that she had business in the country that would oblige her to catch an early train, he deprecated her excursion in view of the menace of the weather. It was spoiling for a storm ; all the signs of a winter gale were in the air. She replied that she would see what the morning might bring ; and it brought, in fact, what seemed in London an amendment. She was to go to Maggie the next day, and now that she had started her eagerness had become suddenly a pain. She pictured her return that evening with her trophy under her cloak ; so that after looking, from the doorstep, up and down the dark street, she decided, with a new nervousness, and sallied forth to the nearest place of access to the 'Underground'. The December dawn was dolorous, but there was neither rain nor snow ; it was not even cold, and the atmosphere of West Kensington, purified by the wind, was like a dirty old coat that had been bettered by a dirty brush. At the end of almost an hour, in the larger station, she had taken her place in a third-class compartment ; the prospect before her was the run of eighty minutes to Poynton. The train was a fast one, and she was familiar with the moderate measure of the walk to the park from the spot at which it would drop her.

Once in the country, indeed, she saw that her father was right : the breath of December was abroad with a force from which the London labyrinth had protected her. The green fields were black, the sky was all alive with the wind ; she had, in her anxious sense of the elements, her wonder at what might happen, a reminder of the surmises, in the old days of going to the Continent, that used to worry her on the way, at night, to the horrid cheap crossings by long sea. Something, in a dire degree, at this last hour, had begun to press on her heart : it was the sudden imagination of a disaster, or at least of a check, before her errand was achieved. When she said to herself that something might happen she wanted to go faster than the train. But nothing could happen save a dismayed discovery that, by some altogether unlikely chance, the master and mistress of the house had already come back. In that case she must have had a warning, and the fear was but the excess of her hope. It was everyone's being exactly where everyone was that lent the quality to her visit. Beyond lands and seas and alienated forever, they

435

in their different ways gave her the impression to take as she had never taken it. At last it was already there, though the darkness of the day had deepened; they had whizzed past Chater – Chater, which was the station before the right one. Off in that quarter was an air of wild rain, but there shimmered straight across it a brightness that was the colour of the great interior she had been haunting. That vision settled before her – in the house the house was all ; and as the train drew up she rose, in her mean compartment, quite proudly erect with the thought that all for Fleda Vetch then the house was standing there.

But with the opening of the door she encountered a shock, though for an instant she couldn't have named it ; the next moment she saw it was given her by the face of the man advancing to let her out, an old lame porter of the station, who had been there in Mrs Gereth's time and who now recognized her. He looked up at her so hard that she took an alarm and before alighting broke out to him: 'They've come back?' She had a confused, absurd sense that even he would know that in this case she mustn't be there. He hesitated, and in the few seconds her alarm had completely changed its ground: it seemed to leap, with her quick jump from the carriage, to the ground that was that of his stare at her..'Smoke?' She was on the platform with her frightened sniff: it had taken her a minute to become aware of an extraordinary smell. The air was full of it, and there were already heads at the windows of the train, looking out at something she couldn't see. Someone, the only other passenger, had got out of another carriage, and the old porter hobbled off to close his door. The smoke was in her eyes, but she saw the station-master, from the end of the platform, recognize her too and come straight to her. He brought her a finer shade of surprise than the porter, and while he was coming she heard a voice at the window of the train say that something was 'a good bit off – a mile from the town'. That was just what Poynton was. Then her heart stood still at the white wonder in the station-master's face.

'You've come down to it, miss, already?'

At this she knew. 'Poynton's on fire?'

'Gone, miss – with this awful gale. You weren't wired?

436

Look out!' he cried in the next breath, seizing her; the train was going on, and she had given a lurch that almost made it catch her as it passed. When it had drawn away she became more conscious of the pervading smoke, which the wind seemed to hurl in her face.

'*Gone?*' She was in the man's hands; she clung to him.

'Burning still, miss. Ain't it quite too dreadful? Took early this morning – the whole place is up there.'

In her bewildered horror she tried to think. 'Have they come back?'

'Back? They'll be there all day!'

'Not Mr Gereth, I mean – nor his wife?'

'Nor his mother, miss – not a soul of *them* back. A pack o' servants in charge – not the old lady's lot, eh? A nice job for caretakers! Some rotten chimley or one of them portable lamps set down in the wrong place. What has done it is this cruel, cruel night.' Then as a great wave of smoke half choked them, he drew her with force to the little waiting-room. 'Awkward for you, miss – I see!'

She felt sick; she sank upon a seat, staring up at him. 'Do you mean that great house is *lost*?'

'It was near it, I was told, an hour ago – the fury of the flames had got such a start. I was there myself at six, the very first I heard of it. They were fighting it then, but you couldn't quite say they had got it down.'

Fleda jerked herself up. 'Were they saving the things?'

'That's just where it was, miss – to get *at* the blessed things. And the want of right help – it maddened me to stand and see 'em muff it. This ain't a place, like, for anything organized. They don't come up to a *reel* emergency.'

She passed out of the door that opened towards the village and met a great acrid gust. She heard a far-off windy roar which, in her dismay, she took for that of flames a mile away, and which, the first instant, acted upon her as a wild solicitation. 'I must go there.' She had scarcely spoken before the same omen had changed into an appalling check.

Her vivid friend, moreover, had got before her; he clearly suffered from the nature of the control he had to exercise. 'Don't do that, miss – you won't care for it at all.' Then as

437

she waveringly stood her ground, 'It's not a place for a young lady, nor if you'll believe me, a sight for them as are in any way affected.'

Fleda by this time knew in what way she was affected: she became limp and weak again; she felt herself give everything up. Mixed with the horror, with the kindness of the station-master, with the smell of cinders and the riot of sound, was the raw bitterness of a hope that she might never again in life have to give up so much at such short notice. She heard herself repeat mechanically, yet as if asking it for the first time: 'Poynton's *gone*?'

The man hesitated. 'What can you call it, miss, if it ain't really saved?'

A minute later she had returned with him to the waiting-room, where, in the thick swim of things, she saw something like the disk of a clock. 'Is there an up-train?' she asked.

'In seven minutes.'

She came out on the platform: everywhere she met the smoke. She covered her face with her hands. 'I'll go back.'

SELECTED BIBLIOGRAPHY

Works by HENRY JAMES

A Passionate Pilgrim and Other Tales, 1875 Tales
Transatlantic Sketches, 1875 Travel
Roderick Hudson, 1875 Novel
The American, 1877 Novel (Signet Classic 0-451-51709-1)
French Poets and Novelists, 1878 Criticism
The Europeans, 1878 Novel (Signet Classic 0-451-51351-7)
Daisy Miller, 1878 Tale (Signet Classic 0-451-00625-9)
Hawthorne, 1879 Criticism
Washington Square, 1880 Tale (Signet Classic 0-451-51766-0)
The Portrait of a Lady, 1881 Novel (Signet Classic
    0-451-51605-2)
The Art of Fiction, 1884 Criticism
The Bostonians, 1886 Novel (Signet Classic 0-451-51285-5)
The Princess Casamassima, 1886 Novel
Partial Portraits, 1888 Criticism
The Aspern Papers, 1888 Tale (Signet Classic 0-451-00625-9)
The Tragic Muse, 1889 Novel
The Lesson of the Master and Other Stories, 1892 Tales
Embarrassments, 1896 Tales
The Spoils of Poynton, 1897 Novel
What Maisie Knew, 1897 Novel
The Two Magics, 1898 Tales
The Awkward Age, 1899 Novel
The Sacred Fount, 1901 Novel
The Wings of the Dove, 1902 Novel (Signet Classic
    0-451-51812-1)
The Ambassadors, 1903 Novel (Signet Classic 0-451-51746-6)
The Golden Bowl, 1904 Novel
The American Scene, 1907 Travel
The Finer Grain, 1910 Tales
A Small Boy and Others, 1913 Autobiography
Notes of a Son and Brother, 1914 Autobiography
Notes on Novelists, 1914 Criticism
The Middle Years, 1917 Unfinished Autobiography
The Art of the Novel, 1934 Critical Prefaces
The Notebooks of Henry James, 1947 Memoranda

SELECTED BIOGRAPHY AND CRITICISM

Anderson, Quentin. *The American Henry James*. New Brunswick, N.J.: Rutgers University Press, 1957.

Beach, Joseph Warren. *The Method of Henry James*. Rev. ed. Philadelphia: Alfred Saifer, 1954.

Bewley, Marius. *The Complex Fate: Hawthorne, Henry James, and Some Other American Writers*. London: Chatto & Windus, 1952.

Blackmur, Richard P. "Henry James." In *Literary History of the United States*, ed. Robert E. Spiller et al, pp. 1039-64. New York: Macmillan, 1953.

Cargill, Oscar. *The Novels Of Henry James*. New York: Macmillan, 1961.

Crews, Frederick C. *The Tragedy of Manners: Moral Drama in the Later Novels of Henry James*. New Haven: Yale University Press, 1957.

Dupee, F. W. *Henry James*. Rev. ed. New York: Sloane, 1956.

————, ed. *The Question of Henry James*. New York: Holt, 1945.

Edel, Leon. *Henry James*. 5 vols. Philadelphia: Lippincott, 1953-1972.

————, ed. *Henry James: A Collection of Critical Essays*. Englewood Cliffs, N.J.: Prentice-Hall, 1963.

Goode, John ed. *The Air of Reality: New Essays on Henry James*. London: Methuen, 1972.

Kelley, Cornelia P. *The Early Development of Henry James*. Urbana: University of Illinois Press, 1930.

Leavis, F. R. *The Great Tradition*. New York: George Stewart, 1949.

Lebowitz, Naomi, ed. *Discussions of Henry James*. Boston: Heath, 1962.

McElderry, Bruce R. Jr. *Henry James*. New York: Twayne Publishers, 1965.

Matthiessen, F. O. *Henry James: The Major Phase*. New York: Oxford University Press, 1944.

————. *The James Family*. New York: Knopf, 1947.

Moore, Harry T. *Henry James*. New York: Viking, 1974.

Poirier, Richard. *The Comic Sense of Henry James*. New York: Oxford University Press, 1960.

Powers, Lyall H. *Henry James: An Introduction and Interpretation*. New York: Holt, Rinehart, and Winston, 1970.

Tanner, Tony. ed. *Henry James: Modern Judgments*. London: Macmillan, 1968.

Great Philosophers from MERIDIAN CLASSIC